TWO JOURNEYS HOME

TWO JOURNEYS HOME

A NOVEL OF EIGHTEENTH CENTURY EUROPE

The Derrynane Saga

Kevin O'Connell

The Gortcullinane Press

Copyright © 2017 by Kevin O'Connell
All rights reserved, including the right to reproduce this book, or any portions thereof, in any form whatsoever, without limitation.
ISBN-13: 978-0997407617
ISBN-10: 0997407611
Library of Congress Control Number 2017903863
Gortcullinane Press, The – P.O. Box 157, Severna Park, MD 21146 USA

Published by The Gortcullinane Press

Cover design by Jennifer Quinlan, Historical Editorial – after a photograph by Laurette Hankins-O'Connell, Derrynane, County Kerry, Ireland, June 2008

For Laurette, again and always, with love and gratitude,

as she has continued to effortlessly play the modern-day role of the
mythical Gaelic muse,
Leanan Sidhe ("My Inspiration")

It is she to whom *The Derrynane Saga* owes its existence

Go raibth mille maith agut!

ACKNOWLEDGEMENTS

I REMAIN INDESCRIBABLY GRATEFUL to (and for!) my extraordinary editor, Randy Ladenheim-Gil, for her continuing patience, understanding and good cheer - as we've yet again wended our way along on our own pair of journeys during these number of months. Her editorial and critical skills, her suggestions, her nudges, her sense of humour have all proven to be invaluable.

In that our travels about Eighteenth Century Europe, including Ireland, are far from over, to have her as a friend and, in many ways, a guide, makes this prospect far less daunting.

Laura Oliver has continued in her role as the consummate mentor. It was she who was present at the very beginning, and remains an integral part of this on-going creative undertaking. My debt to her is – and will always be – immeasurable.

Aboard the Will o' the Wisp—*off the coast of Ireland*—*17 August 1767*

Eileen O'Connell's deep blue eyes widened as she gazed about the magnificent setting for what was a glittering, dazzling ball in Catherine the Great's majestic Winter Palace at St. Petersburg. That she was an honoured guest of the empress compensated, at least in part, for the lengthy, bitterly cold and snowy journey she'd taken from Vienna to Russia. Now, herself stunning in the most breathtaking royal blue velvet gown, the most delicate of French dancing slippers, she glided across a floor that gleamed as if it were intricately coloured ice, in the arms of a striking blond Austrian officer, Major Wolfgang von Klaus, her dear friend, her lover of some years, with whom she had been joyously reunited immediately on her arrival in St. Petersburg. The two were smiling, laughing even, as they performed a newly learnt, somewhat intricate Russian folk dance, not dissimilar to the graceful, elegantly complex Ländler, which they had enjoyed in Vienna, in that both required light foot stomping and small, almost delicate hops and jumps.

Suddenly . . . sensing, possibly even hearing an audible thud, her first thought was, *perhaps it is Wolfgang's boot.*

As the music softened, then became more distant, she drowsily began to realise that the floating sensation she had been experiencing was indeed a literal one, being the movement of a ship beneath and all about her. Eileen finally, unenthusiastically, concluded that, very early on this August morning, she had been suspended in what frequently was a gently blissful place—those idyllic moments in time just before one became fully awake. She took a deep breath and sighed . . . reluctantly bidding Major von Klaus adieu and, with him, the elegant grandeur—and the bitter cold—of St. Petersburg, Eileen rolled over slowly, stretching her six-foot-plus-an inch—or perhaps even two long frame—beyond the footboard of what the master of the ship upon which she was indeed sailing had called a "compact" bunk. After spending her first restless night therein, Eileen had decided it was more correctly, and at best, "confining."

Stirring, she rose tentatively, assuring herself of the absence of any beam directly above her head before standing straight. As she did, her thick black hair cascaded, tumbling past her shoulders, over her full breasts, down her back to her waist.

Eileen went about her toilette in a matter-of-fact way: First emptying her chamber pot overboard, she washed her hands, arms and face, her throat and finally her legs and feet in the saline-laced water from an oval, blue and white salt-glazed basin, which she also emptied out through the porthole. Wriggling into a shift and hip pads, she donned a simple, deep blue dress of medium-weight wool. Not bothering with shoes, she eased open the cabin's substantial door with her left shoulder and clambered along the narrow passageway, padding in the direction of the pleasant morning aromas of strong coffee and sizzling sausages.

Clearing the gangway's few steps, Eileen emerged onto the rolling deck of what was a compact schooner. Scanning the dully brightening heavens, she concluded that it was now shortly after dawn, and she yawned, twice, laughing softly at herself. Despite that she'd caught fleeting suggestions of blue buried in the clouds, there seemed little difference between the leaden sky and the almost methodical rising and falling of the dull grey Atlantic's waves, broken only by the occasional whitecaps.

Those of the ship's small crew on deck, several of whom had known Eileen most of her life, acknowledged the young woman with greetings in English, Irish and, in one case, French—all of which she returned with a broad smile and a genteel, husky-voiced, ". . . and to you, as well!" in the appropriate language.

As she momentarily leaned against the rail on the ship's starboard side, gazing at the nebulous suggestion of a distant landmass, she was joined by Master Charles O'Byrne, who, on seeing her, had descended the six steps from his quarterdeck and, as he passed the open passageway, received a heavy, salt-glazed stone mug of steaming coffee. On his request, the cook's mate quickly handed up a second one, which O'Byrne immediately offered to "my Lady Eileen," with a respectful nod and a warm smile.

Smiling her thanks, the striking young woman's long, elegant fingers wrapped about the welcome warmth of her mug. The pair stepped aside and chatted amiably, as the long-time acquaintances they were, the veteran mariner having been for many years in the service of her family, the O'Connells of Derrynane, in far southwest County Kerry, ultimately coming to play an integral role in their far-flung, and largely illegal, commercial maritime trading activities.

As they discussed the weather and the ship's anticipated course, a booming "Good morning!" heralded the arrival on deck of Eileen's "uncle" as General, the Count Moritz O'Connell of the Imperial Armies of Austria and Hungary, strode across the deck; his firmly tied queue notwithstanding, the chill, blustery wind quickly began to tear at his thick, silver-streaked brown hair. That he wore rough clothing of heavy Scottish tweed in no way diminished the general's dominating presence. The senior officer was actually Eileen's much-older second cousin, the title by which he was known and addressed arising out of the practice of fosterage that was still a part of the sometimes-complex traditional Gaelic family structure, which had resulted in her father and his first cousin being raised as brothers.

"We have made significant time whilst you and"—he gestured towards Eileen— "the ladies have slept, General," O'Byrne announced to O'Connell. "I expect we should be approaching the vicinity of Derrynane by midday, sir," O'Byrne reported to his pleasantly surprised passenger, who nodded as he drank the coffee he had brought on deck from below.

"'Tis good to hear, sir, very good indeed." Morty O'Connell smiled, his sheepishness as obvious as his relief. Eileen and O'Byrne exchanged winks, as both knew well that the immense man—at age fifty-three, O'Connell stood six feet and as many inches, weighing almost three hundred pounds—clearly preferred earth beneath his feet as opposed to the rolling waves of the English Channel or the ofttimes heaving swells of the Atlantic itself, over both of which they had travelled now three days since departing a small, remote harbour in western Normandy. "God Almighty intended man to walk, to run even, and to ride a horse or other beast of burden," O'Connell maintained, pronouncing it frequently and ofttimes loudly, though always with a laugh. "'Tis but man alone who decided we shall traverse the seas!"

Being of an insular land, O'Connell was, of course, aware of the limiting effect his beliefs could have had on his life. Having first departed Ireland as a youth, initially—in violation of the laws prohibiting Catholics, already barred from attaining literacy at home, attempting to seek education aboard—to attend Louvain University in the Austrian Netherlands, thence embarking on what had proven to be a highly successful military career in the Habsburgs' armies, all whilst retaining close ties to Ireland, he had found himself journeying by water far more frequently than he ever thought he would. He began his career as a mounted dragoon, developing into a talented leader of infantry; noticed early on both by his commanders and the Empress Maria Theresa, O'Connell became an ennobled general at a young age. More recently, as the Seven Years War wound down, he had also been serving as a counsellor to the empress.

Despite that the ship's lurching at times challenged his balance, O'Connell peered repeatedly, almost impatiently through Master O'Byrne's gleaming brass spyglass, the ship's captain diplomatically cautioning, as he gestured towards the thick fog bank that continued to obscure the horizon, that the Irish coast would not appear for a time yet.

Noticing the cook's mate smilingly gesturing with a pot of apparently fresh coffee, with a nod of her head and a soft smile, Eileen excused herself and, leaving the men to their talk, padded quietly across the gently rolling deck to replenish her mug.

Intending to return immediately below decks, the young sailor had instead bowed slightly and stepped aside, permitting an older woman of moderate height and full figure to pass, her substantial mass of shoulder-length ash-blond hair tousled in the wind, her long black cloak flapping freely, revealing the heavy grey wool robe she wore beneath.

"A good morning to you, my dear Aunt Maria," Eileen murmured, smiling warmly at Countess Maria von Graffenreit-O'Connell, whose husband of but several months it was who stood on the other side of the deck.

"And to you as well, my dear girl," the forty-seven-year-old Austrian noblewoman managed somewhat drowsily, her delicate yawn followed by a shy smile as she tipped her own stone-glazed mug to Eileen's, observing, "Ah, coffee—it is a gift of the goddess Aurora herself!" Eileen answered with a smile and they both drank deeply, the steam rising from the mugs almost white in the chill air; both the vapour and the aroma of the rich, dark brew it bore being quickly diffused by the winds blowing across the deck.

Their faces brightened at the mate's near-immediate return, now offering them freshly toasted slices of thick, rough white bread. Raising it to her mouth, Eileen noted that the toast was wonderfully redolent with fresh butter and bittersweet Seville orange marmalade. A plate of still-sizzling sausages, more still-warm grilled bread and additional pours of coffee followed.

The women chatted as they feasted until Eileen, seeing that her uncle had gestured for his wife, kissed her aunt on both cheeks and strode forward alone. Since childhood, she had always enjoyed facing into the wind; she was almost immediately leaning against the rail, in the prow of the snug ship, the air singing softly in the rigging, as she heard the soft suggestion of canvas responding to the stiff breeze.

Within moments, it was the whistling trill that heralded the sudden leaping arrival of a pair of dolphins, their joyful presence—especially as they would remain on the port side of the vessel for the duration of the passage to Derrynane—reminding Eileen that no dolphins had been in evidence at the time of her most recent departures and arrivals. *So perhaps the smiling dears herald something special,* she reflected. As she watched them cavorting even as they swam, she could not help but smile, returning, she felt, the warm gestures the animals seemed to be directing to her.

Leaning against the ship's rail, noticing the sun's orb as it continued its struggle to make itself more fully evident in the still-dull heavens, recalling briefly her gentle awakening, Eileen spoke aloud to the wind, and to herself, "These years, these not-quite *six* years . . . They could have *all* been a dream . . . could they not have? Yet to me, *all* of it has actually happened. . . ." A panoply of places and events—and people, so many people!—raced vividly through her mind, as if it were all unfolding as a moving panorama before her.

With the coming of the spring of 1761, General O'Connell's skilful orchestration of arranging opportunities at the court of the Empress Maria Theresa in Vienna for Eileen, now twenty-three, and her ebullient, slightly older sister, Abigail, having borne fruit, it was the Countess Maria von Graffenreit, at the time and for a number of years prior the primary lady-in-waiting to the empress, with whom Eileen and Abby had corresponded, in preparation for their journey to Vienna.

It was also the countess who had greeted them warmly on their arrival at court in October of the same year, following their five-week-long journey from Derrynane, seeing to it that Eileen was presented to her new charges—Their Imperial Highnesses, the Archduchesses Maria Carolina and Maria Antonia of Austria and Lorraine—and Abigail to her own new mistress, the Empress Maria Theresa herself, as well as choreographing a lengthy series of both formal and informal introductions to key persons at court.

In the years that quickly followed, as the sisters flourished at the apex of the glittering Habsburg court and society, Maria von Graffenreit was daily, quietly in their lives. More so, during the same period, the attractive, quietly elegant widow had grown ever closer to the never-married general, such that the two had wed quietly, early in the current year.

It was with, or so it seemed to Eileen, an almost-dizzying speed that immediately following their marriage, the countess had yielded her lofty position as head of the empress's household to Abigail O'Connell O'Sullivan, herself wed less than a year to Major Denis O'Sullivan, an officer in the Hungarian Hussars.

During the ensuing bitterly cold, unusually snowy Vienna winter of the current year, Eileen had experienced what she had come to refer to as *the winter of my own discontent*, marked significantly by the departure from Vienna of her dear friend and lover, Major Wolfgang von Klaus, for an extended tour of duty at the Imperial Russian court at St. Petersburg, an event that had resulted in Eileen unexpectedly sensing herself unsettled, uncertain.

Though in the interim she had become less disconcerted, her state of mind remained such that when in early June the general and the countess announced a late-summer trip to Ireland, Eileen had met the news with an unexpected but profound desire to return to Derrynane herself, if only for a time. Whilst she indicated to the couple that her motivation lay in a simple desire to see the rest of her family, Eileen acknowledged to herself that seeing the O'Sullivans and, more recently, the general and the countess all well-wed—and, she somewhat reluctantly admitted, von Klaus's departure for Russia—had left her feeling to some not insignificant degree uncertain as to what life might next hold in store for her. She felt that some time spent at what she had always felt the powerful sanctuary that was Derrynane might help her clarify her life's future direction.

Though she realised it might be awkward for the newlyweds, Eileen quietly inquired of them if she might accompany them to Ireland, phrasing it lightly, "With the dragoons I shall gladly ride." The general had no doubt that she was, in fact, more than willing to make the trip on horseback rather than intrude on the couple's privacy in a coach. They immediately and graciously acceded to her request, and Eileen rode in the coach.

As Eileen gazed out at the gently rolling ocean, smiling as she watched the dolphins' merry progress, Master O'Byrne joined her briefly at the bow. Uncertain whether Eileen shared her uncle's impatience for the clear sight of Ireland, gesturing in the direction of a still fog-enshrouded sliver of land on the overcast horizon, stepping to her side, the soft-spoken mariner offered, "Soon, m'lady . . . soon the coast of Ireland, of Kerry, it shall be in clear view," and he himself ambled away. Eileen, unlike her uncle, then continued to savour the experience of being at sea, one she had enjoyed as a young girl on journeys brief and lengthy with her late father, Donal Mór, and her siblings, reflecting both on those experiences as well as on her last sea voyage, almost six years before, when she and Abigail had departed from whence she was now returning, on what they had come to call their *grand adventure* to Vienna.

As their final day at sea passed uneventfully, Eileen continued to reflect on what she had experienced in not quite six rather remarkable years: *a grand adventure indeed!*

She had last returned to Derrynane, in the autumn of 1760, a widow at the age of not yet seventeen, having spent the previous seven months away, the result of an arranged marriage to John O'Connor of Firies—one of the wealthiest and most influential men in Ireland and nearly five decades her senior—in the northern part of County Kerry. During this time, she had been Mistress O'Connor of Ballyhar, which she'd frequently spoken of as being *a grand house, a great estate*, only to have her husband die before her eyes of a massive apoplexy. Though the marriage had begun badly, violently even – indeed, so viciously-brutal that Eileen had actually attempted to kill her husband – by the time of O'Connor's death the couple had, quite remarkably, become deeply fond of each other, the extent of which such that Eileen had returned home in mourning.

During her time in Vienna, Eileen had grown from being an occasionally wistful young woman from a barely accessible region of a remote island on the far-western edge of Europe, still recovering from the loss of her spouse and, with him, her own significant social position, into a well-known and widely respected person of consequence at the Habsburg court. She was viewed fondly by the empress herself and beloved especially by her youngest charge, whom she addressed privately as Antoine and referred to affectionately even now, despite that later this year she would mark her twelfth birthday, as *my wee little Archduchess*.

Along with Eileen's towering height, her cascading wavy mane of gleaming, thick blue-black hair and singularly husky voice, her vibrant personality combined to assure her of being amongst the most recognised figures at court, such that she had come to feel very much at home amidst the grandeur of Vienna: the magnificent palaces—the Hofburg, Schönbrunn and Laxenburg—where her apartments were closely proximate to those of her young charges' and the splendid Spanish Riding School, where Bull, her singular chestnut, black-maned Frisian stallion, dwelt when the court was at the Hofburg, sharing barn space with the legendary Lipizzan stallions, and also the site of her at least thrice-weekly riding lessons with the archduchesses.

She moved easily through the glittering balls and the sumptuous banquets, spending numerous evenings at the opera house, for the last several years customarily escorted, until his abrupt departure for Russia, by von Klaus.

Her mind wandering, she smiled at the thought of her Anna, who, along with so much else, saw to her mistress's dressing, changing outfits sometimes as frequently as three or even four times in a single day: Anna Pfeffer, the once-awkward young country girl who had, by the simple decree of Maria von Graffenreit, come into Eileen's service virtually on her arrival from Ireland, her maid now these five years, who in the process had also become Eileen's dearest friend. Anna was now a trim young woman of seventeen, with brilliantly blue eyes and cascading golden locks; together, she and Eileen had grown up, Anna teaching Eileen German whilst Eileen educated Anna in French—the language of the Viennese court—as well as in the complexities of English. In concert, both young women had increased in the unique combination of sophistication, wisdom and no small degree of guile essential for success, if not survival, at court

The day was indeed passing quickly, much to the general's relief, as evidenced by the booming "Land, ho!" he had cried on seeing the Kerry coast grow nearer yet, and that he had practically jumped with joy as, true to the master's estimate, shortly after noon the ship approached Scariff Island, O'Byrne advising as he gestured, ". . . then past Deenish and dead-head towards Lamb's Head and virtually at Derrynane, we shall be!" thus marking the end of their largely uneventful land and sea journey across and around Europe. On this fine late-August afternoon, the small ship was not far from where its master would ease it into a snug, still harbour, just beyond Derrynane, at Iskeroon. It was a now-magnificently attired Eileen who had cried out, "Derrynane, yonder it lies!" as the substantial, dark bulk of Derrynane House had come into delicately misty view. She gripped the ship's rail and, her excitement notwithstanding, stood still momentarily, silently looking at the house in which she'd been born and in which she'd spent the majority of her life thus far.

The ship slipped quietly past the rambling house and the ruins of its ancient abbey, the latter seeming to float on its own tiny, sandy island.

"As you will recall, General, we are carrying cargo, as well as your good selves," Master O'Byrne advised O'Connell, explaining the need to use a larger dock, which, as they eased into Iskeroon's gentle cove, came into view.

O'Connell nodded. "Aye. 'Tis understood, sir. We are grateful for the transport, good Master O'Byrne . . . Indeed, were I alone, I should gladly walk the way to Derrynane."

"Ah, General, no one shall walk, sir," the captain advised. "A small boat we have already sent on to your family, advising them of our coming. I expect transport will await you and your ladies."

Some minutes later, more by reflex than by actual need, he lifted again the gleaming brass spyglass to his eye and nodded in approval. "A cart 'tis already there; several actually," he called over to the general, gesturing, then handing him the glass yet again.

Waving it off with a smile, O'Connell exclaimed, "Several indeed there are! Indeed, much of the house appears to be awaiting us."

At that moment, the countess and Eileen joined the men at the bow; they had been leaning on the rail amidships, where Eileen had been providing the countess, in as much detail as possible, with a preliminary introduction to the area, by which the older woman seemed already charmed.

"So green," she was saying to Eileen as she slipped her arm into her husband's.

"Green it is, my darling Countess!" O'Connell exclaimed as he planted a gentle kiss on her forehead, noticing with appreciation the striking appearance of both his wife and niece.

The "newest O'Connell," as the general had come to refer to her, had chosen, most appropriately he felt, a striking emerald green satin afternoon dress, complete with train, which at the moment she had skilfully gathered quite elegantly over her right shoulder, "like a Highlander's 'plaid,'" exclaimed her adoring husband. Unlike in Vienna, as it had been earlier in the day, her soft hair was again loose and full on her shoulders, something he also noted approvingly. Eileen had herself selected an equally elegant dark blue satin afternoon dress, its train now puddling on the deck, contrasting markedly with the long, traditional hooded dark-green Gaelic mantle, casually draped loosely over her broad shoulders.

The ladies' arresting appearance—they had been wearing relatively simple woollen dresses since boarding the ship—had not gone unnoticed, as the snug vessel's largely long-time crew, a number of whom had known Eileen much of her life, had all taken a respectful look and shared nods of approval. "Like queens they are!" a young sailor from Cork, new to the crew, had observed.

One of the senior mates had added knowingly, "The older lady . . . a true *countess*, remember, lad, indeed she is!"

Eileen's eyes were now fixed on the shore and on the sturdy old pier, as wide as it was long, much of its planking bleached and worn smooth by years of sun, rain, wind and waves, where she and Abigail and their siblings had landed on any number of occasions with Donal Mór and his captains, following brief jaunts as well as weeks'-long adventures to the warm wintertime sun of Spain and Portugal.

As they drew even closer to the pier, she let out a joyous yelp. "Mama! Mama! Hugh!" She waved both arms above her head, her cloak slipping onto the smooth deck. "Anne! Elizabeth! Maurice! Morgan!" completed her happy litany of parent, sisters and brothers, as the general pointed out to his wife who was who, just as the remarkably manoeuvrable broad-beamed ship almost delicately bumped the pier, sailors leaping off fore and aft with lines of dense, heavily corded rope, others trundling the gangplank, lowering it with a solid thud.

The elder O'Connells stood at the rail, Eileen behind them, shedding happy tears and waving gently, as she saw her petite blonde mother, Maire, standing with her eldest brother, Maurice, and his wife, Mary, as well as her other brothers, Morgan and Hugh—now almost twelve—and, her younger sisters, Anne and Elizabeth, both young ladies now, each, she would learn, with a suitor paying her court.

Bending to pick up her cloak, Eileen held herself back, allowing the general and the countess to disembark first and alone. She was enjoying watching the elegant pair, O'Connell in full-dress uniform—into which he'd clambered immediately following his first clear view of the coast of Kerry—and the countess, regal and lovely—*flawless, as always*, Eileen thought—as well as the family's reaction to the sight. As she herself stepped onto the gangplank, she was surprised to see Maire executing a deep, perfect curtsey to the Countess von Graffenreit-O'Connell.

Seconds later, having strolled casually down the gangplank unassisted, stepping into her petite mother's embrace, Eileen couldn't resist whispering, "Why, Mama, never have I seen you perform such an act!"

Unflustered, Maire responded with feigned awe. "Why, daughter, *never* have I had a countess in my own family, sharing my own wedded name." Mother and daughter then held each other for a long moment, for the first time in more than five years.

Maire ní Dhuibh— "Mary of the Dark People," referring to her family, the vibrant O'Donoghues, proud denizens of Robbers Glen, high above Glenflesk, located not quite fifty miles east and a wee bit north of Derrynane, their purported activities in the region having long ago given the place its name—stepped back, still holding her daughter's hands in her own, and looked up, carefully, silently studying the young woman Eileen had become. It was more than merely the difference between her at seventeen and now twenty-three; her face was sharper, her features perhaps even more striking, her eyes, if anything, seeming even more piercingly blue, her hair radiantly blue-black as Maire had never before seen it. Her daughter's richly elegant raiment was also something Maire had never seen the likes of, not even in Dublin; at it, especially its seeming complexity, she could only marvel, at one-point puzzling, *How is it that she is able to dress and undress?* To her mother, Eileen appeared *a grown woman now . . . very much a lady at court, of this I am certain*, and she was quietly proud of her daughter.

It was only when Eileen laughed her familiar loud, throaty laugh as she overheard Morgan joking with the general that a relieved Maire sensed her sense of joy, her playfulness remained unaltered and undiminished, the rarefied atmosphere in which she had been dwelling notwithstanding.

Having done so to the elder O'Connells, Maurice then stepped to Eileen, introducing his wife, who seemed immediately to Eileen to be his perfect mate: tall, slim, quiet, a bit plain but pretty, appearing serious and thus older than her years—as was Maurice—she was, Eileen learnt, a Limerick girl, the daughter of a wealthy merchant. Eileen embraced her sister-in-law warmly, whilst Mary Cantillon O'Connell seemed in genuine awe of Eileen's dress. Taking notice, Eileen smiled her warmest smile. "If you can believe it, my darling, *this*—she held up her skirts and swished the fabric—"is *not* the most formal dress we sometimes must wear. I truly cannot wait to don simple Irish country attire," she said as she draped an arm around the quiet woman's trim waist, adding ". . . and 'tis truly, *truly* lovely to meet you at last."

Morgan led the "wee ones"—as, over their collective, yet again groaningly expressed objection, he laughingly referred to Anne, Elizabeth and Hugh—to Eileen, first gathering her himself in a tight, full and lengthy embrace, his expression one of near-rapture at her appearance, seeming truly joyful at once again having her home.

As he released her, seeming to Eileen now much more like their father, both in the bulk of his physical size and the turbulent condition of his thick, dark-blond hair, Morgan stepped back. "My lady," his bow sweepingly dramatic, "am I to understand that both of my sisters appear attired thus magnificently every day?" He laughed, gesturing at Eileen.

Curtseying playfully, Eileen said, "My dear sir, we do so only when we do not wear that which is referred to as *court dress!*" In response to her brother's quizzical expression, Eileen waved her right hand in a playfully dismissive gesture. "I shall attempt to explain it later . . . It has something to do with baskets."

Expressions of some significant degree of awe on their faces, Anne, who was now seventeen, and Elizabeth, sixteen, cautiously stepped around their large brother and, consistent with what Maire had written of them to Abby and Eileen—that the two had grown into *pretty, poised, but quite serious young women*—both curtseyed to their elder sister, the gesture clearly in no way meant to be in jest. Understanding fully, Eileen returned their curtseys with one of her own, deeply and slowly. "My Lady Elizabeth . . . My Lady Anne," she said softly. Standing then to look at the pair briefly, she affectionately gathered both girls, tall, blond, slender and, yes, very pretty, into a warm embrace. "Talk later we shall . . . alone. I have so very much to tell you!" They did and she did, though not everything she had experienced.

It was Hugh, however, now almost as tall as Eileen as he neared his twelfth birthday, appropriately gangly and a bit awkward, his dark blond hair neatly tied, wearing a not quite fitting dark brown suit, hose and buckled shoes, who literally took her breath away.

As he approached her, nodding somewhat sheepishly, the boy began, "Sister . . ." as, unexpectedly sobbing, Eileen fell into his arms.

"Oh, my darling boy . . . 'tis a man you have almost become; I cannot believe this much time has passed!" she cried out, immediately dissolving in tears, weeping briefly but profoundly, on the lad's left shoulder.

Stopping as abruptly as she had begun, Eileen flashed a radiant smile at her once little boy, whom she had raised from his birth to his fifth year. "Ah, 'tis grand indeed to see you, my darling boy," she exclaimed and arm in arm, brother, slightly bewildered by the range of her emotions, and sister walked to join the queue for their transport.

As it first appeared that there might be a shortage of places in what were called rough carts—basically, sturdy, rectangular wooden boxes set on thick, iron-sheathed wheels, designed and built specifically for short jaunts about the rough, roadless Iveragh Peninsula—Eileen, only partially in jest, volunteered to ride home, "Though never have I mounted dressed thus." She laughed, swishing her long train as she cradled it in both her arms, the end still just barely dancing above the dust, gravel and muck where they stood.

Eventually, everyone, especially those whom Maurice referred to as "our honoured trio from distant Austria," was delivered safely to the massive, iron-banded main door of Derrynane House, the countess having been awed into silence by what she had thus far seen—the looming grey mountains, the even more vivid emerald green land, the dazzling blue sky—and heard—the unexpected resonance of a fresh, sharp, stiff wind and, with it, that of suddenly crashing waves. Perhaps more than anything, it was the talking, the chatter, the loud laughter of her new family, as one and all they interrupted and talked over each other, joking, laughing and laughing yet more. And this gentle noblewoman of Austria, who had never in her life experienced quite anything like the last hour, briefly rested her head against her solid husband and sighed and smiled and looked about in silent, wide-eyed wonder.

The joyful tumult continued even as the travellers' considerable number of trunks was divided between their rooms, more news and gossip shared, including that Eileen's twin, Mary, her husband, Dr. James Baldwin and their three small children would be journeying over from County Cork, as would the three significantly older O'Connell sisters, Nora, Joan and Alice, along with their own large families, two from elsewhere in Kerry and one from a much closer location in Cork than the Baldwins, in the coming week, all eliciting a playfully wide-eyed, "Do you mean to say that there are *more* of them?" from a faux-bemused Maria von Graffenreit-O'Connell, to which everyone who heard her responded with affectionate laughter.

As they strolled into the massive hall, the countess gently touched Maire's arm.

"If I may, my lady," she said softly, and Maire turned and took both the woman's hands in her own, smiling warmly.

"Anything, Your Grace," Maire responded perfectly, and the woman who was now officially the Countess von Graffenreit-O'Connell beamed and leaned closely to, she felt, her new Irish compatriot.

"My dear," she began, Maire instantly enthralled by the rich sound of her German-accented English, in which she already sensed just a wee bit of an Irish lilt. "In no particular order, I should be most grateful were it possible for me to be henceforth referred to and addressed by yourself as simply *Maria*—and, indeed, if I may be so bold as to request, and if your children would do me the honour, by them as *Aunt Maria*."

Maire beamed. "And so shall it be!"

"Secondly," the countess leaned even closer now, her face suddenly scarlet, "the general and I, whilst we are here, before we proceed to Morty's people at Tarmons and upon our return, we shall require but a single bedchamber. As did Her Imperial Majesty, we follow the old German tradition of . . ."

Maire beamed yet again and whispered conspiratorially, "Ah, *Maria*, my darling, 'tis a bit of an old Irish tradition as well, at least in this house it is . . . or," she grew quiet just for a moment, "it continues to be," and Maria embraced the smaller woman warmly.

Maire and the countess—who by the end of the evening had indeed become simply Maria or Aunt Maria to the family, at which she was thrilled: "Other than being addressed as 'Mama' and, more recently, 'Grandmama,' never have I gloried more in a title, familial *or* noble!" she had exclaimed, clapping her hands—quickly became fast friends and spent a great deal of the ensuing weeks together and in conversation.

As the long day, which had included brief tours of the rambling house and grounds, including Maire's exotic semitropical gardens, where the countess marvelled at palm, lime and lemon trees, not to mention her orchids, as well as introductions to Brigid, the housekeeper, Annie, her daughter and second-in-command, William, the new head groom and others, along with seemingly endless offerings of food and beverages, was drawing to a similarly long close, the late Irish summer's twilight stubbornly giving itself up to a drawn-out dusk, itself ultimately to become only a bare approximation of nighttime, Maire leaned to the countess, requesting softly, "A moment, please, my love?" and the two women quietly left the library, where conversations and laughter— though finally grown more muted than in the afternoon—nevertheless continued.

Maire took Maria's hand and led her upstairs to her own rooms, handing her into her bedroom and leading her to the massive bed she had shared with Donal Mór, directing her attention to it: "I feel your robe, and Eileen's, as well . . . they are magnificent, truly, and never have I seen, much less donned such a garment, but . . . with the thought that they might be more for a palace suited than to this"—she gestured with open arms— "wild part of God's world in which you suddenly find yourself, my darling . . ." She then indicated three handsomely tailored, long-sleeved, full-skirted woollen dresses in deep green, dark blue and brown and a pair—one natural, the other black—of long, heavy wool shawls. "If you might wish to try, might perhaps feel . . ."

The countess embraced the diminutive woman, laughing warmly. "How thoughtful, oh my dear, how very thoughtful! How did you . . .?"

"Some time ago your now good husband described you—quite vividly, actually, including your height and form—in a letter, which I was able to locate amidst my papers." Maire smiled almost smugly.

The countess continued, saying, "In truth I was reflecting on perhaps requesting something other than"—she gestured to herself and her striking dress—"but I thought I should first consult the general. Now you have already . . ." She stared in wonder at the simple and, she immediately thought, simply beautiful garments. "Thank you! *Go raibth maith agut*!" she said slowly, precisely. "I am so grateful, *my darling*!"

". . . and slippers . . . and boots as well there are, should you so wish," Maire exclaimed.

To the family's delight, the following morning, the Countess Maria von Graffenreit-O'Connell smilingly appeared at table in her new green dress, her hands thrust into its deep pockets as she had seen some of the other women doing, the light-coloured shawl draped about her trim shoulders, upon which also rested her long ash-blonde hair, an expression of sheer joy on her face.

"Why, Aunt Maria, you remind me so of Queen Maeve herself," Morgan began as he rose to hold her chair. "I shall tell you her story, 'tis called the *Táin Bó Cúailnge* and 'tis part of the Ulster Cycle. So now . . . one night, as she and her husband, King Ailill, lay abed, Queen Maeve said . . ." Over the coming days, he would hold his new aunt's rapt attention as he did indeed tell her the lengthy, extraordinary tale—all of it.

Derrynane—mid-August–early October 1767

Following what had, as expected, proven to be both a raucous and hearty breakfast, as Eileen rose from the table, Maire almost deferentially approached her, "Would you join me for a wee bit of a stroll, my darling?" she asked softly.

As they traversed the wide entrance hall, the early morning air being chilly, and noticing her diminutive mother had gathered a substantial shawl about her trim shoulders, Eileen reached for a once-favoured piece of clothing, one she had left behind when departing for Vienna but which she had retrieved and brought downstairs from the closet in her old room last night—a heavy, rough woollen Scottish-made arasaid, sometimes referred to as a woman's kilt, though, as it was traditionally made with a full nine yards of wool, nothing less than a great kilt could it be, woven of a simple, subtle grey and brown plaid. As she'd carried it down the stairs, Eileen had recalled wistfully that, shortly before his sudden death, her father had brought it to her following an especially successful trading stop at Inverness, one which had involved a complex trade of French brandy and clothing, as well as some gold, for the numerous barrels of whiskey which arrived in Ireland in the hold of Donal Mór's ship. Humming a Scottish air, Eileen skilfully folded it several times and drew it about her broad shoulders as a long, roomy cloak. The women quietly excused themselves and headed outside.

Traversing an expanse of emerald-green lawn-cut grass, they strolled slowly first to the small, sandy graveyard, near the ruins of the medieval abbey of St. Fionán, resting place of a number of the O'Connells, most notably Donal Mór, beloved husband and father of the pair. After gazing reflectively on her father's marker, in the shape, though not the dimensions, of a High Cross, Eileen slipped slowly to the soft ground. Her eyes dry, she kissed the cross reverently, patted it gently and rose, again taking her mother's hand after straightening the plaid across her shoulders.

Neither speaking, they trudged slowly towards the Derrynane strand, Eileen appearing to her mother to be absorbing all that Derrynane had long been to the O'Connells and remained: a remote, heavily guarded sanctuary, cradle of their remarkable family in an ofttimes almost overpowering setting of howling winds and crashing waves, or—as it was this morning—one of a haunting silence, broken only by the roar of several mountain streams. The waves approached the beach quietly, almost reluctantly; there was virtually no wind. Several falcons circled high above, their familiar *scree* seeming sharper than usual.

Reaching the beach, the women then sat silently, closely shoulder-to-shoulder, arms hugging their raised knees in the soft, warming sand. Sensing the sun's warmth in the morning air as well, Maire shed her shawl and Eileen allowed the folds of the arasaid to slip off her shoulders, its yards of fabric sprawled in a pillowlike mound on the sand.

Maire watched as Eileen momentarily leant her head back, her hair falling partially onto the sand as she did, closing her eyes against the sun's glare.

As they began to converse, there appeared to be little need to bring Eileen current on the news of the Derrynane vicinage; the women had faithfully written lengthy letters, sometimes twice weekly, for the years of Eileen's absence. She was thus almost fully up-to-date on local happenings, save for occurrences during the weeks she was in transit: Maire quickly rattled off a litany of births (three) and deaths (happily but one), one or two arguments, quarrels, fights even (more than there should be in such a bucolic setting), one shipwreck (not involving an O'Connell vessel) and, just in the week prior, an unexpected visit from His Majesty's Customs newly appointed inspector, one Josiah Dent, just as a massive load of goods was arriving at the pier where, as she put it, the "Austrian O'Connells" had landed.

As Eileen listened wide-eyed, her mother recounted how "Maurice immediately enveloped the wee little man—pasty, unhealthy, sad-looking . . . like a shopkeeper in the city ofttimes does, aye? He *requested*," Maire winked, "that the inspector tote up duty due on the goods already offloaded on the pier and visible on the deck . . . but no more," her eyes twinkled, "and after some of the lads strolled by, each casually carrying a rifle or a pistol, one lad a dirk as well, all of which Master Dent could not help but see, they then sat a long while on the dock, drinking of poteen and nibbling bread and cheese, as Maurice and he *agreed* that the amount then totted indeed would be the extent of goods landed . . . and that thereafter Master Dent would receive a monthly sum, which Maurice allowed him to believe was some twenty percent greater than that which had been settled on his predecessor."

Maire explained that this was with the understanding that he would some time later report that the O'Connells were, for "some reason known only to God Almighty Himself," she laughed, seemingly no longer offloading so frequently at Derrynane, advising his superiors that he and his men would assiduously, most diligently attempt to locate the family's new port of delivery, ". . . never, of course, fully succeeding in that effort," she chuckled again. Once a suitable period of time had passed, Maurice and Mr. Dent would agree on a small number of shipments, and only those involving goods of little value, upon which Mr. Dent would levy the Crown's customs duty.

Eileen could only smile. "So, the proud 'O'Connell family tradition' of *adopting* the newly arrived senior Customs inspector continues. Papa would be proud, would he not?"

Maire chuckled softly, observing, "Were it otherwise, I would fear that your papa would show his displeasure by causing the sandy earth about the abbey to shift and rumble."

After a long moment of reflective silence, the tiny woman turned towards her daughter, her expression and tone soft as she asked, pointedly speaking now in Irish, "*An bhfuil tú sásta, Eibhlín?* Are ye truly happy, my darling girl?"

Turning to her mother, Eileen returned her mother's smile and nodded, replying in kind. "Aye, Mama. Yes, I am, very happy . . . I have had 'moments,' though," she paused, "of late . . . occasioned, I believe, in part by Abby's marriage and dear Uncle Morty's—do you not *adore* the countess?—as well . . . that . . . and, and . . . also my friend, Wolfgang—the officer, Major von Klaus, of whom I've written . . . he has now departed Vienna for a several years' posting at the court of the Empress Catherine . . . 'the Great' . . . as Wolfgang says she is now referred to by some, only these few years since her accession . . . at St. Petersburg." Noticing her expression becoming distant, in the always-vivid imagination the two shared, Maire sensed her daughter envisioning a lone horseman approaching Catherine's glittering Winter Palace, emerging from a howling Russian snowstorm.

Maire sat, nodding her understanding and forcing her effusive self to remain still, as she listened to the comforting sound of Eileen's husky voice, speaking once again in English.

"My relationship with my 'girls,' 'tis in flux," she continued, "The older one, Maria Carolina, is becoming in many ways a young woman; she makes it clear she has little need for me, that she prefers the services of Countess Brandeis only; she is growing so independent." Eileen sighed, her expression for a moment cloudy. "On the other hand, my wee little archduchess"—her mother smiled at the mention of the girl she knew Eileen called Antoine—"though she approaches twelve, a very young twelve she shall be and 'tis she who remains my darling," Eileen's expression became somewhat distant, her eyes almost dreamy as she proceeded to tell her mother of the young girl's remarkable late-springtime pronouncement of Eileen being more of a mother to her than was the empress, this having occurred in a dramatic public display of sobbing, tear-drenched emotion, begging Eileen to "never leave me." "And since then she addresses me only as Mama when we are alone," Eileen said softly, looking for the moment directly into her own mother's eyes.

Maire's interest obvious from her silence, Eileen continued, explaining that, despite that she loved the girl as if she were her own child, she had experienced an immediate sense of being what she thought of as *ensnared . . . trapped even* by the situation. This, she told her still-silent mother, was relieved when Abby advised her that her obligations to her archduchesses would end when both had moved on to the positions being arranged even now for them by their mother as part of the empress's complex pan-European game of matrimonial chess, in which each girl was, as had been most of their siblings a majestically gilded pawn.

"My, my . . . how your life has changed, my darling girl." Maire smiled, thought for a moment and then nodded. "Ah, perhaps then the time 'tis now approaching when you might be considering adjusting this life you lead so that a mama to your own wee birthed babes you will be, daughter," she said softly but firmly.

Eileen looked at her mother, saying nothing, her lips slightly parted.

"As to this Major von Klaus, daughter, have you feelings? Does *he?*" Maire inquired bluntly.

Eileen blushed under her slightly wind-burnt complexion, and only after a moment's pause did she respond, "Ah, Mama, whilst 'tis dear, indeed *very dear* friends we are, we have not spoken of . . ." she began, though even as she did, she heard her mother's voice arching over her own.

". . . Ah, but daughter, is it that 'dear, indeed *very dear* friends' in Vienna are frequently abed?" Maire winced even as she spoke. *Why did Abigail write to me something of which I had no reason to be aware? Why, oh bloody why, am I never able to keep my mouth closed?* her own cheeks flaming.

Audibly gasping, her eyes wide and mouth agape, Eileen abruptly began to stand, her mother pleadingly—"Oh, Eileen, please . . ."— reaching for her daughter's right hand with both of her own, finally succeeding though only with the strong girl's acquiescence – in tugging her daughter back onto the sand, with a gentle thud, Maire's tone now plaintive, almost pitiful, her eyes teary. "*Please* . . . I misspoke, my darling, I should not, I should never have . . . oh, please, my darling girl, I am so . . ."

Settling back down onto the rough sand, Eileen sighed and sat quietly for a moment, her eyes on the offshore islands. Finally, shaking her head, she patted her mother's extended left leg, then, using her thumb and forefinger, squeezed it hard just above Maire's bony knee, causing the older women to "Ouch!" and bounce in place, laughing involuntarily. Without joining her mirth, Eileen then shook her head sagely and sighed deeply, ultimately displaying a rueful smile, exhaling yet another profound sigh. The ensuing lengthy silence ended only when Eileen began to speak, her tone evidencing a sudden weariness, laced ever so slightly with exasperation.

"Mama, despite that she is now the highest-ranking servant to Her Imperial Majesty, indeed one of the highest-ranking people at court, and said to be a soul of decorum and discretion—indeed, a skilful keeper of secrets; a canny, perhaps even cunning manipulator of minions—that she has become; my dear sister, your dear daughter, Abigail is seemingly still unable to . . ." Her voice trailed off. As the women finally shared a sardonic laugh, a flock of gulls appeared overhead, loudly *kawking*, as if to join in their ironic mirth.

For several long moments they were silent, Eileen gently easing onto her back on the level sand, her head resting on the pillowed fabric of the arasaid, looking up at her mother as Maire gazed down on her daughter, as she once had when she'd watched a dark-haired little girl exploring the wonders of the same sandy beach and always-chilly bay water.

Finally, the tension seemingly dispelled, Eileen sat up, once again hugging her knees; she looked over at her mother and drew a breath, yet again sighing, "As you *obviously* are well aware of him," she began, "and of the, shall we say, *intimate nature* of our relationship, I very much do want you to know that we are *indeed* and perhaps even more than we are lovers, very, *very* dear friends." Maire sat silently, forcing herself, this time successfully, to remain still, to listen, permitting her daughter to speak uninterrupted.

"We share so many interests, Mama: books and horses, music and the theatre . . . ideas even. He has taught me of the politics of Europe," she advised, her eyes widening a bit, "and of the complex interrelationship of the kingdoms, and of diplomacy and intrigue." She smiled playfully now, "And I have taught him . . . I have taught him of the fairies and their bright underground chambers . . . of *Fionn mac Cumhail and the Fianna of*

Ireland." She leaned her head back and laughed aloud, her hair again falling behind her onto the sand. "As a result of which he is come to believe in the fairies, it appears." She shook her head, smiling warmly.

Growing serious again, Eileen related to her mother details of some of von Klaus's military exploits in the Seven Years War, as well as of his seemingly vast wealth and high noble birth.

Maire eyed her striking daughter carefully as she spoke, Eileen more relaxed now, gesturing as she customarily did whilst relating a story, the older woman at one point interjecting, "Playful I am sure you are, my darling, in telling of the fairies and your beloved Gaelic mythical characters . . . but I am certain you speak to him of much more than tales; your own insights, your experiences are likely to him as fascinating, perhaps even as compelling as are his revelations of courts and intrigues to you."

Reflecting for a moment, Eileen nodded, then added, "And 'tis of the more recent history of Ireland that I have also spoken to him at length, such that, as he now believes in the fairies, so, too, does he loathe the *Sassenach*," she said firmly.

Pausing again, at first thinking, *You would be surprised, my darling mother. . .* she only then spoke, her tone firm, certain, "You would be surprised, my darling mother, of what I have come to know of the court, indeed of Europe as a whole. 'Tis like a massive, as sordid as it is majestic, game being played, and, aye, indeed I *do* have insights as to the people, to the players, even their possible motivations, noble as well as malevolent, all of which I *do* regularly share with Wolfgang. She then proceeded to say that von Klaus's departure for Russia had been with but slight notice. "Barely any time, in truth. The emperor, he requested that Wolfgang go . . . and go he did." She gestured with an upward flick of her hand. "Acceding to His Imperial Majesty's wishes—and wishes they were; 'twas not a command, as he is a close friend, a confident of the emperor—but as my own, my dear friend, he . . . within a matter of weeks he was gone."

Drawing her upper lip over her lower one, her mother yet again compelled herself to remain silent as Eileen continued. "In truth, I know not to any degree of certainty how it is that *I* feel, deep down"—she pressed her palms to her breasts—"for him . . . and not at all as to what, if anything, *deep down* . . . he may feel for me. Perhaps when he returns . . . perhaps then . . ." A small boat caught her attention and her voice trailed off.

Maire did not ask any more questions. Indeed, no further significant mention of Major Wolfgang von Klaus was made by either mother or daughter.

Several weeks later, one chilly, foggy evening, the Countess von Graffenreit-O'Connell, freed of her own decades-long burdens of secret-keeping and discretion and suddenly revelling in her newfound freedom and her new, now-dear friend, *Maire ni Dhuibh*, shared copious amounts of fine French brandy before a low but merry turf fire in Maire's sitting room. It was then that she—unaware that Maire already knew, confirmed that Eileen and the "truly dashing—oh, my dear Maire, he is *so* handsome! *So* gallant! Such a wonderful gentleman!"—von Klaus had for some time been lovers, "and a beautiful pair they are." She smiled affectionately. In response to Maire's not at all subtly posed questions, she was unable to opine as to the possibility of any permanence in their relationship. "It is so terribly, almost comically complex . . . von Klaus, you see, he is of ancient Austrian noble blood, and a marriage to a foreigner, not to mention, if you would please permit me"—she lowered her soft grey eyes in genuine embarrassment—"a commoner; it could prove quite difficult."

Maire closed her eyes and the countess nodded in emphasis.

Maire did, however, inquire further about her daughter's overall emotional wellness; though she had not touched directly on the subject in any letter since Eileen's departure for Vienna, she now wanted to reassure herself that the manner in which her ill-fated marriage to John O'Connor of Ballyhar had begun was not impacting Eileen in considering an at least eventual remarriage.

Mother and daughter had ridden for much of a breezy, overcast mid-September Tuesday morning, chatting as aimlessly as they had been riding. As they agreed to stop and unpack the lunch the kitchen girls had packed for them—along with, Eileen saw as she withdrew them from her saddlebags, two hefty stone bottles of good Irish ale—once they were settled with their sumptuous meal of cold meats, cheese and several fresh baguettes, lightly buttered.

Maire wondered aloud. "Think ye, daughter, that the . . . ah, how might I put it? . . . the *unfortunately combative* manner in which your marriage to the late O'Connor began . . . that it might be colouring your view of the institution itself?" she inquired, immediately quaffing a long swallow of ale.

Eileen shook her head, half-smiling. "*Unfortunately combative*, Mama . . . your way with words, 'tis in no way diminished these last years. That the man beat me into unconsciousness within a quarter of an hour of my willingly surrendering my maidenhead to him, following my own verbal attack on him. All leading to my attempting to shoot him to death the morning after . . ." Her voice trailed off and she lifted her eyes towards what was becoming a dreary grey, sunless sky.

Sighing deeply, Eileen pushed back the thick lock of hair that had fallen over her left eye as she finished a slab of cheese. "How it began, 'tis not how it ended. You know now that, with time, I had come to grow fond of the man—fonder than I ever thought possible—and he of my good self, as well," she said firmly, "and, despite that it began in violence and fury, it ended in tears and a spoken lament. Whilst nothing close to the level of affection you and Papa shared, genuinely fond of John O'Connor I was, grown comfortable being his wife; his helpmate I had become. His sudden death alone limited how fond, how comfortable I might eventually have become," she said, her voice barely more than a whisper now. Maire thought she detected a pair of minute teardrops gleaming in her daughter's large, deep blue eyes, though neither fell.

The women sat in silence; Eileen drank deeply of her ale.

"Mama, I view the institution of marriage—and all the good and the not-so-good that goes with such a state—in an overall positive light."

She stood abruptly, picking some gorse prickers and brushing the grit off her rough brown wool skirts, then offered her mother her hand.

As they rode home to Derrynane, they spoke no more of the institution of marriage, save that Eileen shared with her mother her genuine desire for children, "and I assure you that 'tis only in the lawful wedded state that I should seek to achieve this desire." She then gently booted her skittish horse, which caused the mare to sprint sharply ahead. As her mother attempted to catch up, Eileen's singular husky laugh trailed its way back to her, and Maire smiled.

Macroom, County Cork, late October–November 1767

Despite all the near-constant activity at and around Derrynane, including a number of enjoyable gatherings, reuniting with relatives, old friends, neighbours and acquaintances, even her erstwhile suitor, Master Ó More, Eileen found herself growing restive after more than a month at home in County Kerry. She was enjoying the dinners, dances and horse races immensely, but the smallness, the reality of how thinly populated the O'Connells' remote world indeed was, had brought on a desire to see other people and places, albeit she was uncertain how or even if this might be possible.

Though it was not at all what she had been considering, when her twin sister, Mary, who, along with her physician husband and their three young children, had journeyed from their home at Clohina, near Macroom, in County Cork, for one of the large family gatherings, unexpectedly remaining at Derrynane for several weeks thereafter, in discussing their departure plans, suddenly wondered aloud if Eileen would like to spend some time in Cork, a surprised, indeed startled but smiling Eileen had without hesitation accepted and said she would pack a trunk—or several. "It shall be fun!" she told her sister, who was surprised as well.

As the remainder of the pleasant week continued, Eileen reflected that, especially after having watched the continuing dynamic between Charlotte and Antoine and its effects on the younger archduchess, seeing in the relationship many aspects of her own with Mary, she felt an extended visit offered an opportunity to, as she told Morgan, "perhaps right some things between us," as well as providing her with the prospect of becoming acquainted with her brother-in-law, Dr. James Baldwin.

"He is a most interesting fellow," Morgan had informed her. "As you have seen, he is quiet, as is Mary, and bright, as she is as well . . . but he is also to no small degree courageous." This, he explained, stemmed from the doctor's virtually unheard-of conversion from being an until-then lifelong communicant of the Church of Ireland to Catholicism at the time of his marriage to Mary.

As the week, and along with it the Baldwins' lengthy stay at Derrynane ended, early on a sunny albeit cool, breezy Saturday morning, with several of the stable boys hauling a pair of substantial trunks containing a variety of Eileen's clothing, including an array of afternoon dresses, Eileen strode in the lead, the two little Baldwin girls, Sarah and Elizabeth, holding on to her hands, and they all climbed aboard a snug O'Connell river ship for the sail across the Kenmare. A coach there awaited them, carrying the extended family into County Cork and on towards Macroom.

Eileen quickly settled into the Baldwins' comfortable home and household. She enjoyed being with the children, Sarah, who was a precocious three and even little Elizabeth, whom she felt was a very sombre two-year-old, making them laugh by telling them countless funny stories and silly jokes. By the end of the first week, the three had become fast friends, and even, at the age of, as he solemnly advised her, "almost five," Walter, the eldest child, quieter even than his sisters, had joined them on walks and in playing a variety of noisy games.

After the evening meal one night after Eileen had been in residence for not quite two weeks, Dr. Baldwin found himself, as he occasionally and happily was, called to deliver a baby for a neighbour. Having seen the children upstairs, Mary joined her sister in the smaller family parlour for brandy. Eileen had already poured their drinks into two intricately cut Irish crystal glasses and toasted her twin's health, even as Mary was sitting down. Both drank deeply, their cheeks immediately flushing.

Relaxed, Eileen planned on chatting informally, very much hoping to continue their previously begun discussion about their very different lives; she was just beginning to tell Mary about using their own not always easy relationship growing up as a teaching device with her archduchesses: ". . . and 'twas then that I said to Antoine—you will recall that she is the littler one—that . . ."

"*Eileen,*" Mary interrupted sharply, "because you have mentioned this, I have desired to discuss with you . . . I know not how I might best perhaps phrase it . . . the direction of your life, perhaps?"

Surprised at her sister's assertiveness, though instantly intrigued by the topic, Eileen sat back, cradling her snifter in her hands, inhaling the fine French brandy's rich aroma, saying nothing as Mary continued, her tone suddenly chill, sharp even.

"Is not Abigail well wed? Does she not occupy a position of great honour and prominence at the court?" she queried; *somewhat archly,* Eileen thought, though she remained silent, reflecting even as her sister was still speaking.

Before Eileen could respond, Mary continued. "In contrast to our dear sister's exalted position, do you not in fact remain a *servant,* in effect a nursemaid even to these little princesses . . . or duchesses is it, rather? I mean you *wait* on them, do you not?"

"*Archduchesse*s," Eileen corrected sharply, reflexively defensive. "Expressed *correctly,* they are each *Her Imperial Highness,* an *archduchess of Austria and Lorraine,*" she said loftily, firmly adding, "and, indeed, *I* most definitely do *not* wait upon anyone; whether I dine with the archduchesses, with others . . . or alone, it is *I* who am waited upon," she purred.

"Oh . . . yes . . . very well, I stand corrected then," Mary managed, charging on, "but this does not alter your *position*, does it? You are still a *servant*, are you not?" she said again, not pausing for any reply. "What I am attempting to say, Eileen, is," she sighed, with seeming exasperation, "when might it be that *you* will aspire to a good marriage and a position worthy of your talents . . . indeed, one which will, as does Abby's, do honour to our family, to your heritage?"

Eileen, as she rarely ever did, sat speechless, her lips parted, her cheeks flaming, as Mary went on. "Indeed, is not my own position—well wed to a prominent physician, mistress of his home, mother of his children—is it not far, *far* superior to your own?" she asked, then took another deep draught of her brandy.

"Sister," Eileen began softly, "I am not certain you fully understand my role within the Imperial household. Yes, I have cared for both these girls, now becoming young women, since they were wee little ones. I have been their teacher and companion, riding mistress, friend . . . indeed, 'tis quite fair to say that I am perhaps closer to them than is their own mother, Her Imperial Majesty."

Deciding against mentioning that when they were alone, Antoine now regularly addressed her as "Mama," as Mary sighed audibly, Eileen tacked deftly, her tone even. "What you must be aware of is that both these young girls shall eventually, by virtue of their marriages, ascend thrones of Europe—one of them perhaps that of France, even. You must also appreciate, sister, that 'tis I, amongst others—a priest, several nobles, diplomats—who have spent these years preparing them for these positions and all that they will entail."

Eileen noted Mary's expression change abruptly, her sudden albeit reluctant deference now obvious.

Eileen should have left the topic at that point; instead, her ego getting the best of her, she tacked yet again, this time less adroitly. "To be fair—

and though I admit the importance of any of this is perhaps insignificant to you—you must understand I have, by the grace and favour of the empress of course, *three* apartments"—the back of her hand facing her sister, she held up her right pinkie, fourth and middle fingers for emphasis—"in three palaces, I have servants" —she exaggerated—"by virtue of my position, I receive deferential curtseys and bows from my inferiors—of whom there are many, I view operas and concerts from the same seats as are occupied by the Imperial family, Bull is stabled with the horses belonging to the empress and their Imperial highnesses, I dine and dance with . . . " Seeing Mary's eyes roll, Eileen's voice trailed off, and she then cleared her throat. "So, you see, sister, 'tis far from being a mere *servant* that I am . . . I believe you would agree, were you to come to Vienna and . . ."

"As I shall never do so, nor would I particularly care to do so . . . I . . . I shall accept your word as to all that of which you speak," Mary said, her now-impatient tone accompanied by a flat gesture of her free hand. "Though I nevertheless *do* again strongly urge you, Eileen, to consider your future . . . After all, you are aging rapidly now, my dear, and a widow you remain. People will come to believe that . . ." She waved her left hand dismissively, then bending, she poured more brandy for them, as Eileen pointedly changed the topic of the conversation.

After retiring, Eileen sat up in her bed in the flickering light of a single candle. *Widow, nursemaid, servant, husband, children . . . children, husband*—the words and their meanings spun in her mind; reflecting, she thought, *though she is lacking in any number of ways, Mary is not a stupid woman.* Eileen reflected further after she had blown out the candle, settling back on her pillows, lying in the silent dark, recalling now her mother's recent counsel about considering marriage and children, as well, *Perhaps I should reflect . . . indeed, yes, I shall consider . . . I must . . . perhaps even soon.*

It was during the third full week of her open-ended stay in Cork, the Tuesday morning being sunny, with a suggestion of becoming a day of late-autumn warmth, that Eileen, now wearing a simple, full-skirted dark grey woollen dress and a light, loosely woven natural-coloured wool shawl, joined a substantially similarly attired Mary on her ride into Macroom for market day, each woman slinging a pair of commodious baskets, joined by a strap of rough leather across her saddle.

Whilst Mary chatted with a neighbour, and as she was picking through a display of apples, Eileen's attention was caught by the sharp clatter of a horse's hoofs—indeed, by the sound of it, a horse being reined in from a full gallop—this arrival doubly unusual as people more typically arrived slowly, leaving their mounts, as had the sisters, traps or carriages on the periphery, then walking into the market square itself.

Inexplicably, instantly curious, setting her basket down at the apple stand, Eileen eased partway through the animated crowd of marketgoers; standing at least a head taller than most women and many of the men in the square, she had an easy view of what was going on, initially taking note of the just arrived, handsome dark white horse, a striking stallion.

Herself intrigued, especially as she heard hearty calls of greeting, apparently directed at the horse's rider, Mary had followed Eileen and, now at her side, was craning her neck to see the uproar. "What is it?" she inquired of her considerably taller sister.

Her eyes straight ahead, Eileen responded that all that she could readily discern at the moment was that the new arrival was, at least from the back, a tall, trim man in some type of uniform, and that he had a head of flowing golden locks, a queue tied rakishly with a bright red ribbon, the ribbon *a bit too bright, a bit too long*, she thought.

Mary remaining behind, Eileen eased a bit farther towards the centre of the square, stepping out of the crowd just as the man turned and, in doing so, appeared to Eileen to be looking directly at her—as so he pointedly was. Stepping then into the open centre of the square, the soldier smiled at her, a brilliant, gleaming smile, his folded hands resting gently on his hips, his head cocked back ever so slightly.

"*Who* is this man, sister?" Eileen hissed back to Mary insistently, almost urgently. "Do you know him?"

"He is Art O'Leary . . . also called Arthur O'Leary, of Rathleigh House, on the coach road," her sister quickly responded, after a pause continuing, "Do *you* not know him, or at least know *of* him? In Vienna, he is an officer, a . . ."

Eileen was no longer listening; rather she found herself transfixed by the whitest of smiles and the softest of blue eyes set amidst a clear, smooth, tanned face, topped by a head of hair she had already concluded as being like thick, wavy rivulets of spun gold; seeing now the man's left shoulder lowered as he stepped towards her, his left hand pressing his sword against his leg, his hip, his eyes now fixed solely on Eileen—and hers on him.

Eileen stood, facing the soldier, who stood gazing at her, at the most, four feet distant.

A tricorn, dark beaver Caroline hat in his right hand, the tall man bowed gracefully, effortlessly placing the hat over his heart, as it appeared he did frequently. "My lady . . . a good day to you," he said as he rose.

"And to you, as well, sir," Eileen, half-curtseying, responded, in what to O'Leary was a seductively husky voice, the hearing of which caused his lips to part as the voice continued, ". . . Mister Art O'Leary of Rathleigh House, as I am just told."

"I am, indeed, he," a clearly taken aback O'Leary said, "and . . . if I may, my lady . . . you, you are . . . ?"

Eileen seemed to have either ignored or not heard his question as she took yet another step closer.

Taking note of the woman's regal bearing, O'Leary felt Eileen's precise gaze move slowly from his now sweat-sheened face, not quite stark against the stiff sliver of the white shirt band visible at his neck, to his magnificent red uniform coat, which she knew was called a dolman jacket, horizontally paralleled rows of heavy gold bullion-laced braid covering the front from neck to high waist, glinting in the sunshine; a pelisse of similar colour and fabric—though with collars and cuffs strikingly trimmed in fur—worn elegantly loose, draped almost casually on his left shoulder. His buff breeches, she noted, were snug around firm athletic thighs, his lustrous knee-high black boots, she sensed, must encase muscular calves. Most intently, she moved back to his face, his eyes.

An expression of curiosity on her own slightly sunburnt face, Eileen looked deeply into O'Leary's soft blue eyes with her own, much deeper, more piercing.

"It is the uniform of Her Imperial Majesty Maria Theresa that you wear, Mister Art O'Leary of Rathleigh House," she sharply stated rather than asked, sounding perhaps more superior than she actually meant to appear.

"It is indeed, yes," he replied almost brusquely, his surprise at her recognition evident, "an officer of Her Imperial Majesty's Hungarian Hussars I am."

"How is it then," she began, now looking carefully at the understated insignia on the lower sleeves of his dolman, "Left-tenant O'Leary, that never in my own years at Her Imperial Majesty's court have I seen or even heard spoken of you?"

O'Leary stood in silence, immediately closing his gaping mouth, his face nevertheless now evidencing shock and a degree of uncertainty, emotions he was rarely if ever known to experience, much less display.

Eileen now stood a foot or just a bit more in front of him; they were of virtually equal height, eyes looking into eyes.

"*I* am Eileen O'Connell of Derrynane; I—"

To thus unexpectedly learn the identity of this imposing young woman permitted O'Leary to partially recover his bearings; stepping back several paces, crossing his arms, he immediately now affected and displayed the diffidence, the cockiness by which he was far better known, and interrupted, "Ah, yes . . . heard spoken of *you, Eibhlin Ni Chonaill*, in Vienna I most assuredly have. 'Tis the nursemaid of the two youngest archduchesses you are, yes? *Yes!*" He laughed caustically.

A long moment passed, Eileen looking at, in reality looking *through* him. O'Leary immediately felt it searingly, her facial expression arch, despite that she had dismissed her initial thought—*You insolent, conceited, supercilious man* . . . She nevertheless spoke cuttingly into his laughter. "I perform a number of roles in the household of their Imperial Highnesses, Lieutenant, and I am at times, as well, in the direct service of Her Imperial Majesty, the empress, to whom my elder sister is, as I am certain you are aware, now primary lady-in-waiting. Yet never have I heard mention of *you*, sir . . . not from my uncle, General O'Connell, nor from my brother-in-law, Major Denis O'Sullivan, himself an officer in the Konigkrantz Regiment of the Hungarian Hussars . . . ." Her words slashed the air between them.

Approaching her, O'Leary then stood rigid, his cheeks blazing, rendered uncharacteristically mute, his hat abruptly dropping onto the gritty market square. Unsuccessful in his attempt to form any coherent spoken reply, he instead, certainly unthinkingly, perhaps instinctively, in any case without redirecting his gaze, extended his right hand and gently took Eileen's right hand in his own. As he did, not only did Eileen in no way resist him, but her facial expression instantly softened, whatever ire or indignation he had provoked in her leaving it, as, cocking her head to the right, she smiled warmly and, in doing so, moved her own fingers, joining his hand with her own, his fingers strong, firm around hers. Had they reached her pulse, O'Leary would have discovered it was racing.

As he had taken and held her hand, Eileen experienced the sensation of a powerful warm wave washing across her face, which immediately felt burnt. Her breath came then in short, quick bursts as her hand rested with his and she sensed her pounding heart drawing her blood coursing through her body.

Looking into O'Leary's eyes, she spoke with an unusual degree of hesitation, her tone now soft, fully conciliatory, her smile gentle, warm. "Ah, sir, you must . . . please forgive me; perhaps too long have I been a wee bit sheltered at court, I fear. . . . I do not know many people, beyond my limited circle, such as your good self. . . . I now realise that has been to my detriment . . . it is . . . most definitely it is, sir."

Shocked, amazed by Eileen's inexplicable but welcome transformation, the young officer continued to hold her hand, and she in turn his, his own smile now gentle, friendly, rather than mocking. At the same time, O'Leary himself was experiencing what he would later refer to as a sense of lightness, inexplicably sensing a shift, as profound as it was sudden, in his very being.

Feeling light-headed, even a bit giddy, he nevertheless collected himself, responding, "And I, Mistress"—to indicate that he was aware of her history, he spoke the title pointedly, his voice briefly a slight octave lower—"I fear I was wholly out of place in my utterly inartful characterisation of your position at court. Please permit *me* to apologise."

Eileen, her lips still parted and her eyes visibly wide now, nodded slowly and elegantly, as one did at court, responding, as most definitely was not done at court, in Irish, "Och! There is no apology required, good sir, 'tis jesting you were . . . Many days a nursemaid to my girls I have felt myself being," and she laughed, a warm, genuine, almost affectionate laugh, in which a relieved O'Leary joined.

Realising herself somehow profoundly altered, but nevertheless suddenly conscious of how she and O'Leary appeared, holding hands in the middle of the market square, Eileen very gently, most reluctantly withdrew her right hand from O'Leary's, momentarily holding it with her left hand as she did, still looking intently on this tall, striking man.

"Now . . . 'tis so very lovely to have made your acquaintance, Left-tenant O'Leary," she said, now again speaking English. "Staying for a time with my sister, the Mistress Baldwin and the good Dr. Baldwin I am"—she gestured with her now free right hand in the general direction of an unsmiling, flush-faced Mary Baldwin—"so perhaps we shall meet again, whilst I am here? I should like that," she added, smiling with a deliberate hint of sauciness now at O'Leary.

"Since we are so conscious of etiquette at court, sir," she articulated purposely, "please permit me to say, if I may, sir, that should you care to call on me—at your convenience, most certainly—I should be pleased . . ." she smiled broadly, "*most* pleased, if truth be told, *sir*."

"Perhaps—yes, perhaps—that would be . . ." O'Leary attempted, then took a breath, beginning again, ". . . indeed, call on you I shall, then! Might I say at this time on Thursday?" he finally managed.

Nodding affirmatively, Eileen said simply, "That would be lovely, indeed, sir. I am certain you know the Baldwins' location . . . near Clohina it is." She gestured generally in what she believed to be that direction.

O'Leary, now smiling broadly, nodded in the affirmative and watched Eileen as she turned and walked towards Mary, his eyes fixed on her, his arms limp at his sides, still staring as he saw her turn back and look at him once, then twice, and the second time she smiled brilliantly, and though he could not be certain, O'Leary believed she might have winked. His eyes still following Eileen, he bent and retrieved his now dusty hat. He did not turn away until Eileen had rejoined her sister in the crowd.

Mary stepped towards Eileen and almost roughly grabbed her wrist. "What were you *doing*, Eileen?" the much-shorter twin demanded, her voice sharp.

"I simply met and conversed with . . ." Eileen, in marked contrast, said softly, her expression one of disdainful surprise.

"I told you who that man was, sister. . . . You did not listen, you *never listen*, you . . ."

Eileen gazed lightly down on her shorter twin. "But, Mary, listen I did, indeed. 'Twas Art O'Leary—precisely whom you said he was, and he is," she laughed, "indeed, he most definitely is!" She laughed cheerfully.

"What you did *not* listen to me say was that Art O'Leary is an arrogant, prideful young man . . . sent off for education in Flanders and thence to Austria, apparently for military schooling, and there was commissioned, and since his very first return here in uniform from Vienna," Mary scoffed, "trouble he has been, always a source of contention. He is frequently in full raiment, including his sword, as today.

He taunts the authorities, lectures them on something called the Treaty of Dingle and some Lord Desmond in the distant past . . . and his rights. Dr. Baldwin has said that on more than one occasion whilst in the public house O'Leary has openly spoken in a most seditious, virtually treasonable fashion . . . and whilst *not* taken by drink! He is far too bright, far too well-educated, far too conceited for his own good; a dangerous young man he has become, a young man whom one would be well advised to avoid," she finished with a sniff.

Smiling softly to herself, Eileen raised her eyes to the radiantly blue now late-morning Cork sky and sighed audibly. "Perhaps so, sister," she interrupted, continuing quite matter-of-factly, "but . . . arrogant, prideful, contentious, seditious, treasonable *and* dangerous . . . oh, and whatever else you said, though he may be . . . *that* is the man I shall marry."

Wordlessly, she strode away from her abruptly silenced twin, scooping up her still-empty market basket without looking down, and beginning to walk towards where their horses stood tethered. Marketing forgotten, Mary did the same and, both of their baskets bare, the sisters mounted and trotted the horses along the picturesque winding road back to the Baldwin property, largely in silence, each lost in her own—markedly different—thoughts, until Mary, seeing her home ahead in the near distance, finally reined her horse in and stopped.

"I do not know how even to begin to speak to you, Eileen," she began, her voice again sharp.

Hearing her, Eileen stopped and gently turned her own mount, so as to be facing her sister as she did, shielding her eyes from the bright, not quite midday sun, having not worn a hat this day.

"Surely, *I* do not know of what it is that you must so urgently speak to me, sister   . . . at least in *that* tone," she responded softly, almost guilelessly.

Her cheeks blazing, almost stuttering, so great was her incredulity, Mary Baldwin began yet again, her voice seeming to increase in pitch and volume with each thought.

"You ask of me the identity of a man whom you do not know; indeed, a man whom you have never before seen, which I provide, and though I clearly was saying more, many important things more, about this man, you ignore me and walk right towards him. You stand there speaking with him no more than ten minutes—whilst, I must add, holding his hand, in full view of all, like some type of . . . I know not how to phrase it; is *that* how you behave in public places in Vienna?—and the next thing you say, the *very next thing,* is that *he* is the man you shall *marry*! Are you mad, girl?" Mary, half-standing in her stirrups, now shrieked, "Have you left what little sense you seem to possess in your castles in Austria? Have you, Eileen?"

Smiling softly, genuinely, Eileen reached over towards her twin, and, somewhat awkwardly, managed to take both of Mary's shaking hands in her own, "Be calm, sister, please . . ."

As it was Eileen's hope and intention that it would, Mary's agitation did ease ever so slightly, though she almost immediately began yet again, albeit softly, sputtering, "How can you say . . . ? How can you even think that you would—that *he* would . . . ? How can you . . . ?"

Easing her horse closer, without releasing her sister's right hand, Eileen spoke softly. "Ah, Mary, 'tis in this way I am just a wee bit like Mama . . . Sometimes I have a certain feeling about things, I just do, is all . . . ."

Releasing her now silenced sister's hand, Eileen turned her horse's head and they resumed trotting, then walking the horses more slowly now, down the quiet, winding road, Mary occasionally looking over at Eileen in seeming wonder but saying not a word.

As they reached the house, Eileen gently stopped her sister. "If I may, I believe I should perhaps like to go riding tomorrow morning. I have enjoyed being on horseback this morning, and it reminds me I have not ridden enough of late. I should, however, like one of the doctor's more spirited horses—a stallion, if I may—and . . ." Smiling, her voice trailed off.

Mary shook her head noncommittally at her sister, adding diffidently, "Feel free to make your request to the boy in the barn; he is James . . .

although," she sighed, "he prefers *Seamus*," her tone confirming what Eileen had surmised: That the Baldwins were, not surprisingly, thoroughly Anglicised. Mary gestured towards a tall young man who was walking forward to greet them as they approached the Baldwin home.

The subject of this strange sisterly conversation had himself headed out of Macroom in the opposite direction. He allowed his horse to walk gently, his own mind racing:

Eileen O'Connell of the Derrynane O'Connells themselves . . . Yes, oh bloody yes, heard spoken of her in Vienna I certainly have, and certain it is I am now that any number of times 'twas indeed her whom I've seen from afar with her adoring little charges. And, aye, now certain as well it is that 'twas indeed her the many times I took note of the tall girl on that black-maned chestnut Frisian. He shook his head and sighed.

Heard of all of them, the O'Connells, of course I have! And the lad from Konigkrantz's regiment—O'Sullivan, she said—yes, from Kerry he is, as well. . . . Now Major *O'Sullivan he is, he became when he wed the sister . . . Abigail, I believe. All merrily led, I am sure, by the great warrior, General O'Connell himself. . . .* His thoughts trailed off, his mind racing now; after a few moments, reining his mount to a halt, he laughed—at himself and his *foolish ire*, shaking off his bitter-sounding reverie. He knew well he had no reason for indignation—or for envy, of the O'Connells or anyone else for that matter.

Just twenty-one, two years younger than Eileen, he had, at age fourteen, been sent first to the university at Louvain for schooling; afterwards, he, as had Denis O'Sullivan earlier, gone on to The Theresian Military Academy in Vienna, the Imperial Army in Austria believed by some to be a more dynamic and therefore more attractive military force for ambitious young Irish soldiers than others on the Continent, especially as the Hapsburgs had decreed commissions were to be merited, not simply purchased. Though seemingly by choice, he had managed to successfully cloak the extent of his education and his bright mind with the arrogant, cocky persona by which he had become well-known, O'Leary was recognised by his superiors as being an extremely well-educated, and, a number had said, quite gifted young man and officer. At Louvain he had become fluent in French, in addition to Irish and English, though he continued to struggle with German. His few close comrades understood that he was an unabashed romantic and an avid and voracious reader.

O'Leary was regarded in the Hungarian Hussars regiment raised, financed and commanded by Count Leopold Höeninger as being fearless to the extent of often showing a reckless disregard for his own safety or, as the count himself had written O'Leary's father, "At times I fear he is brave to the point of being foolish." Because of his youth, he had not seen action in the Seven Years War, having arrived in Vienna in 1763, the last year of the conflict, though even in connection with training exercises, his general disdain for the detailed study of battlefield tactics or military strategy had proven a disappointment to his superiors. "It would appear that he would rather blindly chance a heroic charge than to have closely considered, thus making available to himself, and his men, the various alternatives—alternatives to what could ultimately prove a disaster," said another officer.

"I vastly prefer to simply *do* rather than to *contemplate the possibility of doing*," O'Leary had said on more than one occasion, and his comrades and troopers alike accurately considered him to be a brave, serious whilst at times fun-loving man, good company in the officers' mess, viewed as being possessed of a quick wit and a rapier-sharp mind.

He was quite conscious that he was attractive to women and availed himself of the opportunities his appearance and personality provided him in Vienna. Initially schooled in the passionate—what were said to be the exotic French and even Italian practices of the erotic arts—whilst at Louvain, and amongst those young women at court who spoke openly of such things, he was said to be an athletic, passionate and altogether satisfying partner, though, as a gentleman, he deemed it necessary for any young woman to understand in advance of, and perhaps more importantly following, any liaison that "'Tis not a wife I am seeking. . . .'" Indeed, truth be told, O'Leary found the disparate assortment of young women at court in Vienna—largely and quite logically being primarily Austrians and Hungarians, but also Spanish, a number from the various kingdoms and republics on the Italian peninsula such as Venice and Naples, as well as a smattering of Swedes, but relatively few Irish—interesting but not compelling.

Gently spurring the animal, Art headed towards Rathleigh House, the O'Learys' home of many years, roughly two miles from Macroom, at a gallop. Arriving shortly thereafter, and barely slowing his horse, he pulled him up short, scattering rocks and raising dust in the still midday air; at the barn he dismounted whilst the horse was still in motion. A young groom came running out of the barn where the surprised animal abruptly stood. O'Leary simply called back, "Thank you, lad!" to one or both of them and raced into the house.

He was surprised to find himself in a virtually empty house. When he finally located one of the younger housemaids, she advised him that his father, whom he regarded as being a close friend, almost a confident, had been called to Cork City and would be gone overnight, he was disappointed.

I should like to have spoken with him immediately of the strange yet tantalising occurrence I just experienced at the market, and of the equally tantalising person of Eibhlin Ni Chonaill, *as Father must know her people.* . . .

Instead, O'Leary spent a largely unfulfilling afternoon wandering about the house and property, trying out a new saddle horse, attempting to read at least three different books, restlessly scanning days' old newspapers and flipping through piles of mail, seeking any circular of interest and finding none.

He considered a ride to Dr. Baldwin's residence, thinking long of it whilst he gently walked a recently injured yearling on a soft, flat field, ultimately concluding, *A very rich delicacy is* Eibhlin Ni Chonaill . . . *best taken in minute portions*, he thought with a laugh.

Finally, early in the evening, in civilian garb, he rode back into Macroom and took an informal meal with several other young men and enjoyed verbally sparring with his favourite serving girl, Alice, a buxom, curly haired blonde of perhaps seventeen. Having consumed his share of the copious amounts of porter and brandy poured at table, upon returning home he slept relatively well, though his last thought before he drifted off to sleep and his first upon awakening in the morning was identical: *Eileen O'Connell*.

That she slept relatively well could not be said of the object of his continuing reflections, as by morning of the following day Eileen had spent a generally awkward and not at all pleasant evening with the Baldwins, followed by a largely sleepless, ultimately restless night.

Whilst Eileen remained at the barn with the young groom, who was indeed called Seamus, making her arrangements for a spirited horse to ride, Mary had immediately sought out her husband, who himself was just returning from seeing several patients.

Locating Dr. James Baldwin as he sipped tea standing in the kitchen, even as she hurried towards him, Mary immediately began, "Dr. Baldwin, speak with you I *must!*"

The physician smiled at his unusually animated wife and set down his teacup; taking her elbow, he walked them both out the kitchen door into the brilliant October late-day sunlight, and then and there heard the details of Eileen's meeting with the apparently notorious Art O'Leary in the market square at Macroom.

". . . and there in the middle of the square she stood—*they* stood— holding hands. *Holding hands,* Dr. Baldwin, like some kind of a—a . . . I told her, I . . ."

"Mary, my dear, I shall speak with Eileen immediately . . . or certainly this evening," her husband said in his best calming-physician manner. "She obviously does not understand the nature of the man, and the undesirability of associating with one such as he. . . ."

Meanwhile, after selecting a mount, Eileen had remained some time at the barn and the adjoining paddock, looking over the other animals and chatting amiably, to his surprised delight, in Irish with Seamus, whom she found to be both bright and knowledgeable in equine matters, as well as good company. They talked horses, and she told him of her experiences in saddle-breaking.

"Talented you are, my lady," the young man had observed as she began to leave, both having agreed that a large, somewhat sad-eyed white stallion named Gallant would be excellent for Eileen's contemplated cross-country ride the following morning. "Spirited he is," Seamus added.

Eileen smiled. "I love *spirited*."

It was not until the three small Baldwin children had been dispatched to bed and the adults had gathered for a light evening meal that Dr. Baldwin took the opportunity to speak with his sister-in-law. He and his wife awaited her in the hall as Eileen slowly descended the steep, simple staircase, attired this evening—as she had been most days since her arrival, with the guided assistance of a young maid who had advised she could not understand why any woman would wear such an outfit—in a quite striking afternoon dress, today's being a deep grey satin. With a playfully wicked smile, Eileen responded to her sister's customary expression of silent exasperation, recalling that when she had first appeared thus attired, Mary had announced that she found her choice of clothing to be "both pretentious and unnecessary." Eileen, of course, dressed formally for dinner almost every evening thereafter.

During the course of the meal, the events of the day had been discussed cursorily, and the physician indicated his concern that Eileen had selected Gallant as her mount. "He is an irascible fellow, Gallant is . . . handsome, yes, but I often find him to be disagreeable. I rarely seem able to get him to cooperate," Baldwin observed.

"Ah, dear brother," Eileen smiled, setting down her fork, "one does not seek cooperation from a horse such as Gallant. 'Tis *acquiescence* one wants—making him do things he has no interest at all in doing—and that capitulation must be earned, taken by a skilful rider."

Noticing a puzzled expression on her brother-in-law's pale face, Eileen continued, "Spoke with Gallant I did this afternoon; walked a bit about the paddock with him as well. I believe he and I understand each other perfectly."

Remaining obviously uncertain as to the topic, the doctor managed only a, "Well, then . . ." and decided that moment was the appropriate time to address the subject of Art O'Leary.

Following what Eileen felt was a rambling, largely unintelligible introduction—focused on Strongbow and the premise that the Irish themselves had requested the English to invade their island!—to the topic, her brother-in-law proceeded with a number of detailed anecdotal illustrations of O'Leary's behaviour and demeanour, which he felt best exemplified the applicability of the words *arrogant, prideful, contentious* and *disloyal* . . . so, as he said to Eileen, "to make you fully aware of the unsavoury nature of the man, and the very real dangers of being even remotely associated with him, especially in the minds of the authorities, 't'woud be most unfortunate for a loyal subject of His Britannic Majesty, our good King George, such as your good self . . . to be thought of or viewed as being in any way, howsoever remotely, connected," he rolled his eyes, "much less wed to this young man. . . ."

Eileen appeared, to both husband and wife, to be listening attentively, in respectful silence, though her smooth fingernails nevertheless formed half-oval indentations within both of her fists, as they rested, clenched unseen in her lap.

Baldwin finally finished his soliloquy. ". . . so you see, my dear, the man is best considered to be precisely what he is—what he has made of himself—one of those undesirable individuals, any association with whom is itself to be considered undesirable . . . and most unacceptable. Now . . . do you understand, Eileen?"

Dabbing her lips with a napkin, Eileen smiled meekly. "Most certainly, Doctor, I fully understand your judgment on the man O'Leary, and the numerous bases you have used in arriving at it. Now, if I may . . ." She folded her napkin precisely and stood, as did Baldwin, he bowing to his sister-in-law. Half-curtseying, she swished out of the room, and though she gently drew the doors tightly closed behind her, she could not help but hear as her sister relaunched her tirade about O'Leary.

Shaking her head, Eileen strolled out the kitchen door and, draping a heavy shawl of warm, rough black Irish wool about her nearly bare shoulders, sat quietly on a wrought-iron bench, watching the final varicoloured streaks of the evening's dramatic sunset fade in the west Cork sky, her only thoughts being of Art O'Leary as she replayed the scene in the market square, smiling, hugging herself several times, more than once whispering aloud into the twilight, "*Left-tenant* Arthur O'Leary . . ."

Awake before dawn, Eileen dressed quickly in what was a high-necked man's white ruffled shirt and, after she'd donned a set of hip pads, a full, flowing black wool skirt. Tugging on, then gartering woollen hose about her thighs, she finally wriggled into her gleaming black boots. Raking her hair with a stiff brush, she reached around with some difficulty to tie it back into a loose, gleaming black rope that hung well below her waist.

Following several well-practised folds of her arasaid, she almost casually flung it over her shoulders. Firmly fastening it over her bosom with a striking heavy pewter broach, the O'Connell stag encircled by an intricately crafted ring of wildflowers and heather, she hurried downstairs, her boots clumping on the thick carpet runner, resounding off the gleaming dark bare wood in the broad hallway leading to the door. Not caring if she were heard, Eileen closed it firmly behind her and strode briskly out to the barn, where she found Seamus and the already tacked white stallion.

"Lady Eileen, here again is Gallant; as I said last evening, he is Dr. Baldwin's strongest and most spirited," said the groom, jumping up as she entered.

Eileen's gloved right hand stroked the horse's flanks, his nose and cheek; looking into his alert, piercing eyes, she smiled—and he whinnied. "Handsome he is indeed, and we shall have a fine morning, perhaps the entire day together, thank you!" Effortlessly, she swung up onto the stallion's back and smiled down at the young boy. "And a good day to you then, Master Seamus," she added.

Just as she began to turn the horse's head, the boy still gently gripping the bridle, she smiled again, leaning towards the young man. "Oh . . . if I might trouble you, what might be the most direct route to Rathleigh House?" Eileen asked softly.

Being somewhat more thickly settled and possessing a primitive infrastructure that included actual roads of some quality, such that her own Iveragh did not, Eileen found the rolling green country about Macroom pleasantly attractive and—especially for her purposes this morning—generally open and easy to traverse.

She immediately gave the stallion his head, and with little direction, he took her back up the gently winding road she and Mary had travelled the day before, though, as Seamus had suggested, continuing on, she now skirted and went beyond Macroom, thence following the route O'Leary had the day prior taken, speedily reaching the crossroads to which the stable boy had directed her.

There, barely slowing the by-then flying stallion—her ribbon now gone, both her hair and her voluminous arasaid streaming behind her, the plaid's dense fabric straining against the heavy broach alone (she, in her haste, having forgotten the substantial leather belt, designed to keep the garment secure)—the horse's hoofs pounding, she completed a wide arc through a rock-strewn field and some wispy ash trees. Gallant cleared an unexpected granite outcrop with ease, thence finally onto the right of the cross, speeding on to Rathleigh House itself, in the distance, a striking, flawlessly whitewashed two-story structure set beyond a grove of mixed trees.

Approaching a gravelled lane, its gates open, which she could see would lead her to the house, Eileen pulled hard as she reined in the panting animal—so that she could catch her own breath, as well. She sat quietly astride for a time, noticing not how long—the morning's chill eased both by a now generous sun and her own intense activity; a breeze, both sharp and then softly whistling—reflecting on the last twenty-odd hours, her thoughts in English, then Irish: *Possessed I must be. By the fairies, is it?* She did not laugh. *No . . . 'tis possessed I am by Mr. Art Ó Laoighaire it is. 'Tis he who is the first man for whom I ever have felt thus. . . Ah, would that Abby were here; ask her I would: What is it that has happened to me? . . . and . . . 'Tis it thus that you feel for Denis O'Sullivan?*

As the white stallion nuzzled at the sparse grasses, periodically chomping loudly, smiling to herself, Eileen reflected, picturing Abby vividly over the last years: beaming at the mere mention of O'Sullivan's name; her giddiness in his presence; the angelic, otherworldly expression on her face at their wedding and the gentle serenity that had become a part of her sister's demeanour in the months since her marriage.

Gazing again down the boreen towards her intended destination, she distinctly heard Abigail's soft voice and easily pictured them in Abby's apartment shortly after her betrothal to Denis had been announced:

"Would you wed again, Eileen?" Abby had asked at the time.

And Eileen heard her own throaty voice in the soft Cork morning air: *"I would   . . . I may . . . but, were I to do so, I should very much wish to feel what I believe you feel and how you feel . . . I should like to feel it is a special thing—as I believe what you and the good captain are and have is a special thing, a very special thing."*

Eileen sighed gently, her eyes brimming with tears and her heart pounding.

I feel . . . I may be mad, but I feel what I believe Abby feels . . . and I feel a very special thing indeed.

She gently booted the horse, who she now knew loved to run; the lane was slightly downhill, so she arrived at Rathleigh House in a clatter of broken stones, a gentle dust rising beneath Gallant's sharp hoofs.

The space before the almost blindingly white house was itself sun-dappled and bright, the air softly cool, the breeze gentle and the sounds of birds echoed from the randomly placed trees.

As Eileen slid off Gallant's back and landed before the centred door with a crunch of stones beneath her boots, the upstairs window farthest to the left opened slowly, and though no face appeared, she heard the dry, papery voice of an older woman calling out in Irish, "Hallo, young woman . . ."

"*Lá maith a thabhairt duit* . . . A good day to you, my lady . . ." whose face I am unable to see," responded Eileen, also in Irish, looking up in the direction of the window, holding her horse's reins. She slowly walked him and herself along the house front, so as to be directly beneath the window. As she walked, she casually draped the right side of her arasaid back over her shoulder.

"What is your business at Rath Laoi House, and at this early hour yet, young woman?" the voice demanded.

Eileen gazed directly up at the window. "Ah, whilst business it may not be, 'tis the Lieutenant Arthur O'Leary whom I seek. I understand this is his home, aye?"

The face of a wildly grey-haired, bespectacled woman of perhaps sixty years appeared tentatively at the window.

"'Tis at the home of Squire Conor O'Leary you are . . . whose youngest son is called Art O'Leary."

Her eyes remaining on the window, Eileen smiled and stood quietly.

"And who might this young woman, this *very tall* young woman who seeks Art O'Leary be, might I ask?" the voice crackled after a moment.

"Eibhlin Ni Chonaill is anim dom, na Doir F'hionáin . . . i gCiarraí," Eileen smilingly responded, her voice ever so slightly louder.

Spare shoulders beneath a dark wool shawl slowly appeared, elbows and thin arms leaning on the sill, the eyes behind the spectacles now observing Eileen carefully. "You say you be Eileen O'Connell . . . of Derrynane, in County Kerry?"

"*Tá . . . agus an inion na Donal Mór Ó Conaill agus Maire.*" Eileen nodded.

Wordlessly, the woman withdrew, and the window closed with a thud. Eileen smiled at Gallant and turned and walked him slowly back towards the entrance.

Within moments, the gleaming black oak door was flung open and the entryway filled—in every way possible—with the person, albeit one now clad in a shirt substantially the same as the one worn by Eileen, dark grey breeches, white hose and dusty black, silver-buckled shoes—and spirit—of Art O'Leary. Stepping onto the stones, his folded fingers resting delicately on his hips, much as they had been the day before, O'Leary nodded and smiled broadly.

"'Twas tomorrow that I was to pay a visit to *you* . . . at Dr. Baldwin's, was it not, my lady?"

Eileen noticed as she had not the day before that though his voice was resonant, it was gentle and not harsh. She returned his smile with a dazzling one of her own. "Indeed it was . . . but *today* is the day I determined to call on *you*, good sir!" She laughed, as did O'Leary.

"A mind of your own, you have, *Eibhlin Ni Chonaill*." O'Leary smiled. "'Tis refreshing, and a wee bit surprising it is, I must add."

"If 'tis approving you are, then pleased I am, sir . . . but why, might I ask, is it surprising to you?"

"Ah . . . my apologies, my lady. 'Tis only that I know your sister to be also your twin, and though perhaps unfair it is for me to judge, even more so to say, I sense her mind is . . . perhaps less *her own* than is that of my lady's hers?"

Eileen again laughed aloud, her head tipping ever so slightly back. "Unfair it may be, sir, but quite accurate it is; and true indeed it is, as it is to the good doctor that my dear sister meekly defers."

"And you . . . to whom is it that *you* defer, meekly or otherwise, Mistress Eileen?"

Eileen stepped closer to O'Leary, her expression thoughtful. "I respect my dear mother, and Maurice and Morgan O'Connell, my older brothers they be . . . and General O'Connell, of course. . . . I serve, as do you, good sir, Her Imperial Majesty Maria Theresa, to whom I regard myself as being fully subject. 'Tis she perhaps the only person on earth of whom I feel thus, but . . . *defer?*" She paused and smiled. "Ah then, 'tis to

God, in His Holy Trinity, I defer . . . *perhaps* . . . yes, but only then as to certain things." She smiled again, this time almost wickedly.

O'Leary stood, straight, rigid—almost at full attention—and, atypically for him, found himself yet again, as he had been the morning prior, fully lost for a response.

Her smile still broad, Eileen stepped towards O'Leary and effectively led him into his own home. As a groom arrived to lead Gallant off to the paddock, she felt she had seen a remarkably similar, curious expression on both the young man and the stallion's faces.

As they stopped just inside the door, the long corridor extending from the broad entryway at the front door to one ajar at the rear, Eileen momentarily felt a cool cross breeze. "Tea?" O'Leary finally managed. "Would you wish some tea?"

"Tea would be lovely, *Art*, thank you, and I should ever so much prefer if you would employ *Eileen* in addressing me. Given that I have already violated so many conventions between yesterday and today, it would seem appropriate that so too should *that* formality be abandoned as well, yes?"

O'Leary nodded in apparent agreement at Eileen, and as he gestured her into a comfortably appointed sitting room, he also nodded to an older woman, the one to whom Eileen had apparently spoken, who stood at the end of the long passageway, an expression of utter incredulity on her pale face. *Tea, please,* O'Leary mouthed, *now.* Quietly unfastening the broach, Eileen permitted her arasaid to slip from her shoulders, casually laying the garment on a side chair.

Again gesturing to Eileen, this time to a high-backed, thickly upholstered chair facing an identical one in which, once she had, O'Leary sat heavily.

"Now, *Eileen*, whilst very pleased I am to see you, 'tis fair to say also quite surprised I am, as you might imagine."

"Not unpleasantly so, I trust?"

"No, no . . . not at all unpleasantly so . . . It is just that I am . . ."

"Not accustomed to unannounced visits being made to your good self by . . . ah, what is it I have been told? . . . ah, yes . . . by a 'headstrong, reckless young woman'?"

O'Leary, frustrated by the lack of his customary witty or cutting ripostes, leaned his head back and laughed very loudly, the sound joining the clatter of a china and tea service as, a still unsmiling face atop the slightly stooped body, the woman, whose name O'Leary would tell Eileen was Anne, appeared with tea and a plate of cakes.

Eileen looked directly into the woman's lovely shamrock-green eyes. "*Go raibh mille maith agut*," she said softly, "thank you so very much." The woman at first stiffened, but then looked at Eileen and smiled, quite tentatively, but she *did* smile and nod in response.

The pair sat wordlessly whilst O'Leary poured the cups of tea and indicated Eileen should feel free to help herself to a cake, which she did. Both sipped their tea for a moment.

"Now . . ." said O'Leary.

"Now . . ." said Eileen at the same moment, and they both laughed.

O'Leary gestured, *please, proceed*, and setting her cup down, Eileen leaned back in her chair.

"I very much enjoyed making your acquaintance in Macroom yesterday . . . and, given that my time here is not to be unlimited, I thought it best simply to do what I felt I wanted to do; thus, my perhaps untoward arrival here."

O'Leary poured himself a bit more tea, listening.

"I wish to know you better, Art O'Leary, because, as does my dear mama, I sometimes sense certain things, things that others do not—and . . ."

O'Leary leaned forward. "I have heard that more than being simply a poet, albeit one of quite some renown, perhaps it is a 'dark woman of the glen' that *Maire Ni Dhuibh* may be . . . 'tis the same to be true of her daughter?"

"Ah, now, one can never be fully certain of an individual possessing such status, of that I am sure you would agree," Eileen said softly, mischievously.

O'Leary nodded.

"As I said, 'tis simply that sometimes I sense certain things, things that others do not, is all," Eileen said softly.

"And if it is not impertinent for me to so inquire, *Eibhlin Ni Chonaill*, might I know what is the 'certain thing' you have sensed that has, I am thinking, brought you here?"

Eileen sat for a moment. She finished the cake she held in her palm and took a final sip of tea, brushing her hands on her rough wool skirts, then abruptly stood. "Walk with me, good sir," she did not request and turned to the hall.

Immediately on his feet, Art O'Leary found himself following the imposing young woman out of the parlour and out of the house, into the bright sunlight, its intensity heightened as it reflected off the whitewashed walls of the dwelling.

Walking alongside Eileen now, he extended his right arm to her, which she immediately took. "Show the way, good sir," Eileen asked, adding almost demurely, "if you would, please?"

O'Leary led them through the grove of random trees that flanked the right side of the striking house and thence into an open field, the sun now brilliantly warm though not quite hot, a fragrant breeze now starting, upon which they could smell gorse and turf smoke, dung and autumn wildflowers as they walked slowly, and as Eileen leaned closer to O'Leary and he to her.

They together climbed a knoll, the grass emerald green, but the myriad flowers on its gentle slopes, and more so those on its crest, showed evidence of the increasingly chilly Cork nights. Eileen gently touched a bunch with the toe of her left boot. "'Tis close to ending their season, they are," she said softly.

O'Leary turned his head, looking at her, his mind racing wildly, his heartbeat suddenly strange and unfamiliar within him.

Raising her voice, Eileen continued, "I very much prefer beginnings to endings . . . the promise of beginnings, 'tis a joyful thing . . . Is it not, sir?" She smiled inquisitively at O'Leary.

"I find it is indeed joyful . . ." he began.

". . . especially when one senses a *beginning*," she finished.

"And am I to now know, *Eibhlin Ni Chonaill*, if 'tis a *beginning* that you now sense? And is this *beginning* then perhaps one of those *things* you . . . ?"

Eileen turned and faced O'Leary, her eyes wide and gleaming, her lightly tanned cheeks bright, her bosom visibly moving as she breathed. She took both of his hands, the right one now rough, as it had not felt the day prior, and looked into his eyes. "Oh, it is, sir, it is indeed very much a *beginning* that I sense," she said, her throaty voice barely a whisper now.

Releasing O'Leary's hands wordlessly, Eileen softly wrapped her own behind his neck, beneath his carelessly tied queue, and gently drew his face to hers, extending her own to his. Their lips brushed, just barely meeting in a most delicate touching—as light as gossamer to each of them—deep blue eyes on fair blue ones, until the four blue eyes closed and all it was that had brought these disparate yet markedly similar people to this time, to this place, detonated a powerful kiss. Their arms came about each other, and the *beginning*—now felt by both of them—the welling stresses and passions, the fears even, all came together as did they in a long, potent embrace of arms, mouths, hands and fingers, her breasts, his chest, their loins . . . until—long, long moments later—both gasping, they broke apart, still connected by grasping hands and outstretched arms.

O'Leary's eyes were now aflame, and his cheeks and forehead as well, his face and neck wet, his lips silently parted. He heard as much as felt his heart beating.

Eileen's bosom heaved beneath the ruffled front of her shirt, her eyes wide and moist and her skin aglow, her own lips parted. She nodded, firmly, decisively. "Yes," she began softly, her head nodding, "yes, oh *yes!*" Her husky voice rose in the still meadow, and a small flock of pheasants noisily took flight behind and well beyond O'Leary's back.

Gripping Eileen's hands tighter yet, as she moved back slightly, and tugging her forward, O'Leary watched and listened in rapt wonder, his mouth forming what was both amongst the simplest and often the most profound of questions: *Yes?*

Eileen's face exploded in a smile, and then the warmest of laughter in which her eyes and cheeks, teeth, mouth and lips all joined, as she managed to say, "*Tá . . . Is ea . . .* yes!"

Tears streaming down her cheeks, she cried out loudly, shamelessly, gratefully, "*Is breá liom tú, Art Ó Laoighaire!* . . . I love you!"

O'Leary's own eyes wide, then moist, he drew Eileen almost roughly to himself. "Oh, yes, yes, indeed! 'Tis true." His voice rumbled as he murmured, "*Is breá liom tú, Eibhlín Ni Chonaill!*"

Eileen's sensual voice responding to his words with a further, albeit almost-whispered proclamation, "*Tú mo ghrá.*"

O'Leary replied with a gentle affirmative nod.

"You are my love," they spoke, they whispered, they felt, as again their mouths, and this time their very souls, came together.

They eventually settled themselves for a time on the side of the knoll, looking at each other, smiling, laughing, softly kissing, touching . . . and sitting, shoulder to shoulder, at times hand in hand, in silence, absorbing, reflecting upon the wonder of the extraordinary thing that had happened, that was happening.

As they thus sat, and after they had begun walking again—"roaming the countryside," O'Leary had said it was, what they were doing—they talked . . . and talked . . . they laughed . . . both shed at first slightly sheepish and then ultimately shameless tears . . . and talked a great deal more . . . of many things.

It was Eileen who first spoke, her voice soft, even. "When first you took my hand yesterday . . . I felt my heart pounding, my blood coursing through my veins; it was as if my very soul was touched. . . ."

"I felt compelled to take your hand, as struck dumb by you I had been," O'Leary smiled softly, "and as I did so, I sensed my very being, the man I had been, ceased to exist."

"Never have I felt thus," Eileen whispered.

"Never could I have conceived *ever* feeling *thus,*" O'Leary admitted.

Each spoke in detail of their childhoods, reflecting on their lives thus far, recalling people, introducing their siblings. Art softly mourned the absence of his mother, Catherine, Eileen of Donal Mór, discussing, as well, his relationship with Conor and hers with Maire. They shared significant past events of their respective lives, including more recent ones each had experienced in what now seemed to them the far-distant kingdoms of Austria and Hungary. Art admitted he had seen her in the distance with her "little archduchesses," and Eileen blushed when he spoke of watching her astride Bull, appearing "regal."

". . . and it is only now that I know for certain 'twas you upon whom my eyes rested, you whom they followed."

"All this time spent in Vienna and we never . . ." Eileen began, and then just smiled at Art, who nodded, *No, never.*

They noted the striking similarities in their backgrounds and personalities, both joining in a spontaneous litany of words—headstrong, proud, loyal, reckless, contentious, thoughtful, loving, caring, arrogant, hopeful, curious, impetuous—and nodded to each other in agreement as to the various descriptive terms' joint applicability to themselves, laughing only when Eileen ticked off, and they both nodded, secretly devout; surprisingly, deeply devoted to God in His Most Holy Trinity and to Holy Mother Church.

"Please tell none in my regiment!" Art cried out, his eyes laughing.

As the hours passed, both felt that he, that she had arrived at a point at which, as O'Leary phrased it, "I believe I know you, Eileen O'Connell: who you are, what manner of woman, of human person you are . . . and, aye, even a wee bit of *why* you are both!"

By mid-afternoon, their hands joined, shoulders and hips touching gently, they continued gently wandering the green land, venturing even further afield. They had walked several winding miles, through fields and woods, on and alongside a rough path, then following a noisy brook, until a shared sense of weariness brought them to a halt at a quiet place where the brook now asserted itself as a quickly flowing stream.

O'Leary sighed as he dropped heavily onto a mottled, leaf-carpeted piece of earth, resting his back, his head against a very old oak tree. Looking up, he extended to Eileen his right hand, and she knelt, her eyes still gleaming, and sat a moment on her heels.

His long legs outstretched, O'Leary patted his lap, and instinctively Eileen turned and lay on her back, her head resting on the indicated place, his muscular right thigh, and smiled up at him. Having talked constantly as they had walked, they both now grew silent, the stream, some birds, the wind gently rustling the heavy oak leaves, and, in the not-near distance, the barking of a single dog the only sounds they could hear.

His eyes fixed on hers and studying her face, save for a long moment, as his slender fingers gently stroked her hair, O'Leary's eyes followed the course of a falcon as it took flight, nobly circled the open sky, arched and disappeared.

Eileen's eyes never left his face; she studied his sun-bleached eyebrows, his high—proud they were—cheekbones; the tiny patch of blond beard beneath his lower lip that had somehow escaped the stroke of his rapier-sharp razor this morning and sensed the delicately perfumed aroma of the fine, French-milled soap he used for shaving.

Just as she was studying the elegant curve of his chin, O'Leary smiled down at Eileen and she reached for him, and their lips met, yet again, but just barely, each murmuring yet again the glorious words *Is breá liom tú,* which they each whisperingly affirmed, *Tú mo ghrá . . . Tú mo ghrá . . . Tá tú mo ghrá, go deimhin;* you are, indeed, my love . . . and nothing that has been said, nothing that has been told to me by ye these many hours has served to alter the fact of this one wee bit . . . Arthur, Eileen. . . .

Taking note that the sun having continued its arc across the delicately clouded blue sky of Cork, and above its emerald landscape, the couple reluctantly acknowledged the need to find their way back to Rathleigh House.

"I suspect your dour housekeeper is wondering to where I have spirited you!" Eileen laughed, as, holding onto O'Leary's proffered hand, he having stood first, she knelt, then herself stood.

"Old Anne, ah, a good soul she is, more than simply dour, grieving these twenty years for her Michael, an exceptionally good soul he also was, I am told, and Michael the Younger in America, I am sure never to return. . . . 'Tis sad," Art explained gently.

Eileen began, "I . . ." and halted, and began yet again. "Maire grieves for Donal Mór each day of her life, I am certain," she responded and then grew silent, the sounds of her boots, his shoes crunching, echoing in the soon-to-be-cooling afternoon air.

Their route back considerably more direct than the one they had taken away from the house, they arrived an hour and a bit more after they'd last stood by the stream, slowly beginning to stroll up and down a series of gentle rises, the sharp white-and-black of Rathleigh House's north side vivid in the near distance.

"'Tis a lovely house, Mister O'Leary," Eileen observed softly as she tugged them to a halt.

"Is it a lovely enough dwelling house for a daughter of mighty Derrynane, one who now resides in palaces in Austria, in which to perhaps someday settle?" O'Leary wondered, in the most matter-of-fact tone he could muster.

Eileen reflexively tightened her grip on his right hand, which she had been holding with her left. "I should think 't'woud depend on the circumstances of such dwelling. . . . Would this girl continue being a *nursemaid*"—she spoke softly, her eyes twinkling—"to the *monarch*'s many children there, for example?"

His cheeks again visibly bright, O'Leary stopped and turned to Eileen, taking both her hands in his own, his eyes looking deeply into hers. He shook his head. "A *nursemaid*? I should think *not*!" Then shaking it again, emphatically, "*No*, 't'woud rather be her duty, amongst many, *many* others, to produce the monarch's children, whether they be many or few, 't'woud not matter . . ." he said softly, his eyes ever so visibly moist.

"Oh, Art!" Eileen whispered, tears flowing down her cheeks, "I believe the daughter of Derrynane would gladly assume that duty . . ." After a moment, her eyes slightly lowered, she added, "I am fully certain that she would . . ." finally managing, "I would . . ." in the tiniest of voices, "I shall."

"I should like that very much," O'Leary himself managed before he drew Eileen's lips to his.

Though they were then but a few hundred feet from the house, it was nearly thirty minutes until they crunched across the broken rocks leading to the main door.

A tumble of practicalities, questions—some easily answered; many, many others not—had filled the air:

"From whom would consent be sought?"

"From Maurice O'Connell, as it is he who is now *príomhfheidhmeannach ár clann* at Derrynane."

"When shall we be wed? Where? Here? At Derrynane? In Vienna?"

"To Vienna we must both return, at least for a time, yes?"

"Yes. I promised Her Imperial Majesty and my sensitive and in many ways still little Imperial Highness Antoine that I would—and to assure them both I have even left my beloved horse in Vienna."

"Is it then in Vienna that you would wish to remain?"

"When both archduchesses have departed, it has been my thought that I would possibly do the same . . . and now 't'woud appear that I may actually have someplace to go. . . ." She smiled softly, her eyes again moist, and he smiled broadly, nodding affirmatively, *Aye, you most definitely shall.*

"What of your sister?"

"Ah, I should miss my darling Abigail so . . . but I have long felt 'tis she rather than I whose life is to be spent in Vienna."

"The thought of possibly being mistress of a fine house in Cork"— Eileen smiled softly, her eyes teary—"that is how I believe I should like to spend my life, with you . . . and our children." She paused, her tone now suddenly wistful. "You know that I once was briefly mistress of a fine house. . . ."

Though O'Leary had heard some of the story of her time at Ballyhar, he waited to hear more.

Eileen was silent for a moment, pensive. She then continued, "Would you at some point leave the army?"

"In time, yes . . . there are rewards to remaining a time longer, though I should intensely dislike leaving you. . . ."

"I should miss you so, though, with your kind-sounding father, I believe I should both feel and be safe and happy here—and I should be pleased to care for him in your absence."

"Then I shall leave here and you only when busy with the first of the few or many children you are and would be," and they both laughed and kissed and laughed again.

From the middle of the three narrow upstairs windows grouped together as one at the centre of the house, Conor O'Leary had been watching the couple at a distance and now as they approached the house, reflecting that it had not been his intention to do so, and even more so that he could not hear them. He continued to watch them until he heard the latch of the door echo in the long hallway below him.

Tall, silver-haired, trim and imposing at age fifty-nine, Conor O'Leary was, like the O'Connells, a devout Catholic who had—no one ever discussed openly how—publicly retained both his cherished faith and his position in society. As it was, O'Leary had for many years been land agent for the prominent Church of Ireland–espousing Minhear family of Carrigaphooka; what was quietly referred to as being the "permanent lease" of Rathleigh House and its not insignificant lands, the rents received from its tenantry being only part of what was said to be his substantial remuneration—along with certain significant "protections" afforded him and his family by his patrons.

Loyal, unsmiling Anne had advised him when he returned from Cork City of Eileen's sudden appearance very early in the morning, and that she and Art had departed on foot.

"An exceedingly tall young woman, the tallest ever have I seen, with the blackest of hair, the longest ever I have seen. She says she is *Eibhlin Ni Chonaill*, that her parents are Donal Mór and Maire of Derrynane in Kerry."

The elder O'Leary had at that point nodded; his mind racing, recalling, concluding, he then felt he had no reason to doubt Eileen's representations.

As he stepped back from the window, he reflected that he had known the late Donal Mór Ó Conaill solely through business and thus not terribly well, acknowledging that it was of the O'Connells' business activities—"commercial interests," they called them—that he himself deeply disapproved. *But matter it perhaps no longer does; the man is dead, the eldest son seemingly dispatched to America, or is it the West Indies? Though why, no one appears to know, and the next son now in charge . . . Maurice, aye? A decent fellow he appears, more loyal, more serious, less obstreperous than the father, he is said to be . . . though a smuggler he remains. . . .* O'Leary shook his head, dismissing the final thought. . . . *And, amidst the huge brood come out of that wee tiny wife of Donal Mór, there is, I know, though never have I seen her, a very tall, dark- . . . I believe, yes, black-haired girl . . . such that 'tis* Eibhlin Dubh, *they call her, and I believe 'tis she and my son who now await me below . . . so, I shall see her now.*

He turned from the window, brushing his sleeves, he walked to the staircase and thence downstairs.

In what was to her Rathleigh House's equivalent of the library at Derrynane, Eileen and Art had seated themselves side by side on a comfortable camel-backed sofa and now faced Conor O'Leary as he himself sat in one of two matching armchairs directly across from them, gently lighting a fresh pipe, his long, lean legs crossed, the silver buckles on his shoes, like the shoes themselves, gleaming, the grouping itself comfortably set perpendicular to a large, elegantly mantled fireplace, a new fire just set and now burning in anticipation of the coming evening's chill.

Educated at Louvain, Conor O'Leary was very much as he was regarded by those who knew or knew of him: a wise, thoughtful, widely read and travelled man, a man soft-spoken and not given to great passions, intemperate judgments or rash actions; indeed, he was the very antithesis of his handsome youngest son.

As he listened, primarily to Art, and also attentively to Eileen when she did speak, in what the elder O'Leary quickly determined was a delightfully seductive voice, primarily of her marriage and widowhood, as they related to him the events of the day, his facial expression remained impassive, calm, at points even mildly amused, whilst his heart thumped and his mind raced.

Such was the length of the couple's discourse that he had emptied ashes from and then refilled, retamped and relit his pipe.

As Art was completing the tale—"and thus it is, Father, that we wished to advise you of these momentous occurrences, and, as a result of them, the contemplated direction of our lives, sir . . ." O'Leary was now drawing deeply on the fresh bowl of tobacco, the result of which he exhaled as a pungent, fragrantly complex blue cloud that momentarily hovered gently above the three of them.

After he had exhaled, Conor O'Leary rested his head back and studied the two indisputably attractive young people seated across from him and saw them join their hands as he sat quietly, almost contemplatively. He bent forward to a low table, cradled his pipe in the upraised prongs of a silver rest and took a deep breath. Looking first at Eileen—*as pleasant to gaze at,* he thought, *as she is to listen to* —as he leaned back in his chair, he smiled and then nodded slowly, respectfully.

"Confess to you both I must, never have I heard a tale such as what you have just related to me; 'tis a story worthy of a great author indeed. . . ." He paused, his own soft blue eyes briefly closing. "And, indeed, the author of *this* . . ." he lifted his rough hands slightly, as if in priestly prayer at Mass, "may, indeed, be the Author of all, eh?" He laughed affectionately, though not at all dismissively.

"What I am attempting to convey is that, whilst there is no logic for any of the events of this day, or of the day prior, it appears that, whatever the reason and whatever the cause, there is a certain, what I shall call *reality* here, a reality that I am recognising and am prepared to accept; all logic, my many years of life and experience, *all* of this aside. . . ."

Eileen squeezed Art's hand and smiled at him, quickly turning her again serious face to the Squire O'Leary's.

"This being said, my dear children, as children indeed you both be, how and whether this . . . this *reality* of yours, which, for reasons unbeknownst to me, I now am come to accept . . . How it will be viewed and whether or even accepted by others . . . 'tis this that remains to be seen.

"Mine are the feelings of an old man who loves his last son and wishes for him a good life, pleased at seeing him come thus with an extraordinary young woman such as your good self, Lady Eileen . . . I would caution you strongly that my own may not be the feelings of your family, who may view the circumstances quite differently . . . I do not wish to seem harsh or critical of the O'Connells, but you yourself, Eileen, make clear that the basis for your union with O'Connor had nothing to do with affection."

Eileen nodded. "Indeed, affection was not at all the basis of my marriage. 'Twas at best a horribly wrong decision made solely by Denis O'Connell, who, as a result of such action, was himself banished by the O'Connells themselves to the island of Jamaica, where he is and there I understand forever shall remain," she replied firmly.

The elder O'Leary nodded. *Ah, so that is what happened. . . .*

"I do not have the answers to any of this; they shall not be clear this night. . . . That said, might I suggest that some thought be given to a meal of sorts, and then to the timing and manner of the Lady Eileen's return to the home of good Dr. Baldwin, yes?"

Assisted by several young women in the simple food's preparation, the solemn Anne oversaw the setting of a hearty though uncomplicated meal of hot vegetable soup, cold meats and cheeses, accompanied by several fresh, warm loaves of bread with butter and a flagon each of simple white and red wine.

The table conversation was similarly simple and uncomplicated: They spoke of horses, the weather and the seasonal change in process. As they finished eating and drained their wineglasses, the elder O'Leary leaned forward on his elbows. "Not that I am especially anxious for an evening's journey, even a relatively brief one, but in the interest of there being, shall we say, a *calmer arrival* at the good Dr. and Mistress Baldwin's residence for our *guest* here"—he gently took Eileen's fingers in his own and smiled—"I am going to request that Art here rouse someone to assist in saddling our horses." He nodded in his son's direction and Art stood, acknowledged his father and Eileen and hastened out of the room.

Within the hour, the O'Learys' mounts and Dr. Baldwin's stallion had been tacked and readied, the O'Leary men had each changed into boots, heavy cloaks draped over shoulders—in Eileen's case, having retrieved her arasaid from the parlour, where Anne had neatly folded it, she drew it about herself, and again fastened the heavy broach—the curious trio had clattered and jangled away from Rathleigh House, up the boreen and onto the roughly adequate roads Eileen had traversed much earlier in the day, their trip beyond Macroom made easier by the gentle sheen provided by an accommodating full moon, which cast the countryside and the evening in a magical light—or at least Art and Eileen thought it did.

Within an additional half hour, the three riders again clattered and jangled, this time up the rough path leading to the Baldwin residence. A sleepy Seamus came racing out of the barn as the front door of the house was flung open, light from the entryway and from a lantern held by Dr. Baldwin endeavouring, with some success, to illuminate the scene, into which rushed a wide-eyed Mary O'Connell Baldwin.

"Eileen! Where have you . . . ?" She saw the O'Leary men and abruptly fell silent, her mouth agape.

The elder O'Leary nodded in a perfunctory manner. "Dr. Baldwin, madame," he said as he removed his hat.

Hatless, Art nodded crisply. "Doctor, madame . . ."

Neither Baldwin responded in words, though the doctor nodded, just barely.

Then Mary Baldwin's almost-shrill voice burst into the chill night air. "Eileen, you will go inside *now!*"

An unspoken tension immediately fell heavily over the dimly lit space.

"And a good evening to you as well, sister." Eileen smiled with cloying sweetness. "I trust you have had a good day." Then, looking scathingly at Mary, she gently took Art's hand and momentarily held it to her right cheek and, whilst lowering his hand at her side, she nodded to Conor O'Leary. "Thank you for a lovely dinner, Squire O'Leary, and for accompanying me home."

She then raised Art's hand again, this time to her lips, and softly kissed it. "Until tomorrow then, *mo ghrá,*" she whispered, and Art nodded gently, his eyes fixed on Eileen as she stepped around the Baldwins and into the house.

As his wife began to speak, James Baldwin, a tall, spare, rather pale man, who, though he was in robust good health often appeared wan and unwell, raised his hand, spoke her given name once—sharply, indicating that Mary should go into the house— which she immediately did, glaring equally at father and son. She stalked heavily upstairs, briefly considered—and dismissed—attempting to speak with her sister and instead went quietly into her own room.

"Now, gentleman," the physician began, "it appears we have something of a . . ."

"Doctor, please, if I may," Squire O'Leary began in an even voice, "I do not believe that *we*"—he gestured to Baldwin and himself—"have anything of an anything." He smiled somewhat ruefully. "Rather, 'tis my son and your sister-in-law . . ." he paused, "'tis rather *they* who have matters to discuss, decisions to make . . . and, I believe, consultations to be had, properly, at Derrynane, not here, not at Rathleigh, but with the O'Connells."

Having formed no thoughts beyond those he had just expressed, O'Leary's mind then proved itself to yet be both quick and highly effective. "In the coming I would say *days* . . . these young people will, as they should, spend certain time together. I shall offer to them an acceptable degree of isolation at Rathleigh, to afford them some measure of privacy for their conversations. I should request that you and the Lady Mary do likewise."

Baldwin nodded, his expression softening.

"At such time as my son and the Lady Eileen determine to be appropriate, they shall journey to Derrynane. I am prepared to accompany them, should that be acceptable to them both . . . and, of course, to the O'Connells."

Art, an expression of relief on his suddenly weary face, silently nodded, as did Dr. Baldwin, who extended a hand to the elder O'Leary and, after they had shaken, to Art as well, and they did likewise, the physician and the soldier looking eye to eye.

As the O'Leary men prepared to take their leave, Dr. Baldwin walked them to their horses, which were quietly nibbling at any easily available mid-autumn grasses.

"Thank you, Squire, very much. I believe you have eased a potentially tumultuous circumstance, though why you have chosen to do so I know not," Baldwin observed and wondered aloud.

"Doctor, when one grows older, one occasionally senses what at least appears to be the correct path to follow," Conor O'Leary said as he pulled himself up into his saddle.

Art smiled as he seated himself in his own saddle. *Ah, now 'tis the squire who is sensing things. . . .*

Baldwin watched the O'Learys depart and then quietly closed his front door.

Once upstairs, hearing nothing and noting Eileen's door closed, he went to his wife's room. A brief, highly animated—as Mary was, after all, an O'Connell—and most unpleasant conversation between husband and wife immediately erupted. It ended abruptly as Dr. Baldwin, his reedy voice purposely sufficiently loud to permit Eileen to hear, told his wife, "You shall do no such thing! 'T'woud be wrong for either of us to attempt to play any role. 'Tis for your mother, for Maurice . . . indeed, I believe General O'Connell yet remains in Kerry, does he not? Perhaps *he* might be able to make sense of this."

True to her word, early the following morning Eileen again rode Gallant, though at a much gentler, less frantic pace than the day prior, to Rathleigh House and was greeted at the shimmering black door by a now-smiling Anne, who ushered her into the dining room where the two O'Leary men were breakfasting.

Consistent with what the elder O'Leary had said the previous evening, after Eileen had joined the men in breakfast and coffee and the three finally rose from table, Art and Eileen did spend much of the day—until he accompanied her home on a slow, gentle twilight ride—in conversation and reflection, the latter both spoken and silent, as to what had transpired and what might, what should next happen.

Indeed it was that Art and Eileen would spend much of the following two weeks, continuing that which they had begun whilst first roaming the countryside, talking for hours, discussing countless matters—both at and about the Baldwins' home and at Rathleigh—as well as purposely appearing in public, riding in the countryside and strolling together in Macroom, Eileen at those times primly on O'Leary's arm, O'Leary himself conservatively attired in dark suits and Eileen in her simple dark wool dress and arasaid.

On only one occasion—an unseasonably warm afternoon—by design did he dress in full uniform—blue breeches replacing his buff ones, and a stunningly high, fur-trimmed busby hat instead of his tricorne—and on that day Eileen herself appeared in a complete, *avec train*, afternoon dress of emerald green satin, heads turning as the couple arrived by carriage in the market square where they had first met, O'Leary himself at the reins, people stopping to marvel as they meandered slowly about Macroom.

However they were attired, whilst in Macroom, they would acknowledge and themselves be acknowledged by friends and acquaintances of their own or of their respective families', all combining to make clear that they were, as it would become known in later times in Ireland, "walking out," formally courting, albeit in this situation, absent both the consent of the young woman's family to do so—and a chaperone.

Derrynane—late November 1767

On a chilly Monday afternoon several weeks hence, a young messenger arrived at Derrynane bearing only a sealed envelope, addressed to *Maurice O'Connell, Esq., nr. Waterville, Derrynane, Co. Kerry*. Receiving it, Maurice graciously directed the young man to Brigid's kitchen for tea, to await— as, having quickly noted the request that he do on the reverse of the envelope he advised that Squire O'Leary had directed him to—a written response. Maurice himself then settled into a wrought-iron chair, set looking towards Derrynane Bay and bathed in the warm afternoon sun; after breaking the plain red wax seal with his long, graceful right pointing finger, his eyes quickly scanning it and, learning it had, in Conor O'Leary's precise, elegant hand, been written, he began to read slowly:

> *Rathleigh House*
> *Co. Cork*
> *20 November 1767*

My dear Squire O'Connell—
Uncertain as to whether your sister, Mary, and/or her good husband, Dr. Baldwin, has communicated with you as to the subject of which I write, please permit me to advise you that your sister, Eileen, and my son, Lieutenant Arthur O'Leary, of the Höeninger Regiment, Hungarian Hussars of the Imperial Austrian Army, have

arrived at, shall we say, an "understanding," one which, if brought to ultimate fulfilment would, I believe, significantly affect both of our families.

Given what in my estimation is the obvious sincerity of these young peoples' feelings for one another and the significant interest that both your house and mine would have given this, I should respectfully suggest that it would appear to be altogether appropriate for us to come together in serious discussion. To this end, I should like to propose that I accompany my son and your sister in coming to Derrynane, perhaps even by week's end.

As he, I trust, has indicated, I have asked the young man who placed this letter in your good hands, to await your written response. I further trust that this is acceptable and in no way an inconvenience to you.

In closing, please be assured that I am now and shall always remain, sir,

Faithfully yours,
Conor O'Leary

Sighing, Maurice folded the letter on the lap of his worn, dusty and bramble-torn brown breeches and draped one long, booted leg over the other, resting his head back and closing his eyes.

Dear God, Almighty God in Heaven, seems this does a harsh, indeed a cruel prank on a family that has only just recently begun to recover from an extended time of tumult, beginning, as Your Good Self is fully aware, with the death of Donal Mór and the horrific events occasioned by Denis, now himself in banishment in the New World, and the subsequent departures of Abigail and Eileen for Vienna, and of Daniel Charles for France, the death of dear Conaill at sea . . . only the joy of knowing Abigail is happily wed to good, stolid Major O'Sullivan and the joyous surprise of seeing General O'Connell himself blissfully wed to the lovely, charming and delightful countess, who, as were he a fresh-faced young man, has brought home to us . . . these events have made us again a happy house . . . and for these, Lord, we are most grateful indeed! But now! Eileen and Arthur O'Leary, as You in Your limitless wisdom must know, no union could be more perfect or more disastrous!

Maurice opened his eyes and sat quietly, staring at, but not seeing, the sunlight dancing merrily on Derrynane Bay. He seemed to be awaiting a Divine response.

Several moments more having passed, he rose and, sighing again, strode slowly towards the dark, rambling house, in search of his mother.

Locating Maire in the kitchen, Maurice and she walked wordlessly to his study, where he simply gave her Conor O'Leary's letter to read, watching her affectionately as her facial expressions evidenced a sense of mystery, surprise, a measure of shock and then a broad smile.

"How lovely, is this not?" She smiled at her son.

"Oh, Mother, how I wish I could share your positive emotions, but I cannot."

"Why can you not, son? Is this man O'Leary not a gentleman? He is in Denis O'Sullivan's . . . in the same army or brigade, or is it regiment, as Denis, yes? Perhaps Eileen and he met in Vienna?"

Maurice sighed. "A gentleman he is, as is his father most definitely . . . but, judging by his reputation in Cork, he also is a brash and hot-headed young man; indeed, he is much talked about throughout Munster. Very proud of himself and his status, he is: Whilst in Ireland, he is frequently in uniform, even to wearing his sword. He speaks openly of his loyalty and devotion to 'Her Imperial Majesty, the empress' and emphasises he possesses neither for King George."

"But, my son, what affect is this *here*"—she gestured broadly about—"on us at Derrynane? Indeed, he and Eileen . . . were they to wed—and it would seem that this is what is contemplated by what the father has written"—she smiled warmly, dreamily, "would they not then return to Vienna? Or even wed *in* Vienna?"

"Mother, would that it were so simple. I see the joy you feel . . . I know how you especially desire Eileen's happiness, but . . . the impact on us could be direct, and, if it were thus . . . it could be severe.

"Young Art O'Leary is well-known and deeply disliked by the authorities in Cork, perhaps even in Dublin, whilst Conor, the father, is viewed as loyal and supportive, the land agent he is for the Minhears, they of Carrigaphooka; the king's men view Arthur as seditious, dangerous and disloyal . . . and I fear they are largely correct in their judgments. He is apparently a bright but strong-willed man. I doubt he could be persuaded to remain permanently in Austria; I know Eileen would not agree never to return here."

The serious man, who seemed so much older than his not-quite-forty years, stared into space. "I cannot—*we* cannot and *we* must not—chance being in any way connected to Art O'Leary, Mama; 't'woud be as if a torch were suddenly held to the entrance to a treasure-filled cave. All that we—you and Papa, and Grandfather and the others—have hidden, secreted and veiled all these years: Our commercial interests, the ships, the people who depend on us, here and in Europe, in the Mediterranean, not to mention our own safety, security and, yes, prosperity, the details of all would eventually become fully known and wholly revealed and all, Mama, all could be lost."

Maire now sat quietly, sadly reflecting, reluctantly understanding and unenthusiastically agreeing, at least to some degree, with her son.

"But . . . 'tis Eileen's happiness . . . Can we not see them? Can we not perhaps dissuade them? Is there nothing . . . ?"

Maurice stood and opened his arms to his diminutive mother, embracing her as she stepped into them. "See them we shall, and see if we can, what we can . . ." His voice trailed off.

So said Maurice's brief though cordial note to Conor O'Leary, which, as soon as it had arrived, he showed first to Art. They then both rode immediately to the Baldwins' to share it with Eileen:

"*. . . My mother and I—and, if you would most graciously consent, also our uncle, General the Count Moritz O'Connell and his wife, the Countess von Graffenreit-O'Connell, now visiting us from Vienna—we should all welcome you and your son to Derrynane, and Eileen, of course, home. Please come at your own good convenience. We shall anticipate and be prepared for you to arrive perhaps by week's end?*"

And indeed it was that late on the next Friday afternoon, carrying their own battered leather satchels, the O'Learys and Eileen stepped off one of the O'Connells' sturdy coastal ships, following a gentle crossing of the Kenmare from what was generally thought of as being "the Cork side," though the lands along the far bank and inland for quite some distance lay still in Kerry. With Eileen leading the way, her long stride fully at home again at Derrynane, they trudged up from the strand towards the house.

They had been welcomed warmly—hands shaken, embraces exchanged; even Hugh, appearing somewhat unsure, shook Art O'Leary's firmly, pointedly looking him in the eye and nodding slightly, O'Leary smiling and nodding in response.

Luggage had been delivered to rooms and unpacked and beverages served; Eileen and O'Leary visited with the elder O'Leary and Maire, and Eileen introduced Art to her brothers and sisters, who received him warmly; in Morgan's case, effusively: "Heard of you, sir, I have; 'tis an honour indeed to meet you. We must talk during your stay here; I have much to discuss with you, sir."

As this was transpiring, Maurice had stepped quietly into his study, rifled through the disarray of papers on his desk and adjacent writing table and retrieved notes and a copy of a document he had prepared earlier in the week. As he did so, he reflected that he had several days' prior summoned a bright young lad named Michael, the literate, highly personable and ambitious eldest son of a tenant family, who had recently begun performing a variety of tasks for the master of Derrynane. Whilst Michael waited quietly by the fire, Maurice had quietly reread the lengthy message he would direct him to immediately carry upriver, the envelope already prepared: *Hon. Geo. Gough, Deputy Under High Sheriff, Kenmare, Co. Kerry.* Declaring himself satisfied with the text, Maurice had then signed the letter with a flourish; immediately dispatching the young man, who placed the envelope containing it in George Gough's rough hand the following afternoon.

He now reread the copy he had made for himself, noting with satisfaction that he had taken broad, but, given the circumstances, he felt *absolutely essential*, liberties with the truth concerning a number of salient facts, such as representing that "this man, O'Leary, of whom I write, has pursued my sister, Eileen, a maiden of barely twenty years, aggressively and unceasingly since he first came upon her in the public market square of Macroom, some weeks prior, to the extent that I now believe that shortly, perhaps even this week, he shall appear at Derrynane, at her very home."

Though the one of O'Leary was based on hearsay and conjecture, he had next provided generally accurately detailed physical descriptions of both Art and Eileen, concluding, "Whilst I shall, of course, continue to make every effort in my endeavour to protect my innocent sister from this man, my concern is that he may have already overpowered her will, and my fear is that he shall perhaps, even as I write, be planning to attempt to spirit her away. My request, indeed, my plea to you, sir, is to have your good self and any trusted, loyal men in your regular or casual service to, from the moment you shall receive this until such time as you shall learn, in writing, from me to the contrary, keep careful watch for and similarly listen for word of either of the persons fitting the physical descriptions above set out, whether they be alone, or as I suspect they may well be, travelling together, whether by boat, animal or even on foot. Should they be seen together, you may act, on my oath herein now given you, under which I swear that my sister will have then been seduced and abducted by the man O'Leary against her wishes, contrary to her will and in violation of the laws of this Kingdom, and I pray that you shall therefore take all measures necessary to apprehend the man O'Leary, charging him with the crimes as alleged, and rescue and return my beloved sister to Derrynane forthwith."

Folding all the papers, his notes, drafts and the final copy, and placing them in the deep left-hand pocket of his coat—he slipped Squire O'Leary's in the right-hand one—Maurice quietly rejoined the family gathering, personally escorting Eileen and O'Leary to the dining room. There the O'Connells and their guests came together at table and a hearty meal was shared, the conversation pleasant, general and largely inconsequential, despite Hugh's awkward efforts to turn it to the topic that he knew was the reason for the unusual visit.

The meal ended, Maurice and Maire had stood in their places at the far opposite ends of the massive table. "If you would please excuse us, we . . ." and he simply gestured to the O'Leary men and Eileen, the general and the countess, and the seven of them quietly left the dining room, an intense buzz beginning even as they were walking towards the doors.

Quickly, and as comfortably as possible, the group was seated in the Derrynane library, in chairs carefully, deliberately arrayed in a half-circle before the fireplace, so that no person was directly facing another, a strange air of anticipation mixed with equal parts of dread and joy immediately settling on them all.

The general looked about and coughed; the countess placed her fingers on his knee, scratching the taut wool of his breeches gently with her fingertips, and smiled: *You are not in command here, my darling general.* O'Connell nodded: *Thank you, I am not.* No words having been spoken, the couple settled back into the awkward silence of the moment.

Finally, Maurice spoke softly, the elder O'Leary's letter in his hand, more as a prop than for any substantive purpose. "We are all aware of the topic of conversation here." He gestured with his hand.

"The purpose is clear, yes, sir," Art O'Leary spoke in a clear, commanding tone. Chairs were slightly adjusted, seated positions slightly altered as all eyes turned towards the young soldier, whose right hand Eileen had pointedly taken in her left. "We have come . . . Eileen and I have come, seeking your"—he nodded slowly, respectfully to Maire, then Maurice—"gracious approval of our desire to wed. We," he lifted their joined hands very slightly, "have only just become fully aware of the depth and serious nature of our mutual feelings of respect and affection. . . . We very much wish to wed, and to do so with the full approval of the O'Connell family."

Gently sighing, Maurice slowly stood, stepping towards the fireplace, his back to the fire; he appeared uncomfortable, divided and almost sad.

"We," he opened his hands, gesturing so as to include the noble couple from Vienna and his mother, "are most grateful for your coming. It is only in this way that this question can be properly and appropriately—seriously, yes—addressed, and perhaps . . . perhaps resolved."

Eileen smiled hopefully, nodding at Maire, as Maurice continued.

"Would that this were but a simple matter of a young couple developing a measure of, as the lieutenant has most graciously expressed 'mutual feelings of respect and affection,' 't'would be an uncomplicated conversation we would be having here. But, sadly, 'tis not the case, as we have frequently said in this house—and, Squire, Lieutenant, I am sure 'tis so said in your own, as well—that we live in sad and troubled times in Ireland and, especially, I would suggest for families such as our own, few things are uncomplicated.

"Speaking for our mother and myself, nothing would make me happier than being able to bless this proposed union, toast the happy couple and . . . toast them again." He smiled weakly at his failed attempt to ease the tension in the still room.

"But, brother . . ." Eileen ventured and immediately stopped herself.

Now looking grave, Maurice began again, softly, even gently. "Our . . . the O'Connells' . . . *situation,* it being the *unusual* nature of our *commercial interests* and activities, remains as it has long been, highly problematic. Given this, I must speak the harsh truth: When first we received Squire O'Leary's gracious letter, my mother and I spoke at length, and in the course of that conversation I likened the situation here to a light being held to a treasure-filled cave, the light being, quite honestly, Lieutenant O'Leary."

Art had just opened his mouth when Eileen firmly squeezed his hand, and he said nothing.

"I mean this in no way as a direct criticism, Lieutenant, but you must recognise that in a relatively brief time you have become quite well known in the small group of families, amongst whom I would include the O'Connells as well as the O'Learys that is still referred to by some as the Gaelic Aristocracy—and, again, I sincerely mean no disrespect, but I am attempting to express facts—as a wild and reckless character, with your fiery temper, taunting the local Protestant officialdom, to whom you are, of course, equally well known.

"You are understandably proud of your well-earned Austrian status, which I agree the English theoretically should be honouring."

"I am indeed, sir . . . as is your good sister!" responded O'Leary sharply.

Eileen, her jaw securely set, nodded, adding in a level voice, "Loyal to Her Imperial Majesty I *am*, we both are . . ." she looked firmly at Maurice, and at her mother ". . . and *not* to the English king and his minions here in Ireland."

Sighing audibly, Maurice leaned back against the mantel to respond; the fire was gentle, not blazing. "This I respect; you have both earned what you have, and your loyalty is placed as it should be, in return for what you have been given by the empress, indeed what you have merited in her service. The reality here," he gestured, opening his arms, "in Ireland, in Kerry, on the Iveragh Peninsula, the reality is a complex one. *This* reality is that Ireland is a conquered territory, and we are to the same extent a conquered people. England rules Ireland, or at least attempts to; illegitimately though she may do so, she *does*. Eileen herself knows that we here, the O'Connells, make much of saying 'the King's writ . . . 'tis not honoured here!' and other fine-sounding, strong declarations, and we pay virtually no customs levies to the Crown on our imports.

"All this being said, the deep truth, the unspoken truth, indeed in many ways a truth that is rarely if ever contemplated, much less acknowledged, is that the *Sassenach* leave us alone because we are so far beyond the Pale, so far from Dublin, and that to do otherwise would require the use of force, men at arms and expenditures that they are better served utilising elsewhere. In return, we foment no discord. 'Tis an uneasy peace between the O'Connells and the Crown, but 'tis peace nevertheless. As opposed to Spinoza's concept of peace not being the 'absence of war,' it is indeed the highest form of 'peace' for which we could reasonably hope. We must do *nothing* to upset this 'peace' . . . *nothing at all,*" he said firmly.

"What is it then that you are saying, sir?" Squire O'Leary inquired in a gentle tone. "Is not the existence and indeed the extent of your family's 'commercial interests' quite well known to the king's men here? You are not saying 'tis any secret, are you?"

Appearing pained and nodding first to the squire, Maurice spoke, equally softly, gently, pointedly looking directly at Art whilst responding to his father's comments, his query. "What I am saying—please be assured, sir, most reluctantly—is that you are, most unfortunately indeed, the light illuminating the activities that are conducted here and from here, our treasure trove of a cave. Simply by being your very self, being married to this good woman"—he gestured with a nod at his sister— "you would bring additional attention to the O'Connells, and a scrutiny the level of which I believe we may well not be capable of withstanding, and thus that we cannot, indeed, that we *shall not* have."

"I fail to see . . ."

"You *must* see, Lieutenant; you have to. We cannot bear this scrutiny. It could mean the end of all we have worked for in this place. Whilst what your father says is wholly correct, much of the time I feel as if the *Sassenach* has largely forgotten us here. . . . We need nothing, most especially the linkage of your name with ours, to remind the king's men of what it is we do here."

"To Vienna we shall be returning, though, brother," Eileen spoke up pointedly, momentarily hopeful.

"Is it in Vienna that you shall henceforth be willing to remain? In Vienna is it that you are willing to *die*?" Maurice asked, his voice firm now, his eyes on both O'Leary and his sister.

"As you yourself have raised the point, sir, is it *this* then . . . our remaining in Vienna . . . the condition for your approval of our marriage, sir?" O'Leary asked, his voice inquiring and, like Eileen's, hopeful rather than challenging. "If so, then I believe we would both be prepared . . ."

Maurice raised his right hand. "Sadly, sir, it is not . . . I did not mean to suggest otherwise. What I am compelled to say is that under no condition am I able to grant this approval, *none at all*, so potentially dangerous do I believe having you recognised as a member of our family could prove to be to our security in this place. Even were you and Eileen to return to Austria, the very fact that she would be and would become known as, your wife would, I believe, bring renewed, most unwanted attention to the O'Connells at Derrynane, and to our activities." His voice was pained, and genuinely so.

Eileen appeared ashen, her mouth half-open, her voice silenced.

"Are you saying that there is an inherent danger in having—I know they refer to my son as such—*the volatile O'Leary* as an in-law . . . that it is for *this* reason that you refuse to approve this union?" the elder O'Leary asked.

Maurice nodded slowly in the affirmative, adding nothing.

Tears streaming down her face, Eileen stood, facing her brother, though still grasping O'Leary's hand, her husky voice firm, determined, as she spoke. "As a child, I was forced, though certainly not by you, brother, into a marriage that as we all know too well came very close to costing me my life. And when ultimately some semblance of a marriage finally did come to exist at Ballyhar, all I had in that place worked for was torn from me in an instant by the death of John O'Connor. It has taken me these five-odd years to recover from this, these years *and* being far away, as in another world. Now, and I speak my feelings alone, whether you approve or not," her right forefinger indicated Maurice, "I shall marry this man, whom I love, and whom I believe loves me."

"'Tis madness, Eileen! This you *cannot* do!" Maurice snapped, his voice suddenly tinged with anger. "It simply cannot happen . . . Indeed, I shall not permit it to happen!"

Shaking her head, her shoulders heaving, Eileen gently dropped O'Leary's hand and stalked quickly away. O'Leary, nodding to Maurice and his father, bowed to the women and followed her, his fingertips catching the door as she was slamming it shut.

At the far end of the hall, with the assistance of an unusually sombre Annie, Eileen had already donned her hip-length riding coat; gathering the folds of her arasaid into her arms, she quickly shaped it as a long cloak even as O'Leary approached. Before he drew on his own long, black military wrap, he helped her clasp the Scottish garment with her heavy pewter brooch, rubbing his thumb over the face of the O'Connell stag. Then, in what was almost a single motion, Eileen abruptly turned back towards Annie, spoke softly into her ear and immediately then rejoined O'Leary. Together they stalked out into the forbiddingly dark night.

In the library, a brief heavy silence filled the void, followed by a somewhat calmer exchange.

"My dear son, is there no way . . . ?" Maire asked, plaintively, hopefully.

"I do not see one clearly."

"But what of the continuing 'arrangement' with the Crown's customs inspectors? Does this not protect us?" she ventured.

"To a limited extent," Maurice said softly, nodding, "Know ye that any inspector is but a single man, one who, at best, may deflect serious notice of us. Yet, again, this is all but a part of the 'uneasy peace' of which I have spoken, acceded to solely because His Majesty's men have better things to do than journey for days overland or by sea to prosecute us."

"What then of the 'doors' Eileen's marriage to John O'Connor were supposed to have opened for us in Dublin, in London even? What of the 'men behind such doors' whom Denis maintained would 'shield us'?" she attempted again, valiantly, and this time, Maurice conceded, *quite brilliantly.*

"Ah, Denis's expectations . . . aye, there were indeed doors in both places and pliable men behind them . . . but then John O'Connor died and most of the doors closed near-immediately . . . and the men behind the few ones that remained, as soon as David O'Connor refused to pay their demands for higher stipends, those portals slammed shut as well." He shook his head, his voice suddenly, markedly hushed, as were he speaking to himself alone. "With their immense wealth, their vast resources, the O'Connors—they have no need of these men and their bloody dammed doors."

Maire reluctantly but finally sensed herself defeated. The mention of John O'Connor's son and heir, whose proposal of marriage Eileen had spurned—realising discussion of which could have opened the painful issue of whether if she had rather accepted his offer and thereby once again became Mistress O'Connor the arrangements in Dublin, in London, might have continued in place—was not a topic Maire wished to ignite.

Undeterred, General O'Connell stood, imposing in his striking uniform, the countess's soft eyes following her husband and remaining on him as his voice rumbled. "Could they not simply depart for Vienna—separately even, to be wed there and remain there? 'T'woud not even have to be made known here; perhaps 't'woud never be known here . . ." he argued in a steady voice, gesturing with his large hands as he spoke.

"Unwilling they are to commit to life and death in Austria, Uncle. You heard them."

"Nephew, they are in love." The general sighed. "'Tis a rare thing, in, as you so well phrased it, 'these sad and troubled times.' Does *that* not have any value?"

"Ah, Uncle, a romantic you are, sir. I never would have believed it. *Love* . . . it is an intangible, a fleeting thing, no? Many believe it not even to be a reality."

". . . and what is wrong with 'love,' with being a 'romantic'? Are you such a sour young man?" the general shot back, the countess unsuccessfully attempting to get him to be seated.

"Whether it is reality or not, neither love, nor anything else for that matter, is worth compromising our security in this place, Uncle."

The general stepped forward and gestured gently to Maurice. "Please, if you would, nephew?" and, his large left hand gently cupping his nephew's bony right elbow, he escorted an obviously more reluctant than willing Maurice through the door, which the officer closed softly behind them.

The chances for whatever the elder O'Connell had hoped to accomplish by stepping out of the library quickly evaporated as Maire, the countess and the elder O'Leary sat in uncomfortable silence themselves, male voices almost immediately echoing loudly in the great hall beyond the door:

"Old fool! – Arrogant! – Vain! – Dangerous!"

"Inexperienced young man! – Unrealistic! – Fearful! – Heartless!"

"I face these realities; you do not, sir!"

"Never in battle have you been, whilst killed men I have! A degree of responsibility, insignificant though you think it may be, for an empire rests in these hands; I am no fool!"

"I am at war each day here, sir . . . a silent, nasty war, without the possibility of glory, General!"

"What would you have for your beloved sister, boy? Condemn her to marriage to some lout in the depths of Kerry or to a feckless Hungarian cavalryman, possessed of a title earned by an ancestor, who will be unfaithful as soon as the vows said? I know these things, nephew!"

"Arrange an appropriate marriage for her, I shall!"

"As was done previously, *to* her!"

The countess smiled uncomfortably at Maire, who nodded in understanding. "Noisy and animated are the Irish," Maire attempted, and she smiled weakly, despite her effort, also uncomfortably, the smile quickly fading, her eyes again studying her hands, resting on her knees.

At that moment, Conor O'Leary wordlessly stood and, bowing slightly, stepped to the door. The volume of the raised voices in the hallway only then softened, but only momentarily, and the women both shook their heads.

Only by slightly lowering their voices did the O'Connell men acknowledge O'Leary's presence, but continued and completed their testy exchange:

"By what means do you propose to, by which resources could you even believe you could prevent what is, to me, nephew, an inevitability?" demanded the general in a hushed growl.

Maurice glared at his considerably taller uncle. "This madness is far from being in any way inevitable, sir! To the high sheriff of Kerry I have already—" He caught himself, quickly tacking, "It is to the sheriff that I shall resort, the law in all its many processes and strengths I shall employ!"

The older man's hands shot up and he shook his head almost violently. "Hah! So *English* law is acceptable *now?* The King's Writ, *at Derrynane* . . . It shall not only be honoured now, but indeed sought out, indeed *beseeched!* Shame! I say, sir, *shame!*"

Taking a step back, the looming soldier finished dismissively, "I think not, sir . . . you shall see!" He turned to the library door and opening it gently, he gestured for his wife. As she stepped out, clutching her cloak loosely, Maurice re-entered and closed the door sharply as the Austrian nobles watched. It was only when his mother inquired as to the man's whereabouts that Maurice realised he had not noticed that Conor O'Leary had removed himself, apparently almost as soon as their verbal eruption had begun.

Far down on the lawn, the night's powerful blackness broken not at all by the flicker of candlelight from the distant house, and only barely by a lantern O'Leary had carried with them; now nearer to the beach than the house, Art and Eileen had been having their own conversation, looking towards arriving at their own resolution—very much their own.

"I have not related to you the full story of my experience at Ballyhar, though I shall, as I desire to keep nothing from you," Eileen began, "but, for now . . . after John O'Connor died, documents came to light by which he—from the grave now, mind you—and my brother, Denis, sought to continue to control my life by having me marry Daniel O'Connor, the heir. Great sums of money and lands in America and the West Indies were involved."

O'Leary's eyes grew wide in the dim light, an expression of true shock on his weary face. He stepped back slightly, allowing Eileen the room to gesture with her hands as she spoke.

"'Twas then that I vowed that 'tis my life and that I must try to lead it as I feel it should be led; to do otherwise in that instance, 't'woud have rendered me a trollop of sorts, would it not? I mean . . . no matter how honourable the intention behind it, it would have meant my being passed from man to man, as decreed, by men! I remember it as clearly as if it were yesterday, my darling love. I was seated on Bull; we had been riding for a long while, in the middle of nowhere, and I was literally screaming into the empty late afternoon, words akin to 'I shall not have it done to me . . . never, never again!' And so it shall not be done to me now, my darling. Rather, I shall run away with you . . . now, right now, tonight."

O'Leary stood silently for a brief moment, looking down at the lantern candles, flickering against the toes of their shoes, their legs, the light barely rising above that level.

Sensing what she thought was a sudden reticence on O'Leary's part, Eileen suddenly gripped his upper arms firmly, her eyes widening, her voice commanding. "But if you do not wish it, so be it, then. Return to Vienna I shall . . . immediately and alone, prepared to remain thus, as I shall never love another as I love you, Arthur O'Leary."

Nodding gently, O'Leary extended his hands to Eileen; releasing his arms, she took both of his hands in her own and appeared again relatively calm.

"We have attempted to do what is right," he began, his voice strong and certain. "What is proper, indeed what is required of us, in coming here to seek consent. Nevertheless, if it is not to be given, deterred I shall not be. I, too, am prepared to depart this very night."

The couple stood in silence, a low, eerie whistle of the Derrynane wind and a heavily thudding tide on the beach the only sounds.

"Your wife shall I be then, Arthur O'Leary," Eileen said, her voice firm though raspy from crying.

"Proud then shall *I* be to be your husband." O'Leary nodded, then added softly, "*Mo ghrá*, the thought that occasioned my momentary silence was my wondering, 'tis it willing you are to lose this?" He gestured about, his arms wide, embracing the whole of Derrynane, though little of it was visible. "All of this?"

"Losing it I am not; relinquishing it most willingly I should be," she said without reflection; in her relief, Eileen surprisingly smiled. "Derrynane shall always have a warm place in my heart and mind, but my *home*, my true home, shall henceforth be with you, Arthur O'Leary . . . wherever that may be."

She turned and again took O'Leary's hands in her own, the wind rising, their cloaks billowing, and she raised his hands to her lips and kissed them softly, then continued. "Home is more than a place where one dwells, more than a piece of land and a house, no matter how lovely the land, how grand the house or how many memories both may hold. I have dwelt in this magnificent place, at the end of Ireland, for most of my life . . . for a brief time, I was, as I have described it, 'mistress of a grand house, a great estate,' though in a much less magnificent setting. Now, in palaces I dwell." She sighed wearily. "And in each of these places I have dwelt because 'twas where I was meant to be . . . by God's will or plan, or perhaps by that of the fairies?" She smiled and shrugged her broad shoulders beneath her heavy arasaid.

"Now . . . as it is, I believe, indeed God's plan for me, as well as being my own choice, soon, as I have just spoken to you, my home shall be with you, Arthur O'Leary, because it is there that I am meant to be . . . as long as I shall live."

". . . as shall mine be with you, Eileen." O'Leary nodded resolutely.

Matters, at least between the two of them, now settled, O'Leary reached down to retrieve the flickering lantern. As they turned and began to trudge up the rough lawn, its whine ebbing, the wind off Derrynane

Bay became steady, rendering the air heavily damp and markedly colder, and they saw a pair of cloaked figures striding towards them.

Eileen recognised a gait similar to her own. *"Mon generale!"* she called out, and tugged Art towards General O'Connell and the countess, who was pulling her cloak more tightly about herself.

The two couples came together, huddling as the wind again became sharper, its sound now a low, mournful wail.

"'Tis not resolved, the matter is not . . ." the general had begun to announce to the young people.

First, however, Eileen, who had heard the countess completing what she correctly concluded was Maria von Graffenreit-O'Connell's personal comment on the turmoil she had witnessed in the library and—though Eileen was unaware of it—overheard in the great hall, the words that the wind had brought to Eileen being, "It is indeed calmer in Austria, my beloved general."

Gently interrupting her uncle, "It *is*, Aunt Maria, *much* calmer in Austria," Eileen said softly, her hand on the older woman's arm. "I am sorry, we Irish . . ."

"We only wish this to be for you as *you* wish," Maria herself interrupted softly. "I offer you my—*our*—castle, should you wish, as a refuge, as a home. . . ."

"Your Grace," O'Leary began, also softly, "we are most grateful. 'Tis your now just expressed support and indeed your friendship, both are valued as much, no, much more than a castle."

"Well, lad, these you have, from both of us," the general interjected. "I have waited many years to experience that with which you young people have been now gifted. I have no choice but to support you, and gladly I shall, *we* shall," he added, holding his wife's hand. The countess nodded. "But now, as I was beginning to tell you, dear children, we have," he nodded slowly to Eileen, "Lady Eileen, advised your mother and brother . . . and," he then nodded in the same manner to O'Leary, "your father, Lieutenant, that it is and will be our honour to stand with you at this time and afterwards. We shall assume full responsibility. . . ." He gestured inclusively with his hands.

Eileen and Art held hands tightly, listening to O'Connell's rumbling voice, which markedly softened as he continued, "What you must know, and must accept, Eileen: This does not amount to being the approval of the O'Connells to your future marriage. Indeed, rather, once you depart Derrynane, you shall not return here . . . for a time, indeed quite possibly a long time; possibly even for many years, I fear."

Eileen nodded; her head held high. "I understand." The wind at that moment caught the ends of her hair, twirling them up, then draping them once again down her back. "'Tis a small price, Uncle, for a life, is it not?"

"Ah, but listen to me, girl, there is more, and 'tis not at all pleasant: Maurice says he is prepared to do all he can to prevent this; as I walked away from him, he was telling me, not as any empty threat, that the high sheriff he will involve if necessary, that to English law he shall resort."

O'Leary's eyes blazed, and Eileen's hands went to her face. "But, Uncle, can he do such?"

"Whether he may succeed I know not, but that he shall attempt to thwart you, of this I have no doubt, my darling girl. Given this, I believe you must prepare yourselves to depart Derrynane . . . perhaps tonight, even." He paused a moment, thinking quickly. "*Yes*, tonight, indeed . . . now, in fact . . . *right now!*" He paused momentarily, continuing almost immediately, "Remove yourselves to Cork. The high sheriff there will surely not do Maurice's bidding, and from thence you may return to Vienna . . . I would suggest with us." He glanced at his wife, gesturing. The countess nodded firmly.

Tears streaming down her face, Eileen's voice nevertheless was strong. "We had already been discussing this. Absent the O'Connells'— more correctly, Maurice's—consent, we have just concluded to undertake an immediate departure, as so now we shall!" Only then did her words quiver. ". . . but Morgan and the girls, and Hugh . . . and . . ." she suddenly sobbed, "and *Mama* . . ." She turned to O'Leary and buried her face in his shoulder, her body heaving, her sobs wrenching to the extent that the countess, too, began to weep.

The general rested his large, powerful right hand on Eileen's shoulder, his left hand on O'Leary's, as he appeared to embrace them both. "Now, whilst 'tis your decision, my children, yours alone, your aunt and I shall assist you in all ways, first, explaining this to Maire . . . and we shall also help your brothers and sisters to understand what has happened . . . and why . . . so that leaving them forever, be assured, you shall *not* be doing by departing this place this night." His words were firm, comforting.

Eileen's tears slowed and she turned to face the general, her right shoulder resting against O'Leary's left, as the two joined hands, both of their faces again strong, their expressions set. As O'Leary began to speak, Eileen nodded at both the general and the countess, "How, General, do you propose . . . ?"

The general stood, looking towards an unseeable horizon, his eyes narrowing, his mind working quickly now, as were he again in combat.

"Very well then . . . To the stables we shall go . . . now, this very moment. The boy, William; if he is not there I shall find him. You are cloaked. You have had an evening meal. Within the hour, perhaps less, you shall be mounted and away." He looked up, scanning the sky. Weak, thin clouds scudded across a not-quite three-quarter moon. "There is at least some of God's light," he indicated, and then paused, reflecting further.

"But first," he looked hard at his niece, "Eileen, and you will *please* speak with all the honesty you possess, not with all the bravery you can summon. In terms of departing County Kerry this night, will you be able to travel swiftly and, whilst at the same time, circuitously so as to avoid any pursuit, as well there might be, and thus able to get your good selves gone and safely away from here, as I suggest?"

Eileen brushed the last suggestion of a tear from her left eye and nodded, her jaw set. "We shall, Uncle, yes."

"Very well, then; you will then describe for me, girl, how you propose to journey at haste from here, out of Kerry itself as speedily as possible and on the way into Cork, where—" he nodded at O'Leary, "I assume you, Lieutenant, will thence lead."

O'Leary nodded firmly. "Aye, sir, I shall."

Eileen bit her lip for a moment, thinking, and then responded, her voice now even, its familiar throaty sound subduing that of the wind. "We shall ride generally north and then east, over the mountains." Lifting her right hand from beneath her cloak, she gestured in that direction. "They are not as rough as those leading to Glenflesk. Beginning from *here*," with her left hand, she pointed down at the ground, "past the Staigue round fort," she gestured roughly eastward, "we shall ride up to the high track," her right hand then gestured to the craggy heights above Derrynane, "so as to be above An tSnaidhm (modern-day Sneem), thence following the rough mountain track to the east, towards, again above and around Neidin (which would become known as Kenmare), avoiding the village, as 'twill be full daylight by then. We shall at that juncture have also avoided the river, Kenmare. I have been this way thus far with Mama, thence going onto Glenflesk   . . . to the O'Donoghues' lair at Robbers Glen . . . and an even rougher trek up and around three mountains there is between Neidin and Glenflesk, but not so I believe on this journey. Though never have I been all the way into County Cork, I believe the ride from near Neidin to where one enters Cork may not be as rugged by comparison. I have heard Morgan mention a place, Kilgarvan, I believe. . . ." She looked at the general, then at O'Leary.

The general nodded affirmatively, based on his recollections of the local geography and apparently satisfied; then he, too, looked at O'Leary, who allowed himself to smile weakly, as he began, "Travelling thus, as Eileen wisely proposes, we shall at that place, past Neidin, be south and west of the highest of the Derrynasaggart Mountains, which is very good." He nodded at Eileen, who smiled tightly. "We shall from thence be able to proceed, indeed past Kilgarvan, which is still Kerry, beyond there, fording the Roughty River, which, being late autumn, should not be high, and proceed due east into Cork and thence on towards Macroom, which is, I believe, perhaps twenty, perhaps a few more miles beyond Kilgarvan. Though the ground will be rough, passing through Renanirree and thence onto Ballyvoge, 'tis all well known to me, and, with this familiarity, we shall thus be able to circle about rather than be compelled to go over a series of peaks, some mere elevations, others hills and two or three being actually mountains, though without names save to those who live on and beneath them.

"When night comes upon us then, in Cork, we shall rest, even if 'tis only laying our heads on our saddles, journeying thence on to Rathleigh House, so as to arrive there in the light of the day following."

O'Connell nodded, again apparently satisfied. "Cork is your country, O'Leary; it appears you know it as well as does your intended know her own."

O'Leary looked the general in the eye. "Aye. I do, sir; travelled this way I have."

The countess stood quietly, her arms folded beneath her cloak, marvelling at the strength of the young people's voices, how sure they sounded, how certain of directions and of the tongue-tying names of mountains and, she assumed, places.

The general turned to his wife, "Maria, you will please return to the house and locate Maire. I must ask that you tell her an untruth or perhaps a partial truth—that I am speaking with the young people—and say no more."

The countess smiled gently. "At the Viennese court I have lived all my life, my darling. I am sadly most skilful in relating, shall we say, incomplete versions of the truth." Kissing both Art and Eileen, she turned to tramp back up the damp lawn alone. She stopped and looked back, calling softly, "Godspeed, my dear children. In Vienna I know we shall meet . . . though I believe the general may have further ideas." She smiled again and began to turn, to re-join the others in the library.

"Aunt Maria," Eileen gestured and leaned close to the older woman, bending slightly, whispering in her ear, Maria von Graffenreit nodding. She kissed her niece again and then trudged back up towards the house.

Though the younger people looked anxiously at him, wondering if, indeed, he might have "further ideas" at this time to relate, O'Connell himself appeared to be preparing for battle. "To the stables," he commanded sharply, gesturing, and turned, the young couple falling in, holding hands.

The general never looked back, nor did he speak as he led them, trudging towards and then abruptly away from and around the looming, slate-sheathed house. Looking at it, Eileen suddenly realised she might never see Derrynane House again.

O'Leary's strong grip leading her by the hand, Eileen could only stare at this place, silent tears streaming down her cheeks. *Slán, Doire Fhíonáin, dearmad orm riamh—le do thoil? Farewell, Derrynane, forget me never—please?* she thought, unable to bring herself to speak the words aloud.

They marched—for it was marching General O'Connell was—making a broad swing farther away from the house, the lights inside of which they could see clearly, and then sharply back towards the stables.

There, a single warm yellow light shone through one still open half door, which O'Leary unlatched and slowly opened.

O'Connell pointed at his niece; instinctively, Eileen called out, "William?"

A rustle of hay and the padding of stockinged feet sounded, as did a slightly gravelly voice. "Lady Eileen?" William whispered, approaching them, a book clutched in his left hand, his finger marking a page and a profoundly wondering look on his tanned face. "General, sir!" he managed, straightening his posture before O'Connell raised his hand.

The general stepped to the young groom. "A difficult night this is, lad. I regret the need to involve you in what is transpiring, but . . . I fear I must. Please, for now, ask no questions."

William nodded wordlessly and gently set his book, spine down, between two oaken feed buckets, on a long, rough shelf holding a row of them.

O'Connell continued. "Now, you will please select the two strongest, most durable animals, those least inclined to weary quickly, and all necessary tack, for a journey." He waved his hands at Art and Eileen and himself. "Assist you we shall in tacking them. But first, you buy and sell animals, yes, lad?"

Puzzled, William nevertheless nodded in the affirmative, again saying nothing.

"You know values, then?" Another nod, eyes gently lowered, no words spoken, the meaning clear: *Yes, sir, I do, yes indeed.*

"As you select the pair of horses, so, too, you will determine a fair value for each of the animals and for the tack they shall require."

William was gifted with a quick and agile mind, such that it seemed almost instantaneously that, his hands holding the sleepy animal's bridle, he was saying, "Now, Lady Eileen, you will remember Daisy? You broke her for the Lady Abigail, aye?"

Eileen nodded and smiled weakly.

He then led a second animal forward, and this time Eileen smiled easily, genuinely. "We finally named this one, did we not?" William said, appearing ironic, as the horse was the once-long-nameless, extremely stubborn grey mare with which Eileen was struggling on the days when talk of Vienna and all of its possibilities was just beginning. The mare's name was Sally.

The general eyed the mares, evidencing a degree of reluctance, which William instantly recognised. "Though they both be mares, General, they are more sure-footed and sprightlier than any of the geldings. The only stallions in the house this night are Master Morgan's and Master Maurice's, sir." O'Connell nodded, satisfied.

As the three men moved towards the horses, Eileen quietly indicated she required a "private moment" outside, smiling ruefully as if she felt the men would—yet again— unfairly judge the capacity of the female bladder. So engaged had they been in gathering the saddles, the tack, none of them had noticed when, just before she stepped outside, an ashen-faced Annie gestured to Eileen from beyond the stable doors. A few words, an embrace, kisses between the young women and Eileen stepped back into the barn.

Within minutes, the three men working together, the sleepy horses—themselves evidencing an equine version of puzzlement—were fully tacked.

General O'Connell withdrew a small leather pouch from beneath his cloak and nodded at the groom.

William sighed. "I believe forty pounds is the value of Daisy, thirty of Sally, two saddles with leathers and irons, blankets, girths, bridles, reins—hardly any of it unused, fifteen per animal . . . but, General, why . . ." He caught himself.

Nodding him silent, the general withdrew a handful of coins and passed them to William, nodding. "You will please place these in the hands of Master Maurice when you next see him, perhaps even this night. You shall explain that I have purchased the animals and the tack."

William nodded his understanding.

O'Connell stood thoughtfully for a moment, his eyes moving towards the far wall of the stable. Gesturing William to the object that had attracted his attention, the officer nodded. "Lad, best I make one final acquisition . . . the saddle scabbard and its contents, aye?" William padded towards the brass hook on which the simply tooled, substantial leather holster hung, snugly resting within it a gleaming rifle. He lifted them, along with a leather bag containing shot and power that dangled off a smaller hook, and handed them to O'Connell. The general dug into his purse and handed the groomsman more money. "This is a fair price, lad. Though not as well as you know your horses and their tack, I know at least generally the values of weaponry." He smiled wearily.

Handing the strap of the holster and the ammunition to O'Leary, he said softly, "I trust you will not need this, but best you be prepared for any possibility, howsoever remote." O'Connell then looked at the couple. "I believe 'tis time you depart, my children."

Unexpectedly, Eileen fell into the large man's arms, and he embraced her tightly as her body again shuddered with tears, his own tears streaking his rough, sun- and wind-burnt face, the two rocking gently.

The general eased Eileen out of his embrace. O'Leary sharply saluted the senior officer and O'Connell returned the gesture, immediately extending his hand to the younger man, which O'Leary gripped firmly. The men nodded at each other, O'Connell's voice comfortingly resonant. "You shall be off now. Consistent with the final words your dear aunt spoke, 'tis in County Cork we shall be joining you, I am thinking at your home," he nodded to O'Leary, "but I shall discuss this with your good father. Though precisely when we shall arrive I am now unsure, but assure you a plan I have; a very well-thought-out plan."

Eileen smiled at him gratefully and he stepped back. In the meantime, O'Leary having been unable to affix the scabbard and its weapon to his saddle, had succeeded in doing so to Eileen's, her saddle leathers seeming more substantial. He then mounted Daisy, whilst Eileen did Sally. Having first fastened the thick, heavy leather belt Annie had delivered about her hips, her arasaid now firmly held in place about her body, settling in her saddle, Eileen gently touched the animal's withers, causing the spirited mare to step towards the general. "Uncle?" she said softly, almost wearily, halting and gently turning the horse ever so slightly.

His eyes on his now-mounted niece, the general nodded. She leaned forward slightly.

"Uncle, you and Aunt Maria . . . when you do come to Cork, will you stand for us at our wedding there, so we are able to return to Vienna a wedded couple?"

O'Connell smiled up at Eileen. "Provided you and . . ." he nodded at O'Leary, ". . . know the ground as well as you appear to, and William here knows horses the way he appears to, in County Cork we all shall very soon be . . . and, yes, child, even without consulting your dear aunt, we shall surely be proud indeed to stand with you there and thus." He gently patted her left knee, smiling wearily. "Now, away with you to Cork, with God's blessing and my prayers."

Both of the younger people smiling, albeit faintly, and then, looking down on the general and William, with a nod to each, they turned their horses' heads and thudded across the packed-dirt floor of the barn and out into the blackness beyond.

The general and the young groom stood silently for a moment, side by side, the older man looming some inches over the younger, watching the pair as the night first absorbed them, and then the sounds of the horses' hoofs, until there remained but black silence.

"Thank you, lad . . . very much," O'Connell said softly. "I shall explain as best I can what has transpired here, but just not this night. Return to your reading you now may, lad . . . and what is it that you . . . ?"

"Ah, 'tis Master Shakespeare, General; of him I have grown most fond, just in the last year, sir, and 'tis in his *Macbeth* that I am genuinely, deeply immersed at present."

"Ah, how fitting for this night, aye? 'If it were done when 'tis done, then 'twere well it were done quickly'. . . ." O'Connell recited effortlessly and, himself smiling weakly, he walked heavily out of the now-still barn, the peaceful, measured breathing of the horses belying the atmosphere at Derrynane this night.

Little peace was there in the looming, brooding house towards which the general strode, the light from which only dimly punctuated the night's gloom.

The only one of the group who had achieved some measure of calm was Squire O'Leary, who, after having excused himself, had ventured off on an ultimately successful search for a kitchen and tea and was enjoying the warmth of the blazing fire, a scalding cup of strong Kerry tea and Annie's effusive company. "Ah, Squire O'Leary, sir . . . your son, what a *man* he is! All the girls, we think . . ." and, blushing, she caught herself, and both she and the elder O'Leary laughed.

"Some thoughts are best left unexpressed, my dear," O'Leary observed with a soft, subtly paternal laugh.

Nodding in agreement, Annie refilled his cup but did allow an afterthought. "I do *so* hope that he and the Lady Eileen will be . . . can . . . may be able to . . ."

"Whilst it will not be without effort, I believe they can and that they ultimately will." O'Leary smiled and sipped his tea, winking at Annie, who beamed in response.

Maire and Maurice alone of the original group remained in the library.

"This could not have been a satisfactory resolution, your uncle's design? Immediately dispatching them back to Vienna, there to remain?" Maire inquired, her voice weary, an unusually drained, worn expression on her face.

Maurice had been resting his head against a high chair back, his eyes following the serpentine lines of a tiny fissure in the ceiling plaster.

"The only truly 'satisfactory resolution' is for Eileen and O'Leary to abandon this entire mad scheme, for him to depart for Vienna immediately and for her to not, remaining here. . . ." He sighed deeply, continuing to study the spidery line on the plaster above.

"This being said, as the two seem so frighteningly similar in their outlooks . . . their behaviour . . . both impetuous, both headstrong . . . 't'would never be that they would, indeed that they *could* part . . . 't'would appear that, amongst a number of things, Dark Eileen has met her match in terms of pure stubbornness. That being said, I shall now . . . beginning this moment . . . tonight . . . *this very night* . . ." he began with a cold certainty, "I shall pry them apart, save us all from this madness, dispatch him and his naive father—I fear the old fellow may be in his dotage, yes? He seemingly approves of this lunacy!—the very first thing in the morning. Rid of them, after Eileen has had time to calm herself, I shall— *we* shall," he gestured broadly, so as to now join his mother with him in his scheme, "begin to reason with her and keep her here . . . safe, indeed safe from herself . . . whilst O'Leary takes himself back to Austria and . . ."

"*We* shall be doing nothing, my son," Maire said firmly. "For the present I shall endeavour not to thwart you—and this, solely out of respect for your position, and though I would vehemently disagree with him as I now do you, because I feel your father would support you, but neither shall I be a part of any effort you envision. Indeed, would that I could, I would fervently aid her—and O'Leary, yes, I would—for . . . for I believe them truly to be in love, that most rare of situations.

"I am loath to lose Eileen again; I so fear this happening, my boy. Throughout much of my adult, my married life, it seems always awaiting a babe I have been . . . but also mourning the loss of a babe." She paused, her lips trembling. "Then later, the older girls; married well, and though not far distant, gone they are . . . and more recently Conaill's death, that on the sea he loved . . . the girls gone to Vienna . . . Daniel Charles to France . . . these all are, in one way or another, losses I have suffered and mourned . . . the loss of my children." She looked quietly at her son, her eyes weary, though her tears unshed.

Despite her plaintive expression, Maurice looked unusually harshly at his mother, shaking his head dismissively, things he rarely did.

"Be assured, indeed be certain, *I shall prevent thi*s, Mother; please know that. I have advised the general that it is to the high sheriff himself that I shall resort. Stop them I shall! I shall see O'Leary jailed before he is permitted to cause any more havoc; I . . ."

Brigid's single knock on the library door was firm. She leaned just her left shoulder, her head barely visible. "Mistress," she said stiffly, unusually formally, "the Countess Maria, may she have a moment?"

Maire sighed, relieved at the unexpected interruption. She stood wearily and exited the room in silence, leaving the door ajar.

The countess was standing across the hall, still wrapped in her heavy cloak, the smell of damp wool filling the area as the women faced each other. They smiled weakly, Maria von Graffenreit-O'Connell slipping her arm into Maire's. "A difficult time, yes?"

Maire looked up at the taller Austrian. "*Ja,*" she said, half-heartedly attempting humour.

"The general, he is speaking with the young people, he has asked me to tell you. I expect that to you he shall also wish to speak, my dear, though it appears well into the night they may talk. It is a difficult time for them also . . . perhaps in the morning after they have rested, once they finish speaking with the general."

Maire nodded. "Yes, yes, very difficult, Maria. I believe, then, that it is to bed I shall take myself. Perhaps it may be less difficult for us all when the sun next appears. If you do not mind, would you please so advise your good husband for me?"

The countess nodded and the women embraced, the countess waiting whilst Maire very slowly, wearily, ascended the massive staircase.

The house had grown still. Maurice remained in the library, the fire blazing anew; having caught snatches of his mother's conversation with the countess, he assumed Eileen and O'Leary remained with the general. Morgan and Hugh, having spoken awhile of all that was apparently transpiring, had gone to their rooms and were asleep, Anne and Elizabeth, abed even longer. Squire O'Leary was in bed, though not asleep.

Seeking her husband, the countess requested a lantern and, the candle burning strongly within its heavy box of iron and thick glass, she exited and circled the house in a wide arc, once and then yet again, finding her way slowly, despite her lantern, through the powerful black of the night. As she began her third passage, low clouds and then a thick, sodden fog suddenly enveloping Derrynane, she was grateful to see O'Connell emerging from the stables, a random, sharp wind gust lifting, tossing their cloaks, even invading the lantern, causing the candle to flicker.

She waited until he grew closer and, setting the lantern on the wet grass, she opened her arms to the immense, now very weary-looking man, and embraced him as he leaned in to her.

As he did so, O'Connell whispered, "*Gone sie sind, meine Liebe.*"/ "Gone they are, my love."

His wife's soft grey eyes grew wide as she gestured in the dank, heavy air with her delicate fingers, whispering in English, "Gone? *Already?*"

"So to bed we should go" was his only response as he draped his right arm around his wife's shoulders and led her into the house.

At that moment, being not quite two ploddingly tedious nighttime miles due generally east and slightly north of Derrynane, they were quite thankful for the measure of God's light, of which the general had spoken earlier, illuminating, if only slightly, their rough path.

Though Eileen occasionally slipped into the lead as a change in direction seemed to her necessary, the couple tried to keep the horses side by side and, once they had finally reached what Eileen had referred to as the high track, they also tried to maintain a fairly steady trot.

"We could not maintain this pace absent even this small measure of God's light," Eileen called across to O'Leary, who nodded his head in full agreement.

"Rough country your Iveragh is, my love," he called out in reply, and Eileen smiled ruefully, nodding.

Indeed, such was the condition of the ground that it was not until they were on a jagged mountain track high above the sleeping community of An tSnaidhm, approximately twelve difficult miles from Derrynane, just before dawn, that they were able to speak briefly, whilst keeping up the pace, talking through a dull, steady rain, Eileen's voice muffled by the wet arasaid's even heavier fabric, now in the form of an ample hood she had drawn over her head.

"Maurice—he could not have reached an undersheriff yet, could he?" she wondered aloud.

"I think not, my love," O'Leary called up over the sound of the horses' hoofs on the rough track as they rode well above the unseen village, "unless one at Derrynane he keeps." For the first time that night they shared a cautious laugh, after which he nevertheless added, "though I believe we still must anticipate and should perhaps prepare as best we can for such a confrontation prior to our being safely out of Kerry."

Eileen bit her lip and nodded in agreement. *Ah, with you, my love, 'tis prepared I am, for anything,* she thought silently.

Easing slowly out of the highest rocky ground, arriving, as the rain itself eased, they reached, in the heavily overcast daylight, a place of relatively open country. Though the stony track itself remained rough they stopped briefly, allowing the horses to graze the wet vegetation whilst they clambered, very briefly, into each other's arms, and Eileen smiled warmly at the man whom, she now fully believed, was always meant to be her husband, whose wife she was always meant to be, joking softly with O'Leary, "*Now* do you understand that I sometimes just sense things . . . is all? *Now* do you believe it?"

O'Leary laughed warmly as he briefly again held Eileen close in the slate-grey, chill morning, whispering, also very softly, "How far to the area above or about An Neidin, do you *sense*?"

Smiling tentatively, Eileen reflected, taking note of the mantle of fog that had originally draped Derrynane and, having seemingly trailed them, now threatened their sight and speed, finally said with certainty, "Seven miles, perhaps a wee bit less even, as we shall skirt up and wide of the village itself. We also need to be certain *not* to head towards what is called Moll's Gap, being careful then to avoid any paths that even seem as if they could be heading north off this track."

O'Leary nodded, *understood*.

Remounting, and riding generally in silence for several more hours, the overall condition of the track very gradually improving, they were able to similarly increase their speed. They also increased their vigilance as, whilst the fog had been dispelled by its coming, the late-morning sun was bright, they had also come first upon a lone horseman, who they greeted courteously—but who also, unseen by the couple, had slowed and looked back at them as they rode away, his eyes following them until they were nearly out of sight. Later they saw three farmers, their animals carrying baskets empty of the butter they had hauled to Neidin for transport out by boat. Nodding pleasantly, they rode on, and remained hopeful, grateful as well for the sunshine, as their clothing slowly dried, the sun's warmth sufficient to cause Eileen's cloak to actually steam ever so slightly.

Though the couple were unaware of the fact, it had not been until they themselves were well beyond the mountain fastness above Sneem that Maurice had confronted the general, as the older man sat alone at the bottom of the massive dining room table, with tea and his small, battered black leather prayer book.

"So, spoke with them well into the night you did, I understand?" Maurice inquired sharply as he entered the room, without first bidding his uncle the time of day.

The general, in rough breeches, boots, a heavy shirt and a thick, tattered wool jacket, did not immediately lift his eyes from his book, purposely taking his time responding, doing so only after he whispered an audible "Amen."

"And a good morning to you as well, nephew." The older man pointedly smiled as he looked up, silently offering Maurice the pot, *tea?*

Maurice, who had not slept well, grunted and, after first lifting a cup off a gleaming sideboard, poured himself some tea., "Forgive me, sir; weary I am, and, if you will believe me, sad I am to a degree, as well. That said, if I may, Uncle . . . how was it that your conversation with the 'young lovers' ultimately concluded last night?" he asked as he took a seat cat-a-corner across from his uncle.

His expression unchanged, the general calmly answered in a level, almost off-handed tone, "I believe the last words spoken by them, as well as by my good self, could fairly be said to have been some variant of 'farewell,' actually." He lifted his cup and sipped.

Maurice's face flushed and his eyes went wide as he half-stood, his palms on the table. "You do not mean to sit there and tell me that—"

"They have departed, nephew . . . left, are gone; they are no longer here . . ." the older man said gently.

Fully standing now, Maurice glared down at his uncle, demanding, "By what means have they *departed . . . General?*" hissing the military title.

The general, who stood at least five inches taller than his nephew, rose slowly, deliberately, the fingertips of his right hand resting on the table top.

"On horseback," he responded, his voice level, even, and—to Maurice—gratingly calm.

"Derrynane horses? *Our* horses? You have no authority in this house, sir; I would remind you that you are nothing more than a guest here, sir!" Maurice's thin voice rasped. "I thus best not next learn that 'twas you who arrogated to yourself the capacity to provide any animals to them."

"I did not, nephew." The general's rumbling voice remained still cloyingly even.

"Then . . . then *stolen* the horses they have! *Horse thieves* they then are! The high sheriff, he shall—"

"Nephew, *please* . . ." O'Connell sighed deeply, a degree of impatience now creeping into his voice and manner. "The high sheriff of Kerry, he shall have no concern of any of these matters. . . . When you next see William, he shall be handing you coins totalling some one hundred pounds, the combined price he set—at my request—for both Daisy and Sally, along with their required tack."

"You . . . ?"

"I have purchased the animals, nephew, at a very fair price, I believe you must agree."

"You old . . ." Maurice began, his face scarlet, his thin fingers clenched into a pair of what appeared to the general barely threatening fists.

"Please be restrained, nephew. I do not intend to grow angry with you over this, as I have no desire for any physical altercation with you, as you would be gravely injured . . . of that I assure you. Now . . . if I may finish my tea and complete my prayers . . . please?" O'Connell said softly as he calmly resumed his seat.

Enraged, Maurice could do no more than fume at his uncle. "You arrogant old fool! All of you: O'Leary, O'Sullivan, Eileen . . . dear sweet Abigail, even! With your titles, your magnificent gowns and splendid uniforms, your palaces and empresses . . . You forget from whence you . . ."

The general was instantly on his feet, so abruptly that his chair turned over, the mahogany of its high back striking the floor sharply, as it tumbled beyond the thick Indian rug upon which the massive dining table and its numerous chairs sat. His temper rising, glaring down at the younger man, his eyes narrowed and cheeks reddening, he roared, "I forget nothing! *We* forget *nothing*, nephew. How dare you suggest otherwise! Compelled by the realities that the occupation of Ireland by the *Sassenach* creates, we all have done what we have needed to do, to live, to thrive, to do more than survive in this blessed, now in many ways this accursed place, which we all nevertheless love and treasure. Departed Ireland some of us indeed have, but only in constraint!" His voice softened. "I would indelicately remind you of the obvious, sir: There can be but one eldest male child in a family. For the younger sons, the daughters . . . life is less certain, eh?"

Stung by the truth, forced to accept it, as well as the reality of which the older man spoke—and seemingly, suddenly aware that he, too, was a "younger son," his position his only by virtue of Denis O'Connell's banishment to Jamaica, Maurice remained silent as the general continued.

"Whilst you have your realities . . . about a number of which you spoke quite vividly, most eloquently last night in this very house . . . others have realities as well; the cause, the curse is the same, the realities as different as the people they confront. I would remind you, sir, as you well know, that the O'Connells resident in Catholic Europe, including young Daniel Charles, now in France, serve your purposes, as well as those of our sovereigns . . . our own purposes last."

Adjudging himself routed at least for the moment, Maurice was visibly shaking as he stood before his intimidating relative. "Stop them I shall! I have prohibited them from . . . they shall not wed!" he nevertheless—albeit weakly—fumed.

The general laid a massive hand on the thinner, younger man's left shoulder. "Lad, let this be. Gone they are, gone they shall be . . . *please. . .*" he ended gently, almost plaintively.

Maurice reached up; thrusting the heavy hand away, he stormed out of the room, his boots thudding heavily as he went.

As they had hoped they would, by the middle of the afternoon O'Leary and Eileen had, without incident, successfully swung wide of Neidin, and from thence descended the foothills of the Derrynassagarts, some distance beyond Kilgarvan.

Having crossed the upper reaches of the Roughty River without incident, thus drawing ever closer to entering Cork, they were, whilst remaining mounted, briefly walking the horses when, thanks to the whim of a just-risen, sharp, suddenly variable afternoon wind, both heard the unmistakeable thudding of several horses being ridden quickly, and the distant voices of men.

Eileen shot a glance back at O'Leary and, shaking her head left, she yanked Sally's reins sharply in that direction, not gently booting the ofttimes stubborn mare, who lowered her head and charged into the tangled brush and up what appeared to be a sharply inclined hillock, followed by O'Leary on a now equally tractable Daisy.

Minutes later, still moving cautiously up the unrelentingly sharp gradient of what they discovered to be a not insubstantial small mountain, they again heard on the wind the resonance of a raw, angry voice. Though they could not clearly hear the words roared out, parsing quickly, they imagined it being something akin to, "You, halt, you ahead . . . the Crown orders you . . ." The voice itself was muffled by the sounds of at least two other mounted horses, and by the fact that O'Leary and Eileen were continuing to climb up and away from it and them.

Reaching a spot on relatively level ground, though not at all far up the prominence, the couple and the mares momentarily stood wordlessly still, the chirping of birds seeming suddenly, shatteringly loud.

There they were able to hear snippets of a brief, foolishly loud discussion amongst what now sounded to be three men, weighing whether their apparent prey had ascended the hillock or had chosen to speed across what were apparently the thinly treed flatlands on the other side of the track, "Humph—I say it is *up* they have gone! Up!" . . . "You err; 'tis on the track we should pursue them, 'tis there or on the flats beyond they have gone . . . if 'tis indeed even *them*. . . ."

The sounds of at least some of the horses and men lumbering up through the rough brush suddenly echoed; O'Leary and Eileen instantly urged their mounts up, both animals immediately responding.

Sensing their pursuers approaching, Art spied an opening Eileen seemingly had not and quickly booted Daisy alongside, flying past her, up and through a stand of scraggly saplings, into suddenly open terrain, reaching which he sharply tugged his horse right, trusting Eileen was behind him.

She was; together they would discover that the ground they reached, though at that point broadly open, ran along a steadily narrowing ridge, the thick undergrowth they had come through on the right, a sharp drop-off to their left. Not looking down, the pair urged their horses—both proving to be as sure-footed as William had said—faster, ever faster, the sound of thudding hoofs behind their backs fading ever so slightly.

O'Leary raised his right forefinger and the two riders slowed to a walk, Eileen casting a quick glance behind.

"Could we have evaded them?" she whispered, though louder than she had meant to.

O'Leary held his fingertip to his lips, nodded *no* and indicated *continue*, as along the steadily shrinking breadth of the ridge they rode for perhaps another ten minutes, managing at least a steady canter until they came to an abrupt precipice, a stark wall of coldly grey granite looming before and above them.

"What a bloody lovely view," O'Leary muttered, looking left in frustrated disgust —as well it was, under a cloud-drifted, misty-blue sky lay a seemingly unbroken ring of sharply falling hillsides, including the one on which they were now halted, tumbling into a deep, in places green, though primarily flint-coloured and starkly bare rock defile. Ominously, they again heard the unmistakable sounds of mounted horses, echoing and re-echoing, glancing off the rocks and scraggly trees now surrounding them—but from where?

Becoming reluctantly certain now of two realities—that the drop-off into the nearly round gorge was too steep to safely attempt, its surface largely devoid of sufficient soil and vegetation that could have provided footfalls for the horses, as well as that there appeared no visible egress from the canyon even were they to successfully manage a descent—they turned their animals' heads away. As quickly as possible, the pair began the struggle back down towards the rough track, still not knowing how far below them and even where precisely it lay, in the process ducking vines and twisting their bodies as the horses' movements propelled random whip-like branches at them.

As they descended, the fortuitous wind gusts again carried the sounds of thudding hoofs and snapping branches growing louder, seemingly both beneath and behind them. Judging from the direction of the sounds, the couple surmised that perhaps their pursuers had not found the mountain's crest, and that quite possibly they had been stubbornly thrashing their way through the in places nearly impenetrable mix of ancient and new forest, thick gorse and other harsh forms of underbrush.

After Art and Eileen had themselves woven through the mountainside's final gauntlet of saplings, finally bursting through a tangled curtain of thick vines, they emerged again onto the track. O'Leary waved a gauntlet-covered right hand, *forward*, as were he leading his Hungarian Hussars, and an unseen smile briefly flickered on Eileen's dry lips as she booted Sally on, both horses effortlessly reaching a gallop as he led her across the track and onto the fringes of the flatlands.

"Let us swing in a wide arc," O'Leary gestured with a sweep of his left arm as Eileen drew alongside him, "and pick up the track when it appears we can safely do so."

Nodding, she called, "Aye!" as he booted Daisy, Eileen similarly urging Sally on. Horses and riders were soon flying, seeming to increase in speed as they made a very wide though forward-directed arc.

After a time at full gallop, they reined in the gasping fillies, sat quietly a moment and listened.

"Perhaps we have eluded them yet, my love?" Eileen wondered aloud, as she had on the hillside, then disdainfully observing, "Many times, *these people* . . . they do not have the best of animals, nor do they seem to care for those they do have very well at all."

O'Leary agreed with a nod, and they headed in the general direction of the track, with still no evidence of their pursuers.

The rough trail ran nearly straight now, as did the riders as they joined it, again at a full gallop; it then took a tight arc around a looming, hoary outcrop of granite, as did they, slowing. At that point, it appeared that it would most likely straighten once more, at which point they would yet again give the horses their heads.

They would have, but for that, some distance beyond, straddling the centre of the track, sat a solitary rider on what was a weary-looking gelding, the man's fully cocked rifle levelled at them. Though the couple could not hear clearly what was being said over the sound of their horses' hoofs, a gruff voice was rasping into the afternoon air, calling out, "Eileen O'Connell? . . . And you, you O'Leary? . . . You will . . ."

Unexpectedly, inexplicably, there was a flash and an explosion as the barrel of the man's rifle spewed smoke and flame, the ball it projected emerging from a heavy veil of smoke, audibly whizzing through the barely three feet of space separating the still-moving pair.

"Bloody hell!" Eileen cried as she reflexively dropped the reins, the horse slowing – though only slightly. With a reach of her right hand, withdrawing the rifle resting in its scabbard near her left knee, without hesitation she cocked and pointed it, immediately firing. Almost instantly toppling from his saddle, they heard the man screech, "I am kilt!" even as he hit the uneven ground.

Never having halted, as she quickly approached the moaning man, Eileen managed to grab Sally's reins in her left hand, such that in a clatter of dirt and small rocks she sharply reined her in, a wispy cloud of dust rising out of the thin, sandy soil. Realising this, O'Leary, who displayed no intention of checking on the wounded man, had pulled up some yards beyond and reluctantly walked Daisy back, shaking his head.

As a still-mounted O'Leary drew up, he saw Eileen kneeling by the now-sitting, wounded man, his eyes still wide, his face streaming with sweat, his left palm gripping his right shoulder. Looking plaintively at her, he managed a wimperingly pathetic, "I am kilt." Pulling the dusty coat off his injured shoulder, Eileen ripped open the man's shirt, exposing a bleeding flesh wound.

Her face displaying some reluctant measure of relief, perhaps grateful the rifle had apparently contained less than a full charge of powder, Eileen concluded, "Fortunate for you, sir—whomever you may be—you are nay *kilt*," she sharply turned his upper arm, and the man screeched in seeming agony. She shook her head. "Rather, 'tis but a minor wound, the ball having just harshly, though quite deeply, scraped through your skin." Whilst Eileen was removing his coat completely, the spent rifle ball pattered onto the ground; she shook her head and sniffed at it. Rid of the coat, she ripped the left sleeve of his shirt, daubing the wound with its fabric. Tearing the several-days-worn soiled cotton shirt further, she made and tied a rough bandage around her victim's upper right arm.

The man seemed relieved, then suddenly angry. Just as Eileen was standing, he looked up at her, snarling, "You could have killed me, you bloodthirsty Papist bitch!"

Reflexively, her eyes wide with rage, Eileen bent and wordlessly smashed the back of her right hand across the man's right cheek. "You bastard, you fired upon us! Would you expect garlands, you . . ."? The man had fallen over on his uninjured side but screeched nevertheless.

O'Leary standing to one side, Eileen now looked directly at the thickset, pale man as he unsteadily tried to sit up, reaching for his battered tricorn hat, noting random wisps of red hair flecking his otherwise bare pate, seeing that both his dull face and head shone with sweat.

Calmer, though only slightly less irate, she haughtily announced, "I am the Lady Eileen O'Connell," as she purposely drew herself up to her full height, looking scornfully down on the man. ". . . and you are?" she demanded in an equally proud tone.

"It matters not who I am, but with whom I ride," the crude voice responded somewhat shakily, Eileen glaring at him, the now-unsteadily sitting man's eyes remaining downcast.

"Ah, you are wrong, sir, as it *does* matter. I always wish to know the identity of whomever it is I am obviously fully prepared to kill," Eileen purred.

Before the man could respond, O'Leary stepped closer. "Your *other* weapon . . . you will please indicate where it is, sir," he probed, on a sound hunch. Sighing in obvious frustration, the man gestured with a reluctant cock of his head to a saddlebag, from which O'Leary reached over and withdrew a heavy old pistol.

The man muttered, "Not loaded; 'tis not loaded. Just leave it be, eh?"

O'Leary eyed him warily. "Ah, is it not now?" He fully cocked it. "I believe perhaps we should verify that fact." Leaning towards the captive, bracing it on his left forearm, he pointed it at the man's chest. Waiting a long moment, he aimed it.

"Sir, *no*! Please . . ." the profusely sweating man stammered. "Please, sir, please do not . . ."

Smiling, O'Leary shook his head, slowly lowered, then uncocked the loaded weapon and rested it in the deep pocket of his riding coat. Together he and Eileen had observed the appalling condition of both the pistol and the man's rifle, with which he had shot at them: dull, uncared-for metal, the stocks dirty, the rifle's stock perhaps even cracked.

"So now, once again . . . who might be the individual with whom you ride, sir, the identity of whom you say should matter to me?" Eileen resumed calmly.

The man looked at her, his expression one of contempt.

Removing the weapon from his pocket, O'Leary placed the cold metal of the tip of the man's own pistol barrel at his temple, cocking it.

"Who is your companion?" he demanded precisely, his voice chilling.

"A deputy high undersheriff of Kerry," he spluttered quickly. "We are seeking you both. Along he shall . . . *they* shall be coming."

Eileen quickly eyed O'Leary.

"The precise reason for this pursuit being what, sir?" he snapped.

There being no response, O'Leary again pressed the pistol barrel's tip against the man's head, harder this time, causing him to wince.

"Assuming you are Arthur O'Leary, you are charged with the crimes of seduction and abduction, sir, of . . . assuming"—he cocked his head—"*she* is Eileen O'Connell . . . and we, we are to take you into custody and . . . and return your . . . ah . . . *victim* . . . to her family."

Incredulous, Eileen spontaneously laughed. "I . . . you say *I* . . . am alleged to be a *victim*?" She theatrically laid her left palm on her bosom. "The only potential victim I see present here is you, sir . . . and of what ultimate fate I shall leave it to you to conclude." Gesturing at his still-bleeding shoulder, she laughed cruelly again as the man flinched. "You shall also think of and refer to me *only* as *the Lady* Eileen O'Connell, do you understand?"

The man then looked up at her from where he sat and nodded reluctantly, his eyes narrow with loathing, an expression Eileen had frequently experienced and could thus easily surmise its probable verbalisation: *Goddammed accursed Papists . . . the rich ones especially.* Her own expression now became one of regally derisive contempt, the emotion it conveyed so powerful that it caused the man to avert his eyes, focusing on the muddy toes of his boots.

"Enough of this!" O'Leary snapped impatiently. "Bloody well enough, I say! You are most certainly 'nay kilt,'" he gestured coldly to the nevertheless still-bleeding man, "and we shall now be on our way," he indicated to Eileen, even as he was remounting, returning the pistol of which he had disarmed the man back into the deep pocket of his long riding coat.

At that moment, just as Eileen had placed the tip of her left boot into Sally's stirrup, a pair of men rounded the arc, one man roughly pulling his foamed mount to a panting semi-halt, the other man swinging to the other side, turning his horse and sweeping the small area with a fully cocked rifle, the butt crooked in his right shoulder, his right finger on the trigger.

"Bloody accursed fucking hell!" O'Leary roared, smacking the pommel of his saddle with such force that Daisy's head snapped towards him, eying O'Leary wonderingly; "So sorry, little lady," he patted her flank gently. Eileen sighed as she removed her boot from the stirrup, releasing Sally's reins, the horse at once nuzzling the gravelly grass.

His horse still in skittish motion, "*Arthur O'Leary!*" cried out Deputy Under High Sheriff George Gough, a florid, red-faced, thick man of perhaps fifty, the descendent of an early Cromwellian planter, well known in Kerry for being, as it was said, "in a permanent state of rage."

By his demeanour, his language, indeed his reputation, there was no doubt that he held all native Irish Catholics in utter disdain, possessing a singularly strong contempt for the vestiges of the onetime Gaelic Aristocracy. *Aristocracy? They deem themselves such because they have shoes. . . . Some are even able to read!* he was often heard to sneer.

But to those who took more than casual notice, it was readily apparent that he felt distinctly uncomfortable around "these types," as he called people such as O'Leary and the O'Connells. "*These types* . . . they think they are better than we are, loyal Protestants, servants of the king, they do," he would rage, whilst all the time believing in his mind, feeling in his very heart, that indeed they *were*, thus fuelling his fury.

His horse pawing the ground with his front hoofs, he began again. "Arthur O'Leary, I arrest you in the name of the king, on the charges of . . ."

At that moment, Eileen, who had, as she'd begun walking towards the still-mounted Gough, in a casually subtle gesture, drawn the right folds of her arasaid to her left side, interrupted sharply. ". . . Should you complete your sentence, Sheriff, you are a dead man," she said calmly, still moving forward. Drawing her gleaming pistol from beneath the left side of her cloak, where it had been resting in a deep, lined, inside pocket of her riding coat beneath, she fully cocked it, and unhesitatingly aimed the weapon at his chest, standing so close that her gloved left hand now rested calmly on his visibly anxious horse's flank.

Evidencing shock and not a small measure of fear, Gough managed only an unguarded, hesitant, "Now, girl, go easy with that. . . ."

Meanwhile, the still-mounted, rifle-bearing deputy had levelled his weapon on Eileen.

"Attempt it and you risk death," O'Leary announced calmly. His eyes on Eileen, the deputy held his rifle level, only then noticing that the young Corkman, but a few feet distant, was now pointing the wounded man's fully cocked pistol directly at him. "Uncock and gently lower your weapon to the ground," O'Leary commanded. As the man did so, O'Leary stepped closer to his horse, picking up the just-dropped dusty rifle. O'Leary sharply ordered him to "Dismount!"

On the other side of the awkward tableau, looking up at Gough, her expression remaining arch, still aiming the weapon at him, Eileen called out, "A wise decision by your man, sir, as this is loaded, and I assure you that I am wholly able to kill you . . . have no doubt, sir, of *that* being your reality. *You*"—she shot a quick look at O'Leary's prisoner, then back to Gough, speaking then to the pair of them—"may *both* ask your companion here. . . ." With a cock of her head, she gestured to the still-sitting wounded deputy.

Silence was each man's sole response.

At that moment, presumably sensing an opportunity that did not exist, with his right hand, Gough abruptly, inartfully, reached for his own weapon, deep in the right-hand pocket of his long riding coat.

Without hesitation, Eileen fired, her pistol spewing smoke and flame as its nasty little report, and then the acrid smell of burnt black power filled the still air.

"*Fucking Popish bitch, arrogant, filthy, heretical spawnofawhore* . . . !" roared Gough, his arm spasming jerkily in mid-air, his uncocked pistol thudding heavily to the ground, just as his wide-eyed horse whinnied loudly and reared back. Violently red-faced now, grabbing his bleeding right upper arm, moaning incoherently, he tumbled backwards off the frightened animal, landing heavily with a painful thud, sprawled in the gritty dirt.

Not noticing that she'd had the presence of mind to grab the terrified horse's bridle, Gough struggled to sit up, bracing himself unsteadily with his palm in the dirt. "Ye shot me, ye fucking Romish slut!" he screeched, looking woozily up at her.

Reflexively, even whilst still gripping his horse's reins with her left hand, Eileen smashed his jaw with the butt of her pistol. "Indeed I did. You should be thanking me that I did not bloody well kill you!" she stormed, as he lurched heavily to his side—and lay motionless.

Dropping to her knees, she unsympathetically pulled the at best semiconscious, unhearing Gough back up to a semi-seated position, muttering, "You stupid, arrogant bastard." She then roughly drew him forward, such that his head and arms hung between his spread legs, their weight and the manner in which Eileen had positioned him preventing Gough from toppling backwards.

As Gough slowly, woozily regained consciousness, several feet distant, O'Leary was ordering the third man, ". . . And now, your second weapon, please, as well, sir."

"I am now unarmed!" loudly squawked the man, his arms wide, hands empty, indicating his innocence.

Feeling almost sorry for the sallow, sad-looking fellow, a wispy former tailor, a Catholic until several months prior, when his shop had closed for lack of custom. O'Leary nevertheless barked, "Comply or I shall shoot you!"

Ashen-faced, the third man did so; unsteadily withdrawing a pistol from beneath his tattered coat, he turned it, his fingers then gripping the barrel, his eyes never raised, he tremblingly offered the stock to O'Leary, who now had three loaded, two fully cocked weapons—the wounded man's and the tailor's pistols, as well as the tailor's rifle—whilst Eileen had at hand Gough's weapon, as it rested on the ground near where she tended to him.

Gruffly ordering the unharmed man to join his wounded companion on the ground, O'Leary knelt next to Eileen, concluding, as had she, that Gough's wound, though considerably nastier, was in one small degree similar to the one she'd inflicted on the first mounted man, in that it was not, at least at the moment, serious, "The ball, 'tis passed partially through your arm and lies imbedded in the fatty layer beneath," he advised unsympathetically. "You are in no *imminent* danger—albeit that lead must be removed, and quite soon." He looked harshly at the sweating, enraged man. "I assure you, had the Lady Eileen desired to do so, she could and most definitely would have killed you."

Evidencing that he doubted nothing O'Leary had just said, Gough's expression was one of impotent fury.

Rising, O'Leary then strode back to where Daisy stood, munching on weeds. Returning with a small stone jug he uncorked, he bent wordlessly to a now-whimpering Gough as, having torn his left sleeve, Eileen was daubing the wound. Removing her hand with his own, O'Leary poured a stream of clear, powerful poteen onto the lawman's wound.

"Jesuschrist, you fucking sonofastinkingpapistwhore! Poison me now with that liquid fire, you worthless fucking Irish call whiskey, I should . . ."

O'Leary grabbed his wounded arm, shaking it roughly, causing Gough to moan aloud. "You ignorant bastard, ye know nothing of *septicus*, do you?" he sneered. "For sure you do not . . . for 'tis with *this*"—he mockingly shook the jug with his fingers—"that I may have aided your eventual recovery, you worthless *stupid* sack of shit!"

Disgusted, he stood, stalking towards the first wounded man; first asking and receiving the man's consent, he poured some of the liquid onto his wound. The man winced but said nothing.

The winds that had been blowing having abruptly, entirely ceased, the damp afternoon air now grew thick and pungent, a nearby waterlogged bog reeking, the odours of a thousand years of muck and treasures—of history—now dominating the space.

Eileen, having almost violently bandaged Gough's wound, stood and brushed the dirt and dust off her skirts, eying O'Leary uncertainly.

O'Leary gestured with the rifle gripped in his right hand. "Now . . . *Mister Deputy Under High Sheriff of Kerry*, you will please stand and step, very slowly, to that oak." Gough hesitated. O'Leary leaned forward and pulled him roughly to his feet. Gough moaned and then stood still, seething at the couple.

"*Now!*" Eileen called out, pushing her again-gloved right hand against Gough's chest, such that he turned unsteadily and lurched forward four or five steps. At O'Leary's direction, with a nudge with his own pistol in his lower back, the tailor, walking forward, immediately joined him.

Looking at the two men, O'Leary appeared pensive. Turning his attention to the tailor, he said firmly, "You shall untack your horse. Once he stands thus, you shall then smack his rump, causing him to depart . . . riderless." He laughed harshly. As the pair stood dumbly, O'Leary snapped, "*Now!*"

Gough leaning weakly against his own mount, the tailor did as he'd been ordered most reluctantly. Within minutes, the untacked horse bolted freely away, quickly disappearing as he raced across the lightly treed flatlands, in the direction of nowhere his rider would have wished him to go.

Once the animal was out of sight, O'Leary, with an eye to the sky, continued, "Now, gentlemen, you shall begin what to your misfortune I fear will be a rather lengthy nighttime trek towards Kilgarvan," in the general direction of which he gestured with the pistol in his right hand.

"Bloody goddammed *arrogant* Papists! . . . Fucking bloodthirsty murderers!" Gough roared, gesturing to his arm, and to the wounded man, "You cannot compel us to . . . you shall *both* be hanged!" then adding, "How dare you!"

"Oh, I dare for several reasons actually, sir," O'Leary said matter-of-factly, almost playfully continuing, "I hold two," he nodded at the first man and the tailor, whose pistols he gripped, "of them . . . whilst, as you will of course note, the Lady Eileen holds two more." Eileen smilingly raised Gough's pistol and the tailor's rifle, pointedly aiming one at each man.

"The *fifth* it is, however, the most critical of all reasons," O'Leary continued, his voice now gravely serious. "This reason being that there has been *no* seduction, nor has there been any *ab*duction, the warrant, the writ—if, indeed, any has issued, which I believe none has, thus void. I strongly suspect you have come on a private matter for the master of Derrynane, your actions being based on, at the very least, a lack of understanding of certain salient facts; at the very worst, on a perjured oath." Gough's mouth again fell open.

"My sworn testimony to the contrary will disprove that of my brother, sir," Eileen suddenly volunteered, "and almost twenty-four years of age I am." She nodded for effect.

Noticing the gathering dusk slowly but pronouncedly coming upon them, O'Leary calmly commanded the tailor, "Now . . . should you wish to haul it with you, you will please collect your horse's tack." The man appearing uncertain as to what to do, O'Leary then ordered, "Get your man aboard his horse and bloody well get the both of you along; depart!

"Your companion shall accompany us into Cork, at which time, after assuring ourselves that he remains in satisfactory condition to ride, we shall release both him and his horse. Should you and/or anyone at your behest attempt to pursue us into Cork—which is beyond your jurisdiction, do you not concede, *Mister Deputy Under High Sheriff of Kerry?*—you shall by your recklessness imperil the life of your man here." Eileen pointedly aimed the tailor's rifle barrel at the still-seated, wounded man's head, causing him again to gasp aloud.

"Our weapons!" the painfully thin tailor cried out.

"Your weapons?" O'Leary paused. "They shall be handed over to the high sheriff of Cork. You may pursue the matter of their possible return with him."

Keeping the rifle aimed at their hostage, Eileen gestured at the other men with the pistol in her left hand. "I believe it is best you depart, gentlemen." Gough, with the tailor's assistance, having managed to unsteadily mount his horse, appeared ready to speak. "*Now!*" Eileen snapped, extending her left arm, her voice icy.

Wordlessly, the tailor hoisted his heavy saddle, to which, after first fastening the cinch, he'd tied his horse's bridle and reins. By balancing the tack over one arm, he was able to grasp Gough's horse's cheek strap, and, albeit with some difficulty, turn the animal—and himself. They finally began to trudge back down the rough track, the stirrup leathers swinging, the irons themselves thudding against the tailor's bony side as he tramped away. Gough, wobblingly mounted, seethed silently.

"Godspeed!" Eileen called out caustically, "and a very good evening to you both now!" Neither man looked back. O'Leary stared at her. She winked at him.

O'Leary then walked a few paces forward and picked up the spent rifle. Examining it, he shook his head at its yet still-seated owner. "'Tis in very poor condition," he opined; he then discharged the man's pistol up into the still, wet air, after which he observed, "Very poor condition as well."

He waved as the unhappily trudging, heavily burdened tailor and the sheriff both swung clumsily around in shock at the sound of the pistol's firing.

After first picking up their captive's hat and setting it on his head, O'Leary helped the man to his feet. Eileen removed the poteen-soaked first bandage and carefully examined the still-slowly seeping wound. The man having consented to O'Leary again disinfecting it with the clear, powerful liquor, Eileen skilfully folded the remainder of his left shirtsleeve into a thick bandage and tied it with a bow. O'Leary then helped him to remount. In the meantime, after returning her own pistol to her riding coat pocket, Eileen divided their small cache of pistols between her pair of saddlebags. With O'Leary already cradling the still-loaded rifle, once she returned her spent one to its saddle holster, they headed out.

With virtually no conversation, save for their occasional inquiries as to how the man was feeling, the hostage volunteering that his name was

Craig and at one point suddenly, loudly protesting that he had been "impressed" into joining Gough, to which neither Eileen nor O'Leary responded, the trio followed the by-now relatively smooth track over a series of hills and around several small mountains, until at a point recognised by O'Leary alone he halted, the darkness of an Irish autumn evening falling heavily about them.

"Ah, 'tis in County Cork we now are," he said softly, Eileen drawing up her horse next to him.

As they had promised, after both examined the man's wound, around which Eileen then tied on a relatively clean handkerchief she'd unexpectedly found in her saddlebag, with few words, the couple immediately released Craig, O'Leary securing his battered weapons, placing the rifle into a worn saddle holster, the pistol he slipped into his saddlebag, muttering "Retain whatever powder and balls you may have."

As Craig began to turn his horse's head, he stopped; looking at both Art and Eileen, he paused, then touching a finger to his hat, nodded respectfully and said, "My lady, sir . . . a good evening to you both, then."

Art nodded, Eileen adding, "And a safe journey home to you, then," and they turned, as did he. Neither the man nor the couple had given any thought to remaining together for the night. Despite—or perhaps it was on account of—his wounding, Craig simply appeared relieved to be free; the couple, to be rid of him, happy to be travelling again alone.

No mention was made of the wounding, nor of Eileen striking Craig afterwards.

"In Cork we truly now are, my love?" Eileen finally asked softly.

"Indeed yes, we are!" O'Leary replied gently, though when they came upon a tiny cottage set amidst a plethora of in some cases tiny stone-walled fields, he hailed a ruddy older fellow, a hay rake over his shoulder and a nondescript but pleasant dog at his heels, the pair just heading inside.

After greeting the fellow, bidding him the time of day and, despite the poor light, the man taking a smiling special notice of Eileen, O'Leary inquired, "Might I trouble you to advise my lady as to the county in which we have just recently arrived?"

"Ah, 'tis Cork, my lady, blessed Cork indeed." The farmer smiled, bowing and doffing his hat to Eileen.

She smiled down. "Thank you, good sir, very much."

They continued riding until the evening had fully gathered and they could no longer travel safely, stopping then in a lightly treed grove, seeming to have perhaps at one time been the entrance to a boreen, just off the track, that now apparently led nowhere. Once they unsaddled and loosely tethered the grazing horses so they might continue to forage, O'Leary unexpectedly produced part of a loaf of bread as well as a thick wedge of cheese, and the two sat on the ground, leaning against a pair of middle-aged elm trees.

"My love, how well prepared you are!" Eileen smiled, breaking off some bread.

"Not as prepared as you, my darling," responded O'Leary, gesturing in the direction of Kerry with his head.

Holding her bread, Eileen responded in an even voice. "When we journeyed to Derrynane, I certainly did not want it left amongst my remaining belongings at the home of the Baldwins"—she rolled her eyes—"nor could I have abandoned the weapon at Derrynane the night we hastily departed, so when I saw Annie in the hall, I asked her to retrieve from my rooms there my weapon and my . . ."—she gestured at the heavy belt still about her hips—"So tucked well into the special wee pocket in my riding coat it has been since before we departed Derrynane . . . and indeed, useful it proved, did it not, my darling?"

O'Leary nodded, smiling, in his weariness saying nothing further, other than expressing his relief that "at least a corpse it did not create."

Within moments of their small meal, warmly bidding each other a good night, the two were soundly asleep.

County Cork, Ireland—November–December 1767

The following morning, O'Leary awakened slowly to a dull grey sky, weak early sun providing but thin light and little warmth. His saddle hard beneath his head, despite that he had draped Daisy's saddle blanket over it, he shivered slightly beneath his dew-dampened cloak and stiffly sat up.

As he looked about, he smiled. His fellow traveller lay sprawled on her side, cat-a-corner across from him, a long figure wrapped in the thick wool yardage of her immense plaid, an abundant cascade of hair askew on her own saddle.

He knelt over the still-sleeping figure. "My Eileen of the raven locks, 'tis your very first morning awakening with me in County Cork," he said softly, just barely touching her right shoulder.

As O'Leary knelt up, Eileen turned slowly onto her back, smiled sleepily and yawned. He laughed as she sat up stiffly and stretched her arms.

"Ah, good sir, now you see how I shall appear every morning." She smiled again, running her long, elegant fingers through her tousled hair and pushing it out of her eyes.

O'Leary nodded. "Ah, 'tis not at all how you shall appear, my love. You shall awaken in a massive high bed, with only the smoothest of linens, the finest of pillows and coverlets, and you shall . . ."

Eileen had by then knelt up, placing her fingers behind his neck ". . . and I shall not be wrapped in a dew-misted cloak but rather naked and warm with my darling love," her lips whispered to his own.

The pleasant prospect shared, they devoured the remainder of the bread and cheese O'Leary had brought from Derrynane; their morning hunger satisfied, they would nevertheless be thirsty until they reached a brook sometime later. They were quickly saddled and away, the country beginning to open up and the quality of the track improving as Cork soon both lay open before them and fell quietly away behind, separating them from Kerry and from the events of the days prior.

It was the barking—*yapping!*—as Conor O'Leary frequently referred to the chorus as being—of Rathleigh's polyglot brood of a half-dozen dogs, accompanied by the pall-mall racing of most of them through the depth of the house, from the back to the gleaming front door that heralded the arrival of General the Count and the Countess von Graffenreit-O'Connell one still, suddenly bitter cold early December evening.

And it was the now only occasionally dour Anne who came hustling on the heels of the noisy pack, prepared to immediately order the itinerant tradesman she believed to be the cause of the ruckus to the kitchen house door. "If any sale you expect to make, any meal you expect to be offered . . ."

As she opened the door, the dogs raced out and away from the house, their attention now fixed on the scents riding on the just-rising wind, or perhaps it was the scurrying foxes the lead one had presently noticed in the gathering dusk; nevertheless, she gasped at the sight, as she later related it to Conor O'Leary: "A massive man, mounted on an obviously hired horse, so small it was for him, and himself in raiment similar to, but, ah, so much more elegant than Master Arthur's, 'twas he that I first saw   . . . and then, mounted sidesaddle on a second animal, in size more suited for this rider than her companion's was his, I saw her, this lady . . . regal and beautiful she, the most delicate of smiles and a tumble of not blond but not silver hair on her shoulders, her travelling hat ever so slightly askew . . . and I realised 'twas I myself at whom she was smiling, not at her companion. The officer reached up and held her waist, lifting her groundward as effortlessly as were she but a wee child!"

By the time General O'Connell had assisted his wife down from her horse and the returning dogs had dispersed, Art, Eileen and Conor O'Leary himself now filled the entryway for a grand, loud reunion of sorts. As Eileen and Art gathered up the arrivals' satchels, the countess indicated that the rest of their belongings would arrive, "I hope very shortly . . . as virtually all our . . ." she looked archly at Eileen, ". . . finery is in those trunks."

Over an informal tea and, afterwards, a hearty meal, indeed well into the evening, the two couples and Squire O'Leary shared their respective stories of "that night at Derrynane," and the colourful and, in the case of the younger couple harrowing, aftermath.

The general and countess briefly related that, prior to departing for Cork, they had together spoken at some length with Maire and the girls, Anne and Elizabeth, whilst the general alone had spoken with Morgan and Hugh, also for quite some time. The couple was pleased to learn that they were all fully supportive, even though General O'Connell reported that Morgan, despite that he had indicated he liked O'Leary, had cautioned that, "Maurice's concerns, they are genuine, and definitely not wholly without merit."

Before the night ended, the general advised that, though he had obviously been unable to recall the under sheriff, Maurice had "most reluctantly abandoned all other attempts to prevent the marriage," telling him, "I have far more serious matters with which to be concerned."

Maurice had also told the general, "Your new obligation, indeed your primary obligation to this family, General, is to assure that they shall remain in Vienna . . . and that they shall never return to Ireland." The general did not relate this part of the conversation to the young couple, nor that he had made no such commitment to Maurice.

Rathleigh House, near Macroom, County Cork—19 December 1767

Very early on the still, grey morning of 19 December, the countess quietly slipped into the comfortable small bedroom that had been Eileen's since she and Art had returned from Derrynane. Barefoot and in a heavy dressing gown, she smiled as she saw Eileen still soundly asleep, curled up like a little girl.

The countess climbed up the small steps to the high bed and knelt next to her niece. Bending, her ash-blond tousle tumbling about, she gently laid her fingertips on Eileen's left shoulder and leant to the younger woman.

"Good morning, bride; today is the day for which it would appear you have always been destined, my good niece," she whispered.

Eileen came slowly awake, rolling onto her back and smiling up at the countess and reaching for her hand. "This day could not have come without your help, and the good general's," she almost whispered, "my dear Aunt Maria."

The woman who had comfortably become simply Maria O'Connell during her stay in Ireland smiled and squeezed Eileen's hand.

Art, she told the soon-to-be bride, had returned home from an apparently night-long celebration with some of his friends. Eileen could only smile, momentarily wondering *where . . . with whom . . .* then just as quickly dispelled the thoughts as Maria advised that the priest from Macroom would be at Rathleigh in time for the wedding to occur in the mid-afternoon, and that Art's sister was due to arrive during the morning.

O'Leary himself had retired to a small cottage down a side boreen from the main house, there to sleep, bathe and perhaps dress for the wedding, whilst his father had been out since dawn on a horse-trade, so Eileen breakfasted alone, awaiting the arrival of Art's sister, Catherine, about whom she knew only that she was older than Art by more than a few years, lived, apparently quite comfortably, in Cork City and had never married. She was said to be informally associated with at least two of the large Cork merchant houses, her precise role never discussed.

It was just as Eileen was finishing her solitary breakfast, skimming a several days-old newspaper as she drained her coffee cup, that the front door of Rathleigh was unexpectedly flung open with a slam, and there appeared Catherine O'Leary, accompanied by the loud thudding of her baggage being deposited hastily by a seemingly harried, thence immediately departing coachman, and followed by the woman's sharply delivered command to the young housemaid who had rushed to the entrance, to "see that my belongings are immediately and properly cared for, girl!"

Hearing the slight commotion, Eileen stepped to the door of the dining room, the women immediately, almost instinctively eying each other critically before a word was spoken.

Catherine O'Leary was several inches shorter than Eileen, her complexion glowing, her fiery-red hair equally so as it rested just below her shoulders. Her grey eyes were more piercing than pretty, her shoulders narrow, her body trim, *hard even*, Eileen thought, as she concluded that she must be at least thirty-five.

Catherine spoke in a slightly rough-edged, blunt tone. "Well now, if it is not the *grand lady herself* of whom my father has written me much!" she said as she remained in the entrance hall, without bothering with introductions.

Eileen smiled warmly and, stepping into the hall, extended her right hand and dipped into a gentle, almost-playful half curtsey, fully expecting the woman who would soon be her sister-in-law to reciprocate. Her eyes narrowing, Catherine archly waved off the younger woman's proffered hand with a flick of her own, turned and walked into the comfortable parlour across the hall, followed by a now-wary Eileen.

"How lovely your gesture was, my dear," Catherine said, mimicking Eileen's greeting, "but I think not." She dropped casually into a high-backed padded chair and added diffidently, "I know well the *pretensions* of the O'Connells of Derrynane, and I fear your years in domestic service to the Habsburgs have done little to disabuse you of your affectations . . . but 'tis nevertheless mildly pleasant to finally make your acquaintance."

Eileen walked slowly to a chair across from the older woman's and sat cautiously, purposely saying nothing other than a very correct, but quite chilly, " . . . and yours as well, *dear*." Atypically, she sat quietly, her hands folded, her expression inscrutable, simply watching and waiting, thinking, *I wish to hear what else this woman will say.*

"My brother is such a dear boy, but 'tis certain I am that you are aware of that," Catherine began. "You might not, however, be aware of . . . actually, I suspect you are largely unaware of much concerning Arthur, though you certainly shall be—and quickly." She smiled almost cruelly.

Eileen's eyes were squinted just slightly, as she began, precisely, "*Actually*, I know a great deal, Catherine, and my understanding of the man, *as his wife*, will most certainly differ from that of his sister, do you not agree?"

"No, I do not; Arthur is and always has been closer to me than to any other woman. I have long believed, and frequently expressed, that in many aspects of life—most, really—we are as one."

The statement hung heavily in the still air of the closed room. Eileen, parrying now, said, "Is that not an *unusual* view of life, as it appropriates to a man's sister the role that is properly that of his wife? This I find to be . . . unusual, highly unusual, especially as, even had it been the case prior to a man being wed, 't'woud at the time of his marriage then properly pass to his wife." Her voice even, her impression of Catherine O'Leary quickly forming.

"A wife bears a man's children, dear, and does virtually nothing else, including, save in the rarest of cases, providing any significant quality of physical pleasure at the time of the acts leading to the conception of such children." Catherine continued dismissively, "Which is why I have never desired to wed . . . to be a broodmare I have never fancied myself." She sighed.

"Though some women are said to find fulfilment in things domestic—cooking, sewing and the like—you will of course finally have a household, so the domestic abilities I am certain you have perfected whilst a servant in Vienna will come to be of little use . . . and what is it precisely you do there? Do you actually . . . ?" She interrupted herself, again waving a dismissive right hand.

Eileen continued to listen, her mind whirring, *Could it be this woman is slightly mad? Or more than slightly?*

"My brother has emotional, and, yes, intellectual needs to which I have always responded . . . indeed, were it not for the unfortunately restricting practices of modern society, I am certain I should be quite capable of caring for his physical requirements as well, I should think." Her expression, her laugh were both caustic.

Eileen's cheeks flamed. Noticing this, Catherine spoke again. "I have often thought of the utter joy we would bring to each other . . . a truly perfect union in all ways."

At first her lips had parted in shock, but Eileen's expression was quickly, venomously searing, evidencing both rage and revulsion. The woman was indeed raving mad . . . and perverse.

"Does that offend your delicate sensibilities, dear?" Catherine finally purred.

Her expression unchanged, removing her hands from her lap, where they had been, folded, Eileen now rested her arms, her hands on the arms of the chair, her head straight, her shoulders barely touching the back of the chair. She sat as regally as she had when assisting her little archduchesses to perfect their formal sitting, appearing, the empress had observed to Maria von Graffenreit on more than one occasion, "more regal than any woman of this family."

The impact immediate, Catherine felt herself suddenly uncomfortable, shifting slightly in her own seat, no longer looking directly at Eileen.

"Whether or not it offends my sensibilities, delicate or otherwise," Eileen began, "is quite immaterial, though I find it wholly beyond my comprehension that any *civilised* person could maintain such thoughts, much less speak of them. What it *does* offend is my sense of boundaries . . . as deciding how to properly care for a man's 'physical needs,' as well as the other roles you describe, all of which you appear to have arrogated to yourself, are properly left within the realm of any marriage."

Now it was Catherine's cheeks that grew flushed as Eileen continued, her tone aggressive, "It is for a wedded couple to agree, or"—and Eileen herself smiled archly now—"for the woman to decree, if it is her decision—as well it may be—that all or any part of a husband's needs, including his physical ones, as you put it, are to be cared for outside of the marriage. So shall it be in the marriage to be celebrated in this house today, *Catherine*," she ended, slowly, precisely and—by the expression on her face—most definitely.

Her face blazing, Catherine O'Leary stood quickly. "Arthur is the dearest of persons to me. I shall not *ever* agree to—"

Eileen stood now as well to her full height, regal and icy. "You *shall not ever*," she gestured with her right forefinger, her left hand clenched into an obvious fist at her side, "intrude *anywhere*, encroach *anyplace*, in which you are neither desired nor needed." She stepped forward, disdainfully looking down on the now visibly diminished older woman. "Do you understand me?"

Catherine's eyes flashed and she turned abruptly, wordlessly stalking out of the room.

Eileen stepped towards one of the windows, an Irish winter pastoral before her now: a leaden grey sky with but a few tentative wisps of blue; even darker grey clouds spinning in from the Atlantic; rolling open country, even in December still evidencing slight suggestions, subtle vestiges of the prior season's vivid greens; two romping horses, several fleece-chubby sheep and a widely circling dog, its barking perhaps in frustration at being ignored by the other animals.

Smiling at the rotund-appearing sheep, unconsciously her mind moved quickly, inexplicably to Firies, and the first indication that John O'Connor might be truly unwell. As she focused, she realised it was neither the setting nor the event but the words she had thought and spoken at the time: *We shall have to be aware and vigilant.* She shook her head, smiling coldly; so 'twas aware and vigilant she would once again be. Then she went to complete her preparations for the wedding.

In the midst of changing into full court dress with the help of a wide-eyed new young housemaid named Silé, who struggled to follow Eileen's slow, precise instructions—*Please pull the cinches tighter and tie the laces at my lower back; yes, dear, like that!*—the bride realised how disturbed she was by Catherine's remarks. Aware of his return, having heard his boots thudding on the stairs, she sought out her soon-to-be husband. Arriving at his rooms, she knocked sharply, immediately announcing, "'Tis I, my love; with you I must speak a moment, please."

A surprised O'Leary, in his uniform breeches and shirt but otherwise not yet dressed, quickly opened the door, and Eileen stepped in, her complexion and expression evidencing that she was uncomfortable, unusually agitated. The door clicked softly.

Sitting on a chest at the foot of the high bed, she indicated she had had a "quite out-of-the-ordinary, indeed extremely bizarre conversation" with Catherine, without providing details save to observe that his sister appeared to be a "highly strung woman, with a seemingly vivid imagination."

Somewhat uncertainly, O'Leary began to respond, speaking briefly about Catherine as a young girl, "odd and difficult even then." Collecting his thoughts, he spoke more definitely, indicating that "She is indeed quite strange. I hear stories repeated about her . . . such that she favours women over men," he actually blushed, "whilst at other times she is said to prefer multiple partners of both sexes in her bed." He shook his head.

"Not knowing for certain whether these and other public-house tales are merely calumny or truthful—though I sense that truthful indeed they are—I nevertheless fear she is in many ways delusional. Indeed I have for some time considered that she might even be slowly descending into madness."

Eileen sat silently, her expression now one of sadness. He appeared pained but continued, "I am aware that she holds eccentric and indeed disturbing views on a variety of subjects: She opposes all executions, no matter how egregious the crime, would have institutions, all forms of government, the Church even . . . done away with, and marriage as well! She cloaks and thus justifies—in her own mind—her beliefs concerning marriage and relations between the sexes in a confused and highly selective understanding of Brehon law, she . . ."

Noticing Eileen's continuing dark expression, O'Leary paused, taking her hand. "Has she said or suggested anything that specifically troubles you?"

At first, despite the fact that she had sought O'Leary out, and given what he had thus said, Eileen was prepared to say nothing further but, concluding that to do so would not be the best way to commence a marriage, she did then share with Art in general what Catherine had said. "So, yes, *husband*," she smiled briefly and concluded softly, "*that* troubles me."

O'Leary's face went scarlet, "Never has she spoken thus to me, and were she ever to do so, her face would feel my open hand. That she harbours such . . . such *thoughts* is both shocking and troubling. Happy I am that we shall soon depart for Vienna, indeed that she shall even sooner return to Cork City."

They sat quietly for a long moment.

"So be troubled no longer, my darling; 'tis you who have captured my heart . . . my very being, and that both shall you possess forever . . . you and no other."

Reassured, Eileen departed somewhat awkwardly to re-join Silé in completing their dressing protocol; after she'd gone, O'Leary completed his own and, quickly burnishing his boots, stalked down the long corridor to his sister's rooms, his ornate uniform coat open, the stiff gold-braided front flapping as he walked.

Rapping his knuckles sharply once, though unbidden, he admitted himself and remained for almost an hour. The voices within were initially muffled; though Catherine's was heard clearly not at all, O'Leary's was—throughout much of the house, several times: "How dare you? . . . Shocking, even for you! . . . Persist and I shall have you declared a lunatic and put away . . . finally, once and for all!" When O'Leary left, he closed the door with a gentle click and calmly returned to his own room.

Father Martin O'Mahony, a tall, ascetically thin priest, had arrived at Rathleigh— aboard a tall, significantly more robust-appearing grey gelding—and was welcomed warmly by Squire O'Leary and the count and countess shortly after noon.

At the appointed time, Art, in his splendid red-and-gold Hungarian Hussars full-dress raiment, including the unique fur-trimmed pelisse delicately draping his left shoulder, joined the priest at the far end of Rathleigh's library.

General O'Connell, his uniform, though striking, far less dramatically detailed than Art's, Squire O'Leary, soberly dressed in a simple suit as black as the cleric's cassock and a now surprisingly serene, gently quiet Catherine O'Leary in an elegant dark blue gown, all awaited Eileen's arrival at the foot of the house's steep, gleaming main staircase. A rustle of fabric and muted women's voices above silenced the soft chatter amongst the three.

After a moment, delicate feminine steps and the gentle swish of a heavy, deep emerald satin court dress heralded the countess's descent of the stairs, her train full, her expression one of stately joy as she beamed at her husband. Catherine O'Leary's eyes grew wide as she absorbed the woman's appearance with each precise step the countess took, and wider still as Eileen O'Connell herself appeared, her court dress considerably more elaborate than her aunt's, being the one Eileen had first worn on what now seemed to be the long-ago day of her presentation to her then-little archduchesses.

Her bearing regal, her expression serene, Eileen descended slowly in her thickly embroidered, heavy, long-sleeved robe of deep blue-and-gold thread, a full train flowing from the waist and ample décolletage.

As she reached the entrance hall, her uncle stepped forward and bowed to Eileen, then offered his arm to his wife, who before she took it gracefully curtseyed to the bride. The two, followed by the squire and his daughter, entered the library, where Anne and the household staff waited in the back of the room, along with twenty-odd friends and neighbours of the O'Learys, men and women alike. As she passed her soon-to-be sister-in-law, Eileen smiled warmly, conciliatorily. Though Catherine's expression was tight, she appeared calm, perhaps embarrassed even, certainly grateful for Eileen's smile. She, too, curtseyed flawlessly.

The priest and Art, joined by the two couples and the members of the household, briefly awaited the bride, who walked the length of the room, her eyes filled with unshed tears. She stepped next to O'Leary and reached down for his hand.

Eyes on each other, Eileen and O'Leary now stood before Father O'Mahony, the general and the countess flanking them, though standing closely and ever so slightly behind them, almost protectively, so the two couples were arrayed in a gentle arc rather than a straight line.

Unlike her wedding at Firies, Eileen made certain she listened to and absorbed every word said, every gesture made, every feeling experienced. *. . . I shall remember these moments, indeed this entire day, until I die. . . .*

She heard Art's deep, gentle voice, *I take thee, Eileen, to be my wife . . . to love, honour and protect . . . for better or worse . . .* and then her own familiar, husky one, *I take thee, Arthur, to be my husband . . . to have and to hold, from this day forth . . . 'til death do us part,* as they repeated the simple vows slowly, precisely, looking deeply into each other's eyes.

So profound was the experience, she thought several times, *yet, 'tis as if I have never heard, much less spoken, these words before.*

Amongst the many images and emotions of the day that she would indeed carry with her for the rest of her life was the moment O'Leary, according to the Catholic rite and Irish custom—advancing the ring from finger to finger—*In the name of the Father . . . and of the Son . . . and of the Holy Ghost . . . amen*—finally slipped a fine gold band on the fourth finger of her right hand, though she saw it only through a veil of joyous, unshed tears. Later she would recall that she was certain that at that very moment her heart had stopped, missing a beat, perhaps even two, resuming only after she had looked at her husband and again at the ring now gleaming securely on her finger.

I shall always believe that at that very moment I was reborn on this earth!

The vows complete and the blessings bestowed, the small family group and the guests, joined by Anne and the rest of the household, serving but also celebrating, enjoyed the remainder of the afternoon and into the evening with a variety of wines and spirits before, during and after a light but lengthy supper, all accompanied by pleasant and enjoyable conversation.

Squire O'Leary proved himself a most effusive, jovial host; at one point he nudged the general, observing warmly that "Beneath all that bright red wool, gold braid and lace of a noble officer of imperial Austria there beats the very heart and soul of Ireland!" His eyes ever so slightly moist, the general delicately clinked O'Leary's glass. *"Shláinte . . . agus Erin go Bragh!"*

Maria O'Connell meanwhile had succeeded in captivating a now fully subdued and surprisingly charming Catherine O'Leary, along with a number of the ladies—and indeed some of the gentlemen guests as well—with what she said were "some of my favourite tales of Vienna," laced with exotic, magical-sounding words such as *empress and emperor, archduchess, the Holy Roman Empire, castles, balls* and *sledge rides in the snow.* When she explained the intricacies of the formal dress she and Eileen wore, the group's eyes drifted between the countess and Eileen as, gesturing gracefully with her hands, she contrasted the robes.

It was evident she had overheard Catherine's references to Eileen's "years of domestic service" and her role as a "servant" to the Habsburgs in Vienna, as well as "the pretensions of the O'Connells of Derrynane." At one point after first advising the woman that, "I am customarily addressed only as 'Your Grace,' though at the moment—" she elegantly flicked her right hand dismissively. Now deliberately speaking very softly, indeed in an intimate, almost conspiratorial tone, the countess made it quite clear to Catherine that, "Whilst servants to Her Imperial Majesty we all are"—she gestured broadly, including the entire tiny Viennese contingent—"on the most intimate of terms with the imperial family *we all are*, as well!"

She related Eileen's years in the schoolroom, the riding rink and in their Imperial highnesses' lives overall, pointedly using the sometimes-convoluted Irish sentence structure with which she was becoming familiar. She went on to inform a by-now-wide-eyed-and-open-mouthed Catherine O'Leary that, "'Tis Eileen who is the true mother of these once little girls, now both soon to be queens; indeed 'twas today's bride who told these dear Imperial children of the death of their beloved father, the emperor."

Absorbing these and similar stories, strategically related by the countess as the late afternoon progressed into evening, Catherine became cloyingly deferential to her new sister-in-law, addressing her now as "dear sister" as she refilled her glass and offered her food. In return Eileen was gracious and also used the term "dear sister" effusively, nevertheless reminding herself of the need to remain *aware and vigilant*—though perhaps a bit less than she had originally envisioned.

The elder O'Connells—both of whom, to their bemusement, Catherine was by that time addressing as "Your Grace"—and Eileen and Art continued to regale the others with funny stories from Vienna.

At one point, after Art had quietly told Catherine the story of their experience with the deputy under high sheriff of Kerry and his men. As Art related how Eileen had effortlessly shot two men as the couple had struggled to reach sanctuary in Cork following their failed attempt at Derrynane to win approval for their marriage, Catherine took her new sister-in-law's hand, exclaiming, "You really *are* quite an extraordinary woman!"

The O'Leary men and the general shared their experiences of continental education and the officers delighted the squire and a number of the guests with tales of the army and their time in the field.

Only briefly during the afternoon and evening did Eileen dwell on those whom she thought of as being the "absent O'Connells." *Would I have loved to have had Mama and Morgan, Hugh and the girls come from Derrynane, and Abby and Denis to have suddenly magically appeared from Vienna, and Daniel likewise from Paris? Certainly* . . . *but,* turning away from the gathering, she reflected as she watched the December night closing blackly about her new home . . . *no more joy could I feel even were all of them here than at this moment I do! My happiness is,* she thought, turning back to the room and quietly looking towards her gallant horseman. As O'Leary, as elegantly arrayed as he was when first he had entered the room but now with a glass in his hand and his other arm resting affectionately on Maria O'Connell's shoulder, her eyes glowed. She and the general flanked Art as he was apparently enthralling his listeners with an account of some feat of the Austrian cavalry during the Seven Years War, cautioning, "Now, present I was not at this heroic event, though my brother-in-law, Major Denis O'Sullivan, serving then, as now, under Count Konigkrantz, was himself . . ."

Welcome to the family, Lieutenant O'Leary. Eileen strolled over to re-join the celebration.

As the evening wound down, the newly wedded couple appeared to be delaying their departure, until finally General O'Connell gently though not terribly subtly observed, "This has been a full and memorable day indeed! I should think our young friends"—he gestured at Art and Eileen—"they must be weary. I believe we should permit them to retire."

Hearing this, his wife instantly attempted to get his attention, loudly whispering, "But, darling, her robe . . ."

Conor O'Leary, as if on cue, added a precise, "Indeed!" and, taking his son's hand, gently kissed his new daughter-in-law on her blushing right cheek.

Catherine led everyone in gentle applause as the couple almost sheepishly joined hands and climbed the stairs. As they did, Maria tugged at her husband's sleeve. "I was endeavouring to remind you, my darling, her dress—it requires . . ."

The general chuckled and shook his head. "Ah, quite capable they are to disassemble her!" and he laughed aloud, walking then towards Squire O'Leary so as to share the joke with his comrade.

The countess, shaking her head, thought to herself, *Ah, but they are not!*—though then she, too, could not help but laugh softly at the prospect.

Immediately upon entering Art's rooms, Eileen and he began what would prove to be a joyous but in some memorable ways wonderfully awkward wedding night.

"My love, should you wish me to assist, I . . ." said Art softly, gesturing at Eileen's complex raiment, knowing full well he could not.

Eileen blushed and began, "Oh, no, sir, I believe that I shall be able to . . ." knowing full well she could not, which resulted in the new Mistress O'Leary clumsily and uncomfortably directing her husband of but hours through the intricate series of steps necessary to liberate her from her ornate outfit. Art muttered as he fumbled with the seemingly endless array of hooks, eyes and stays, as well as gossamer-seeming strings and tiny ribbons, and both of them ultimately laughed a bit then—and much more so in the days that followed—at the effort required for Eileen's magnificent robe to ultimately become an elegant mound of fabric on the carpet. Now barely clad as she was, she helped Art remove his suddenly tight, gleaming boots.

Ultimately shed of most of their clothing, they clambered up onto Art's bed—the "massive high bed, with only the smoothest of linens, the finest of pillows and coverlets" of which he had spoken the morning of their first awakening together in a Cork boreen—and yet again became self-conscious, awkward and, incredibly, tongue-tied, as if neither wished to acknowledge to the other—so singular, so exceptional was this night—that, as Art related to Denis O'Sullivan weeks later in Vienna, "We had each been abed with others and both fully aware of it! Indeed was Eileen not a widow?"

Finally, after lying quietly, saying little for a time, in the seductive light of a single candle, the firelight from the hearth dancing on the walls, visible in each other's eyes, O'Leary, by then clad only in his open shirt, turned and wordlessly, gently, lifted Eileen's loose chemise over her head and arms. Naked, she rested her head and shoulders back against the mounded feather pillows, her hair askew, and opened her arms to her new husband.

Their expressions joyful in the soft candlelight, O'Leary rolled onto her, her arms and legs immediately, instinctively embracing him, as they now joined their bodies as had they already joined their hearts, their souls—passionately and powerfully. Given the joy they felt, fuelled by the passion both had in common and coloured by the not-insignificant, highly athletic erotic experience both possessed, the night exploded in a dizzying blend of sex, love, affection and humour, punctuated by laughter and the sounds of true ecstasy, utter joy.

"'Twas not a night for sleeping!" Eileen would almost blushingly confide to Abby once back in Vienna, the thought originally having come to her as she slowly awakened—some slumber having inevitably come to them both, though just before dawn—amidst a tumble of coverlets and pillows, recalling her own words in the Cork boreen that she would henceforth awaken "not wrapped in a cloak . . . but rather naked and warm . . . with my love."

As so she was and so she did, very early this cold morning of 20 December, her love himself slowly awakening, smiling as he saw Eileen's tousled raven locks spread across the pillows, drifting over her bare broad shoulders as she, her own sleepy smile wickedly seductive, teasingly, very slowly, lowered the quilts to expose just a bit more than a hint of her round, full breasts and O'Leary drew the covers over both of them, murmuring just as his lips touched his wife's, "'Tis quite early, indeed, Mistress O'Leary."

A small notice would appear in the next edition of the *Corke Journal*, a weekly newspaper published in Cork City, cuttings of which both would retain for the rest of their lives:

MARRIED,
MR. ARTHUR O'LEARY, MACROOM,
TO
THE WIDOW O'CONNOR OF IVERAGH,
19 DECEMBER 1767

On the evening of St. Stephen's Day, 26 December, as the extended household quieted, its members gathered in the large front parlour considering perhaps a final tea or brandy, Eileen quietly excused herself. Within moment she was settled alone with a hefty snifter of brandy and a writing box, along with a freshly cut quill and a nearly full ink bottle, near a quietly burning turf fire in the cosy library. She had told Arthur earlier in the day, "There is a letter I must write, my darling . . . one I have delayed," she qualified, her smile softly sheepish. O'Leary nodded, his voice gentle but firm, "Aye, so you must, my love, von Klaus . . . he is a good man."

Smoothing the full skirts of her heavy grey wool long-sleeved dress, Eileen almost fiercely dipped her pen, and in her distinctively looping, flowing hand, began:

Rathleigh House
Co. Cork, Ireland
26 December 1767

My dearest Wolfgang—

She immediately paused, eyed the salutation, sighed and continued:

I have been remiss in my communications, this I know and must acknowledge—and do so, with apologies.

She looked deeply into the fire, visions of a handsome couple, laughing, side-by-side on horseback, frolicking in bed, dining in the company of the empress and other notables, many eyes upon them as they danced at spectacular balls . . . the turf popped, and with it the images. She drew a deep breath:

I have thought over and over—and indeed over again!—how to tell you, as tell you I must, of the momentous events that have occurred during my time here in Ireland. Part of my delay lies in that I have been seeking desperately to find the right words, the best phrases to convey . . .

She eyed the meaningless serpentine fissure on the eggshell white wall just to the right of the mantel, shook her head and muttered, "Bloody hell, Eileen, just tell him, girl!"

and I have at long last concluded there are no perfect words, no ideal phrases. The fact is, my dearest friend, I have wed—would that I could see your face at this moment, and take your hand and tell you how much you have meant, how much you will always mean to me, but of course and alas I am unable.

Since October, following a chance meeting in the market space in Macroom, the wee town located near where I now write, my world has changed in ways that I still cannot fathom, much less adequately explain. 'Tis as if the world in which I dwelt, so ordered, so familiar, had been by some mysterious force destroyed—and replaced by a new one. As if an explosion of sorts had occurred, as I stood in this public square, I was struck by some emotional force that consumed, as well, the man across from whom I was then standing, changing us both, transforming us, in fact. By the day following, I confessed the most profound love I could even imagine to this man, as did he to me.

She lay her pen on the writing box, resting her head against the high back of the wing chair in which she sat—gazing into the fire, she saw only Art O'Leary, now—and she permitted scalding tears of profound joy to flow, smiling, laughing, even as she wept.

She picked up the nearly dry quill and dipped it firmly:

He is the most wonderful man, my dearest—the events of this autumn and winter are made even more confounding by that, as do you, so too does he proudly wear the uniform of Her Imperial Majesty! My love, my husband—she stared at the word and smiled broadly—*is a lieutenant of Maria Theresa's Hungarian Hussars, his name being Arthur O'Leary.*

She momentarily considered attempting to explain that his given name really was Art, an Irish word meaning *bear*, fitting for a strong man, a strong personality—shaking her head, she saw no reason, as at court, as well as frequently in Ireland, she learnt that he was indeed Lieutenant Arthur O'Leary, as even she had begun to occasionally address him.

Being a junior officer in a regiment of horse, I am certain he is unknown to you, but I assure you he is a gentleman and a gentle man, and my feelings for you, my dear, are such that I pray you will approve—and knowing you as I believe I do, I am certain you will wish me the happiness I already enjoy, in which I revel.

Eileen drew a deep breath, weighing whether, now that she had written the words she had in many ways dreaded, she could—or even if she perhaps should—set the letter aside, *for tomorrow, or the next day, even,* but decided she could not.

Pouring another snifter of brandy, taking a deep draught, she wrote on, the almost-idiosyncratic loops and curls of her handwriting filling several more sheets of the rough, heavy writing paper used at Rathleigh—as it was at Derrynane—as she related in greater detail her being unexpectedly at Mary's home, of the commonplace nature of their marketing venture into Macroom, then describing O'Leary's appearance and manner, his elegant ways, his playfulness, explaining how incredible she felt it was that they had both been in Vienna for some years but had never even known of each other, much less met. She told of their ill-fated trek to Derrynane, of their effort to seek and obtain the O'Connells' approval, failing which, with the aid of General O'Connell and Countess von Graffenreit, of their nighttime flight through the blackness of

Iveragh. She described in detail their confrontation with the sheriff's posse, emphasising, *Kill these men I would have indeed done—killed them all, I would!* and of the arrival of the general and the countess at Rathleigh and the *simple, beautiful wedding we experienced shortly before Christmas.*

After inquiring of him, of his well-being and of his work and diplomatic efforts at the court of Catherine the Great on behalf of the Habsburgs, Eileen informed von Klaus of their plans to return to Vienna with the elder O'Connells shortly after the turn of the new year. *I shall anxiously await your response, though, given the contents of this letter, should you feel that one is not warranted, that I should understand as well.*

Recalling the entry on her desk calendar for the month of February 1767, when von Klaus had departed Vienna for St. Petersburg and the Empress Catherine's Winter Palace, Eileen saw no reason not to close her letter in the identical words, *Adieu, mon cher Wolfgang—a bientôt!* and so she did, the smoothly flowing words that followed being the first time ever she had written *Eileen O'Leary.* She looked at them and smiled. *'Tis indeed who I am now, is it not? No longer O'Connell and indeed the Widow O'Connor . . .* she *is at long last gone as well.*

Within less than a quarter of an hour she had set the brandy and glass on the sideboard, returned the writing desk and instruments to Squire O'Leary's study, snuffed the remaining table candles, from the last one of which she lit a small one to illuminate her climb upstairs. She quickly disrobed in the tiny dressing room off the room she now shared with her husband; the chill of the air almost piercing on her skin, she hastened nude into bed, snuggling gently against O'Leary's naked body. As the sleeping man reflexively draped an arm around her, Eileen smiled into the dark. She was quickly, quite soundly asleep.

The Hofburg, Vienna—February 1768

Shortly after celebrating Christmas and welcoming the new year of 1768 with Squire O'Leary and a continuingly pleasant Catherine at Rathleigh, the countess, the general and the now wedded O'Learys departed for Vienna, arriving there in the first week of February after a generally unremarkable journey, anticipating being warmly received by the empress and by Abby and Denis O'Sullivan, all of which ultimately proved to be the case. A rider having been sent on to the Hofburg when the party was estimated to be perhaps a day away from Vienna, as the compact but comfortable gleaming black—with a single stripe of Hapsburg yellow at the roof line—enclosed sledge they had shared during the journey through the increasingly snowy Habsburg states to Vienna swooshed across the rough, crystalline, largely icy surface of one of the small private entrance courtyards at midday on a Thursday, Lieutenant O'Leary was instead greeted by a serious young orderly bearing a set of terse orders, requiring him *without delay* to re-join his regiment, then encamped for late winter exercises at Schönbrunn, whilst Eileen was handed a rigid card written in Abby's careful hand: *Please come immediately to me!*

The couple parted awkwardly. As he turned from sharply saluting General O'Connell, O'Leary's expression was tense, whilst Eileen's was one of surprise and dismay. The countess held her waist as the young bride raised a hand to her husband whilst he mounted the animal just brought for him from the stables, and with a wave back at her, turned and rode briskly away, looking back once, and then again.

Following O'Leary's departure, Eileen said somewhat ruefully, "It would seem we are indeed returned." She kissed the elder O'Connells warmly before they departed for their small castle home beyond the city and entered the Hofburg, instantaneously finding herself in altogether familiar surroundings, greeted warmly and effusively by many courtiers, as well as familiar attendants, guards, maids and other factotums, thinking, as she no longer strode but walked precisely and elegantly down one corridor, *But a few months only in the life of man have passed, yet so much indeed has occurred.* As she climbed the ornate staircase that would take her to Abigail, she felt even then *strangely alone without my darling.*

The sisters were reunited warmly in a very pregnant Abigail's own ornate audience hall—only recently having belonged to Countess von

Graffenreit—with many kisses and tears, thence retiring to Abby's cosy sitting room, at which point the primary lady-in-waiting to Her Imperial Majesty, the empress—fuelled by even more than her customary several afternoon cups of thick Viennese coffee—proceeded to, as she told her younger sister, "catch you up as best I am able," a process that ultimately seemed to Eileen to have been more of an assault with facts—and words, so many words—an experience that left her emotionally exhausted.

"First of all, as to your 'wee little archduchesses'—they have been separated, since August. . . . Indeed, 'twas accomplished almost immediately after your departure, though not in anticipation of Her Imperial Highness Maria Carolina's imminent departure . . ." Eileen could only manage barely spoken words—*separated? departure?*—before Abigail, refilled cup in hand, charged ahead, advising that, within weeks, Charlotte was to depart Austria to become Queen of Naples. Abby initially did not attempt to inform her sister that this, too, was more complex than it sounded, as it was the now-only very recently deceased Archduchess Maria Josepha who had originally been destined for Naples, Charlotte having become the replacement after conversations between the empress and the king of Spain, whose son, Ferdinand IV, the Neapolitan monarch was. "'Tis all very complex; I shall tell you more of it later, but . . ." As her words drifted Abigail's expression became distant, then sombre. She shook her head and, tacking, instead continued, " . . . suffice it to say that the months of 1767 when you were absent, they were horrid ones." She sighed. Whilst Eileen had been present for the death of Emperor Joseph's second wife in May, she quickly became ashen-faced as her sister related the details of the brief, brutal autumnal attack of smallpox that had been visited upon the Habsburgs, one of which had killed Maria Josepha on 15 October and, though she had been spared death, cost the strikingly beautiful, understandably vain Archduchess Elizabeth her future by leaving her horribly disfigured.

Breathlessly continuing, Abby then delivered the news that Her Grace, the Countess Brandeiss, had left Maria Antonia's household— Eileen's face was instantly red, her forehead soon gleaming with sweat—

and had been replaced by Her Grace, the Countess Lerchenfeld. Eileen's head rested against the high back of her chair, her eyes on the ceiling, as Abby finished with, "I do *so* wish my letter had reached you! Until I heard from your good self via the letter you wrote at Christmastime, which itself arrived only last week, I knew not even where you were for certain . . . and certainly not all of what was happening."

Eileen murmured something that sounded to Abby as perhaps being "Later . . . we shall discuss all of that later . . ." and then stood and wordlessly walked to a high window, looking out over Vienna. Sighing, she turned back. "I am not certain how to resume . . . or . . ." She suddenly took a sharp breath. "Or is it that I no longer have a position here, my lady?" She began to cry softly.

Her temporarily rotund state notwithstanding, Abby was instantly on her feet, her arms immediately about her younger sister. "Oh, my darling, my dearest love, *of course you do!* As soon as I was able to inform the empress of the momentous change in your life," Abby smiled broadly, "and assure her that you were indeed en route back to Vienna, preparations for your return began immediately. The Archduchess Maria Antonia is well and vibrantly healthy; she anxiously awaits you this very evening, whilst Her-soon-to-be-Majesty, the Queen of Naples continues to inquire of the time of your return."

Eileen smiled now, tears undried on her pink cheeks.

". . . and as for the Countess Lerchenfeld, she has asked me even as recently as this morning when she shall have 'the gift of Lady Eileen's presence and talents,' so, yes, sister—indeed, *Mistress O'Leary*—you very much have a position here." Abby smiled and embraced her sister again.

Next, however, the conversation turned to both the momentous events of November and December just passed, as well as what Eileen referred to as the "wee new little life amongst us." It was not until some two hours later that Eileen had pronounced the night of 19 December as having been "not one for sleeping," causing her sister to smile impishly, "Such a night is traditionally *not* meant for that purpose," she laughed wickedly. "Mine was surely not!" Sitting quietly for a moment, Abby laughed aloud. "The only individual thing I recall of the entire night was that in a moment of, shall we say, *calm* I suddenly experienced the most profound necessity to confess to Denis my true baptismal name." She shook her head.

"You mean you'd never . . ." Eileen began.

"Indeed, I had not," Abby admitted, feigning shame, "But the vows pronounced, the marriage duly—and *repeatedly,*" she again laughed wickedly, "consummated, only then did I advise Denis that he was truly wed to *Gobnait Ni Chonaill* . . . or, as Mama always pronounced it, Gobinette!" She leaned her head back and laughed heartily, adding through her laughter, "In either case 'tis my good self who is the one who *brings joy* . . . or *whose father is joy!*" she proclaimed, thus explaining that the Irish had looked to the original Hebrew in anglicising the saint's name.

After a brief discussion of the very early Irish saint, who'd dwelt, Eileen told her sister, "at Ballyvourney, which lies barely ten miles from Rathleigh House!" and was, amongst a number of other things, known for her skills at beekeeping, and once Abigail had assured her sister that "the wee one and I are doing quite wonderfully . . . 'Tis as natural as breathing; indeed, did Mama not do it more than twenty times! As I suspect you shall yourself be seeing very soon," did the sisters part. Abigail smilingly took note that Eileen had worn her distinctive arasaid on her journey from Ireland, rubbing her thin, almost delicate fingers almost reverently over the O'Connell stag in the centre of the garment's brooch, as Eileen gathered it in her arms.

As Eileen finally made her way to her own apartments, drawing near she heard the most unusual sound in the corridors—that of running feet; as she turned to her own corridor, racing towards her was Anna, her skirts and her long golden hair both a-fly, the young girl's arms open wide. She did not slow at all, colliding happily with Eileen such that both women struggled for their collective footing, laughing and crying at the same time.

Anna admitted Eileen to her comfortable suite, its fires ablaze, its porcelain stoves silently burning and the atmosphere cosy, and then curtseyed. "My lady, Mistress O'Leary," she said softly, precisely, in English, her pronounced German accent tinged with the slightest Irish lilt, as was now Maria von Graffenreit's. Eileen beamed at the younger woman, who added quite firmly, "Each day now . . . I do English."

"How wonderful!" Eileen exclaimed, her arm draped over the shorter girl's trim shoulders. "But . . . how? Who?"

Anna flashed a bright smile. "She is Helga, a new maid. Her mama is Eng-lish, she come from Eng-land. Helga, her Eng-lish is good, yes?"

Eileen nodded as they closed the apartment door. "Anna, *your* English is good, *yes!*" The younger woman blushed.

Resuming her soft German-laced French, Anna advised that she would await Eileen's belongings and, easily reverting to English, that "I shall then settle you back in," she twinkled, only then bemoaning that Eileen had been abroad in harsh weather, her winter cloak having been left behind in Vienna.

Eileen first gestured to her arasaid draped over a chair, then offered the immense, densely heavy Scottish garment to her friend. "My darling girl, this article of clothing has served its purpose, I assure you!" Amazed at its weight and dimensions, holding the plaid in her arms like a large doll, Anna could only nod in agreement as Eileen added, "I have so very much to tell you."

"But first, but now, Mistress," Anna said, "her Imperial Highness awaits my lady as soon as you are ready." Settling the arasaid on a chair, she gestured in the direction of Maria Antonia's apartments. Starting for the door, Eileen suddenly stopped and turned about, her fingers over her mouth, and raced to her dressing room, from which, through the closed door, Anna heard the unmistakable sounds of retching.

"Ah, 'tis just the hard journeying, my love," Eileen said dismissively as she emerged and accepted a proffered glass of water, proceeding then to the archduchess's apartment.

Eileen once again walked the familiar corridors, her event-filled absence rendering her surroundings suddenly vivid, making them seem almost novel. As she reached the end of her own hall, she turned right onto a broad one, instantly noticing that it was, even by candlelight, almost shockingly carpeted in bright red, made more so by the starkest of lightly adorned white walls, thence less than fifty feet and right again into a broad foyer, which itself opened onto an ornate double doorway, the wings of an elegantly carved pair of Hapsburg eagles spread protectively above the entrance. Eileen nodded to the bewigged doorkeeper, who stepped inside, entering the archduchess's formal audience room. Through the partially open door, Eileen heard spoken in French, for the first time, "Your Imperial Highness, the Lady Eileen O'Leary . . ."

The door was then fully opened for her. Her eyes on the archduchess, who appeared prepared to race to her, Eileen nodded respectfully, as if to say *wait*, and quickly dipped into the deepest, most elegant of curtseys. She remained bowed until still-small shoes padded quickly across the thick carpet, smooth, slender fingers closed gently about her right hand and a familiarly soft German-accented voice said very carefully in English, "My Lady Eileen, Mistress O'Leary, welcome home." Only then did she rise, as she felt herself being tugged to do so.

Standing, she saw that the archduchess's arms were wide and lifted, the still little girl's eyes flowing with happy tears, and Eileen knelt and embraced her. The two remained thus for long moments of tears, laughter and murmurs: "I have missed you so," "I have so much to tell you," "Oh, my darling . . . *Mama*, you are home!"

When they finally, slowly, almost reluctantly separated, Eileen stood and took Antoine's hands in her own and stepped back, looking at the slim, luminously lovely girl, who appeared much the same as she had six months before, though enough height had been acquired in that time that Eileen could not resist saying, "You have grown, my darling." The archduchess smiled and stood a bit taller, her fingers gently touching her as-yet-nonexistent bosom. Nevertheless, sensing something there must be changing, Eileen cast her eyes down and nodded approvingly.

The two then moved into the archduchess's warmer, much cosier sitting room and settled on a comfortable settee facing a blazing fire and shared hot chocolates and pastries and hours of joyous conversation, mostly in French. After proudly telling Eileen that it was the Lady Abigail herself who had assisted her with her greeting, Antoine indicated her wish to hear all about Lieutenant O'Leary, adding in a conspiratorial whisper, "The empress has been inquiring of Count Höeninger all about him," smiling smugly. Eileen then told the girl of their chance meeting in Macroom, providing very selective details of their whirlwind courtship and much about the wedding; she refrained, however, from telling her young mistress—who, she had always known, would have no choice in deciding to whom she would be wed—of the flight from Derrynane and their encounter with the high sheriff's men.

As the evening grew late, and whilst making allowance both for why they were together at this hour as well as for the fact that her charge was now six months older—remembering that in the fall she would turn thirteen—Eileen noted the first archducal yawn. Despite the child's continuing animated chatter, when the second and third quickly followed, she gently resumed her duties. "Might I suggest, Your Imperial Highness, that we now prepare for bed? I should so welcome the opportunity to again assist you." Maria Antonia stood and reached for Eileen's hand, and they once again completed the routine they had followed for so many nights, at the close of which Eileen happily read the archduchess to sleep, as she had when she was a very little girl, this night finding herself yawning as well.

As she and the archduchess were at their lessons the following afternoon, Eileen received a brief message from O'Leary in which he advised that the urgency behind his hasty departure on their arrival was actually a summons to a celebratory dinner in his honour, attended by virtually all his fellow officers, including Count Höeninger himself. Her husband wrote that, as he bedded down in his tent after enjoying multiple courses of excellent food, actually prepared in the Schönbrunn kitchens, and copious amounts of drink, all he could think of was that *to be abed with my treasured Eileen of the Raven Locks on this night of our return would have been vastly more enjoyable than . . .* and she chuckled softly as she read that *across the tent, within mere feet of where I write, my brother officer, Lieutenant Fritzemeyer, has just commenced yet another round of his infamous snoring. . . .*

Vienna—late Winter–Spring 1768

Charlotte and her former governess had been reunited several days after Eileen's return to Vienna, and it became immediately apparent that, whilst pleased to see her, Maria Carolina had clearly progressed well beyond the time when Eileen could accurately speak of "my two little archduchesses."

Markedly taller, and seemingly very certain of herself, she appeared to have become quite mature, seeming more a woman than a girl, almost detached; indeed the young monarch-designate displayed little interest in discussing in any detail her upcoming marriage, concurrent with which she would join her husband, Ferdinand, on the Neapolitan throne, or any aspect of Eileen's changed life, other than a casual, "I understand that you have become wed." She indicated rather matter-of-factly that her proxy wedding to King Ferdinand was contemplated to occur in the spring and that she would shortly thereafter depart for Naples.

The conversation became animated only when the archduchess began making surprisingly pointed inquiries of Eileen about sex, in an arch tone that seemed an early attempt at haughtiness. "Explain to me how it is done, my lady; how precisely is this act accomplished?" In response to which a slightly shocked Eileen cautiously proceeded then to do, and in quite some detail, which elicited a series of what Eileen felt were largely amusing observations, including "That does not seem something that is easily achieved! Could not one injure oneself by attempting to remain in such a position?" Eileen found herself truly hard-pressed to avoid laughing at, "What, my lady, does one say whilst such activity is actually occurring?"

Between that time and her departure in late April, the two would rarely see each other, as Eileen anticipated would be the case when Maria Carolina had almost casually, though in a soft tone, advised her, as Eileen was about to withdraw, "You are, after all, no longer of my household."

That being true, and Antoine appearing to need her in many ways perhaps even more now than before, Eileen returned to the now-separate household of Her Imperial Highness, the Archduchess Maria Antonia, with relish. Though she quickly learnt that, sorely missing the benign, indulgent Countess Brandeiss, the archduchess did not at all care for the woman, Eileen found Countess Lerchenfeld to be quite pleasant, even to a degree charming, and more than happy to leave the daily care of the archduchess solely to Eileen.

Anticipating that the arrangement would lead to an even greater degree of intimacy between her and her Imperial charge, balancing the child's age against the realities of their close relationship, as spring progressed Eileen sat quietly with the archduchess after breakfast one magnificent early spring morning in a sunny and windswept hillside garden.

"Your Imperial Highness," she began softly, her precisely correct form of address immediately capturing the young listener's attention, "there is something of which I must speak to you." The girl's expression instantly became serious. "It is something of which I must ask that you not speak to anyone, including Her Imperial Majesty, unless you ask and I tell you that you may."

Antoine's eyes widened, her small hands forming small fists in her lap, which Eileen reached over and patted.

"'Tis a *baby* . . . I am to have a baby, in August . . . or perhaps September," she began, not certain what, if indeed anything, else she might say.

Her face immediately evidencing delight, the archduchess jumped up and enveloped her with embraces and kisses. "So wonderful, my dearest

Mama!" she cried out. "So wonderful indeed! You know how we love babies here!"

As Eileen momentarily pulled the child close to what would very soon be her steadily shrinking lap, she softly tapped Antoine's lips with her fingertip. "This must be our secret, just for a short time, yes?"

The girl pursed her lips and nodded solemnly. "*Oui*, Mama."

Before they strolled back to the palace, Eileen explained to Antoine that the principal practical effect of her advancing pregnancy would be her eventual inability to ride Bull, and the child nodded.

Given her arrangement with Countess Lerchenfeld, Eileen and the archduchess became virtually inseparable, from meals and the classroom to their shared harp lessons and practises, as well as the three afternoons a week now devoted to riding, during which Eileen, at least until midsummer would gently mount a set of steps and ease back onto the sidesaddle with which Bull had been tacked. As her pregnancy progressed, she would simply remain in the small carriage in which she and the archduchess had arrived, which would be placed in the middle of the riding ring.

Despite the archduchess's separate music, singing and dance lessons, their schedule also permitted a great deal of nonstructured time, hours Eileen had come to refer to as being "ladies' time," when the two would walk—Maria Theresa's physician, Dr. Gerhard Van Swieten, having indicated to the empress during her later pregnancies that gentle walking was actually good for an expectant mother, it had become a regular practise for expectant mothers at court—or be driven about in a carriage. They even, a number of times, left Vienna so as to enjoy a full day's outing in the countryside about Laxenburg or up into the foothills of the surrounding mountains, whilst at other times they simply sat in a garden or in their rooms. Through all of it, they were free to simply talk; the value of this complete access and the extensive opportunities for conversation it provided would be much more important than Eileen could have imagined, as, during the course of a lengthy audience, attended in part by Abigail, very much in her official capacity, Eileen would be formally told what she already knew, that her little Antoine was well on her way to becoming dauphine of France. More importantly, for Eileen, she would begin to learn the significant role she would be expected to play in preparing the young girl for all that lay ahead.

Gathered around the empress's large, paper-strewn writing table, the three women sat for several hours during the course of an otherwise largely nondescript, drizzly grey afternoon in early April.

"We have much to advise you, my lady Eileen, and you have much to understand," the empress began, her gown, as always, severely black, her manner more formal than usual, quite business-like, almost brusque, as she nodded to her principal lady-in-waiting, whose afternoon dress, Eileen noticed, was now of the finest fabrics and couture.

"Indeed," Abigail continued, addressing her sister, her tone unusually precise and equally formal. "You will perhaps recall in February of last year that the Marquis de Durfort arrived as the new ambassador from the court of Versailles, yes?"

Eileen vaguely recalled the fact and a reception, perhaps even a dinner, so she nodded affirmatively.

"It was with the marquis's arrival that conversations commenced concerning the possibility of one of our archduchesses . . . shall we say, *joining* the royal family of France." A smile fluttered on Abby's unusually serious face. "The thought was that Maria Carolina would perhaps be the one, and . . ."

"And, indeed, yes," the empress gently interrupted, leaning forward towards Eileen. "At one point, I considered that it was to become the wife to the recently widowed Louis XV that she would go, to become queen. It was in connection with this arrangement that I considered a second archduchess would at the same time be offered as a bride for the dauphin . . . all of this until I learned that the old roué's fancy had turned to a young woman whom he had no reason for wedding . . . and, in truth, that he had no interest in marrying anyone. I was thus left with the decision as to which of the archduchesses I would send to France."

Eileen sat quietly, though she did bite her lip several times.

Abby resumed. "As events have progressed, as you are aware, Charlotte is bound for Naples, and the topic of the continuing conversation with France has now turned to your Antoine . . . and your particular responsibility for advancing this process is quite critical, Lady Eileen."

Reflecting momentarily that never had Abigail addressed her as she just had, Eileen nodded, almost gravely. "I am prepared to do all and anything I can to further the archduchess's advancement, my lady . . . " and, looking quickly at the empress, "Your Imperial Majesty . . . indeed, anything at all."

The conversation continued well into the afternoon, embracing a detailed, hour-long soliloquy by the empress on the complex, delicate relationship between Austria and France, of their long-standing status as what the empress characterised as "brave enemies," as well as their much more recent rapprochement, this being, as the empress softly but firmly declared, "in the interest of Europe . . . as well as of our respective houses." She ended with a somewhat critical discourse on the current state of the Bourbons of France, taking special note of the fact that the family was minute when compared to her own, concluding, "What we envision is a better future than has been our shared past."

As apparently scripted, Abby rose and smoothed her elegant skirts. "Very well, then . . . if I may, Your Imperial Majesty, I must tend to young Master O'Sullivan." She smiled broadly as the empress reached for her hand. Eileen nodded and smiled as well, pleased that Donál O'Sullivan had arrived safely, lustily, several weeks before, and had been happy to learn that the empress herself was his godmother.

As Abby swished out of the room, Maria Theresa indicated that Eileen should remain, "for just a brief moment, my dear. You will please consider over the coming weeks how and in what manner you propose to accomplish the charge you have been given, realising that you shall not be alone in these efforts."

Eileen nodded, precisely, and the empress inclined her head, indicating that she might withdraw. As Eileen rose to curtsey, the empress stood and extended her hand, not to be ceremonially kissed but to hold the young Irishwoman's. "I believe that we shall dispense with curtseying . . . at least until, oh, shall we say, October?" Her tone was playful as she leaned towards Eileen and gently patted her abdomen.

Blushing, Eileen smiled broadly. "October will be quite fine, Your Majesty."

Relatively late the following evening, Eileen was pleasantly surprised when Anna slipped into the archduchess's bedroom, where Eileen and she were reading aloud to each other, advising her that O'Leary had unexpectedly arrived, that he had been in Vienna selecting new horses to replace older, less agile ones in the regiment—the senior animals destined for what the young officers all thought were living quarters of a quality superior to that of their own—the fine-blooded horses' only remaining responsibility being to assist in producing the next generation of regimental mounts.

"What a near-perfect existence!" O'Leary had observed after explaining his horse-selection mission, his arm gently around his wife's waist as she returned to the archduchess's apartment.

"I shall be but a few moments, my love." Eileen smiled at her husband.

Anna escorted him back to Eileen's apartment; as she led him away, she advised an initially puzzled O'Leary, "A tall young man you are, sir, you have . . . blond . . . yes, blond hair, sir!"

Eileen heard her husband's laughter echoing in the hallway as he exclaimed, "Your English . . . 'tis wonderful, Anna!" though she could not see Anna blush scarlet.

Within a few moments, Eileen returned.

Anna awaited her at the door, glowing. "The lieutenant, mistress, he pronounced my English as being *wonderful*."

Eileen observed a bit briskly, "And so it is, my love, and a good night to you then." She kissed the shorter woman on her forehead, then stepped into her sitting room as Anna closed the door with a gentle click behind her.

Having doffed his coat and unbuttoned his waistcoat, O'Leary was leaning against the high arm of a camel-backed sofa that faced the pair of high double doors leading out to the apartment's small terrace, his legs crossed, gazing into the Viennese night sky. Noticing him beginning to stand to greet her, Eileen stopped him with a gesture and gently eased herself onto his lap, her fingers around his neck, beneath his carefully tied queue. Before O'Leary could say or do anything, Eileen's lips had covered his own, a languid, sensual kiss following, his hands gripping her broad shoulders as he responded, equally so.

Gently breaking the kiss and placing her own hands on his shoulders, Eileen smiled. "So, 'tis envious you are, sir, of the animals who will leave active service, yes?"

Amused by her question, O'Leary nodded. "How could one not be? In magnificent stables they shall live, far lovelier even than the domain over which your good man William presides at Derrynane. Their days spent frolicking in limitless pastures . . . their sole obligation to make love to young, fecund mares, all of whom I am sure they shall consider to be beautiful!" He laughed softly, his eyes twinkling.

"Ah, sir, just imagine what satisfaction these equine Lotharios shall have, as they see their beautiful, handsome progeny cavorting about in their own limitless pastures. The pride of fatherhood is a profound one, is it not, sir?" she teased coyly.

O'Leary's cheeks were suddenly aflame; very early in their relationship, he and Eileen had discovered that, much of the time, they seemed to possess an almost mystical singleness of mind, and as he began to speak, certain she knew what he was going to say, Eileen gently placed the tip of her right forefinger on his slightly chapped lips. "So now, when, in the late summer, you see these fellows, you shall then be able to share with them your own pride of fatherhood, Lieutenant O'Leary."

Smiling broadly, O'Leary compelled Eileen to stand and, taking her hand, with his other hand at her waist, he danced them in some semblance of a slow reel several times around the perimeter of the sitting room and out onto the terrace and back, laughingly humming several tunes strung together. Both shed happy tears as they slowly ended their impromptu celebration in a long, gentle embrace, gazing into each other's eyes and sharing whispers:

"'Tis wonderful!"

"Is it not now?"

"But . . .when?"

"Ah, the doctors, you know they can never be certain . . . August, perhaps September . . ."

A suddenly weary Eileen then insisted that they undress and prepare for bed. "For reasons unbeknownst to me, her Imperial Highness arises very much earlier these days." So it was only as they were stretched out on the high bed they had so infrequently shared since their return to Vienna, which O'Leary laughingly pronounced far superior to his own at regimental headquarters, that the young wife shared the details of her recent first visit with Doctors van Swieten and von Koester with her husband.

"Dr. van Swieten is her Imperial Majesty's own physician," she advised. "Abby arranged for me to be seen by him. Dr. Paulus von Koester is a younger physician, schooled at Leipzig and trained by van Swieten himself. He shall be my doctor, as he was Abby's for Donál. She says he is wonderful, and I have found him to be so.

"I am well, wee Master or Mistress O'Leary is quite well indeed, and, other than the change that has occurred within me, as am I . . . though I must confess that I felt compelled to tell Anna before even your good self, sir, so concerned has she been with my frequent 'morning upsets,' as she called them, especially as I have been declining my coffee. Truth be told, sir, I have also felt it necessary to take the archduchess into my confidence, as I am no longer permitted to ride, and I was certain she would begin asking questions, particularly of others, so . . ."

O'Leary gently shook his head, whispering, "'Tis of no matter, my darling; you were compelled to tell them." He stretched and kissed his wife softly. "You are well, the wee one—he or she—is well, that is all that matters, and I am quite overjoyed, Mistress O'Leary."

"As am I, sir, *as am I*," she said, as she turned her bare back to him, and O'Leary snuggled up against her, his skin against hers, a light quilt drawn over their bodies, the gentle sounds of an Austrian early spring night in the far distance.

It was a quiet late afternoon in May when Abigail arrived unannounced at Eileen's apartment; the archduchess was at her painting lesson and her increasingly rotund governess was shamelessly perched on her bed, quietly napping.

Awake immediately when she heard the gentle click of her door, Eileen roused herself and appearing, Abby thought, *beautifully dishevelled*, she padded into her parlour, a warm, sleepy smile for her sister, who smiled broadly, gesturing with an envelope.

"I believe this warranted a personal delivery, my darling," the elder sister allowed as she handed Eileen a considerably worse-for-wear envelope, the sender's name and location slightly water-splattered but readable: *Maj. W. von Klaus, Austria Haus, St. Petersburg.* Eileen's cheeks immediately blushed as she rolled her eyes.

"Thank you—I think." She smiled ruefully at her sister, gently waving the envelope, "This is in reply to my 'news' of December."

Nodding understandingly, Abby said quietly, "Then take my leave I shall, my love."

Eileen sighed and eased herself into the corner of the camel-backed sofa facing the open windows, the breeze warm, the springtime sounds subtle, gentle even.

She was relieved that the first words she read, beneath a sprawling *26 February 1768*, were *My darling Eileen, my dear friend forever* . . . she exhaled, in some degree of relief.

Von Klaus was at his almost-military best in terms of brevity, being very much to the point, *While I cannot say that I was not surprised, shocked even by your momentous news, so, too, could I not feel anything but joy and happiness for you, as I most assuredly do!—and for the very fortunate Lieutenant O'Leary!* Eileen exhaled again, deeply this time, as she read on: *This said, my darling, to say that I do not feel a twinge, a pang—might it be of regret?—would be an untruth. We had grown so close in those Vienna years, yes? Yet never did we speak of the "ultimate closeness" of the wedded state. In truth, when I did think of it, I dismissed it—knowing the difficulties it would present, fearing that I could never adequately explain to you the chasm between an Austrian such as I and a fair Irish lass such as you, feeling you to be as noble—no, more noble than I—but alas also aware that your nobility is Irish, not Austrian.*

"Oh, Wolfgang!" Eileen said softly, her thoughts spinning. *I, too, never spoke of marriage and I, too, then and now perhaps even more so understand the* chasm *of which you write. I know, my dearest friend, that I am a* commoner— *there, it is I who said it! We could never have been, so* . . . "So, *Leb wohl, auf Wiedersehen,* my dearest friend." She smiled, somewhat sadly, somewhat gratefully, more than slightly relieved. Laying von Klaus's letter aside, she rested her head back and fell asleep for a short time.

Eileen and the handsome, blond Austrian noble would remain dear friends and regular correspondents for many years—and during all this time, von Klaus never wed.

Laxenburg—Summer 1768

What had been a precariously early Austrian spring having by then arrived in earnest, the Imperial household had removed directly to Laxenburg, as opposed to a customary Easter time sojourn at Schönbrunn in late April. Maria Antonia had, as early as Eileen's first spring in Vienna, transmitted her love of this special place to her governess, so Eileen was thrilled at the move and the relative informality of their life there, and was especially pleased when she learnt that it was in the third week of May that Lieutenant Arthur O'Leary of Her Imperial Majesty's Hungarian Hussars was to be there formally presented to the empress.

Even as they were preparing to depart the Hofburg, Eileen had begun suggesting possible topics the young archduchess might wish to consider exploring with her or about which she might have questions, which she would feel most comfortable asking her, as opposed to, for example, her Imperial Majesty. The archduchess responded positively. "I wish to speak about everything!" she told Eileen.

So it was almost immediately upon their arrival at Laxenburg that they resumed talking, in wide-ranging, great and intimate detail.

One unexpectedly chilly evening, the archduchess and Eileen shortened what had become their customary early evening stroll along the edges of broad fields where sheep and horses often grazed and played, a walk that had been enjoyable on the recent warm evenings, but not so this one, as the winds off the mountains had again turned sharp, the air abruptly becoming almost cold.

They instead returned to Eileen's small apartment, in close proximity to the archduchess's, and slipped into soft, warm wool dressing gowns before Eileen added logs to the fire already set and lit whilst they had been out. The pair now settled in large facing chairs at angles to the fire and resumed their outdoor conversation, during which the young girl had indirectly begun to raise what Eileen thought of as being delicate, though timely topics.

Antoine eyed Eileen almost sheepishly. *"Eileen,"* she began, pointedly not employing her customary form of address, *Mama,* indicating to Eileen the degree of intimacy the archduchess felt she needed to raise this matter, much as Eileen's use of *Your Imperial Highness* would set the tone for a serious discussion, and Eileen looked up gently at her, smiling softly and nodding, *yes . . . anything.*

"How is it to be wed, how does one *feel?* . . ." She paused, obviously being careful in phrasing her question. "Are your feelings for the lieutenant similar to the ones you felt for your other husband, the one who died?" she finished, her voice barely above a whisper.

Eileen continued to smile softly at the girl, and then looked deeply for what seemed to them both to be a very long time into the blazing fire before leaning back in her chair, her elbows on the arms and her fingers raised, the tips touching. "My darling girl, you have indeed become a young lady, no longer a little girl."

The archduchess raised her eyes up from her lap and looked again at Eileen and smiled tentatively.

"'Tis a good, indeed a significant question . . . a question you *should* be asking," Eileen reassured her. "'Tis also not an easy question to answer, but try I shall.

"First, as you have asked from deep in your heart, I shall respond from deep within my own." Her fingers touched her left breast. "My feelings for Arthur O'Leary are unlike any I have ever had, could ever have imagined having . . . and, I believe, are most unusual in this world, so deep, so profound are they." She looked at Antoine who, as she feared she might, appeared uncertain.

"Please permit me to put it this way, my darling: My mama always spoke of my papa as being a huge part of her heart, a huge part of her soul, and I believe *that* is how I would describe my feelings for the lieutenant . . . and, as I said, I believe this is not typical. I love him dearly, and I have since first I saw him, as I told you on my return, in the market at Macroom."

The girl's expression had become soft, almost dreamy. How Eileen wished for her what she had found in O'Leary, but she knew . . .

"The circumstances, however, of my first marriage were not unlike those with which you are and will continue to be faced, so, as I have told you before, when I say that I *understand* or that I *know* how you feel, I actually do, for I have experienced in many ways what you are experiencing."

The archduchess looked intently at her, her expression urging Eileen to go on.

"I did not even know who he was, had never heard his name until I was told I was going to marry him . . . and obviously had never seen, had no idea what my husband would look like. 'Twas decided by my eldest brother that I would wed John O'Connor, the sole reason for this being that it would greatly benefit the O'Connells; no thought at all was given to me. Mr. O'Connor was a very wealthy man; he had many commercial interests and lands, properties in the New World even"—the child's attention was rapt, total now—"and an alliance would thenceforth exist between our two families."

"Such as there will be between the Hapsburgs and the Bourbons, Eileen, yes?"

"Yes, my darling Antoine, *precisely*, though the one of which I speak was of far less import to the world." Her smile was ironic. "So, a small party led by Mr. O'Connor's eldest son came to Derrynane to escort me to the O'Connors' home called Ballyhar, some five or so days' riding distance away, as I have told you, and upon arriving, then and there, for the first time did I meet John O'Connor. For the first time ever I saw him was on the very day of my wedding."

Maria Antonia stared in silence now at her beloved Eileen, her lips parted, her eyes fixed on her face, but Eileen could only imagine what the child was envisioning.

"Thus I was wed that very evening; within hours of my arrival I had become Mistress O'Connor, and . . ." thoughts, images—not pleasant ones—spinning in her mind, in her mind's eye, Eileen paused, thinking, and sighed. "And no, I did not feel for John O'Connor as I do for Art O'Leary, not at all, nothing even approaching. . . . In truth, my darling, I did not even *like* Mr. O'Connor, not that night and not for quite some time thereafter.

"*Total* truth being told, Mr. O'Connor and I quarrelled, quarrelled quite bitterly that night; he said things and I said things . . . and for many days—weeks, actually, thereafter—we hardly spoke."

"But . . ." the archduchess ventured.

Eileen nodded softly. "*But* in time he apologised, indeed most sincerely, to me. When he did I was astride Bull, he on his shining black stallion, Champion; ah, such a magnificent horse, you would love him! . . . And I, too, then apologised to him for my part in our quarrel and slowly," she smiled somewhat ruefully, "*very* slowly, we began to speak, and began to come to know each other, discovering shared interests even, and in time a measure of affection came to be. We had grown close . . . in truth, very close indeed, and when he died, I mourned him aloud in a poem spoken at his grave, as the Irish sometimes do, and later, for some time, I continued to mourn. I . . ." As she looked at the archduchess, the girl saw that tears glowed in Eileen's eyes: what would prove to be her final tears ever for John O'Connor.

As she brushed them away with a flick of her fingertips, she quickly told Antoine, "So you see, affection does come, does grow . . . sometimes very slowly . . . but if two people are good people . . . as you I know are, and as I must believe that the dauphin is . . . and they care and try, affection will come, a true marriage will come, and that, I believe, is at least part of what it is like to be wed, my darling girl."

The room grew momentarily silent, the popping and crackling of the logs, the comforting aroma of cedar mixing with oak—both filling the brief space—until Eileen smiled at the young lady now and drew a breath. "Now, my darling . . ." and the archduchess smiled and almost immediately yawned and was shortly thereafter sound asleep.

Having seen the archduchess to bed, as Eileen strolled back to her suite, she wondered if she should perhaps raise the topic of the wedding night itself and its many challenging complexities. Then, remembering her conversation with Maria Carolina, who appeared somewhat versed in the basics and comfortable enough with the topic to discuss it, Eileen dismissed the thought, as she was falling asleep, drowsily reflecting, *'Tis quite likely the empress has people responsible for such matters . . . no need . . . no need for me . . .*"

Since the archduchess never raised the topic, leading Eileen to conclude her assumption was perhaps accurate, Eileen gave it no further thought, as they had much else to discuss.

The soon-to-be parents had spent relatively little time together since their return from Ireland. O'Leary had been largely on manoeuvres and training exercises, whilst most of Eileen's time had been spent with the archduchess. The fact that the officer resided at his regimental headquarters or in a field tent limited them to but a few nights a week in Eileen's apartments, and even then, when O'Leary was there, virtually all of the evenings, up until bedtime itself, were spent, though not at all unpleasantly—as Eileen would laughingly advise Abigail—*en famille*.

Eileen later elaborated on her characterisation, sharing with her sister how an at first slightly awkward but quickly quite comfortable little family of three, consisting of O'Leary, herself and a wonderfully happy archduchess, again relishing the type of doting attention she had once received from her own parents, had come into being.

Depending on the time of O'Leary's arrival and the length of his proposed stay, the trio would walk in the gardens, or, more frequently, enjoy a leisurely carriage ride before dining together; afterwards, Eileen and the archduchess would sometimes entertain O'Leary with harp music, both classical—played primarily by Antoine—and Irish, which Eileen had been teaching her, which he quite enjoyed, as he did the child's singing. They occasionally played games, but most of all they talked, as all of them loved to talk, primarily in French—O'Leary smilingly noting that the child's words continued to be spoken with a marked German accent, though now coloured by the slightest of Irish lilts—but sometimes in English.

They spoke of horses and riding, a shared love, and the child asked O'Leary detailed, almost technical questions about the challenges of horsemanship in the Hussars, and the different types of cavalry manoeuvres. "I believe I could do that," the archduchess once exclaimed. "Lady Eileen could teach me how!" Antoine also asked O'Leary much about Cork: "How does it differ from the Lady Eileen's home?" more than once wistfully regretting that she would probably never visit Ireland, "although it seems almost a second home to me," she said on one such occasion and leaned back against Eileen for an embrace that caused the baby to kick and them all to laugh.

Relatively early on, O'Leary frequently had begun to draw the archduchess onto unfamiliar ground, inquiring of her various thoughts and feelings relative to what he simply referred to as "France." The girl's responses were at sometimes light, even silly, whilst at others quite thoughtful. "My fear is that I shall not know how to be a queen, and my hope is that that time will be far distant from now." More than once she had observed, "I have no doubt that the empress was always prepared to rule; I pray that I shall be a helpful queen to my husband, though I do not know whether I shall be."

Eileen cautioned her to remember that "Daily we are working on acquiring knowledge and learning and practising skills so as to prepare you for this eventuality," and reminded her that "a very bright young cleric will arrive from Paris in the fall whose sole responsibility it shall be to prepare you in all ways for the future."

O'Leary wondered aloud whether she would consider Louis XV as a gentle *grand-père* or solely as the king of France, and the girl smiled guilelessly. "I should think both!" she said, though she was far less certain when asked about the dauphin. "We have not as yet corresponded and I know nothing at all of his appearance, but . . ."

"Ah, soon you shall . . . *both*!" Eileen interjected, smilingly rescuing her from her thoughts.

As spring and Eileen's pregnancy progressed, more often they would take a carriage into the countryside and perhaps picnic. O'Leary preferred to drive the light carriage himself; though, despite being in uniform and well trained and well-armed as he was, a party of young Hussars nevertheless discreetly accompanied them. When the various arrangements—as well as that at Laxenburg, the three were now commonly being referred to, not unkindly, as *la petite famille*—were brought to the attention of the empress, she indicated she not only approved but that she was "most pleased, as this young couple is able to provide the archduchess with their undivided attention to a degree that I myself cannot."

Given her positive response to all she had learned about Eileen's husband from his commanding officer, as well as the favourable reports she continued to receive from Laxenburg, the empress was perhaps even more intrigued at the prospect of meeting the young Irish officer who had become her youngest daughter's surrogate father than O'Leary was at being presented to the sovereign, and his anticipation was considerable.

The twenty-seventh of May was a Saturday; late in the afternoon of what had proven to be a flawless day, O'Leary in his magnificent red wool and gold-braided full-dress raiment, including his hat tucked under his left arm and sword gently thudding on his left hip and thigh, along with Eileen, in the prettiest—and roomiest—of the several afternoon dresses Anna had seen to being constantly altered, walked quietly from one end of the Laxenburg palace to the other, strolling slowly, holding hands and chatting softly. It was only when they drew near the empress's formal audience rooms that they grew silent and appropriately serious.

They stopped inside the massive double doors, Eileen slipping her arm out of her husband's. She stepped quietly to one side as he was formally announced and directed to enter. She watched him walk the long deep purple carpet from the double doors to the empress's throne, his gleaming boots thudding gently over the smooth wool surface. She recalled later that *a wee bit astounded indeed I was*, as she noticed, in addition to her Imperial Majesty and the archduchess and, as expected, the general and countess von Graffenreit-O'Connell and the O'Sullivans, most surprisingly, was Count Leopold Höeninger, O'Leary's commanding officer.

As he reached the designated place, O'Leary dropped effortlessly to one knee, as Abigail, now in her official capacity, stepped to his right side, curtseyed deeply and rose. "Your Imperial Majesty, it is my honour and—" Abby smiled softly—"indeed my *pleasure,* to present to you the

Lieutenant Arthur O'Leary, presently serving in the Höeninger Brigade of Your Imperial Majesty's Hungarian Hussars . . . and husband of the Lady Eileen O'Leary." She smiled again and in Eileen's direction, whilst, at her mother's side, the archduchess beamed delightedly.

Maria Theresa rose and, taking several steps, stood before the kneeling officer, extending her right hand, which, with his eyes still lowered, O'Leary took into his own, gently touching it with his lips. Her right forefinger immediately thereafter went to his chin, which she lifted, Art O'Leary of Rathleigh House, Cork, now looking upon the woman he considered his sovereign from inches away. Spontaneously, most unceremoniously, each immediately smiled at the other: broad, glittering smiles. From their vantage point, Eileen's fingers went to her lips, which she was biting. Rolling her eyes, Abby's head lolled back gently as she and O'Sullivan, too, smiled broadly.

"You may rise, Lieutenant," Maria Theresa said softly, still holding O'Leary's hand as he came to stand before her and, placing her other hand on top of his, she now smiled even more dazzlingly.

"It is indeed our pleasure, good sir, to be able to formally welcome you to our court, one which I have learned you have been serving devotedly and . . ." she gestured, and Count Höeninger and Denis O'Sullivan both stepped forward, "in recognition both of this day and of your faithful service to us and to our empire, we are pleased to recognise your advancement to the rank of captain in our Hungarian Hussars of the Imperial Armies of Austria and Hungary."

O'Leary bowed deeply and as he rose, Count Höeninger handed him his delicate captain's sleeve chevrons, and both the count and Major O'Sullivan returned the new captain's salute as the others applauded.

The formalities completed, the empress led the little gathering out onto a broad terrace, under a warmly benevolent sun, a gentle breeze soft on their faces and hands, with views over Laxenburg's expansive grounds and gardens, a three-man consort providing what all noted were an appropriate mix of German and Irish airs and melodies. At one point, hearing a piece familiar to him, General O'Connell grandly announced, "I believe that I shall now sing!" though, as the countess laughingly shook her head and affectionately squeezed his hand, immediately corrected himself, "I believe I shall *not* sing!" his deadpan delivery causing everyone to laugh.

Abby and O'Sullivan warmly congratulated their brother-in-law, and the count indicated that the promotion was a timely one, "deserved, indeed merited, Captain," but it was the empress herself who spent much of the time speaking with the tall young Irish officer. So focused was their conversation that Eileen slipped quietly towards her own small family group, Abby observing, "*Taken* with your good husband, her Imperial Majesty certainly appears to be!" She laughed affectionately, as Eileen, a faux rueful expression on her face, shook her head, lifting her eyes plaintively to heaven.

The monarch was indeed very much taken by Art O'Leary, her experience on meeting him being a very slight version of Eileen's own. She found herself drawn to his eyes, to his strong yet gentle voice, feeling that *a very special young man he is*, though she did not dwell on how or why he was.

As they spoke, easily, fluently, Maria Theresa continued to gaze warmly up at O'Leary, occasionally taking his hand, gesturing broadly with her own, her expression at times girlish, even coquettish, to the extent that more than once the two O'Connells and two O'Sullivans found themselves enthralled, simply watching the two.

They spoke of his background, education and time in service, much of which she was already quite well aware, having learnt as much as she could about Eileen's new husband from Count Höeninger himself, as Maria Antonia had advised Eileen on her return.

"I was interested to learn of your progression from Ireland to Louvain, Captain," the sovereign said.

"'Twas my father, Majesty, he had studied at Louvain, and 'twas he who urged me to do the same. I learned much, though. . . ."

"Had you decided upon a military career by that time, sir?"

O'Leary lowered his head wordlessly.

"I must think that the strong Irish presence amongst our officer corps was a factor in this, yes?"

"Indeed, Majesty, yes." O'Leary smiled.

"Though you were then attracted to our court. Other than the Irish, why do you suppose, sir? Of what—or perhaps *of whom*—had you become aware?" the empress asked, almost in a flirtatious manner.

"I had learnt, Your Imperial Majesty, of the strength, depth and traditions of the Imperial Austrian armies and of the quality of service," he paused, "and, in utter candour, of the quality of life at Your Imperial Majesty's court," O'Leary replied with a nod, and the empress nodded as well.

"And of . . ." she added almost playfully.

"And, indeed if I may, of Your Imperial Majesty yourself . . . intrigued I was by the prospect of serving, in even the smallest of ways, the most powerful woman in the world," O'Leary ventured.

The empress visibly blushed, her fingertips fluttering girlishly in the air, then parrying in her own way, "So it is to strong women you are drawn, Captain?"

O'Leary smiled down at the sovereign and his eyes drifted subtly, briefly towards where Eileen stood. "Strong women, indeed . . . strong and brilliant . . . and passionate," he smiled, ". . . as is your good self."

Noticing the empress's immediate expression of surprise, O'Leary feared it was rather one of displeasure. His cheeks scarlet, he quickly appended, "Your Imperial Majesty," and her smile immediately reappeared. She once again took both of his hands in her own, her cheeks still quite noticeably ablush. She later regretted it, but she was unable to stifle a wholly audible giggle, though she nevertheless reflected, *strong and brilliant . . . and passionate*, she mused, *indeed, young man, indeed!*

The pair stood for a moment in a somewhat awkward silence, until the empress inquired, "And what now of your first child, sir; have you a preference for a son?"

"I do not, Your Imperial Majesty. Drawn as I am to strong women, a daughter of mine and . . ." he gestured again in Eileen's direction, "I should think would be every bit as challenging as a lad. I shall, however, be grateful for the wee one's arrival."

The empress laughed warmly now. "'The wee one,'" she repeated in precise English. "Such an Irish reference . . . so charming and dear."

Only half-listening to Aunt Maria and Abby, Eileen could not help but note that the empress and O'Leary had arrived at the topic of the new baby when she overheard the empress's reference in English to *the wee one*. That was how she and Art had been referring to their firstborn, and the empress was repeating his phraseology; Eileen's warm laugh carried across the terrace.

Noticing that fact, Maria Theresa spread her right arm wide and gestured to Eileen, who feigned embarrassment at being caught listening, to join them, taking the younger woman's hand as she stepped close and announcing, "I approve! Very much so, I do!"

That night, following an early evening meal on the terrace and after the archduchess had retired, as O'Leary was positioning Eileen in bed with a variety of pillows and puffs, making her as comfortable as possible, she said mischievously, "I believe the expression I have heard used at court is an 'instant favourite,' my darling Hussar. 'Tis that which 't'woud appear you indeed are: an instant favourite!" She laughed warmly, and his red face notwithstanding, O'Leary neither protested nor disagreed. He and Eileen agreed that 'twas not at all a bad thing that he was.

Laxenburg, July–August 1768

Though the empress and her court would divide the summer of 1768 between Laxenburg and Schönbrunn, Eileen and the archduchess were both delighted to learn that they would be remaining amidst the smaller, more intimate surroundings of the former. As summer progressed, Eileen was more and more restricted by what all agreed was a very large baby. "'Tis the shape of a massive round gourd I have taken on!" she moaned, only half in jest, to Abby one still, hot July Sunday when the O'Sullivans made the approximately twelve-mile trek to Laxenburg for the afternoon.

On 15 August, O'Leary was formally ordered to Laxenburg, arriving at midday in full raiment, an orderly leading a horse bearing the new captain's belongings, which were immediately brought to Eileen's apartment. A smiling Anna received them happily. "The new papa, he is here, yes?" she jested with the young orderly.

Eileen was pleasantly surprised as she looked up from the book from which she was reading to Antoine as they sat by a small lake, to see O'Leary, bearing a flower for each of them, with a maid from the kitchens in tow with a light meal.

"My darling, flowers and food!" Eileen exclaimed as she struggled to rise, having to catch her balance when she finally did stand, laughing and causing her husband and the archduchess to join her. "'Tis like a round ball I am!" she observed, patting her rotund belly, and O'Leary leaned to kiss her softly as Maria Antonia took her hand.

As they sat at a small table, O'Leary offhandedly remarked, "I am here."

"Of that fact I can see, my love." Eileen set down her fork, and then her lightly sweat-sheened face lit with a gleaming smile. "Ah, you are *here*! For the wee one's arrival, yes?" She reached for him, hampered again by her stomach, and O'Leary stood, bent and kissed her lightly on her head.

"Indeed, yes, for the wee one . . . and, even more so, my love, for you."

The young archduchess stretched her arms around both adults. "We are *all* here now!" she exclaimed, softly but joyously.

As indeed they were; within several days, an altered familial routine had evolved, focused largely on whether the baby would arrive that day. The three breakfasted together, short walks were taken and, in late morning O'Leary went for a vigorous ride and took his midday meal with the officers of the infantry regiment then in residence at Laxenburg. This proved a respite for him, as he told a fellow captain: "There is little I am able to do at this moment, other than wait.

The same was true for Eileen, who had shared with the Countess Lerchenfeld, "The poor man, he paces, gazes anxiously at me and paces yet more!"

Even the archduchess was showing some signs of impatience, each morning inquiring of Eileen, "Will it be today, Mama?"

The week after O'Leary arrived, both physicians—Maria Theresa's own doctor, van Swieten, as well as the younger von Koester—examined Eileen and, as they stepped out of her bedroom, advised an anxious O'Leary and an equally so archduchess, "Within days now." O'Leary appeared relieved yet anxious and Maria Antonia clapped her hands in delight.

The twenty-fourth of August had been an unusually torrid day, airless and heavy. The little household barely moved: O'Leary forwent his midday ride and Eileen napped, something she rarely did, and in the afternoon O'Leary and Antoine went for a slow walk through the still, sultry air.

As the long twilight ending of a Viennese summer day came on, the sky had grown dark and the alpine wind began to whistle down on Laxenburg, shrilly announcing a change, which arrived in the form of a series of dramatic thunderstorms, the wind's whistle becoming a roar and remaining a moan, the mountains silhouetted against repeated lightning flashes, rain flowing in torrents, the rapidly cooling air fragrant with electricity and wet vegetation.

Having just settled the archduchess back into her own apartment, and as the wind shifted yet again, Anna, with O'Leary's assistance, closed some of the apartment's high windows against the rain. Eileen was following the progress of the latest storm in bed, leaning against her high pillows, a gossamer-thin summer coverlet across her legs, an open yet unread book on the bed beside her and her face gleaming in the candlelight. An expression crossed her face, ever so slightly evidencing a measure of concern as she felt yet another twinge. The first ones she had experienced had been in mid-afternoon, those being spaced many minutes apart, but now after but a few moments came the next one, and yet another, and . . .

"Ouch!" Eileen said aloud, her tone more one of annoyance than anything else, then, some moments later, there was a much sharper, deeper, involuntary *mmmfffhh*, followed almost immediately by "Annn-naaa!" echoing against the high walls and ceilings. In response, the golden-haired young woman strode purposefully past a now-standing O'Leary. Stopping, she turned quickly and smiled. "Sir, I believe it is time, and such is it that I must ask you to leave . . . now, sir."

O'Leary's face immediately evidenced surprise. "But Anna, I . . ."

Calling out, "One moment, my lady," Anna handed the soon-to-be father his uniform coat, draping it over his left arm, and began to button his waistcoat.

O'Leary's hands fluttered. "I can . . . I shall—" he said, and the young woman decided that he indeed could, and smiled tightly at him and hastened instead into the bedroom, whilst O'Leary, drawing on his coat, stepped through the still-open door, gently shaking his head and proceeding, as planned, to the Archduchess Maria Antonia's audience room, where a camp bed, an ample array of reading materials, both books and a number of several weeks' old London newspapers, as well as some refreshments, awaited him.

Within minutes, having correctly determined Eileen's status, Anna rang for a breathless young page, who, in turn, raced almost soundlessly on padded slippers through the wide palace's sometimes-labyrinthine corridors and up several staircases to the temporary quarters of the youthful Dr. von Koester.

Instantly drawing on a tan cotton coat, he raced through the palace. Leather satchel in hand and a calm, determined expression on his pale, sweat-sheened face, the young physician was at Eileen's bedside within a quarter hour, quickly examining, feeling, asking what Eileen thought were many questions, his first being, "We are certain you do *not* wish to use the birthing chair, my lady, yes?" He gestured to the rather severe-looking wooden appliance in the corner.

Similar devices were quite commonly used in Austria and elsewhere in Europe, as they were believed, not without good reason, to assist the mother's movements during the birthing process, especially thought to facilitate her pushing. The empress herself had delivered most of her vast brood using one. When first shown it, Eileen contrasted it with Maire giving birth many times in her and Donál Mór's huge, high bed and quickly expressed her desire to have her baby in bed, the fact that Abby had delivered Donál in the empress's own chair notwithstanding.

As he expected she would, Eileen indicated she had not changed her mind.

The physician's inquiries then became clinical: how she felt, was she in pain? For ease in communication, Anna translated them into English from von Koester's softly spoken German, until Eileen waved her hand. "Please . . . if you would, Herr Doctor . . . 'tis not easy to respond, sir. *Ahhhhhhhooooooooooo!*"

Von Koester then took his patient's hand in his smooth right one and nodded. "I understand. . . . Soon, my lady, very . . ."

"Ohhhhhhhhhhmyyyyyyyyy—ooooooooooooooo!" she cried as her eyes closed, her fists clenched for the first time and "*Gawddddddddddddddddd!*"

The physician determined from Anna that O'Leary was elsewhere and directed her to quickly advise him that he should remain thus, then to bring in the hot water and towels she had prepared and to close the bedroom door, all of which she accomplished speedily. As the doctor directed, she gently slipped well-wrapped, puffy down pillows beneath Eileen's thighs and others under her bottom, protective sheeting already having been placed on the bed.

Whilst Anna held Eileen's hand, von Koester lifted her nightdress to her waist, soothingly rubbed with his strong fingers her lower thighs just above her knees and calves, then gently elevated and spread her legs. The doctor took a short, thick candle, snug in a reflective examination glass chimney, its light bright, steady, and noted her already fully effaced, now nearly completely dilated cervix, as for the first time so sharp was a contraction that Eileen actually screamed—loudly, passionately—and grabbed Anna's hand so tightly, the young girl winced.

What would seem to Eileen to be many hours then began to pass . . . very slowly. . . . The pain of the contractions seeming to be growing progressively more exquisite with each successive one, Eileen shot her clenched fists over her head and arched, a low *mmmffh* escaping her lips as she tried to remember to take deep breaths as Anna continued to remind her would help.

As the long minutes passed, Eileen heard what she knew was von Koester's soft voice, speaking soothingly in German, little of which at the moment she understood; then, she noted gratefully, he returned to French, which she did. At one point, breathing, writhing in place, trying not to cry out, she even managed to smile at his gentle attempt at English, as, lifting his head, he spoke to her between the powerful contractions. "Is good, lady, will be good, fine, excellent, yes," and she was grateful for his hands on her and for Anna, whose gentle, concerned face and smooth hands remained near.

Mostly she remained acutely conscious of the stabbing pain of the contractions and the pressure *down there* . . . and she vehemently and, she hoped, silently, cursed *Arthur O'Leary, how could you bloody well do this to the one whom you profess to love with all your heart, whom you say you adore! Ohhhhh, gawddddddd! . . . How . . . could . . . you?*

The process seemed to have slowed. Anna heard the clock on the mantel in Eileen's sitting room strike midnight . . . and then one o'clock.

It was shortly after the clock chimed its single melodic *ding* that Eileen's contractions suddenly began coming quickly, the waves of pain almost constant. Anna held her hand and stroked her hair, Eileen moaned. . . and writhed . . . breathed and screamed lustily, "*Gawwwwwddddddddddd . . .*"

Her eyes were half-closed . . . fuzzy, fleeting images appearing . . . of a little girl, already with long black hair, squirming in her diminutive mother's arms . . . of the same little girl, being placed on a chubby Kerry

Bog Pony by a massive, tousle-haired blond man, his hands so large they almost encircled the child's waist . . . of a young woman, her face ghastly pale, her hair and dress shockingly black, her eyes distant, her . . . of, it seemed, the same young woman, magnificently attired . . . was she at a palace, a ball? . . . but . . . *Finally*—had it been hours or even days? . . . Just as she saw Art O'Leary himself, again in the Macroom marketplace, the pressure and pain now beyond intense, Eileen suddenly heard von Koester's voice, no longer soft and gentle but urgent, commanding, almost harshly: *"Drücken! Drücken hehr!"* The words crackled sharply in the room.

The image of O'Leary vanished; her eyes suddenly open wide, looking up at the doctor, Eileen called out anxiously, "No! *Nein*! I don't underst—"

Anna immediately looked down at her and cried out, *"Push!* Push *now!"*

Retaking Eileen's right hand, sensing the relief coursing through her mistress's very being and the same expressed on her gleaming face, Anna caught the slightest flicker of a smile as Eileen gritted her teeth . . . and pushed . . . and . . . as she again heard the command, *"Drücken hehr!"* she immediately did so again . . . and yet again . . . and again. . .

Until, heralded by a final roared *"Ahhhhhhhmyyyyyyyygawawwwwwwddddddd!"* from his mother, Conor Donál O'Leary made his own quite piercing, squirming entrance into God's world at, as the young physician's report to the empress would reflect, "some thirty minutes past one o'clock, on this, the morning of 25 August 1768," noting, in his precise, stark handwriting, "mother and child quite well."

As his head, followed by his shoulders, then his arms appeared, and crying lustily, the little boy permitted himself to be brought into the world, into the physician's firm, gentle hands. Von Koester made note of pinkness and noise, of tiny kicking legs and feet, with ten toes as well as waving arms and hands, with a total of ten fingers as Eileen gazed in wonder, her chest heaving, sweat-soaked, her eyes wide, her mouth open.

The young physician then passed the infant to an equally wide-eyed Anna, who took him and held him on the corner of the bed in an open wrapper whilst the doctor severed and tied off the stub of the umbilical cord; then, as directed, she wrapped and briefly embraced the squirming infant as she smiled at Eileen, who herself now smiled weakly, rolled her eyes and struggled to sit up. The doctor assisted her in doing so, and Anna laid her son in Eileen's arms, the women sharing tears and a sense of wonder.

Oblivious to her physical appearance and sweat-soaked, bloodstained gown, Eileen gazed down at the minutes-old little boy in her arms. She saw Arthur O'Leary and herself, Donál Mór and Maire, whilst from her childhood emerged her O'Donoghue grandparents as well as her ancient great-grand-uncle Turlough Ó Conaill from Tarmons—he who had never abandoned the *ould ways*, even steadfastly refusing to adopt English dress—misty memories of the ancient Ó Conaills of Ballycarbery Castle and of her Hugh as an infant and of the O'Learys, her dear father-in-law and peculiar, though recently less troubling Catherine. She saw Ireland, in all its glorious, heroic, mystical and tragic past, as well as its sad, ofttimes bitter present, and, as her son cooed and fluttered his barely seeing eyes, she sensed Ireland's future, its hopes, its prayers, resting in some small part of this tiny, wee gift from God she gently rocked now.

Leaving Anna, Eileen and the infant briefly alone, von Koester raced down the corridor to inform O'Leary of his son's safe and healthy arrival and of his wife's condition being excellent, and asking him to wait just a few moments. When the physician returned with a young woman who had been waiting through the hours, they moved quickly, so that all would be ready to receive O'Leary.

As the two, joined by Anna, speedily cleaned the birthing area, Eileen, now happily exhausted, quietly leaned against her pillow, gazing down in virtual awe at the now-dozing infant, gently, just barely touching each of his fingers and then his chubby cheeks with the tip of her own right forefinger, grateful for a cooling breeze on her gleaming face and arms, which seemed to rouse her from her weariness and silent reverie.

"Ah, so welcome to God's world, young Conor Donál O'Leary, as you journey through which the names of your grandfathers, two fine men indeed, you shall bear," she began, holding the baby's right hand and speaking then in what Anna softly explained to the doctor was Irish, "*Tá mé do mháthair*/I am your mother . . . and as good a one as my own I shall hope to be to you . . . my son. . . ."

She rambled softly, briefly, of Ireland, of Vienna, of Maire and Abigail, suddenly laughing weakly as she informed the infant, "You must know, little man, even an older sister of a sort it appears you have, as well. . . ." Hearing that, Anna smiled as she approached with a basin of warm water and soft French body towels, as well as a fresh nightdress and a summer-light shawl.

Quickly then, the infant left softly fussing, then soon dozing in his cradle, Anna bathed Eileen, dried her and assisted her in dressing, such that the sweat and other liquids-soaked nightdress and all other evidence of the reality of human birth would be swept away, and the room proper for O'Leary's first visit, as it was when a quickly changed Anna escorted the visibly nervous young father into the room.

With her, O'Leary, buttoned into full uniform, walked slowly, gracefully to the apartment, where a beaming Anna opened the door, silently stepping aside to let the anxious new father pass, hurrying ahead to open the bedroom door.

Standing in the doorway, O'Leary saw that Eileen was sitting up, a mound of fresh pillows behind and about her, a fresh nightdress replacing the one in which she had given birth, her face washed, glowing, a dazzling smile for him. He approached his wife and son almost reverentially.

As he reached the bed and his lips barely touched Eileen's forehead, she gently, ever-so-slightly lifted her summer-blanketed bundle, her husky voice now weary, softly announcing, "Captain O'Leary, sir, a delivery for you, sir!" Her tears streamed silently down her cheeks, as did O'Leary's his, as he sat at her shoulder and together they saw their son for the first time, each taking a tiny hand in fingers of their own, marvelling that the minutes-old little boy would grasp his mother's and then his father's forefinger with his own minute hand.

They sat and contemplated their miracle until Eileen began to doze and O'Leary somewhat shakily lifted their new son out of her arms. He gently opened the door and a waiting Anna took the baby. "Sleep, sir, if you are able. I believe the world now is different for us all."

Schönbrunn—Autumn 1768

The remainder of the summer passed gently, indeed quite uneventfully, as Conor O'Leary, to whom Abigail and O'Sullivan stood proud godparents as the child was christened in the small chapel at Laxenburg, quickly became assimilated into the rhythm of life in the palace, the archduchess fully enthralled with the infant and enjoying every moment she was able to spend with him.

To be sure, given that Antoine wished to spend as much time as she could with Conor, she made virtually no demands on Eileen's own time; they simply shared what Aunt Abby had dubbed as being baby worship, and continued to read and walk and talk, taking the infant for his first carriage ride in early September, O'Leary proudly riding alongside.

By mid-September 1768, after all had returned to the Hofburg, Eileen met with the empress, in preparation for the anticipated arrival of Abbé Jacques-Mathieu Vermond from Paris.

"Amongst my many hopes is that I shall be viewed by the French as having sent them an angel in sending them Antoine. . . ."

Eileen smiled, nodded and, perhaps more casually than she meant to, observed, "But perhaps should not an angel entering the French court be properly equipped, say, with something intellectually akin to the sword of the Archangel Michael?"

Maria Theresa appeared more interested than taken aback, as she knew well that Eileen adored her youngest daughter, had been the child's advocate and protector over the years, yet that she had also urged upon Maria Antonia greater effort in her studies.

"That is a *most* unusual thought, Eileen. . . . What is it you mean?" she asked softly.

"I am concerned that my little archduchess, now destined, as I knew she was from my very first day here, to ascend a throne—as we now know, the throne of France—that she be fully and properly prepared for what lies ahead, indeed prepared to rule France."

The empress's puzzlement remained, as she observed what she knew Eileen already understood, that "It shall be as the dauphine of France that she shall arrive, only to ascend the throne as queen *with her husband. . . .*"

Eileen lowered her eyes slightly and, very softly, continued, "Your Imperial Majesty, if you would indulge me, please, I believe I shall be better able to explain my concerns."

"I know you have only the best interests of my daughter at heart."

"I do, most assuredly. As Your Imperial Majesty is well aware," Eileen's eyes were warm on her sovereign, "I am a reader, still a wee bit of a student, 'tis even said."

The monarch nodded knowingly.

"My readings during the summer just ended, as well as my conversations with many individuals knowledgeable of the ways of the French court, all whilst awaiting the wee one's arrival—" she smiled, "have included as much as I could locate about the house of Bourbon, which even of late has suffered from a series of early and untimely deaths."

Though the empress had made herself fully aware of the history, particularly the recent history, of the Bourbons, as well as of the complex, in many way, strange workings of the French court, she was nevertheless interested in what Eileen had to say and gestured for her to proceed.

"Not only have both the present dauphin's parents died—indeed, his father, Louis Ferdinand, died as dauphin but three years ago—and, some time ago, his elder brother, the Duc de Bourgogne as well—thus, as Your

Imperial Majesty well knows, the present dauphin was not at birth destined to be king, though now, surviving his brother and father, he is."

"And your concerns, my dear, they are . . . ?"

"My concern is that when Antoine and her husband ascend the throne of France and presumably then have a male child, were the dauphin, who would then be Louis XVI, to tragically continue his family's sad tradition . . . and suffer an untimely death, our Antoine, as queen of France, might very well then become regent.

"I have come to learn, from several of monsieur the count d'Mercy's gentlemen, that there is uneasiness—yes, tensions even, within the Bourbons, indeed that the house of Orleans seems anxious to make mischief as and whenever it can. The current duc de Chartres, called Louis Philippe, appears an exceptionally nasty young man, and 'tis upon him that the title of duc d'Orléans shall rest when the present duc dies. Whilst my prayer is that the archduchess will never be confronted with difficulties or suffer any unhappiness . . . the reality is that she shall be going into a court that appears to spawn far more intrigues than that of Your Imperial Majesty . . . and that she be prepared for these realities."

The conversation ended shortly thereafter, the empress rising when she deemed it completed, gesturing to Eileen that no curtsey was required. The older woman stepped forward and took Eileen's hand in her own, looking up at her to say softly, "I must reflect and consider the wisdom you have shared with me, Mistress O'Leary. I shall request that you come to me in several days . . . and we shall speak further." Smiling, the empress turned to her desk, and Eileen quietly withdrew.

Indeed it was later in the same week when Abby herself was dispatched to personally bring Eileen to the empress. As the women entered, Maria Theresa appeared to them, as she was, extremely busy, and she apologised to Eileen for being brief. "I did not want to merely send you a written message, but nor am I able to speak in detail at this moment . . . so permit me to say quite simply that, beyond what you and the Abbé Vermond shall jointly and individually endeavour, I realise that you may see a need for additional instructions to more fully prepare our little archduchess for her future life. I also recognise that, no matter how bright and talented the priest may be, your love and concern for her well-being are paramount. Accordingly, you shall be free to do . . . to tell her to do . . . have her read or read to her, if you must, virtually anything you see fit, so that she shall indeed be better prepared to become the queen of France." She sighed, but then smiled. "Thank you, Mistress O'Leary," and gently dismissed the O'Connell sisters.

Abbé Jacques-Mathieu Vermond finally arrived in Vienna in mid-October 1768, seemingly a genial French cleric in his mid-thirties with a pleasing personality and an easy, elegant manner. He appeared to take an instant liking to the archduchess, whom he addressed as Madame Antoine.

The priest focused primarily on the archduchess's substantive preparation, his remit being an extensive one: He was especially focused on her at-present uneven command of the French language, but he was also charged with educating her about French history, the Bourbons, the customs of the monarchy, the various chateaux in the Île-de-France amongst which they shuttled, the intricate etiquette in place, especially at Versailles, as well as the personalities the very young woman would confront there and elsewhere.

Eileen was interested to learn that Abbé Vermond was even teaching the presumptive dauphine about the regiments of the French Army, including the colours and designs of their flags and uniforms, and was surprised to hear that the archduchess had quickly come to love the topic.

Given this, as she worked both with and independent of the priest, Eileen occasionally mentioned "my brother, Daniel Charles, who is himself a commissioned officer in the Royal Suédois Brigade of the armies of His Majesty." Appreciating this fact, the archduchess almost immediately made the effort to learn, and then proudly related to her beloved governess that the regiment, founded in 1690, was distinguished by its handsome dark blue uniform coats, with buff collars and cuffs, unique in that the colour combination largely matched the uniforms of most infantry regiments of the Swedish Army itself.

It was to Eileen that a miscellany of issues and topics as broad, it sometimes seemed to her, as human nature itself fell. It was in an effort to at least begin addressing what Eileen had characterised as her "study of France, of all things French," that she again encouraged the archduchess to reflect seriously on matters perhaps personal to her, or beyond the abbé's charge, as she looked towards her eventual departure for France.

One breezy late-autumn afternoon, after the archduchess's work with Abbé Vermond had been completed for the day, she and Eileen, wrapped in what had become gracefully billowing cloaks of smooth, light wool, strolled in one of their favourite small gardens of the Hofburg, the vast palace at their back, the mountains seemingly suspended in the far distance before them, the archduchess began tentatively, "My lady, the empress last evening said something that was and remains quite confusing to me."

Looking down at the girl, Eileen nodded: *Yes—what is it?*

"She says I am to avoid familiarity with servants," the girl continued, puzzlement, even a degree of discomfort clear on her face. She stopped, as did Eileen, and they turned to face each other. "Are *you* not a servant, Lady Eileen? Are we not familiar?"

Eileen thought a moment before beginning. "Indeed I am; do I not always refer to you as Your Imperial Highness in public, and, save when we are alone, I walk only behind, never with you, yes? But, as to your second query, I would say, indeed we are!" The archduchess appearing less uncomfortable, Eileen took both of her hands in her own, the wind teasing their hair so that momentarily each saw the other as through breeze-tossed vines. "But ours is a unique, even an unusual situation, as you were a wee little girl when I first came into your service, yes?"

The girl nodded and smiled.

". . . and my roles were from the outset several: companion, teacher, riding mistress . . . and we have become, I daresay, very dear friends."

The archduchess smiled warmly now, nodding, and she took a deep breath and leaned quite close to Eileen. "Though never could I—never, *ever* shall I—say so to the empress, at times . . . many, perhaps even, in truth, most times in my life . . . and in ways known only to us, as I have frequently said, I feel more a *mother* than a servant or even a friend have you been to me . . . and thus you shall ever remain," and they both sat quietly, the now rising late-spring breeze swirling pollen and the smell of mountain wildflowers about them.

As the girl sat back, it was Eileen who leaned slightly towards her young mistress, about whom, she admitted, she had long felt most maternal, early on becoming her protector, her advocate. "I understand, my darling, and it is in this depth of feeling, which I am certain you are aware that I share, where the uniqueness of our relationship . . . lies, 'tis one that, as now a young woman you are become, you must understand will not repeat itself," she said with a firm expression on her face.

The archduchess's expression indicated puzzlement, and Eileen took her hand as they resumed walking.

"What the empress is saying to you is a very wise caution: You must approach both servants and courtiers with care. I have learned that more so than here, especially in other large courts such as Versailles; there is much intrigue, many people who have little to do other than to promote themselves and their positions at court. They continually seek out ways to advance themselves, often using relationships with other people; cultivating a young princess—indeed the dauphine of France, she who is destined to become queen of France . . . and, given your youth and that of the dauphin, as well as the age of Louis XV, a queen likely to reign for a very long time—would be tempting to such grasping, ofttimes unscrupulous persons, I assure you.

"You must remember, my darling, that as dauphine, even more so as queen, other than your husband and the king, you will have no equal." The young girl's eyes became visibly wide. "Virtually *everyone* will be your servant; I believe this is what the empress is saying. You must choose your friends very carefully, my darling, avoid untoward intimacies with both women and—most especially—men, take great care with what you say and always consider appearances: a relationship, or even a simple gesture, may appear to others very differently from what you intend. I believe 'tis not easy to be a princess, but I also believe you are a good person and will be a good queen; a great one even."

The archduchess smiled gratefully and took Eileen's hand in her own.

"Lady Eileen, what is *duty?*" Antoine inquired as their carriage slowly pulled away from the confines of Laxenburg.

Eileen's mind's eye immediately shot back to the seemingly long-ago night of her return to Derrynane from Firies, standing in her mother's rooms, telling Denis O'Connell, "I fully understand what my obligations are as an O'Connell. . . . I have done my duty."

She did not speak immediately, the horses' hoofs clattering on the gravel drive, thudding on the pounded dirt of the road to which it led, their harnesses jingling, the thudding and jingling of the Hussars' horses behind the carriage all filling the silence . . . and when she did, she spoke very slowly, very precisely.

"Duty, my darling girl, is, I believe and as I have experienced, an obligation one bears because of who one is and, in some instances, perhaps also because of one being a member of a certain family." She paused. "When one hears the word *duty*, I think most would picture a military man, yes?"

The girl appeared thoughtful and nodded.

"Lieutenant O'Leary, Major O'Sullivan and," she said, "General, the Count O'Connell," and Antoine, who adored the general, smiled broadly, "each of these men has a different rank and different duties: In simplest terms, my husband has a duty to carry out the major's orders, whilst both Lieutenant O'Leary and Major O'Sullivan must follow General O'Connell's orders, and all three gentlemen have an identical duty: to obey the empress.

"Now, these men have chosen lives, careers for which duty is a significant part . . . but there are also people who have duties they have not chosen to assume, but which they must nevertheless perform, because they are an O'Connell or a Hapsburg." She nudged the archduchess's right knee with her left, and the girl nodded.

"She must do something because it is her duty?" the archduchess asked, "even if she does not want to do it?"

Eileen nodded.

"So, it is to France that I must go . . . though I may not wish to?"

Eileen smiled and turned slightly. "Yes, my darling, as that is your duty . . . indeed it is your destiny as an archduchess of Austria . . . though I know, unlike my husband, you did not choose this life or this duty."

Antoine shook her head, a sombre expression, perhaps even the slightest twinge of resentment, on her face. Eileen took the archduchess's hand and they rode in silence for a time, the sounds of hoofs on the packed dirt of the road and of jingling tack again dominating.

Schönbrunn—June 1769

It was one gentle evening towards the end of May when Eileen received a battered, water-stained but still quite intact envelope from Derrynane. Looking forward to reading the letter it contained alone and hopefully in a peaceful setting, she waited until she and the archduchess had dined and she had been excused, feeling it every so often in the pocket of her afternoon dress. As she entered her own apartment, Anna, with Conor in her arms, greeted her warmly. Kissing both Anna and the now ten-month-old little boy, who smiled and cooed at her, appearing to be trying to clap his chubby hands, Eileen was pleased when Anna advised that he had been fed and his linen changed.

"That is wonderful, my darling," Eileen said, taking the baby into her own arms. "I believe he will shortly be abed, and so shall I, so . . ." and she wriggled her fingers, gesturing that Anna, too, was free for the evening.

"Very well, my lady, but we shall first undress, *ja?*" said Anna, who would soon be nineteen. Shaking her head, Eileen laughed, at having momentarily forgotten, as she still sometimes did when she was weary or excited, that she could neither dress nor undress alone. As they had both gotten quite adept at the process over the years, Eileen was quickly in her chemise, Conor in her arms and Anna, humming, out the door and down the hall.

Chattering to the occasionally babbling little boy, safely propped up and encircled by pillows in the centre of the huge bed, Eileen stripped, washed and drew on a dressing gown. As had become her habit most evenings when O'Leary was with his regiment, she snuggled up on her high bed with the baby and read softly aloud one or two selections from *Mother Goose,* sometimes making him laugh with funny voices and silly faces, and ultimately causing them both to become drowsy.

Lying him in his cradle, now moved from the foot of the bed to a corner of the comfortable room, Eileen blest him in Irish and kissed him, "Once . . . from Mama and once . . . from Papa," who, she saw no need to advise the little boy, was again somewhere in Upper Styria—*or was it Lower?*—on manoeuvres. As she watched Conor fighting sleep, his deep blue eyes flickering as he finally lost every child's nightly battle with the inevitable, she sighed softly. *I miss your papa, Master Conor, I do so when he is not here . . . he, my beloved horseman of the bright eyes.*

Starting to clamber up onto the bed, she suddenly remembered Maire's letter, still tucked in the pocket of her afternoon dress, and gently, almost stealthily, padded across the deep carpet into her dressing room to retrieve it, carrying her bedside candle rather than relighting others.

She finally settled back against her mounded pillows, and as she turned to tear open the envelope and saw, frozen in heavy green wax, the strutting O'Connell stag, she smiled, as she invariably did, wondering . . . *or is he tonight prancing?*

Unfolding the thick sheaves of the rough paper used at Derrynane, she smiled warmly at the sight of her mother's careful, almost precise but nevertheless elegantly unique flowing hand.

She nodded sometimes, smiling often, frowning occasionally as her eyes moved over the pages, images of people, the weather, animals and happenings vividly appearing, all against the backdrop of great Derrynane in its many meanings and moods. Maire wrote well and Eileen imagined well, which made reading her mother's letters a largely enjoyable experience, despite that this one advised that *"Brosnan Óg, the son of the short, stout Squire Brosnan, has been killed in a riding accident—so your old friend, Master O'More has advised, whilst stopping here Monday last. He sends you, I believe, sincere good wishes and protests—in jest, I am satisfied—that he daily mourns your marriage!"* and that *"the youngest McMurrough girl— Betsy, I believe she is— has lost yet another baby. She and Tom have now buried more children than there are around their hearth."* Eileen closed her eyes and then gazed gratefully in the direction of Conor's cradle.

More news, better news followed, as did a series of questions, inquiring of everyone's state of wellness and of news *"from your glittering palaces."*

It was not until she neared the end of the letter, which, given its length, she knew Maire had most likely written over a period of several days, that Eileen's eyes grew wide and she had to force herself not to cry out.

As you may be aware, we have been honoured with a lovely, though far too brief, visit from Major O'Sullivan, who has brought us much news of our Viennese O'Connells, O'Learys and O'Sullivans, and has now departed, hastening back across Europe to Abigail and all of you, I know.

I write to advise that the major is not, however, journeying alone, but rather has in his good company our little boy, though little no longer, as you saw whilst last you were here, who—after many, many conversations—and in the absence of Maurice, I must add—convinced his aging mama that 't'woud advance his "education and learning in the ways of the world"—I believe that was the lad's very grown-up sounding phrase!—to journey from hence to where you are reading my words, there to remain for a period of time, perhaps . . . ? Your elder brother, unhappy, displeased even, he shall be upon his return, I am sure, but . . . I believe the lad will truly learn much from this, and I have dealt with far worse than a displeased Maurice O'Connell!

Eileen smiled broadly, hugging herself: *Hugh! He is indeed no longer my little boy!* and thought quickly. *'Tis fourteen he shall soon be turning!* And then smilingly remembered, *he is virtually the same age as my little Antoine!*

Before she dozed off, she looked again at the date of her mother's letter—"20 April 1769"—calculating when, considering perhaps time in Paris, but also that uncle and nephew would be riding rather than in any conveyance, they might arrive shortly. She smiled . . . and finally fell asleep.

The intricate diplomatic dance involving the possible marriage of an at that time still undetermined archduchess of Austria to the future king of France that had been engaged in since the February 1767 arrival in Vienna of the Marquis de Durfort, as the ambassador from the court of Versailles, reached its initial, though most definitely far from its ultimate, culmination on 6 June 1769, as the marquis made application for the formal betrothal of the dauphin of France to the Archduchess Maria Antonia, or as the elegant French script of the prescribed written document now reflected, Marie Antoinette.

On 12 June, the monumental step was marked in celebratory fashion by a dazzling fête on what was the eve of Antoine's name day. The painstakingly complex protocol of the occasion was such that it was Countess Lerchenfeld who alone would—indeed it was only she who properly *could*—attend the archduchess, leaving a nevertheless, serenely content Eileen, little Conor O'Leary in tow, watching some of the glittering event from slightly afar, happily in the company of her dear friend Anna and, as Eileen philosophically reflected, a goodly number of her fellow servants.

As the excitement at Schönbrunn surrounding both the formal betrothal of the archduchess and the aftermath of the sparkling fête was slowly receding, Major Denis O'Sullivan and his young travelling companion were more than midway on their journey from Paris to Vienna, in O'Sullivan's mind the entire trip having thus far been both pleasant and productive.

It was apparent to the Irish officers, including now-Captain Daniel Charles O'Connell of the Royal Swedish Brigade of the armies of His Majesty, Louis XV, both those whom they met as well as those with whom the travellers had stayed in Paris, that the brothers-in-law genuinely liked and were enjoying each other's company, as Daniel had written to Maire, "indeed quite immensely."

O'Sullivan had quickly come to find Hugh to be bright, engaging and revelling in all-male company, his recent time at Derrynane being principally with his mother and two youngest sisters, Elizabeth and Anne. Hugh, he noticed, was also enthralled with all things military, as the three of them—the O'Connell brothers and O'Sullivan—had strolled towards the officers' mess on the grounds of the École Militaire it was clear that Hugh was already alternatingly picturing himself in the French uniform and the Austrian.

To both Irish officers, each resplendent in his Austrian and his French uniform, Hugh seemed a perfect candidate: Slightly taller than six feet, "albeit I doubt anywhere close to being finished in his growing," O'Sullivan had observed; possessed of the pleasantly typical O'Connell good looks—blue eyes, a ruddy, outdoors complexion, a tousle of dirty-blond, wavy, on some days curly, hair; and an erect, at times striking posture, evidencing, though he clearly was a country lad, an obvious self-assurance unusual in an adolescent. He displayed a sometimes almost wry, gentle sense of humour and spoke smoothly, precisely, moving comfortably amongst English, Irish and French, "his Latin indeed quite good," Daniel remarked to O'Sullivan, "though not as good as Eileen's," and they both laughed, as hers was acknowledged by all of them to be extraordinary.

As they travelled, the boy's command of history and literature would prove to O'Sullivan to be impressive—his education, like that of his siblings', largely the product of the "imported Jesuits" Donál Mór had begun bringing to Derrynane when the older O'Connell offspring were quite young.

To O'Sullivan, he seemed—and Daniel confirmed the fact—"a sensitive, thoughtful lad, more so than many his age." The men agreed that those facets of his personality were directly attributable to his being raised, at least in early childhood, by the remarkable combination of Maire and Eileen, and that Eileen's influences on him had continued past that time, as he had remained very close to his elder sister, exchanging increasingly detailed letters several times monthly after she had departed for Vienna.

"So, brother, is it to Vienna that you are going, a Hungarian Hussar to become?" Daniel Charles pointedly asked Hugh as the three sat to a hearty Normandy-styled meal, O'Sullivan looking up from his plate at the younger brother.

"Our brother O'Sullivan," he smiled at him, "has indicated 'tis a possibility, yes," and O'Sullivan nodded, putting down his fork.

"An excellent one . . . should you wish it," he said sharply, immediately thrusting his fork back into the ample plate of boeuf bourguignon, still steaming, before him.

As they were completing their meal, and their wineglasses refilled with what O'Sullivan pronounced as being a *burgundy extraordinaire,* he smiled at Daniel and pointedly inquired, "So, brother, are you still finding *Le Royal Suédois* to your liking?"

"Indeed, sir, I am, most certainly. I feel we are well trained, well officered, the Swedes being quite delightful under and with whom to serve, and *l'esprit* is excellent, amongst the officers and the men as a whole." He looked across at Hugh, whose expression was one of awe and a slight degree of dreaminess, as the youngest brother continued to take in his surroundings, and impressive they were, as the hall in which the men dined was resplendently hung with colourful regimental and individual company banners, as well as displays of battle-scarred shields and still gleaming armour from armies of earlier French monarchs and strikingly large Swedish and French flags, the latter gleaming white with the Bourbons' gold fleur-de-lis. Hugh was thoroughly enjoying his time with his brother and brother-in-law and revelling in his near-total immersion in all things military.

Smiling at his younger brother, Daniel continued. "I take liberty to tell you, lad, and certainly meaning no offense to our esteemed elder brother"—he smiled at the major—"you would be equally welcome here, were you inclined to consider offering your services to Louis XV, as opposed to her Imperial Majesty, the empress," and he nodded, the message in his eyes, his expression, quite clear to Hugh: *You should seriously consider this as well.*

The usually talkative Hugh's eyes went a bit wide, and he did not immediately respond.

"'Tis fine for you to do so, boy," O'Sullivan ventured into the momentary pause in the conversation. "Maintain an open mind: It appears you like what you are seeing here . . . and at Versailles as well. . . . Let us see what your reaction will be to those things in Vienna to which you shall similarly be introduced, though," and now he smiled broadly, "in addition to everything else, Vienna comes with other attractions—or might it be *distractions?*—in the persons of the Ladies Abigail and Eileen." All three men laughed at the prospect of the sisters lovingly pouncing on their favoured youngest brother.

O'Sullivan and Hugh nevertheless revisited the topic frequently as they crossed France riding into, and then making their way across, the vast, complex realm of the Hapsburgs. "'Tis your choice to make, lad," O'Sullivan cautioned yet again, even as they were approaching Vienna itself, having just pointed out the direction of Laxenburg. "Eileen and her youngest archduchess, that is their favourite place to be; 'tis quite lovely, as you shall, I am quite certain, see," then indicating, "though 'tis to Schönbrunn, the larger of the summer palaces, ornate where Laxenburg is simple and pastoral, that we are headed," and they rode on.

The travellers arrived at their destination in mid-afternoon, the palace and its environs evidencing a relaxed, indeed almost a holiday atmosphere, as confirmed by the young Galway-bred orderly attached to one of the infantry brigades then in residence, who had hurried to greet them and take their horses. *"Yessir,"* he said sharply to O'Sullivan, "much excitement has occurred, sir, as the Archduchess Maria Antonia, she has been . . ." Hugh, gazing all around, did not follow the exchange.

The orderly had just finished relating the news when O'Sullivan heard a booming "O'Sullivan, *O'Sullivan,* I say!!" as up strode Major John MacCarthy, still attached to the Imperial mission at Paris, with whom O'Sullivan had spent some months early on in his career, and of whom Abigail had spoken warmly when she had first arrived in Vienna. Nodding to the orderly, who saluted both men and they him, O'Sullivan then turned, and the officers warmly shook hands, slapping arms. MacCarthy expressed his regret that he had missed seeing O'Sullivan in Paris, ". . . as I assume you passed from thence to here, yes?" Confirming that indeed they had, O'Sullivan introduced Hugh to his brother officer and indicated that they must hasten, "to introduce the lad to my son, his nephew . . . and to O'Leary's new boy as well!"

MacCarthy sweepingly bowed to them both as he and O'Sullivan agreed to meet for beer on Tuesday, week.

As they resumed walking, O'Sullivan drew off his gauntlets and draped a long arm over Hugh's shoulder. "We must now hasten indeed, lad, as the thought of keeping your sister Abigail waiting is not a pleasant one at all." He laughed, and they quickened their steps, their boots crunching on the rough, broken stones spread across this part of the courtyard.

Hugh would experience a pair of noisy, tear-filled greetings from each of his sisters, Abby's being louder and involving a degree of jumping, as little Donál O'Sullivan, who, too, was excited and loud, was nevertheless in the arms of his nurse – standing behind Abigail, whilst Eileen's was equally tearful, albeit less animated, as a sleeping Conor O'Leary rocked in her arms.

Within days, Hugh was well settled, quartering with the O'Sullivans, as their apartments were significantly larger and more opulent, being part of the empress's residential complex, than Eileen's. "Our sister," Eileen smiled at first playfully to her dearest young brother, "you will understand she is indeed the *loftiest* of all women here, save for her Imperial Majesty herself and the remaining archduchesses still in residence with us, 'tis true! But even more importantly, I believe she is perhaps the most beloved of any person, no matter rank or station, in this palace, in this entire court!"

He had quickly come to enjoy spending time with both of his sisters and playing with their little boys, and was overjoyed when O'Leary returned, indicating that he, too, would be at home for a time. Hugh seemed to immediately attach himself to his brother-in-law, talking constantly of things military, seeking his advice, his opinions. O'Leary quickly came to enjoy the boy's company and their many conversations. "The lad, he is bright," he told Eileen one night in bed, "a brilliant future I believe he has, whether 'tis here or in France."

They had all merrily trekked out to the von Graffenreit-O'Connell castle one lushly warm Sunday after Mass for a sumptuous feast, enjoyed on a large sun- and wind-swept terrace, the luxuriant mountain scenery striking on all sides, the edifice itself seeming to a now-fully awed Hugh virtually identical, albeit smaller, to the many storybook castles he had seen, and thus appearing gentle where Irish castles were rough, and considerably more ornate, as those in Ireland were quite simple. General O'Connell laughed warmly with O'Leary and O'Sullivan as they enjoyed the spectacle of the O'Connell sisters, joined by their elegant Aunt Maria, all three effusively fluttering, hovering about the handsome adolescent, seeing to his second or third, perhaps, in the case of the pastries, even fourth helping.

After dessert had been taken, Hugh felt privileged when General O'Connell leaned over to him and suggested they might take a ride, "just we two, lad, providing that is acceptable to you." Hugh had bobbed his head enthusiastically.

For better than an hour they had ridden gently about the verdant countryside, speaking—"as two men," Hugh proudly confided to Eileen that evening—in detail about the boy's future, the general echoing

O'Sullivan's thoughts that whether he wished to serve in Vienna or in Paris was largely Hugh's decision to make. "There is much to be said for both courts, both military establishments," the general had said, confessing, "as there are healthy—and, at times, not healthy—rivalries between the armies of the empire and of France, but in truth there are also rivalries within armies, between cavalry and infantry, and even amongst the various regiments within the same service, so you will see that there is no perfect situation . . . so you must decide on how it feels to you, lad, yes?"

Hugh nodded, and they agreed to return to the castle, and did so at a healthy canter, Hugh's mind spinning, twirling with all he continued to learn, all of which he would reflect upon as he lay awake that night in the luxurious surroundings of the O'Sullivans' quarters.

It was one afternoon the week after their castle visit that they all learned, via Abigail, that Her Imperial Majesty wished to formally meet their distinguished young visitor from Ireland, the announcement immediately igniting a giddy, joyous firestorm of activity by "the O'Connell girls," as both of their husbands now referred to them, at one point joined by the countess, who had herself driven to Schönbrunn for the sole purpose of "providing any and all assistance that I am able" to prepare the overawed boy for an event that O'Leary had reflected was being treated as if "it were to be with the Blessed Virgin Mother herself, stepped down from the clouds for a wee visit." The three officers were additionally bemused by the fact that the precise nature of the occasion was indeterminate: "As *I* understand," O'Sullivan smilingly advised both the general and O'Leary, "from the *primary Lady-in-Waiting herself*, 'tis not that he is being presented formally . . . though neither is it a casual greeting in public, so . . ."

". . . So, to *whatever* the occasion may be said to be, he shall go, and he shall comport himself quite well, of that I am certain," concluded O'Leary.

The general added, "We are all to be treated to a supper, the same lady-in-waiting has advised my good self, and we know well that the lad certainly knows how to eat!" All three men laughingly agreed.

As prepared as the three happily frivolous women could help him to be, and walking slowly with O'Sullivan, Hugh, looking all about, awed by what he saw, approached the entrance to the palace to which they had been directed late on a breezy, gloriously sunny Thursday afternoon in the last week of June.

O'Sullivan had outfitted Hugh in a simple dark blue wool suit, a fresh white shirt with ruffled cuffs and jabot, white stockings and the black shoes with silver buckles Hugh had brought from Derrynane, the shoes now gleaming as a result of the efforts of O'Sullivan's valet. Hugh's wavy, dirty blond and—usually—unruly hair was brushed and carefully tied back in a neat queue, with a matching blue ribbon. Unlike O'Sullivan, who was in full-dress uniform, he was hatless.

Stopping some distance from the entrance, O'Sullivan turned to his young brother-in-law, speaking softly. "Now, you remember what I have told you, lad, aye?"

Hugh turned, his demeanour deferential, his tone respectfully soft. "Yes, sir, I believe so: I shall walk in beside you, sir; I shall kneel as and when you do. I shall speak in French, but I shall not speak until I am spoken to."

O'Sullivan nodded proudly; looking the boy directly in the eye, he clapped him on his left shoulder, "You are quite ready, then," and, cocking his head in that direction, turned them towards the entrance.

Hugh quickly brushed his sleeves, following O'Sullivan into what appeared to be a seldom-used entrance, two Irish soldiers standing guard. They smiled warmly at a now very serious-expressioned Hugh, and one cocked his head towards the building, loudly whispering, "Ah, fear not . . . she's a good 'un, lad!" and Hugh smiled. The guard stiffened slightly as the officer then looked sharply back at him, O'Sullivan having a reputation as being something of a stern leader, and quickly offered a crisp "Sir!" in response to which, to the soldier's relief, O'Sullivan winked.

The door opened for them by two lightly liveried boys both approximately Hugh's age, the Irishmen now strode down a long, simple hall, O'Sullivan's boots clicking, his sword sheath clanking softly against his boot tops, his cavalryman's stride longer than his young brother-in-law's.

The hall had taken them to a broad marble staircase, its brass railings gleaming. Climbing quickly, they reached the landing, at which an ornate, carved door stood immediately before them, and a footman, very German, very formal in an elegantly severe black satin suit and white wig bowed deeply and, as he did so, reached back effortlessly to open the tall door. As it swung wide, he turned and announced in German, "Major O'Sullivan and page," then closed the door almost silently as they entered.

At the end of a smallish, simply furnished and quite narrow room stood the Empress Maria Theresa—Hugh recognized her from the portraits he had seen already in his brief time at the palace—before a high desk, starkly regal in her black widow's robes, holding a large paper in both hands, which, as she saw them, she placed on the desktop, her fingertips settling it, her eyes remaining on her visitors as they slowly approached.

O'Sullivan halted at the proper place and Hugh, just one step behind him, did so as well; exchanging quick, subtle glances, both gently dropped to their right knees.

Gesturing to them to rise and approach and speaking softly in French, the empress began, "Major, as always, it is so very lovely to see you." Smiling at Hugh, she continued, "And this young man is . . . ?"

Hugh immediately responded, in English, "I am . . ." before catching himself, his cheeks turning scarlet, and the empress smiled warmly.

To the monarch's amusement, the always militarily formal O'Sullivan could not help but smile himself, finishing, "Your Imperial Majesty, this gentleman is the youngest of the numerous O'Connells of Derrynane, Hugh O'Connell."

Having stepped forward, the empress extended her right hand. "We welcome you to Schönbrunn, Master O'Connell."

Hugh correctly knelt once again and, raising his eyes slightly, his lips grazed the back of the empress's hand, she immediately drawing him up.

"You have journeyed a very great distance to us, Master O'Connell," she said, her voice gentle.

"Ah, from Ireland, yes, mum," a smiling Hugh spoke brightly, his French lilting, as did Eileen's. "'Tis indeed *quite* a long way, actually. We took ship; in truth, you see, it could be said that we were smuggled away from Derrynane; that is where we, the O'Connells, you know, mum, live, and thence to France and . . ."

O'Sullivan cleared his throat as the bemused monarch again smiled very warmly, interrupting maternally, "We are confident it was an interesting journey. We are truly so very pleased to have you here."

Hugh lowered his head again. "Thank you, Your Imperial Majesty; it is my honour indeed," he remembered to add.

At that moment, through a side door and with a rustling of the skirts of a striking mauve afternoon dress, Abigail entered the room. Marking the occasion by deftly curtseying to the monarch, she exchanged a quick smile with her husband, who shook his head gently, sharing a slightly rueful smile of his own. The empress immediately joined the silent exchange with nods to them both, almost saying, *It is fine; he is doing very well!*

Maria Theresa inquired, now speaking in German, "My Lady Abigail, am I to understand that refreshments are set on the terrace, and a light supper afterwards, once we are joined by the others?"

"Yes, Majesty," Abby replied, also in soft German.

"Excellent . . . then let us be comfortable," ordered the empress, gesturing to them with slightly spread arms to an open set of leaded-glass, wrought-iron doors, which were opened immediately by a footman's white-gloved hand.

The empress, O'Sullivan and Hugh followed Abby through the doorway onto a long terrace that appeared to Hugh to run the length of this wing of the palace, a prospect of verdant pastures, gardens and, in the distance, blue, hazy mountains, seemingly an entirely different place than the bustling panorama of courtiers, troops, servants, visitors and hangers-on on the opposite side of the building.

The empress looked back at Hugh, saying in halting English, "Forgive our use of German; we meant no rudeness. We shall speak French . . . though I so wish I could speak at least some of your Irish; it is so musical when I hear your family and the soldiers . . ."

As she was speaking, the shrill yapping of a small dog sounded behind them, immediately followed by the dull but loud thud of what was another heavy wrought-iron door, opening and thence almost instantly slamming against the palace's masonry, a small pug racing past them, as from behind there echoed, "Mops, *stoppen*! . . . *stoppen*!" in a girl's lilting voice.

In pursuit, a fair, trim adolescent girl in a relatively simple light blue dress, her long, ash-blond hair flying, sped past them.

The small group halted and the empress looked to heaven, shook her head and laughed, somewhat louder than she had intended. She inclined her head, stating the obvious to the O'Sullivans, though not to Hugh, whose facial expression was one of clear surprise: "My child, her animal . . ." adding in only a semi-faux rueful whisper, *"Madame la Dauphine de France!"* as she again laughed aloud. She then sharply clapped her hands. "Antoine! Antoine!"

The girl halted and turned—as, albeit without slowing, much less halting, so, too, did the sprinting pug—who abruptly now raced back towards the group at full speed. As the small dog flew by, Hugh bent and, seemingly effortlessly, intercepted the animal, scooping it into his arms, where it squirmed and yipped softly, almost plaintively.

Walking briskly now and smoothing her hair was Her Imperial Highness, the Archduchess Maria Antonia of Austria and Lorraine, an apologetic, indeed somewhat fearful expression on her flushed face, which became scarlet as she saw Hugh. She stopped and curtseyed deeply. "Mama," she said in German, the words tumbling out of her trembling lips even as the empress raised her, "Your Majesty, I am so very sorry, I did not know that you . . . " She appeared to her mother to be on the verge of tears.

"*En Francais, s'il vous plâit, Antoine,*" said the empress softly, easing her daughter's fears by the tone of her voice, by her facial expression and by placing her arm lightly on Hugh's shoulder as he continued to cradle the fidgeting dog. She continued, "Our guest has journeyed all the way from Ireland and our common tongue is French."

Her mind racing, the archduchess knew immediately who their guest was. *I did not know . . . Lady Eileen has never said how . . . attractive her brother is, though I should have . . . Oh, my. . . .*

As the two stood awkwardly, the empress introduced them informally. They eyed each other warily, silently, each smiling tightly, Hugh bobbing his head slightly after the fact, and each of them quickly turned their attention back towards the adults.

"Antoine, you will join us for a light supper?"

Stealing a quick glance at Hugh, the girl nodded slowly, respectfully, to her mother. The empress then gestured with a nod of her head to the squirming animal, still tucked under Hugh's arm. He awkwardly handed the dog to the archduchess who, receiving him sheepishly, though now with a nod and a quick, nervous smile, took a hurried few steps to a waiting servant, his arms already extended to receive the dog. Thanking him with a nod, the archduchess rejoined the group.

As she and her guests approached a pair of tables, the empress gestured casually to the O'Sullivans to take seats. "We shall sit and visit . . . then, when General, the Count, and Her Grace, the Countess, and the young O'Learys join us, we shall dine, yes?" Knowing full well he did not, she diplomatically inquired, "I trust you have no pressing matters, Major?"

O'Sullivan smiled. "No, Your Imperial Majesty."

As the empress took her place, she nodded to her still-standing daughter. "We are not yet ready to dine, so, Antoine, if you would, please take Master O'Connell to the end of the house," she gestured, "and there describe for him what he is seeing. He has only just recently arrived in Vienna, never having been here before."

The girl self-consciously bobbed her head respectfully to her mother, and, gesturing, said, "Sir . . ." and Hugh turned with her.

Watching the adolescents, still appearing ill at ease as they walked slowly, wordlessly away, the O'Sullivans took their own seats on cushioned, wrought-iron chairs, arranged around a small circular table, a second identical table similarly set.

"So, Major, my lady and her sister have both indicated the young man was anxious to come to Vienna, yes?"

"Yes, Majesty, indeed. . . . He is quite taken with our presence here, he corresponds frequently with the Lady Eileen, with whom he remains quite close . . . and quite taken he appears to be with Captain O'Leary, despite only having met him briefly in Ireland, before they were wed."

"Ah, Captain O'Leary, yes." She suddenly smiled, her eyes sparkling. "How well met he and the Lady Eileen appear to be. So very good it is to have both of them with us here." Abby stifled a giggle as she fondly eyed her sovereign, who continued to speak warmly of O'Leary, approving of his dashing appearance and graceful manner.

"I fear the lad perhaps has an excessively romantic notion of military service, Majesty," O'Sullivan advised.

"Perhaps it is you and Captain O'Leary, in the magnificence of the uniforms your sovereign has chosen for you?" the empress chided O'Sullivan, who laughed dryly, respectfully. "So the young man will remain with us then, yes, Major? General, the Count, will . . ."

"Actually, Majesty, I know not for certain. I brought the boy with," he nodded at Abby, "their mother's acquiescence, yielding to his pleading to her good self . . . my thinking at the time perhaps being more of how I would feel, were I he than perhaps how I should have been thinking . . . being not."

Abby added softly, "Our eldest brother had forbidden the boy from going anywhere until he himself decided the appropriate destination. He believes Hugh is both dreamy and impetuous, unschooled in the world. Though Eileen indicates that the captain had suggested he consider Louvain, Maurice's plan, I believe, had been to send him to Salamanca, but our mother perhaps had *forgotten* this." She rolled her eyes.

Her eyes brightening again at the reference to Art O'Leary, the empress diplomatically said, "Ah, Salamanca, warm and sunny Spain, but perhaps fewer chances for military adventure, I think." She laughed softly. "My dear, should he wish to remain with us, the count, your good uncle, my faithful Irish warrior, I am certain he could impress upon your brother the fact that . . ."

At the far end of the sweeping terrace, the sun bright, though not glaring, a warm breeze in their faces, teasing their hair, the conversation was not about the barely visible, seemingly distant sights of Vienna, being primarily church steeples peeping above luxuriant trees. Beginning to respond to what had been a precise, staccato string of questions posed sharply by the archduchess in her distinctive, German-laced French, Hugh, when finally permitted to speak in full sentences, first advised her, in his Kerry-inflected version of the tongue, which she instantly found delightful, wonderfully similar to Eileen's own lilt, that, "I am fourteen years old and I am going to be a soldier."

Attempting to appear diffident, she sniffed, "All boys want to be soldiers. . . . Do they not have armies in Ireland?" she inquired archly. "So many of the officers *und*—I meant *et*—officers *and* men of the empress's armies are Irish." Hugh now noticed her hesitancy, as if her mind were searching for the correct French word; concluding that his own French may be superior to hers, he spoke more slowly, more precisely.

"The armies in Ireland are the English king's; Irishmen cannot become officers."

"That appears to make no sense." She frowned. "But then, so often, things . . . so then they come here?"

"Indeed yes . . . and to France, yes, and Spain," Hugh answered, adding, "*Catholic* Europe," with a firm nod.

The archduchess grew quiet, now looking up at, she thought, *this very handsome boy.*

Making then a valiant effort to establish some commonality, Hugh began, "And *you*, Archduchess . . . or . . . I truly apologise, please forgive me . . . in the excitement of the moment, I fear that I have forgotten the proper form of address," continuing haltingly, "My brother-in-law has told me that we—you and I"—he gestured, "are of approximately the same age."

Her soft eyes still fixed on Hugh's face, Antoine smiled warmly, beginning in faux hauteur, "Actually, sir, the *sole* appropriate way to address me is *Your Imperial Highness.*" Her tone then purposely softening, she added, "Though as your sister, the Lady Eileen, has long been permitted to address me as Antoine . . . I decree," she stretched her right arm out in her version of an Imperial gesture, "that so shall you be!" Immediately wishing she had not, she giggled, quickly finishing, " . . . and I was born in 1755, Master O'Connell, sir."

"As was *I*," Hugh responded with a smile, "in July."

"You do not say, really?"

"Really, I *do* say," he continued playfully.

"And I in November," the archduchess advised, relaxing even a bit more, "*Hugh*," and she smiled, quite dazzlingly. Hugh returned her smile with a sparkling one of his own.

"So . . . Hugh, a soldier you shall be—here, as your brothers are? . . . of the empress?"

"Perhaps, yes . . . though . . . as we journeyed from Ireland, Major O'Sullivan and I stopped for a time in Paris. . . ." He noticed a sudden expression of interest on the girl's clear, luminous face.

"Our brother—mine and Eileen's and Abby's—Daniel Charles is an officer in *Le Regiment Royal Suédois* of the armies of Louis XV. He has urged me to also consider service in France, and Major O'Sullivan took no exception to the thought."

I am aware of Daniel Charles, she thought but did not share, her eyes still very much on the boy, her small, elegant hands resting on the back of a wrought-iron chair, similar to the ones the adults occupied at the far end of the terrace. Antoine brushed back some of her thick, ash-blond hair, which had blown over what to Hugh appeared quite lovely light blue eyes. "How very interesting, how coincidental . . . of sorts," she said softly.

Hugh's silent response was an expression of puzzlement.

"You see, my future . . . it is quite a bit more settled than yours. Although . . ." she laughed, not meaning to, "I, too, am . . . actually, I shall be compelled to leave my country."

Endeavouring to appear casual, Hugh had leant his back and elbows against the terrace's granite and wrought-iron perimeter; he nevertheless immediately seemed to the archduchess to be clearly interested.

"Why would *you* leave Vienna, Antoine?"

"As awkward as it is for me to do so, speaking thus to one whom I have just met, indeed to one whom I do not at all know . . . the fact is that, actually . . . you see, I am to become the queen of France," she allowed, almost casually hurrying the final three words, immediately attempting to gently cloak the enormity of what she had just said with the softest of laughter.

Hugh's eyes widened, his jaw visibly dropping. "Not . . . not right now . . . Louis XV, he is . . ."

Antoine laughed aloud. "Oh no! It is to the king's grandson, the Dauphin Louis Auguste, that I have just become betrothed to be wed, and, as dauphine, I will become queen when Louis Auguste becomes king. . . Louis XVI, he will be."

Hugh exhaled an involuntary whistle. "And I have been thinking that my life was . . ." He shook his head as his voice trailed off, then wondering aloud, "This is fact, this has already occurred?"

"Earlier this month, and indeed on the sixth, the eve of my name day, a grand fête was held here to mark the occasion. It was quite lovely; it . . ."

"So, you will go to Paris . . . to Versailles, yes?"

The girl nodded affirmatively, though, Hugh immediately discerned, not at all enthusiastically. He would like to have attempted to discover *why*, but, instead he continued, "Versailles, it is . . . it is beyond words."

"You have been there? *Versailles?*"

"Ah, yes, whilst stopping with my brother in Paris, he took us there. The building, the chateau . . . it is truly magnificent. There is a hall, a huge hall . . . 'tis all mirrors, if you can imagine . . . *mirrors!*" The archduchess appeared to Hugh to be enthralled; unbeknownst to him, she was rather purposely not mentioning the existence of a similar gallery at Schönbrunn, permitting him to continue. "There are so many people about everywhere, and I saw the king himself; even though from a distance, 'twas quite exciting. And it is there that you shall live?"

Wide-eyed now, Antoine nodded, again though, Hugh thought, seemingly more in surprise that he had been to Versailles rather than evidencing any true eagerness on her own part to be there.

"And the dauphin: what does he speak to you of Versailles? How was it that you came to meet him? Do you like him?" Hugh asked guilelessly.

The archduchess's cheeks went immediately scarlet, her fingers gripping the chair back. "We . . . I . . . mmm . . . we have not actually . . . met. I do not know . . . him . . . yet. You see . . . decisions as to whom an archduchess of Austria or the dauphin of France is to wed are, as the Abbé Vermond has taught me, *matters of state*. . . . This is indeed difficult to . . . you see, my sister, my dearest Charlotte, she is Queen of Naples now since April; she did not meet her husband until she arrived there. . . . It is difficult to explain; I myself do not fully understand . . ."

Hugh looked gently at, he reflected, *this quite attractive girl*. "Please permit me to apologise, I did not mean to . . . I did not know . . ."

The girl flicked her right hand casually rather than dismissively. "Nor do I, of much of what is occurring to me. . . . I am taught by Abbé Vermond, my tutor, that this is a *marriage of countries*, of houses . . . 'the Bourbons and the Hapsburgs,' he says . . . It is . . ." She shook her head, looking away for a moment, her eyes now, though unseen by Hugh, ever so slightly moist. She cleared her throat and redirected her gaze to the boy's genuine, open face. "You shall remain in Vienna, Hugh, *ja?*"

"There is some question about that, but for now, yes."

"Perhaps then, whilst you are here, we might see each other again." She smiled warmly.

"Yes, yes . . . perhaps yes. Though . . . would it not be inappropriate, given your . . . what is it that you said, *betrothal,* is that what it is?"

"As for there being any inappropriateness . . . or not . . . it is in the gentle care of your dear, dark-haired sister that I am, as I have been since a little girl, and it is with her . . . and indeed with *your wee nephew,*" she spoke the words precisely in English and then laughed softly at herself, "that I spend much, indeed most, of my time . . . so you may simply join us!"

Hugh nodded. "That would be . . . quite lovely, yes. As I am at present . . ."

". . . residing with Lady Abigail and the major . . . that I know. Indeed I was already made aware that you were here . . . I just did not know at first . . . that is, before today, that you were so . . ." She stopped abruptly and blushed and then continued, ". . . that you would be here today, now . . . only that you had arrived . . . as, though your sister, Lady Eileen, is quite discreet, the Countess Lerchenfeld, who is the actual head of my household, though I rarely see her, is a terrible gossip. She knows all manner of things and speaks much of what she learns to me . . . when I *do* see her."

Hugh had listened carefully, wordlessly, as her words nervously cascaded. They were mostly French or a close approximation of it, some German, the sprinkling of Italian he used his Latin to grasp, so he believed he understood much of what she had said. When she finally did finish, he smiled.

"So then, sir, we shall indeed be seeing each other." She smiled, though to Hugh it seemed almost to be a command.

"We shall indeed, Your Imperial Highness," he nevertheless managed, and they both laughed.

As they had noticed that O'Leary and Eileen and the von Graffenreit-O'Connells had arrived, they then began to stroll very slowly back towards the adults. Watching the young people approach, Eileen and Abby exchanged nods, wordlessly agreeing that they appeared to be chatting quite amiably.

As they grew closer, the general's arm now raised in greeting to the young people, his familiar, booming voice sounded. "Ah, see, 'tis such a handsome young couple coming now to join us!"

The countess winced visibly and squeezed his thick hand as hard as she could with her own delicate one, hissing quietly, "Morty!" and the general's face reddened. The radiantly refined countess could only look up lovingly at her massive husband and smile, shaking her head softly and whispering, "*Protocol*, my beloved, protocol. . . ."

The general shook his head in response, as by then the handsome young couple, their faces as red as the general's, had indeed joined the group for what proved to be a wholly enjoyable evening, with excellent food, fine wines, delightful conversation, all the more enjoyable as the elegant sounds of a string consort filled the soft air of an Austrian summer evening.

It was only as the general and his wife were taking their leave of the gathering— "Our day today began early; our day tomorrow even earlier," General O'Connell indicated—and as the empress strolled, her arms joined with each of them, towards the doors, she then stepped to the general's left side, taking his hand, and the three of them stopped in the fluttering light of two small torches on the side of the building. "My Irish warrior," the empress began affectionately, her eyes up on the striking man, as the countess watched, wondering, "your most genuine greeting of the young people, so observant, was so true, that indeed I saw them as did you . . . as a 'handsome young couple. . . .' Your spontaneous words, they spoke my thoughts. . . . Truth be told, I felt a pang in my heart; would that my dear Antoine were able—if so she desired—to select her own Irish warrior, in the person of your handsome boy, or another . . . or a Hungarian warrior even!" She smiled almost sadly. "Yet she is not, and that is . . ." She coughed.

"I merely wished you to be aware of . . . that I had taken no . . ." She now looked almost plaintively at the countess, her oldest and dearest friend, and as the women's eyes met, the countess nodded her understanding. In grateful response, she wished them "A good night, my dearest friends," and the empress added softly, "God bless you both. . . ."

As the older O'Connells strode the familiar corridors of the palace to their overnight lodgings, the countess could be seen in deep conversation with her husband, his right shoulder lowered, his head cocked down, nodding occasionally as he listened intently to all she was telling him.

The summer of 1769 would thus proceed; whilst without major incident, it was never boring. With two very little boys, the younger of whom not yet a year old, and a spirited adolescent in their midst, not to mention the continuing daily active presence of the archduchess, the lives of the O'Sullivans and O'Learys were far from dull.

Well before Hugh's arrival, Antoine had settled easily into her self-determined role of older sister to Conor, playing with him, taking him for walks in an elegantly cumbersome carriage, even assisting Anna at his mealtimes, though the archduchess drew the line at linen-changing—all leading to much good-natured banter amongst the servants about Anna having an "Imperial helper." As the weeks progressed, a bemused Eileen suddenly found that she had much less to do: The archduchess in her care was, after all, herself caring for her child. Once Eileen became as comfortable with the situation as she could, she found the sight of Antoine playing with, even feeding the infant whom she frequently referred to as "my little brother," to be heart-warming.

The officers arranged for Hugh to join them as they led detachments from their respective regiments on patrols or manoeuvres about the sprawling Hapsburg states. The boy concluded patrols were shorter times in the field than manoeuvres, and the former primarily involved seeing to it that the peace was kept and the countryside calm, whilst part of the latter was spent in practicing actual cavalry exercises and drills, the Hungarian Hussars being in constant preparation for any conflict. Both of the younger officers took time to explain to Hugh that in battle they were used in such light cavalry roles as reconnaissance, harassing enemy skirmishers, overrunning artillery positions, and pursuing fleeing troops, with all of which Hugh appeared awed.

As a relatively senior officer, O'Sullivan possessed greater authority and more prestige than did the younger, more junior O'Leary, and Hugh was also able to observe the different manner by which each officer commanded his men: O'Sullivan was invariably crisp, militarily precise, sometimes quite demanding, brusque, cold even. There was little evidence of O'Sullivan's warm laughter and gentle sense of humour in the field, except when he and Hugh would bed down in the major's tent and he might tell Hugh humorous stories about General O'Connell or laugh heartily as Hugh told him tales of Abby, of which there were many . . . and the two continued to explore Hugh's continuing interest in a military career.

Whilst O'Sullivan was clearly respected and, at least to some degree, Hugh could tell, feared by his men, O'Leary, though obviously acknowledged as their leader, was clearly additionally embraced by his men, leading them more by cajoling, nudging . . . or, as he told Hugh, "'tis akin to a sheepdog an officer, if he chooses, is able to be, circling about, keeping the men together, moving forward, ever forward." Hugh could not picture Denis O'Sullivan commanding in that manner, though it appeared to work superbly for O'Leary, and both men were respected by their troopers and their brother officers, as different in their methods of command as each was from the other.

Additionally, Hugh was regularly invited by the general and the countess to join them at their castle, with which Hugh was enthralled. Each time there, he felt very much like a little boy, fully awed at the towers and turrets, the looming grey walls, the colourful standards of General O'Connell and the ancient von Graffenreit counts aflutter, all set amidst a verdant, pine-scented dell, gentle mountains on sentinel. What surprised him the most, however, was how comfortable, even intimate a number of the rooms were.

The extended visits permitted the boy to spend significant time with the general, who proved to be excellent company, a fine riding companion and "a source of much wisdom," Hugh would tell Eileen upon his return from one of his visits.

The general was equally pleased with Hugh: "a promising lad the boy is," he advised the countess on more than one occasion.

General O'Connell's detailed elaborations on various topics—including the positives and negatives of a military career, the various branches of service, a military career's impact on oneself, one's family—"Ah yes, one's family: You can only imagine the devastation suffered by Her Grace, the countess and their daughters, then your age, when Colonel, the Count von Graffenreit was killed in battle"—they were exploring during the course of a number of wide-ranging conversation also led Hugh to unexpectedly develop an interest in the infantry. This was especially true as General O'Connell related that he had in fact begun his own military career as a cavalryman, only later transferring to the infantry, where he had earned great respect and achieved a not-insignificant degree of fame as a strategist, a tactician widely regarded for what many said were his extraordinary leadership abilities. Indeed, though O'Connell himself would have disagreed, had he been made aware, it was with General O'Connell in mind that many said the empress's late husband, the Emperor Francis Stephen had written: *The more Irish officers in the Austrian service the better our troops will be disciplined. An Irish coward is an uncommon character. Even what the natives of Ireland dislike, they generally perform through a desire for glory.*

It was Denis O'Sullivan who expanded on the general's leadership. "He has come to be regarded as quite singular, actually. Indeed, he is regularly referred to as 'the warrior general.'" Correctly seeing a question in Hugh's eyes, O'Sullivan added, "As, during an engagement, whilst a number of generals remain—and quite rightly so, I would add—at the rear, amongst their staffs, studying their maps, receiving information from the field, giving orders . . . General O'Connell is known for often being at the head of and amidst his men on the field, sabre and pistol in hand, the light of battle in his eyes. And, as many say, 'pity the foe,'" nodding in agreement as he saw the pride in the boy's eyes.

As his time in Vienna progressed, Hugh would learn from O'Sullivan—as well as from Eileen and Abigail, and indeed from General O'Connell himself—that, his courage under fire and leadership abilities notwithstanding, the general was far from being the leading Irish officer in Her Majesty's armies.

"'Tis Field Marshal Franz Moritz von Lacy," O'Sullivan shared one quiet evening when Hugh was at home with his uncle and aunt, "who is the true Irish star in the Austrian military firmament." Born in St. Petersburg in 1725, von Lacy was the son of Count Peter von Lacy—also known as Pyotr Petrovich Lacy—himself a Russian field marshal, who had, during a military career of more than five decades, served under Peter the Great as well as Empress Anna.

The major then recounted that the younger von Lacy had received his military training in Germany, afterwards entering the Habsburgs' service. Though during the Seven Years War, von Lacy had grown—far closer than had General O'Connell—to Field Marshal Daun, the two had at some point fallen out. This notwithstanding, von Lacy's career had over the long-term flourished, both under Maria Theresa and Emperor Joseph II.

Abby, who had been quietly toying – she did not particularly enjoy the pastime – with a needlework project as she listened to her husband's tales, looked up and smiled, "My darling, you must tell Hugh of the grand St. Patrick's Day Ball of two – or was it three? – yes, 'twas indeed three years – of 1766, hosted right here in Vienna by the Spanish ambassador himself!"

Laying down her work, Abby smiled as she watched Hugh listen, seemingly enraptured, as her husband spoke of what had indeed been a glittering affair – sometimes subsequently referred to as "The Ball of the Wild Geese" – held on Monday, 17 March 1766.

"Aye, 'twas indeed a grand occasion . . . and fortunate we were to be in attendance," O'Sullivan began, the "we" being he and Abigail, Eileen (who was escorted by Major von Klaus) and General O'Connell and the Countess von Graffenreit, "The Empress was there, the Emperor as well, virtually the entire imperial family and, indeed, much of the Court – all sporting what they were calling 'Irish Crosses' in honour both of the saint and of our land.

"But it was Count Lacy, as President of the Council of War, who was clearly regarded by all as the host, he being the preeminent Irish officer in attendance," O'Sullivan explained.

Abigail's eyes twinkled, ". . . and let us not forget to have Hugh know the *Spanish* envoy's name and identity, my darling," she laughed."

O'Sullivan gestured for his wife to chime in, as he rose and refilled the trio's wine glasses.

"Our host on this spectacular evening was . . . ," she took a deep breath, and to Hugh's surprise deftly continued in a gentle Castilian tone, (having learnt basic Spanish from a Salamancan riding master at Derrynane), *"El Excelentísimo Señor el Embajador de Su Majestad Carlos III de España, Demetrio Conde Mahoni,"* after a purposeful pause, speaking the final word slowly, precisely and again for emphasis, absent her soft Castilian accent, *"Ma-hone-ee,* aye!" she smiled, her eyes sparkling as Hugh's own eyes had gone wide, causing O'Sullivan to chuckle.

Between the two of them the couple informed their nephew that the ambassador was the son of "a Kerry lad, from up near the Gap – Daniel O'Mahony, who after the Williamite wars had fled to France and Louis XV's armies in 1690 . . . or perhaps '91," said O'Sullivan, Abby continuing, telling her nephew that O'Mahony had subsequently gone on to Spain, becoming a general and Count of Castile, finishing with that "Demetrio chose diplomacy over soldiering . . .and here . . ." she spread her arms slightly, ". . . here he was as Spanish ambassador and our host on the good Saint's own day!"

O'Sullivan swallowed a sip of wine and cleared his throat, "The point of this tale, my lad, is that you will know there were and are generals – all senior to our beloved Uncle Morty," he smiled affectionately, "named Brown, Maguire and Plunkett and O'Kelly . . . one even called O'Donnell . . . indeed, of Donegal, and on that night, him only recently become Inspector General of the Imperial Cavalry."

Abby lowered her eyes in feigned modesty and giggled, "The *real point* is that we, the O'Connells and O'Sullivans, we were fortunate indeed to have attended . . . us being of the 'lower classes'," she laughed.

"Ah, woman, speak for yourself, and . . ." O'Sullivan said sharply, playfully gesturing at Hugh, "'Tis of the *O'Connells* and certainly *not* the O'Sullivans whom people are referring when they speak of a clan being *'mere graziers, not to mention smugglers, thieves, murderers, cattle-rustlers* and *God knows what else in addition!* Are they not?" he laughed heartily. Abby laughingly buried her face in her hands in faux shame, lifting it finally to admit, "Wed above myself I have indeed!" O'Sullivan feigned a haughty tone, an officious appearance and laughed, "Indeed you have, woman! Indeed you have."– and Hugh sat in wondering silence.

It was on another occasion, some weeks later, as Hugh dined with Eileen and O'Leary in their own apartment at Schönbrunn, as the topic again returned to the members of the family and their respective roles at the Viennese court, his interest and curiosity now piqued, that Hugh had inquired, "But what of General O'Connell, how is it that he has advanced?"

Somewhat to his surprise, it was, with O'Leary's nodding immediate assent, that Eileen then smiled warmly, "As much as – perhaps even more than – anything else *Our* General is a truly beloved man. Though brave and military astute he was and is, I believe his strength lies in the affection he always has maintained and displayed for his men, and they for him, as well as in his gentle manner, a warm self-effacing sense of humour and, believe it or nay, lad, in a genuine lack of raw ambition, an attribute so common amongst military officers, and one viewed by many as necessary to one's advancement."

As she finished, O'Leary, who had nodded several times as his wife had spoken, offered that, "Our great and good uncle General, the Count O'Connell possesses an innate common sense, absent in many men of arms. It was more than his affection, indeed reverence, for Her Imperial Majesty that caused him to instantly agree to leave active military service and join her at court, even before your dear aunts came to Vienna. I honestly believe that he realised as the war was gradually drawing to a close that opportunities for purely military advancement would become more limited. As he did on the field, in his career he has displayed a strikingly good sense of timing, which along with, as your aunt has said, his total lack of the all-consuming, patent striving that is so terribly common amongst so many, many officers, has yielded career results that have eluded many men having far great ambitions than he."

Hugh sat quietly for a moment.

"One final fact, if I may, my loves," Eileen requested, "The Lacys, even before becoming ennobled in Russia and then here, they were of ancient Irish nobility, ultimately in Limerick, I believe, but descended I do know from one Hugh," she smiled at her now wide-eyed brother, "aye, . . . Hugh de Lacy, who was Lord of Meath in the Twelfth Century." Her husband swallowed a sip of wine and nodded, "Impressive, my darling!" Hugh's mouth momentarily fell open.

Eileen raised her right forefinger, "The point I make, my darlings, is that the Lacys were noble in a way we never have been, *and*, indeed, of course never shall be. In the 1100s, I suspect even the highest ranking O'Connells were, at best, mere bowmen or spearman to the MacCarthy Mór. *Our* dear general, he realised this early on I suspect– he knew he would never advance above, beyond a von Lacy and he conducted himself accordingly . . . *and*, I would say, he did *bloody well good* for himself, did he not?"

Uncle and nephew could only laughingly agree.

His admiration for his uncle perhaps even greater after learning of such things, Hugh continued to avail himself of any opportunity to spend time with the general, who enjoyed their conversations and the opportunities they provided him to teach a bright young lad with military ambitions.

One breezy morning as Hugh breakfasted outside with his uncle and aunt at their castle, the von Graffenreit and O'Connell banners fluttering, the general, responding to his nephew's well-thought-out questions as to why he had become an infantry officer, advised, "I found leading ever increasing numbers of men—both in battle and peacetime—to be challenging, captivating . . . perhaps even more so, the complexity of devising—and then successfully, much of the time, executing—battlefield tactics and strategy for foot soldiers, 'tis most appealing."

"More so than *horse*, Uncle?" Hugh had asked.

"'Tis a different form of military organisation indeed, a totally dissimilar way of waging war. I personally came to believe it to be more satisfying, though our own bold Hussars, your brothers, my nephews, would, I am certain, disagree." The general smiled. "Additionally, you will understand that an army involves much more than men trained solely in the ways of war, as, for example, engineers, who design and construct buildings, fortifications, roads permanent and temporary, the latter two often in the midst of actual engagements, which I also find fascinating. I must tell you, as I have only recently learnt from a letter received from Paris, your dear brother, Daniel Charles, has begun additional studies in engineering."

As he shuttled pleasantly back and forth between Schönbrunn, and later in the summer, Laxenburg and what he came to call the O'Connell castle, Hugh also availed himself of ready access to General O'Connell's significant library of military topics and found himself reading, indeed studying, infantry troop movements and even joined by the general, sitting on the floor, kneeling over detailed maps of famous battles and becoming engrossed in the idea.

As fascinated by the entire experience he was having—seeing and learning how his sisters, their husbands and indeed, as he would come to know, a select number of other Irishmen and -women lived and played a variety of roles at and near the apex of Imperial Austria, not to mention all he was being taught by his brothers-in-law and uncle—Hugh was perhaps most surprised, and pleasantly so, by the fact that he was spending considerably more time than either he—or, he imagined, or at least wondered, *she* —had ever expected with the pretty girl whom he continued simply to call Antoine, though in public he was precisely formal, *Your Imperial Highness.*

Though, as she applied unequal measures of protocol, etiquette, propriety and common sense to the unusual situation, frequently out of Eileen's sight, the attractive but somewhat curious pair—the tall, gangly Irish boy with an easy gait, a gentle, loquacious manner and a rollicking laugh, and the trim, in all ways precisely elegant archduchess of Austria and Lorraine, with a flawless complexion and large, soft blue eyes that seemed nearly always to be fixed on Hugh—would stroll in a variety of garden or other appropriate outdoor settings, occasionally ride, well escorted by a covey of cavalry or simply sit: talking, it seemed constantly, talking a great deal, about a number of things.

They spoke of growing up in very large families and of their shared loss in the deaths of their fathers whilst both were relatively young children, ". . . and yet both of us benefitted from the Lady Eileen being intimately a part of our lives at those sad, sad times," the archduchess observed, and she related how extraordinary she and Charlotte had felt Eileen had been during that dark, grim summer of 1765.

"Yet both of our mothers appear very strong women, do they not?" Hugh questioned, quickly adding, "I do not, however, believe Maire an empress she could be considered. . . ."

Antoine cocked her head questioningly. "From some of what you— and Lady Eileen as well—have told me, how she reigns over vast Derrynane, I believe she is a monarch of sorts, is she not?"

They agreed she was.

They both loved riding and horses, whilst Hugh was clearly the more bookish, more intellectually inclined of the two. Both loved to dance and all forms of music, though Hugh did not play an instrument.

As the weeks passed and their near-daily meetings continued, they began to touch on more personal topics, thoughts, feelings even, Hugh frequently wondering aloud how it was that she could possibly look forward to the marriage, the life that awaited her. The first several times he gently, almost diplomatically, especially for a fourteen-year-old boy, raised the topic, the archduchess, though not quite as diplomatically, refused to discuss it.

One dazzlingly sunny, windy afternoon as they rode near Laxenburg, the breeze gentle in their faces and hair, the competing aromas of numerous types of alpine wildflowers on the wind and the cavalry detachment at a discreet distance, Hugh yet again attempted. "I continue to wonder . . ." he began over the clatter of hoofs, the jangle of tack, and the girl drew her gently cantering horse to a halt in a scattering of dirt and stones.

"What is it that you *wonder* so, my dear friend? Why are you pondering what is after all, as your own dear sister, the Lady Eileen herself, has said to be my destiny?"

Reining in his horse as well, Hugh, as had become his habit, exhaled deeply, whistling softly in the process as his gloved hands rested on his saddle, looking intently at his companion as she perched comfortably atop her left-facing sidesaddle, her full eyes soft on him, drawing her gloves off. "Why do I? Why am I? I have *wondered* that myself," he chuckled somewhat uncomfortably, "and I conclude that it is because you *are*, my dear friend, the first such friend ever have I had," he tugged at his soft riding gloves, "and that I wish only your happiness . . . as I have grown most happy in your good company these months." By gently kneeing his dappled-grey mare slightly, Hugh placed himself on the archduchess's left side, never taking his eyes off the girl's glowing face.

He reached for and gently touched, softly taking her gloveless hand in his, and she immediately thought, *rough, strong hand.*

They sat in a nearly still tableau, save for the breeze and the random insects, the gentle, synchronistic flicking by the horses of their tails, eyes fixed on each other, their breathing deeper, faces pink and expressions soft and wonder-filled for what seemed to them both an extremely long time, until Hugh cleared his throat. "I am certain that I have breached all manner and form of protocol," he began, "and if it would be required, I should . . . and do indeed . . . apologise." He nodded, but then immediately smiled softly.

The youngest current archduchess of Austria, whose ungloved small, smooth hand remained in his larger, callused one, at first said nothing; rather she continued quietly looking at him until she began, "Your apology is not nor would it be accepted, as it is not at all necessary, sir." Her voice was soft, whist being firmer than Hugh had ever heard it. "I am grateful for the friendship"—she lifted their still-joined hands just slightly up in the air—"that we share, as you have expressed and now shown to me. . . . I, too, have never had a friend such as you are, have become, and . . . I trust that you will know that I am similarly your dear, good friend."

As Hugh began to speak, the girl, perhaps instinctively, lifted her free hand, the tip of her forefinger just barely touching her own lips, effectively silencing him, then smiled and nodded ever so slightly. Though Hugh did not smile, he, too, nodded, and they slowly, reluctantly released each other's hands, though they remained sitting as before until Hugh finally noticed movement by their escort and nodded at the archduchess. Turning their horses' heads, they nudged the animals into a gently rocking walk in the general direction of the palace.

In the days, the weeks following, each time they were together they would frequently though delicately touch on the subject of their "dear friendship," that each was the other's "dearest friend," about which each expressed true happiness, despite an air of wistfulness that pervaded the space about them each time the topic arose, both sensing that things remained left unsaid, as so, even in their immaturity, they also sensed they should be. Ironically, though, little mention seemed to have ever been made of the fact that, by the following spring, the girl would have been married in a proxy wedding to the dauphin, and thus virtually immediately to depart Vienna as the dauphine of France.

Rather, she frequently said to Hugh, "We shall always be the dearest of friends, of this I am certain," whilst lying, waiting for sleep to come, she had begun to think almost every night, *Would that it were possible, is it possible? . . . to become dauphine, and then queen, as I must . . . but to retain Hugh O'Connell as my closest, dearest friend?*

Hugh had already begun to seriously reflect upon joining Daniel and General Dillon in Paris, though more frequently thinking, *Were I to do so, I shall be there . . . even as she arrives in France!*

Of their thoughts, neither spoke to anyone—including each other.

"Ah, do not I wish I could know of what they speak so intently, at such length . . . There is a sense of unreality about it all—about *them*," Eileen said softly, almost reluctantly to O'Leary, just home from a lengthy stay in Styria, as they lay abed late one night as summer moved slowly towards autumn. "Daily now it seems I see them together; they are become dear young friends," she said, suddenly sitting up, her loose hair, which she thought she had tied back after putting Conor in his cradle, now tumbling over her shoulders, her bare breasts, "and I must confess to you alone, my beloved, when I dare to watch them carefully, to look at their eyes, study their subtle gestures . . . I fear they could be becoming, indeed may already have become, *more* than dear young friends. Yet they *cannot* be. . . ." She sighed, her husky voice quivering slightly in the near black stillness of the room.

O'Leary raised himself wearily up on the pillows. "No," he said, matter-of-factly, "'tis true that they cannot be; 'tis to devastating heartbreak either or both would then be headed." He then sat up, leaning against Eileen. "But is it ye, my darling, who shall dare tell your little archduchess as months pass quickly in this place?"

"Perhaps, sir, yes . . . but would it then be *ye* who would similarly speak to our little boy?"

They then lay back wordlessly and were shortly asleep, though, immediately upon awakening to Conor's early morning sounds, Eileen's mind began to whirl. *If . . . how . . . what can I possibly say . . . or do . . . and when?*

As had been frequently the case over the years at Derrynane, whilst others reflected and considered a topic or a concern, it was Abigail who took it upon herself to address it. It was the same in this instance, *this* topic, *this* concern about the handsome young couple, as she did one just slightly chilly September night, first knocking on the door of the comfortable bedroom Hugh occupied in their sumptuous apartments at Schönbrunn.

Hugh stretched out in his large, high bed, several military texts open, though, as Abby sensed, he appeared to be faraway, deep in thought.

As his older sister closed the door, and he noticed that though she was wrapped in a long, elegant dressing gown, her thick hair was loose on her shoulders and that indeed, she was barefoot, Hugh smiled; he had grown so used to seeing her fully immersed in and elegantly gowned and coiffed for the rarefied atmosphere in which she now lived and worked, to the extent that he had taken notice that a number of the servants actually would bow or curtsey to *her*, it was refreshing to see her as she was tonight.

"Why, dearest sister, in my months here yet have I to see you thus." He gestured. "'Tis almost as were we in your rooms or mine at Derrynane. The sight is a welcome one!"

As she had frequently done at Derrynane, Abby clambered up onto the bed and sat at the foot, leaning back against one of the bed's high posts. "I admit, so terribly formal have we been, so terribly busy have we been—because of both, so glad it is I am that your time with us continues."

Their conversation ranged from the physical settings and layout of the three palaces and the reasons for movements amongst them, Hugh's questions and comments about the many people he continued to meet, and Abby's about his decision making in terms of soldiering and his activities. "You are happy, my love, yes?" she asked, and he nodded, *very much so.*

Abby wandered verbally just a bit longer, finally very softly saying, "I cannot help but take notice that you seem to very much enjoy the company of a special friend, yes?"

Hugh's face immediately blazed scarlet, and Abby reached over and squeezed his leg just above the knee as hard as she could, and he jumped and said, "Yeow, girl!" and they both laughed.

"I apologise if I have misspoken; it is just that I observe much, I learn much from many people; this as a result of the unusual position I hold, yes?"

The boy nodded but said nothing further.

Abby sighed. "My darling boy, you must understand that very little occurs in these palaces that is not known by many more people than I, that does not become a topic of conversation. . . ." She waited for him to speak but he did not, though he did nod.

"I want to make certain you understood these facts . . . and understand that . . ."

"Abby, the archduchess and I *are* become friends," Hugh interjected almost sharply. "I do not particularly care who knows that, observes that. Never before have I had such a . . ."

Abigail interjected softly, "I know, my darling, and I assure you my concern is well beyond palace chatter, for 'tis my fear that you have become more than friends, perhaps more even than *very dear friends.*" Her right hand hovered about her heart. "Do you understand?"

Hugh's face remained scarlet. "It is *friends* we are, Abigail, *friends!*" he said, his tone firm, the message certain—or at least so they sounded.

"But, darling, you must ask yourself . . . and, when you do—as, I say again, you *must,* answer yourself wholly in truth . . . is it that as a friend only how you feel for the archduchess . . . or could it be more? What you must remember and understand is that in mere months she shall be wed, and will thus, at that moment, *here,* become dauphine of France, to then be gone from here forever . . . for the remainder of her life, most of which she will spend as the queen of France!"

Hugh's heart was racing, thudding so hard beneath his nightshirt and dressing gown that he was certain Abby could see it. "But, sister, never have I . . ." he began almost shrilly, paused and then continued, his tone softer, more even. "I understand the course of her future life . . . I assure you, I do . . . truly," he said as firmly as he could, nodding for effect.

Abby sighed in obvious relief. "You do then, *yes!*" she declared resolutely, as if by simply doing so she had made it fact, and the basis for her relief. "*Of course* you do!" She knelt up, kissing her brother gently on the cheek, slid off the bed and scurried back to her own suite, clambering up to the massive though this night empty bed she and O'Sullivan shared, as the major had been called to Vienna, her final thought of this day being a very simple one: *Please God he does!*

Hugh O'Connell slept very little that night, several times relighting his bedside candles, his intent being to lose himself in one of General O'Connell's military texts, but each time he found himself gazing into the near darkness, and each time the beguilingly smiling, laughing face of his dear good friend appeared, and so vivid was it that he could practically hear her soft, German-accented French, almost see his reflection in the clear sparkle of her eyes.

After a long discussion with O'Leary, though without speaking to Abigail, some days later Eileen had undertaken a substantially similar, equally uncomfortable conversation with the archduchess, whilst Hugh was again spending several days with the general and the countess.

There had been much blushing, any number of uncompleted sentences and repeated protestations of *simply friendship*, and when Eileen had finished, and after she had left Madame Antoine to her French history lesson, unlike her older sister, she did not even attempt to convince herself that all was well, and so advised O'Leary upon his return from several days' patrol.

Speaking some days after Eileen's conversation with Maria Antonia, the sisters talked around the topic, ultimately acknowledging that each had discussed the situation with one of the young people, indicating roughly that each appeared to understand the realities of it all and that, whether they did or not, there was little else that could be done by the adults.

It was only when the countess von Graffenreit-O'Connell—or, as she continued to prefer to be called, Aunt Maria—arrived at Laxenburg for a brief stay whilst the general was occupied in a special late-summer multiday meeting of the empress's close circle of advisors, was the topic revisited.

Eileen had approached her first, and in an unusually clipped, precise and wholly factual manner informed the older woman of what she believed was the case. Sitting quietly by Eileen's fire, the only sounds in the room the gentle ticking of the mantel clock and—the day having turned abruptly chilly—the hiss and occasional popping of not-quite-seasoned wood in a hastily laid fire, the Austrian noblewoman nodded and occasionally bit down on her lower lip. Without waiting for Eileen to ask, she said, "I shall speak with each of them . . . or perhaps, I believe, yes, it would be better . . . with just her Imperial Highness, in as dispassionate and direct a manner as I am able. Human feelings, particularly of affection and especially by the young, they are complex, yes? This, of course, is yet further complicated by the personalities involved," she sighed, "and the life one of them is deign to lead."

When Eileen had smilingly informed Antoine that "The countess von Graffenreit-O'Connell is unexpectedly at Laxenburg and would be grateful for a few moments of Your Imperial Highness's time," the girl smiled back broadly, standing immediately.

"Is she in the palace now? I should love to see her, today even! I shall go to her!" she said, and expressed delight when Eileen offered to bring the countess to the archduchess "in a moment," and, as soon as she did so, she left the warmly elegant noblewoman and adoring girl to themselves.

They chatted informally in French—de Graffenreit noting some improvement in the young girl's command of the language—for some time, the countess gently creating a path by mentioning different topics, at one point recalling the dazzling celebration of the betrothal in August, looking forward now to "Your Imperial Highness becoming dauphine of France . . . you must view the prospect with much anticipation, yes?"

"Your Grace, I do in truth, . . . yet, also in truth, I grow sorrowful that it will involve me departing here . . . forever." She teared up, and the countess rested a palm softly on her right knee, as the girl sniffed. "And it is leaving Austria, and the people, who . . ." and tears streamed down her luminously fair cheeks.

The countess sat silently, though she remained seated across from the girl, as she wished to continue to speak facing her, which she did, removing her hand as the archduchess's tears were stanched and the girl smiled weakly.

"Departing one's home and one's family and friends; I am unable to imagine how difficult it must be," the countess admitted softly, having lived her life at the Viennese court, always being amongst her ennobled parents and numerous siblings, marrying a man whom she had loved from afar since childhood, happily discovering he had felt the same way for her. She sighed. "You are very brave, my darling archduchess, very brave indeed."

The child's expression abruptly changed to one of mild anger. "I am *not at all* brave, Your dearest Grace; the Lady Eileen has told me that it is my destiny as an archduchess of Austria to do"—she gestured with her fine hands—"*this*, this what I am doing . . . and I am doing it because it is my duty," she said firmly.

It was when the countess began to speak more particularly of "special friends" that the archduchess's expression became sadly resolute. "There is but one *special friend*," she began, "whom I cannot conceive leaving," and the girl began to cry, the countess moving to then sit alongside her, her right arm gently draped over Antoine's shoulder as the girl sobbed profoundly, the countess tenderly rocking her as her tears slowly ebbed.

"Tell me, dear child . . . I shall speak to no one, I assure you."

The archduchess turned, leaning back against the high corner of the settee, her eyes moist and wide, facing the older woman, whose delicate hands were now folded in her lap.

"I believe that; I trust you implicitly, Your Grace . . . *Aunt Maria*, as our special Irish refer to and address you." She smiled wanly. "Aunt Maria, indeed it is one of *our special Irish* for whom I care deeply, it is the thought of leaving him that tears at my heart."

The countess sat silently, her expression one of affectionate calm, permitting the girl to continue. "As *they* say, 'tis of Hugh O'Connell that I . . . oh, Aunt Maria, what am I, how am I possibly able to . . . ?" she spoke plaintively, pointedly speaking German,

The countess cleared her throat gently, as she changed her language as well. "And the young man; he is aware of this?"

The archduchess nodded. "*Ja*, he is . . . indeed, he has expressed similarly gentle feelings for me." The girl's small, fine fingers pressed her breasts, her expression now one of agony.

"And Her Imperial Majesty, she of course does not?" de Graffenreit almost whispered.

Her soft pink lips pursed, the archduchess shook her head firmly in the negative.

"Nor shall she," the countess assured her, her voice strong. Von Graffenreit sighed, closing her eyes momentarily. When she opened them, she was looking deeply into the girl's soft blue eyes, which brimmed yet again with tears. "How I wish I could remove this burden from you, my darling, how I wish I could say that 'all things are somehow possible,' yet *this* is not." Her voice grew firmer, more resolute. "As to what Lady Eileen has said, it is utter truth; you are indeed an archduchess of Austria and, as such, it is indeed your destiny to do what you will indeed do: unite the house of Hapsburg with that of the French Bourbons. There is no other way; you are betrothed to the dauphin, it is to him that you shall be wed and it is with him that you shall ascend the throne of France, and with him as king you shall rule as queen of France," she finished firmly.

The gentle adolescent looked solemnly at the older woman and wordlessly nodded slowly several times, sighing as she did, her mind whirring. *I understand; I shall do that for which I am destined . . . but Hugh O'Connell, he shall somehow . . . I know not how . . . remain in my life.* Then, her face brightening, she smiled at Aunt Maria, her familiar soft smile.

The Hofburg—Autumn 1769–Winter/Early Spring 1770

By late September, coincident with the return of the Imperial court to the Hofburg, a briskly sharp, colourful autumn having arrived, cloaks had begun being worn and the O'Sullivan and O'Leary little boys found themselves being bundled when their parents or their servants took them out.

As the warm weather faded, Hugh and the archduchess came to understand that the idyllic times they had spent in the various gardens and other relaxed settings at Schönbrunn and, even more so, of Laxenburg, and frequently on horseback at both palaces, were inevitably beginning to come to an end. As a result, they saw far less of each other as the seasons changed, and changed yet again, as what would prove to be a snowy winter descended on Vienna just as the Christmas holidays commenced.

The Imperial family—more particularly the empress and Archduchess Maria Antonia—included the O'Connell-von Graffenreits, the O'Sullivans and the O'Learys in several of their many celebrations at the Hofburg, at one of which Hugh, himself elegant in a new black velvet suit, for the first time saw the archduchess attired in full court dress, a magnificent red and gold brocade robe. As soon as his eyes settled on her, he smiled warmly from across the room, and as he approached her, gently bowing, his lips touching her extended right hand, he whisperingly confessed the sight had "rendered me virtually speechless," quickly adding, "Your Imperial Highness," which caused them both to laugh and set the mood for a pleasant evening, during which they would dance, which provided the archduchess an opportunity to introduce a blushing Hugh to the playful intricacies of the Ländler—even several times switching partners with the O'Connell girls and their magnificently uniformed husbands, many heads turning to watch the archduchess as she danced with Hugh and his brothers-in-law—and dine, talking constantly, it seemed, even as the archduchess warmly cuddled both Donál O'Sullivan and Conor O'Leary, both of whom nevertheless eventually squirmed away.

Shortly after the arrival of the new year of 1770, in the midst of a spectacular blizzard it was that Hugh requested from Eileen permission to call on the archduchess, in response to which she promptly arranged an afternoon visit, complete with coffees, teas and pastries. Pointedly leaving the door to the archduchess's sitting room open, Eileen indicated she would be in the formal audience room with Countess Lerchenfeld.

The young people greeted each other warmly and chatted pleasantly whilst Antoine played the hostess, pouring the beverages, though the carefully arranged pastry tray remained untouched.

Avoiding the topic of their special friendship and the inevitability of their April parting, they spoke of the Christmas holidays just concluded, presents received and given, of how fast Conor O'Leary was growing; in short, anything other than what was on both of their minds.

At a lull in the conversation, Hugh turned slightly so as to enable him to face the archduchess a bit more directly, smiled and took a deep breath. "So, my dear good friend," he began, "'tis news that I have, news which I wished to share with you before virtually any other."

The archduchess smiled tightly, a bit perplexed. "If it is news you have, my dear friend, please . . ." She gestured with her right hand.

Nervously clearing his throat, Hugh began again. "A decision has been made in terms of my future. Following much thought and discussion, and an even greater amount of correspondence, it has been decided that I shall join the Irish Brigade of the armies of Louis XV."

The girl's hands went to her mouth, stifling a shout, as she smiled, her eyes wide, sparkling.

After the fact, Hugh quickly added, "Dillon's Regiment," almost in a whisper. "I am told that I shall depart for Paris once some extended interruption of these seemingly constant snows is perceived." He sat back, taking a deep breath.

"So, it is in Paris that you shall be in the springtime, Monsieur O'Connell," the archduchess said almost saucily. Hugh's face reddened as he nodded affirmatively.

The atmosphere in the room became warm, hopeful.

"So, monsieur, I believe that once she is near there settled, the dauphine of France shall be summoning a certain Irish cadet from the École Militaire to Versailles . . . so he should expect such a command." She smiled.

"I shall answer the dauphine of France's summons as promptly as I am permitted to do so by my superiors," Hugh said softly, speaking for the first time to her of the reality of military life. "I fear my movements, they shall be restricted . . . at least until I achieve some measure of advancement, towards commissioning," he nodded surely, "and then . . ."

Antoine added as she nodded knowingly, ". . . and certainly when I become queen, nothing shall be impossible. *Nothing at all!*"

The conversation then grew more relaxed, continuing in a wonderfully naive, happily guileless spirit of hopefulness—and at least some unconscious measure of denial, as what neither could know was that, prior to any decision being made as to Hugh's resolutely expressed desire to join the Irish Brigade, the O'Connells had carefully explored with and had it definitively determined by General Theobold Dillon himself, that it would indeed be virtually impossible for the young people to meet.

You must appreciate, my dear friend, General Dillon had written General O'Connell, with a request that he circulate it amongst *all of your family there,* that *the court at Versailles is much less relaxed than that of Her Imperial Majesty. . . . Life here is governed by the strictest, most rigid forms of protocol. . . . In addition, I shall see to it that once your archduchess is become our dauphine and in residence at Versailles* any *correspondence she may send to your young cadet at École Militaire shall be immediately delivered to me.*

Nodding knowingly to the countess, to whom he had read it aloud as soon as he'd received it, General O'Connell observed, "This being blessedly the case, I believe to otherwise oppose the boy's aspirations would be cruel." His wife agreed, as would the O'Sullivans and O'Learys upon learning of it.

With General Dillon's firm assurances, the adults had relaxed, though Eileen had indicated, and the group concurred, that she would mention the *unusual relationship* in her next letter to Daniel Charles, despite the fact that he was in a different brigade.

As abruptly as the seemingly daily onslaught of snow and wind suddenly stopped, General O'Connell unexpectedly announced that Hugh was to depart for Paris within the week coming.

The general indicated that he himself would accompany the boy to France. "An aide de camp and not less than two orderlies are required to accompany an ennobled general of the Imperial armies of Austria on a journey such as this," he boomed in a deliberately officious manner, so unlike him that it caused Eileen, Abigail and the countess, whom he collectively had come to refer to as "the women in my life" to laugh aloud.

"And perhaps a standard bearer as well, dearest Uncle?" Eileen called out, as Conor wriggled free of her hand and raced to the general's open arms.

Both Hugh and the archduchess were stunned by the suddenness of it all, as well as by the brevity of their last meeting, which occurred late in the afternoon of the day just prior to the boy's departure.

With snowflakes lazily drifting past the high windows that faced the terrace, they sat facing each other by the fire in Eileen's apartments,

Anna necessarily, though quite diplomatically, present nearby and not obvious. Their expressions were sombre, the mood one of loss, sadness and uncertainty.

"Simply knowing that you shall be there, awaiting my arrival in France, that is enough," the shaken archduchess allowed to her very dear friend, who chose not to remind her of the realities of the situation as he understood them.

"I shall write once I am arrived at the École Militaire," he pledged.

Her soft blue eyes cloudy now, she gently held his hand, looked up and promised, "And I shall reply immediately!"

Hugh, bowing deeply, his lips barely grazing her small hand, then took his leave as reluctantly as she granted it, their eyes moist, their hearts sad.

Neither young person slept well during the cold, eerily still, snowless night that followed. For the first time in several years, Maria Antonia cuddled a treasured large, softly stuffed doll with long black yarn hair she had fittingly named Eileen, as she tried to sleep, her tears dampening the doll's sewn-on smile.

The following morning, the archduchess stood alone at a distant window in a room in which she had never before been but to which she had asked Countess Lerchenfeld—who, though she had not been well of late, had recently returned to the household—to find for her, it being a location from which she might observe her very dear friend's departure—in what was a just-begun light, powdery snowfall.

The gently moving and, to her, silent tableau featured all her special Irish, about whom she suddenly felt, *they actually are my family!* An atypically solitary Eileen, unmistakable in her dramatic red winter cloak, her hair streaming down her back, now flecked with the large, fluffy snowflakes that drifted past the young girl's solitary windowpane; the little cousins, Conor and Donál, frolicking, chasing the snow and each other, as Anna chased them both, her golden tresses vivid against her own long black cloak; the younger officers, O'Sullivan and O'Leary, resplendent in their brilliant gold braid-faced red uniform coats and high boots, their ofttimes decorative pelisses today actually being worn as the fur-trimmed coats they were. They appeared to be in deep conversation with a grey-cloaked Hugh, his head moving slightly from side to side as they spoke, O'Sullivan gesturing with a gauntleted left hand, O'Leary with both hands, his ungloved. Abigail O'Sullivan, dazzling in a new heavy black wool, fox-trimmed cloak, the garment made magnificent by its simplicity, joined the threesome; as she took his hand, O'Sullivan's attention turned to her. Antoine could not tell if they were sad as they stood still, speaking just between themselves.

Suddenly what she knew to be a heavy door was flung open and, Countess von Graffenreit on her husband's arm, her deep royal blue cloak stark against the falling snowflakes, the general burst forth, instantly dominating the scene, striding to the group, his dark blue cloak billowing, the dismounted soldiers all snapping to attention. The huge man enveloped his much smaller wife in a long embrace, a slow kiss; then, quickly kissing his nieces, bowing to Anna, he solidly clapped his right hand on Hugh's shoulder and gestured to him, as if to say, *Mount up, lad, 'tis time.* As the tall boy did so, the general shook hands with and returned the younger officers' salutes.

As soon as General O'Connell swung himself up onto Conqueror, his white charger's broad back, the procession formed and, yet again stunned at its suddenness and overwhelmed by an immediate sense of loss, the archduchess sobbed as she watched Hugh, in the company of the general's small but impressive contingent—which did include a standard bearer, albeit in the person of one of the orderlies—depart, now regretting she was not there below, with and amongst her *family*.

That evening she invited Eileen, O'Leary and little Conor to dine with her in her apartment. The adults could not help but notice how quiet and withdrawn the archduchess was; even when Conor clambered onto her lap, she simply held him, rocking gently and kissing his soft dark blond hair. She barely touched her food, though she insisted her guests eat and fed Conor his dinner as he perched on her lap.

Eileen returned alone when it was time for the archduchess to retire, and it was then that the young girl dissolved into bitter, heaving weeping. So profound was her grief that Eileen could barely understand what she was saying through her sobbing; all she could do was hold the young girl, rocking her gently, until finally her tears slowed and then ultimately stopped, her eyes red and swollen, an expression of utter desolation on her usually luminous face.

Eileen began to speak, and Antoine gently placed her forefinger on the woman's lips, tears again welling in her eyes. "Nothing you could say, my darling Mama, *nothing* could alter the sense of tragic loss I feel. . . ." Eileen nodded, and they completed their evening routine in an eerie near silence. Once alone in bed, weeping softly, the archduchess finally drifted off to sleep, her arms again wrapped around her large rag doll, Eileen.

As the days followed, Eileen experienced a sense of what she told O'Leary was profound change. "I believe things here are already altered, overwhelmingly so . . . never to be the same again, my darling." O'Leary did not disagree.

It seemed indeed with Hugh's leave-taking that the pace of the winter quickened, inexorably passing into what all felt would be a hopeful, lengthy spring, the minds of many at the Hofburg appearing now to be focused primarily on mid-April, the time set for the archduchess's proxy wedding and for her, as Madame la Dauphine, Marie Antoinette, to depart for France.

At the same time, both Eileen and O'Leary were completing their own reflections on what would be next. As early as the beginning of their whirlwind courtship, Eileen had spoken of feeling that when Maria Antonia departed Vienna, so should she; they now frequently revisited the topic, the possibility, the alternatives. O'Leary enjoyed military life, though he, too, had begun to consider ultimately returning to West Cork.

Eileen had ultimately concluded and felt strongly that her "wee Antoinette" was the primary, if not the sole reason for her being in Vienna. "I cannot conceive of serving in another position," she finally admitted to her husband, who indicated that he would respect whatever she decided.

Nevertheless, Eileen, whilst—for a time—keeping quiet from Abigail, the countess and the general what had come to be her final decision—that she would indeed leave Vienna when the dauphine departed for France—judiciously began to seek the opinions of several of her contemporaries and her superiors, though it was with Anna that she had spoken most openly.

"We have been together since my first weeks here." Eileen had smiled to the younger woman as they together strolled with Conor on a warmish, almost humid afternoon in late February. As they did regularly now, Anna's English having become superb, they conversed in that tongue.

"Indeed, we have, m'lady." Anna had smiled back. "We have grown up together, have we not?" she continued, her gleaming blue eyes brimming with tears, which fell as Eileen wrapped her arm around the shorter woman's black-cloaked shoulder.

"We *have* grown up, yes, my darling, that indeed we have, from girls to women . . . which is why I am speaking to you thus, as I feel you are become closer to me even than is my beloved sister."

They then grew quiet, their boots thudding softly on the grainy, mostly wet paving stones, as Anna continued to try to prevent Conor from jumping into the numerous puddles of melted snow and ice, crunchy with the grit, rough sand and dirt spread for traction at the height of the harsh winter now ending.

Stopping, Anna gazed up at Eileen with a questioning expression on her smooth, healthy face.

"That is the reality, to be sure," Eileen responded to the girl's unspoken question. "Love Abby dearly I do, but she is the primary lady-in-waiting to her Imperial Majesty the empress, and I am her younger sister, who is also her inferior; we both knew that some distance between us would be inevitable. Additionally, from our first years here I came to believe that 'twas Abigail's life that was meant to be spent here, not my own." She resumed walking.

Anna's eyes grew wide then, as she stopped and looked up at her mistress, her friend. "So, is it that you contemplate departing Vienna, mistress?" she asked very softly, her voice wispy, uncertain and sad.

As they both decided to allow Conor to splash in a barely there puddle, the women turned to face each other, and Eileen took Anna's smaller, more delicate hands in her own. "I am, my darling, and I have for some time been . . . The captain and . . . he and I . . . we both felt that, prior to the time when this shall occur, I would not do so without requesting that you join me on what would be the next phase of my own life . . . which I believe could prove to be as great an adventure for you as my coming here has been for me. I believe this is the time then, for me to . . ."

". . . and I would be most honoured and so very grateful to be able to join you, mistress," Anna said without a moment's hesitation, her eyes wide with hopeful excitement. The women laughed and cried and embraced as a wondering Conor gazed up at them. Then they all went inside.

This conversation had led to a number of others between the women: Anna had expanded upon many of the facts Eileen had learned over the years about the striking golden-blond girl: She came from a large—an even dozen surviving children—peasant family, living in a tiny hamlet near Laxenburg. Her parents were, as Eileen had correctly surmised, distant and weary people, fatigued from many children and a life of struggles. They had been relieved when a relative who was a member of the small staff in permanent full-time service at Laxenburg made it possible for Anna to obtain a very minor—as directed, she was to clean floors, dust furniture and maintain certain, largely decorative fires—position at the Hofburg, from which, primarily because she found her to be both bright and quite beautiful, the minutely observant countess von Graffenreit had plucked her upon Eileen's arrival there in the fall of 1761.

During the nine years that had followed, Anna had grown from a shy, at times awkward country girl of twelve into a poised young woman of almost twenty-one; she had become fully literate and was fluent now in German, French and, more recently, English. She clearly adored Eileen, the feeling being fully returned by the older woman.

"I could not conceive a day without you, my darling," Eileen had said.

". . . and I without you, m'lady," Anna responded.

Her eyes grew wide and wonder-filled when Eileen proceeded to tell her, "Should you at some point meet a young man—say one with a good farm in Cork—I would never . . . indeed I would be most pleased were you to . . . shall we say, become a neighbour. My hope, of course, would be that you would also remain my dear friend," she added, her eyes twinkling mischievously.

From that moment, Eileen felt that Anna Pfeffer stood a bit straighter, held her golden-locked head a bit higher—as well she did, for Eileen had provided an opportunity for a life Anna could only have dreamt of whilst in service at the Hofburg.

O'Leary, too, had grown fond of the pretty girl, having, as a result of their rambling conversations, come to believe she was extremely bright and felt very comfortable with their entrusting Conor to her, so he embraced them both when he returned one evening to learn that Anna would indeed accompany the family to Ireland.

Eileen had informed him of the fact that she'd advised Anna that she would not be expected to remain permanently in service at Rathleigh, and he heartily approved of that as well, playfully telling the girl, "I believe you shall like Cork, and Ireland . . . and 'tis my firm belief that you shall soon find yourself there become 'Mistress Anna,' the 'Lady Anna,' your new name begun with an *O* or a *Mac* almost for certain," to which prospect the usually loquacious girl had no response but a wide-eyed, open-mouthed half curtsey and a speedy exit.

In the world shared by the archduchess and Eileen, aside from beginning in a blizzard and ending in something that felt like an early spring, February was marked by a series of radically different events.

On 3 February, a messenger had delivered a thick envelope, which Anna then placed on a small silver tray, set on a shelf just inside the door of Eileen's apartments, though not before she noted with a broad smile the words École Militaire, Paris, and, looking closer, the to her now-familiar O'Connell stag, its movements frozen in heavy plain, uncoloured wax.

When her mistress next returned in mid-afternoon, Anna immediately handed it to her. Given its heft, Eileen anticipated a lengthy, news-filled letter from her youngest brother; instead she received one of two pages, briskly summarising Hugh's trip to Paris and first weeks at the French king's military academy. She quickly noted that the letter was itself wrapped around a thick envelope, also sealed but addressed, in a much more careful, strikingly precise version of Hugh's customary sprawling hand, to, "H.I.H., The Archduchess Maria Antonia of Austria and Lorraine." Rolling her eyes, she showed it to Anna, who smiled sweetly and then made a noncommittal face as she took the envelope to the archduchess.

Eileen did not inquire and the archduchess did not volunteer the substance or indeed any particulars of the communication from Hugh, though some time later a young man now briefly in Vienna, a member of the staff of the Count de Mercy-Argenteau, the Austrian ambassador to the French court, sought her out, making her aware that a similarly thick envelope, addressed in the still cryptic, not terribly attractive hand of the archduchess had been brought to him for forwarding to France, addressed to "Monsieur Cadet Hugh O'Connell, Brigade Irlandaise, Régiment de Dillon, École Militaire, Paris." Eileen nodded her thanks.

Contrary to General Dillon's expectations, the archduchess's letter was delivered directly to Cadet O'Connell. Despite that Eileen never pressed the issue with her, had the correspondence been read—as, despite that it passed from Versailles to Vienna only by Count Mercy's secure couriers—it surely had been, though most likely by only the count himself—by other than the intended recipients, little untoward or shocking would have been disclosed: Both Hugh and Antoine were generally circumspect in expressing themselves, mutual protestations of the other "remaining always in my thoughts, my heart" and longing "for the moment we are reunited in France, never again to be separated" being perhaps the strongest indication of the shared feelings of two very young people, both on the verge of entering a world neither could fully understand.

Mere days after Hugh's letter had arrived at court, on 6 February, though she had been ill only a few weeks, the Countess Lerchenfeld died and was immediately replaced by Countess Trautmannsdorf, a warm, effusive woman in marked contrast to her predecessor, a crisp, precise individual, though generally viewed as being coldly efficient, thought by the archduchess to be heartless.

Since her return from Ireland, Eileen had maintained a generally pleasant relationship with the now-deceased noblewoman, primarily because the countess had largely left Eileen and the archduchess to their own devices, save when strict protocol required that it be otherwise. Eileen was thus not emotionally affected by her passing. She quickly found her new superior to be an altogether indeed quite charming woman, as she advised Abigail, deeming her perfect for the short-term assignment as head of the soon-to-depart archduchess's household. The archduchess pronounced herself quite pleased, expressing little more than perfunctory, as required, regrets at the deceased woman's passing.

One chilly morning in early March, whilst the archduchess was studying with Abbé Vermond, a quiet-eyed, very young page gently, almost tentatively approached Eileen as she was returning to her apartment for a midmorning visit with Conor. "My Lady Eileen," the boy said softly, virtually whispering in genteel French, "I am come to you from Her Imperial Majesty, Madame." Handing her a small, rigidly elegant envelope, he bowed and wordlessly withdrew.

As she removed the stiff notecard within, Eileen was surprised to see the message, written in the empress's distinctively regal hand:

As soon as you are able, please come to me.

Eileen slipped the unsigned, quite unusual missive into her pocket, stopped momentarily at home, leaving Anna to read to Conor, and quickly headed downstairs, reverting to her Derrynane stride in a successful effort to cover the massive breadth of the palace as quickly as possible.

Maria Theresa greeted her warmly, asking after Conor, inquiring as to O'Leary's location in the field, but, once both women were seated, she proceeded to quickly— indeed so quickly it shocked Eileen—and immediately inquire as to her plans ". . . once the dauphine, Marie Antoinette, leaves us."

Though clearly evidencing surprise at the monarch's directness, nonetheless prepared, as she had been for some time, with her response, Eileen looked fondly at her sovereign and began softly, "Your Imperial Majesty, if I might speak freely . . . please?"

The empress smiled warmly. "Certainly, my darling . . . I have typically learnt much when you speak freely."

Eileen sighed, took a deliberate breath and began, her husky voice very precise, 'I believe, Your Imperial Majesty, that once the dauphine is on her way to France, I, too, should most properly be on my own way . . . to Ireland."

Her eyes unexpectedly growing moist, she looked at the empress, who said in an equally gentle, maternal voice, "You realise that were you to remain with us you could, in all fairness, perform such activities and possess virtually whatever it may be that you would desire, yes?"

Her mouth partially open, Eileen sat silently as the empress continued. "Your service here has been invaluable, Eileen, your fine husband already a truly gallant Irish warrior, possessed, we believe— indeed we are told by his superiors and *their* superiors as well—of the makings of a great officer. Were you and he to aspire to titles, rights, privileges, lands . . . whatever would be in our power, we should gladly, unquestioningly bestow on you both, virtually anything you would ask of us."

Eileen audibly gasped, her eyes now wide, her lips fully parted; as she began to speak, her words came at first very slowly. "Your Imperial Majesty, you may recall that once . . . and indeed it seems now a very long time ago . . . I was mistress of a grand house, a great estate in Ireland, and it is in a similar role . . . though of a less grand house, a smaller estate," she smiled, "that I wish to live the rest of my life.

"I could be no more grateful for Your Imperial Majesty's boundless generosity   . . . but the greatest treasure you could ever bestow on me would be your blessing, when it is finally time, to depart Vienna and become the mistress of Rathleigh House in County Cork."

She smiled warmly again, though this time through her tears, which became profound sobbing as the empress rose to embrace her, saying softly above the weeping, "Indeed. We bless you now as we shall then . . . and always thereafter."

After Eileen had withdrawn, the empress sat quietly, her fire gently crackling and popping, the windows and their heavy draperies open, despite the day's chill, the fabric gently rustling in a steady breeze. *What an extraordinary place it must be, this Ireland from whence they come! Would that I could grasp, could understand the power of the call so many of them feel for it.* Gently shaking her head, she returned to the papers on her desk and the matters they brought before her.

Some days later, Eileen had joined Abby before a gentle fire in her sitting room, O'Sullivan in the field and Donál O'Sullivan sound asleep. The sisters had not spoken at length for some weeks, and Abby had seen to an ample decanter of brandy and two Irish cut-glass snifters.

After sitting quietly for a time, cupping it with both hands, resting her heavy glass on her knee, her eyes looking deeply into the fire, Eileen looked equally expressively at her beloved elder sister.

"I have spoken recently, as I am sure you are aware"—she smiled knowingly—"with Her Imperial Majesty. . . ."

Sighing, her expression serious, almost grave, Abby responded. "I understand the substance of your conversation with the empress. That said, I fear you may well find daily life in Ireland dramatically different from that to which you have grown accustomed here these last eight, almost nine years, my darling," she cautioned.

"I know not of the position of the O'Learys in Cork, but, with respect, I doubt their home provides the powerful sanctuary that Derrynane does for the O'Connells." She did not wait for Eileen to respond. "The questions you must ask of yourself are to me clear, and the answers at which you arrive must be wholly honest:

"Are you prepared to be again subject to the *Sassenach*? Will you be able to accept the fact that, once again and seemingly forever, inferior you shall be to the very type of men who pursued you and Arthur out of Kerry?"

Eileen sat quietly, thoughtfully, for a seemingly long time. "I have considered this, yes, and I continue to do so. . . . Should we ever be required to take steps to protect ourselves, as we did then, yet again I am and we are both fully prepared to do so. I have no fear of those people . . . only utter disdain for them and all they represent. . . ."

A genuinely pained expression on her gentle face, Abby leaned towards her sister. "*That* is my fear, my darling, your *utter disdain for them and all they represent*. . . . Not to mention Arthur's attitude, which, more than disdain I feel is more accurately loathing, hatred even. This could lead to your living in some form of a state of war, could it not?"

Eileen did not respond directly beyond a soft, "It could perhaps, yes," spoken into the room, but after a long, deep silence, she continued. "But, my own darling, Ireland is *home*, is it not? I have loved—and shall treasure—virtually every moment spent here in this quite singular place . . . but the call of the southwestern corner of Ireland, 'tis so strong to me, to Arthur as well—though I expect he shall continue to return here for extended periods."

"Are you not perhaps being overly romantic, dearest sister?" Abby inquired softly. "Is it truly the 'call of the southwestern corner of Ireland' that you are hearing, or is it rather the emotional tug, perhaps even the voices of Maeve and Cúchulainn, of Fionn and all the Fianna, perhaps Bran's barking even"—she smiled—". . . of the many wonderful people who populate your beloved legends and treasured tales? I caution you, darling, the 'minions of the English king,' as you yourself have long referred to them, and the system they represent, both remain strongly in entrenched in Ireland. . . . I believe it shall not change in our lifetimes, perhaps not even in the lifetimes of our little boys."

Eileen's expression turned both distant and determined. "This I understand, yes, but you must know, my darling, that I told Arthur not long after we had first met that I have always felt that 'twas your life the one destined to be spent here . . . not mine."

Abigail grew sombre, for she understood what Eileen felt, and of what she was now speaking,

"The person who has been virtually the sole reason for my entire life here is to wed. As is that of my beloved 'wee little archduchess,' my time here is nearly at an end," she sobbed, and Abby rushed to embrace her, as Eileen's broad shoulders, her very bosom shuddered . . . and they continued to speak long into the night, of many topics but no more of Eileen's decision, which that night became irrevocable.

As April grew closer yet, O'Leary found himself engaged in what developed into a series of similar conversations with General O'Connell, who was strongly, unalterably, opposed to their decision.

"You propose to return to a place you refer to as 'home,' yet it is a place that nevertheless denies you the very things you have achieved here, as it remains a place where you shall have few if any rights, indeed where it at least technically remains illegal to even practise our Holy Faith. . . . I believe that, as was I and your father, as were you as well—your little boy, too—will have to be sent to Catholic Europe for his schooling," he said, his fists clenched, "Assuring that the Irish people remain illiterate, landless and impoverished is the only chance the English have of retaining the illegitimate position they have in Ireland.

"I ask you, sir, if it is indeed Eileen's wish, her desire . . . how are you, as an officer, as a husband and father . . . to accede to this, how is it possible that—" He stopped, noticing O'Leary's wholly respectful silent smile, and the older man nodded sombrely and then smiled as well, sighing. "Ah, lad, *Eileen's wish, her desire* . . . I understand, my dear man, I do. I do not agree, but I *do* understand." The general smiled ironically. and the veil of tension over the men ever so slightly lifted.

After they finished their brandies, just before he rose to take his leave of the general, O'Leary's expression grew serious, thoughtful. "Your Grace," he began, his choice of address purposeful, "should the situation in Cork prove to be as you suggest—and I agree that there is every reason to anticipate it may well indeed—I assure and commit to you that I shall unhesitatingly return Eileen and our child or children to the safety of this place."

Minimally satisfied, the general bid the younger officer the time of day and they shook hands. When General O'Connell spoke of their conversation to the countess, she became incredulous, her soft grey eyes wide, then angry, something she rarely ever was; finally, she wept.

Each of March's windy days seemed to pass more rapidly than the day prior. The time between Eileen's announcement of her decision and the scheduled departure of the soon-to-be dauphine was approximately six weeks, and it seemed to all concerned to, in many ways, be an *untidy* period.

Whether it involved Eileen and Abby or the archduchess, or her siblings and other members of the household, carefully planned visits or even walks failed to occur or were brief, almost abrupt; conversations thought to be necessary prior to any departure became less so, and, in some instances, though not amongst the O'Connells, then not at all. The atmosphere became daily more electric: with tension and stress as well as excitement.

Amongst Eileen's more bittersweet experiences during this period of farewell was a Sunday she, Arthur and Conor spent with the general and the countess at their castle. She had seen little of the couple since

General O'Connell's return from Paris, though she and her uncle had exchanged frequent chatty notes with highly personal observations concerning events and the people around them, including, of course, the archduchess and Cadet Hugh O'Connell.

Despite the fact that one of the purposes of the visit was to permit them all a private, extended farewell, rarely had the older couple seemed happier, the countess's demeanour reminding Art of her giddiness at the time of Hugh's arrival and introduction to the empress.

Whilst Conor played on the floor with an array of toy soldiers the general had collected for years and with which he had always permitted any children who visited to play, both he and the countess began to speak at once.

"I am . . ." she began.

"My darling is . . ." he began.

". . . *expecting*," both cried out—and the room erupted with joyous laughter, whilst little Conor looked up in puzzlement. The youthful-looking but nevertheless middle-aged countess, already twice a grandmother, was indeed with child, some four months into her uneventful pregnancy, and the general was beside himself with pride and love.

As the days progressed, Eileen's wardrobe and belongings, including virtually all of the furnishings of her apartment at the Hofburg and most from her quarters at both Schönbrunn and Laxenburg, including the artwork and carpets, all being gifts from the empress, as well as her entire extensive wardrobe, were carefully crated for shipment to Ireland; clothing necessary for the time remaining in Vienna as well as the journey to France being carefully set aside, along with the much simpler clothes in which she would journey to Ireland, much of the time on Bull's back.

O'Leary's possessions were eventually removed to officers' quarters in the regimental barracks; he would journey to France and on to Ireland in uniform. As it was expected that he would for a time return, only selected items belonging to him would be shipped to Ireland now.

Anna's far fewer possessions were packed carefully with Eileen's; General O'Connell saw to it that she would have a fine, sturdy animal for the journey to Cork. Though the younger woman remained sensitive to her mistress's swirling, conflicting feelings during these days, her own were largely focused on having the freedom to lead a wholly new life. She had spent a dreary day in late March in her little village near Laxenburg, at the conclusion of which she bid a warm but largely unemotional farewell to her parents and those of her siblings present and, as she left, though she realised and acknowledged that she would never see any of them again, her primary thoughts were solely of Ireland and the possibility—a very real one, according to the O'Learys—that it was there she would meet and wed a young farmer and become mistress of her own small Irish estate.

Acting on her own, the empress had personally seen to it that Eileen, O'Leary and Anna would formally accompany the soon-to-be Marie Antoinette on her journey to France; Count Höeninger had himself given O'Leary command of a detachment of Hungarian Hussars, advising the empress that "the lad is as impressive on the parade ground as he is in the field; he possesses a sense of drama, understands the effect that beautifully uniformed, superbly well-led troops has on people. He will represent the empire well on this journey."

Wholly disregarding, indeed, uncaring, about the reaction she was fully aware the gesture would spark—"She is a mere servant!" one incredulous courtier would exclaim, whilst another correctly observed that her very presence would violate all protocol—the empress's handwritten directive, personally delivered to him by the Lady Abigail herself, to Count Khevenhüller-Metsch, the high chamberlain, provided in no uncertain terms that "the strictures of court practices, protocol and precedent notwithstanding, you shall please make all such efforts as may be necessary to assure that the dauphine shall make this journey in the company of the Lady Eileen O'Leary." The count immediately requested Abby to advise the empress that he knew precisely what to do.

When she returned to the empress, a relieved Abby smilingly advised the monarch, "It shall be done!"

In the meantime, Anna was simply informed she was to be a travelling maid, though her sole duty appeared to be to care for Conor O'Leary; she was also told that she would receive garments suitable for making the journey.

As the day of her leave-taking grew closer, Eileen grew more reflective, wistful—sad even—until she reminded herself that "my little archduchess shall no longer be here," and thought of Rathleigh House, of returning to live in Ireland—so thus it was that often she wept, then smiled and wept again.

Ironically, as April began and quickly progressed, she saw less and less of the archduchess, the empress having seemingly taken possession of her, even to having the young girl sleep in her bedroom, about which Antoine had observed to Eileen, as the governess packed her trunks with personal items for the great journey, "I enjoyed it so! . . . though never have we done this previously. It is sad that she had waited until now, to do . . ."

Though they had had several extended visits and a number of quiet walks, many of them abbreviated, as it was, Eileen took her leave of Abigail amidst the organised chaos of the proxy wedding, which both attended with their spouses, and the formal departure of the now dauphine of France the following day. *We know and are secure with and in each other's feelings, though there is an inevitable sadness in parting; our bonds are strong, unbreakable,* Eileen had written in a note left for her sister to read after her departure.

In Vienna, Saturday, 21 April 1770, dawned overcast, with a sharp, spring-like chill, one that remained until well after the Austrian cavalcade's departure. Dominating the seemingly vast open space in front of the public side, as opposed to the gardens and inner courtyards of the Hofburg was an array of not quite five dozen carriages and coaches of varying size and appearance, arranged in a striking serpentine pattern.

Around the periphery had formed a colourful crowd of lesser courtiers, townspeople, servants, the extremely interested as well as the merely curious. At one of the principal entrances to the immense palace, the imperial family had already begun to assemble in advance of the dauphine's anticipated nine o'clock departure.

Unnoticed by all but a few on that dazzling, chaotic and in many ways poignant morning, walking slowly, almost awkwardly towards Abigail, who, standing with O'Sullivan, herself was required to join the empress for the dauphine's formal farewell to her mother, her family, was Eileen, magnificent in a royal blue robe, a matching, flowing travelling cloak. She appeared ashen, numb, holding tightly to Anna's hand, the younger woman obviously in her own state of awe at the day, not to mention the splendid medium-blue gown she wore, one of three she had been given for the journey; her own black mantle draped over her shoulders, her golden locks dramatically flowing over her shoulders, her appearance attracting a degree of attention of which she was blithely unaware, being somewhat distracted by the need to retain a firm hold on the permanently squiggling Conor O'Leary.

Once she had watched Eileen and Anna embrace, and after Eileen had lifted her son one last time, Abigail herself bid adieu to Anna and her nephew as they were directed to the now distant carriage in which they would travel. Haltingly, the elder sister then attempted, her usually even voice trembling, to speak. "So much more to say I feel there is," she endeavoured, even as the doors of each carriage in the massive cavalcade beckoned. "I cannot now believe . . ." and she dissolved utterly in tears, her magnificent robe splotched, spotting.

Eileen felt herself struck dumb, her heart was so full, yet no words would come. Likewise, she could form no words of farewell for her brother-in-law, for whom she had come to care deeply, with whom she finally exchanged slow, wordless nods.

A number of courtiers now watched in respectful silence, suddenly sombre, as Eileen and Abigail stood now in a long, largely wordless embrace, both in tears, gently rocking, murmuring promises of letters and travel.

As a young officer gently escorted Abigail, tightly linked to her husband's arm, away— "I am, I fear, compelled to escort you now to the empress, madame, please. . . ."—the sisters' hands gripping tightly, then just fingertips touching, then not at all, her eyes on her sister, who though on the arm of her handsome husband nevertheless walked gazing back at her.

Eileen, on the other hand, experienced the sensation for an extended moment of being utterly alone, this being mirrored in her expression of loss, agony and, inexplicably, given the wholly familiar surroundings, she also was gripped by at least some degree of actual fear. She felt as if she were standing on a precipice, and indeed she had no idea what she was to do: Told only to await an escort, having seen her friend, her servant and her child depart, her husband being nowhere in sight, somewhere with his small troop of cavalry; her beloved sister having, she thought, *just been taken from me*, her cloudy eyes darted about the eddying mass of courtiers, servants, well-wishers, anxious for a hand, a face, some direction.

After several long moments, from behind her right shoulder, "My lady," purred a polished German voice in soft English; turning, she gasped, "Wolfgang!" as she found herself unexpectedly facing—for they were of the same height—the magnificently uniformed, recently promoted now-Colonel Wolfgang von Klaus, her lover some years before, still her regular correspondent, but today, in this moment, she strongly believed him to be her emotional rescuer. She smiled gratefully, touching his right arm gently, as he bowed to her.

Shocked, rendered virtually speechless, all she could manage was a stammering, "When did you . . . ? When last you wrote you were to remain indefinitely in St. Petersburg, and now . . ."

Taking her smooth hand in his own much larger one, von Klaus gazed with a degree of wonder on his friend, whom he had not seen for more than three years, finally being able to advise, in his only slightly German-accented English, "I am just yesterday arrived from Russia. I was recalled by the emperor with the same abruptness that I was there dispatched by him! I travelled with the greatest alacrity—especially as I learnt of your impending departure with the archduchess."

Eileen whispered, "I am so very glad that you are here, especially . . ." and she gestured at the chaotic pageantry in the midst of which they stood.

"You have not been forgotten; I am sent by the emperor himself at just this moment to tell you," von Klaus then said crisply, offering her his arm. "We have not far to go," he assured her, his grey eyes soft, deep.

As indeed they did not, for in less than five minutes he stopped and turned them next to the magnificent first carriage in line, appearing as a wheeled jewel box, which would carry the dauphine to France. Eileen's eyes, though now returned to their sharp blue, at once widened as a bewigged footman, his eyes lowered respectfully, extended a rigid right arm, whilst with the other he effortlessly opened the as-yet-unoccupied carriage's right-side door.

At that moment, "My lady," the handsome colonel said, indicating that she should step up into the coach, "my dearest friend, Eileen, Godspeed to you and your girl"—he smiled—". . . a safe journey to you both . . . and a long and happy life to you in your beautiful green homeland . . . which I believe I shall yet see . . . and to your most fortunate spouse, indeed I have already bid the good captain adieu . . . and, your handsome son, *ja*?" Eileen's expression was questioning. "Ah, and yes, I also located pretty little Anna, who introduced me to Master Conor." He smiled broadly.

He then nodded warmly, genuinely, as he handed a visibly shaken, very grateful Eileen into the striking coach, softly kissing her hand as she sat very tentatively in the centre of the front-facing seat.

The officer bowed yet again, the door closed and he was gone; Eileen remained seated gingerly on the edge of the sumptuously cushioned bench where she had been placed, her eyes taking in the magnificence of the coach's interior, her expression now one of wonder, focusing briefly as well on the colourful throng of people milling about on the fringes of the scene. Though she remained alone amidst the tumult, she was no longer apprehensive or gloomy, especially as within moments, the door was briskly reopened and a familiar, lustrously glowing face shone at her.

"It is *you*! *You* are my *gift*!" Marie Antoinette, dauphine of France, cried out joyously, reaching for Eileen's automatically extended hand. "The empress," she said breathlessly, wriggling up into the carriage, not yet sitting, ". . . she told me a 'wonderful gift, perhaps the best, the most wonderful gift possible' for my departure awaited me in my coach . . . and so *you are*!"

"Madame la Dauphine," a gentle voice sounded urgently.

"If Madame would please be seated," half-ordered Count Khevenhüller himself, "we may thus progress," and the dauphine did as she was requested, her skirts rustling as she sat to Eileen's right, by the window.

Countess Trautmannsdorf then entered from the left-hand side of the carriage and took the place facing the dauphine. As she settled into her seat, the countess indicated that the dauphine and Eileen alone would share the occupancy of the carriage's front-facing seat for the duration of the lengthy journey towards France.

Count Khevenhüller having deftly crafted a creative response consistent with the empress's directions, the occupants of the remaining two spaces on the rear-facing seat of the coach would be different each day, assuring that as many worthy Imperial nobles as possible were allocated the privilege of travelling with their former archduchess on her great journey to France.

Whilst they were joined almost immediately by a pair of noblewomen—Eileen recognised only the Princess Starhemberg, whose husband had been entrusted with the actual movement of the cavalcade—the dauphine's eyes yet again grew cloudy as the empress stepped closer to the coach, Emperor Joseph at her side, the Lady Abigail, holding tightly to O'Sullivan, directly behind Maria Theresa. As Eileen impulsively raised her fingers in a delicate gesture of farewell to her sister, she mouthed her feelings at the same time: *I love you.* Abby O'Sullivan began to weep shamelessly, the empress reaching behind and taking hold of the younger woman's hand in her own tremulous one.

Commands were then being sharply called out, footmen standing to the right side of each of the fifty-six carriages strung out to the rear of that of the dauphine peered into each vehicle, nodded up and down the delicately winding line and, virtually simultaneously, each of the fifty-six doors was sharply snapped shut.

The emperor, along with those of the Imperial family present, as well as Abigail, her arm now linked in her husband's, remained on the steps behind, whilst the empress alone stepped to the window of her youngest daughter's conveyance and clasped the young girl's trembling hand with her own. "Remember, my beloved daughter . . . an *angel*; may the French believe I have sent them an angel in gifting them with you." As the empress's usually commanding voice faltered, the girl held her mother's hand and, gazing into her eyes, nodded, barely managing the softest "*Oui,* Mama, *oui* . . ." her other hand gripping that of her seatmate so tightly, her small nails actually hurt Eileen momentarily, until she placed her left hand over both of theirs and the new dauphine's grip eased.

Just as she prepared to step back, the empress peered into the coach and looked at Eileen, who leaned forward in her place. The sovereign nodded and smiled at her. Eileen's lip-quivering expression of gratitude was one Maria Theresa would long recall.

The empress resumed her place next to the emperor. As she did, in response to a sharp, almost harshly delivered command, the coach lurched forward, then moved firmly as the horses settled in their traces, lowered their shoulders and pulled. The speed of the magnificent carriage, and the dozens behind it, was initially very slow, then quicker, albeit not fast. Though Eileen would be unaware of the fact until she alighted from the coach later, in the afternoon, leading the procession on its departure from Vienna was Captain Arthur O'Leary. Though she was uncertain where her husband even was, she smiled as she noticed troopers in the familiar Hungarian Hussars' distinctive, heavily gold-braided, short red-jacketed uniforms, their distinguishing pelisses draped elegantly off their left shoulders, began to fall in alongside the berline as it pulled away from the Hofburg.

She managed to elicit a brief smile from the dauphine as she advised, addressing her for the first time as such, "Your Royal Highness is in good and safe hands," gesturing out the window as one of the young Hussars fell in directly outside. "You see the captain and his men; we are in their care." Marie Antoinette nodded tightly, a grateful expression on her otherwise sombre face.

As she sensed she would before she heard her former charge begin to sob, Eileen could only hold the girl's hand, and that was what she did as the dauphine alternated between leaning out of the window, her eyes fixed on her mother and her home, waving and occasionally easing back inside for a moment to wipe her eyes with the handkerchiefs Eileen held. It was only when the figure of the empress and those people gathered about her and the reassuring expanse of the Hofburg itself finally slipped out of sight that Marie Antoinette rested back against the thickly padded velvet cushions, her red-rimmed eyes closed, her left hand holding—no longer gripping—Eileen's right, and they rode in silence for a time.

The sense of calm was interrupted when the noblewoman whom Eileen did not know offhandedly remarked, before Countess Trautmannsdorf could interrupt her, to the Princess Starhemberg, who was similarly unsuccessful, "Ah, see . . . Schönbrunn, it approaches," gesturing out the window. The dauphine roused herself and attempted to stand in the uneven motion of the coach to see her beloved Schönbrunn in the distance on the left side of the carriage. Her tears flowed again as her hand rested on Eileen's knee; half-standing, she struggled to remain so and keep the gentle palace in sight, ultimately sinking mutely back into her seat, her elegant French-coiffed head this time resting gently against Eileen's shoulder, the two continuing to hold hands, the sounds of the postillions' horns saluting Schönbrunn echoing in the damp, chilly air, as a gentle but soon steady rain began to fall.

A journey of not quite two weeks, a number of the days being rainy or at least terribly dreary, followed, taking the massive procession across a significant swath of the Habsburgs' vast domains until they would reach Schüttern, across the Rhine from Strasbourg; they traversed indeed much of Europe. It seemed to Eileen, as it did to a number of her confreres as well, that very quickly one day melded into the next, and the day following that one into another, and yet another . . . each featuring some variant of genuinely warm, sincerely gracious welcome. Troops of inevitably beautiful little girls, seemingly all of them blond, offered their former archduchess equally lovely sheaves of at times stunning flowers; bands, music, flags; and the people—Eileen had never seen so many people—of all stations gathered together in so many places, displaying a seemingly limitless excitement, enthusiasm—indeed sheer joy, it appeared to her—at seeing Marie Antoinette, the daughter of their empress, who would become the queen of France, and to wish her well.

There would be dinners and concerts and endless receiving lines, even specially written plays and performances of local dance and music in some of the places in which they stopped.

The accommodations ranged from magnificent and luxurious to better than adequate, although Captain O'Leary and his fellow officers were generally quartered with their mounts, whilst the other ranks slept outside unless the weather was poor.

The foods and wines provided were generous and by and large excellent; it was a historic and memorable continuing occasion, yet another once-in-a-lifetime experience for Eileen, she reflected. Wondering often of Anna's feelings, she would learn that her young friend spent much of each day enthralled, watching, taking notes of seemingly everything she saw, attempting to assure she remembered as much as she could of the singular experience. The girl had enchanted her companions in the coach, which remained far distant from that carrying the dauphine and Eileen, on this, the longest journey she had ever undertaken, her first trip from Laxenburg to Vienna being the longest before that. The other women, more senior servants, shared in her delight and also shared caring for Conor, who, Anna would ultimately be able to tell his anxious mother, proved to be an excellent little traveller.

Yet, despite all this, Eileen soon found herself growing weary, and the young woman who she, with a wistful smile, had begun to think of now as being her "little dauphine," she, too, grew weary—and bored . . . the weariness, brought on as much by spending at least eight hours of each day travelling in her coach than anything else. It and boredom, compounded by a nasty little cold that appeared on the morning of their fourth day in transit and remained stubbornly with the princess through much of the balance of the extraordinary expedition. This notwithstanding, the dauphine proved herself an impressive performer, displaying appreciation and excitement and showing a genuine interest in all that was done for her, only in the most private of moments, and then briefly in passing, indicating to Eileen indeed how dreadfully bored she was with yet another performance of local music and dance, and how genuinely weary she had grown of the always effusive remarks of welcome delivered by members of the local nobility or officialdom. "How many different ways is it possible to greet one?" she wondered aloud, but she and Eileen steeled themselves by concluding that the warmth was indeed genuine and the message in each location equally sincere and, as Eileen phrased it, and Antoinette agreed, "Most likely never again would any dauphine of France visit any of these places."

The dauphine's cold had passed and some measure of enthusiasm returned as the cavalcade, having traversed the Black Forest, finally arrived in mid-afternoon of 6 May at the looming, somewhat intimidating abbey at Schüttern, where the dauphine and her retinue would spend their final night together.

The evening before the formal handover—the more elegantly delicate French term *remise* now being the way to which it was referred—of the former Austrian archduchess to the kingdom of France—was, for Eileen, a strange experience: Countess Trautmannsdorf had softly, with obvious reluctance, indicated to her that "your services will not be required tonight, my dear. . . . Matters of protocol of both courts now control our actions, yes?" In response, Eileen could only nod *yes*, and the countess then gently touched her arm. "I wish it were not thus, dear girl; I know and understand that Madame la Dauphine would much prefer that you rather than I were with her this night," and Eileen lowered her eyes in an expression of gratitude for the older woman's sensitivity.

As it was, after enjoying a pleasant meal with the lesser nobility and senior servants, she spent much of the remainder of the evening exploring, not unhappily, the abbey, including making a visit to the Blessed Sacrament in one of its smaller chapels, fervently praying for a good life for her dearest Antoine, brushing away tears as she stood to leave the church. She had even hoped to perhaps find Anna, but Anna was much further removed than Eileen from the centre of activity. Later, Eileen caught a glimpse of a procession of sorts, composed, she could tell, solely of nobles of impressive, in some cases ancient titles and the dauphine, moving from a glittering dinner to what she was told would be a musical performance of some type. She returned to her small, comfortable room and was soon asleep.

The morning of 7 May dawned overcast and cool; sporadic claps of thunder rolled out of the Black Forest as the Austrian participants in the *remise* rose, dressed, breakfasted if they chose to and came together for their final act in the as yet far-from-completed drama in which they had been taking part.

Eileen was assisted in dressing—in a magnificent cloth-of-gold robe with a lengthy train—by a young, polite, but largely uncommunicative German girl, who was markedly efficient and gone as quickly as she could manage to be. As Eileen called *"Danke!"* to her as she hurried out the door, the gesture went unacknowledged, and she merely sighed, reflecting, *This—all of it—is now nearly at an end. . . . I believe I am quite ready for it to be thus.*

Eileen was advised by a young page in slow, precise French, a language with which the boy was clearly not comfortable, "Your belongings, they shall be delivered with those of the Captain O'Leary, your son and of the Lady Anna"—Eileen smiled at the reference, *for someday soon I believe she will be thus!*—"for your departure this day, madame." Eileen thought of asking for Conor but decided against doing so, assuming, hopefully, that her husband and child, Anna, their horses and whatever equipage General O'Connell had arranged for would be in a certain place at the correct time. Thus having reassured herself, she went to seek out Countess Trautmannsdorf.

"We are quite ready!" the countess, standing outside the dauphine's suite, called effusively to Eileen as she saw the younger woman approaching her.

"May I have a moment with Madame la Dauphine, Your Grace?" she asked.

"Madame la Dauphine, ah . . . she has just now proceeded to our carriage. I saw to her dressing and escorted her, as I am required to," she added, and Eileen understood, "and now we must . . ." She made a sweeping motion with both hands, signifying they, too, were to leave. The countess slipped her arm through Eileen's and the pair made their way to join the dauphine.

Entering for the last time the memorably ornate carriage, Eileen observed that Marie Antoinette, as she had now at last come to think of her former charge, appeared apprehensive, perhaps a bit nervous, though she smiled warmly, her eyes brightening especially at the sight of her beloved governess, greeting the two women with an effusive "My ladies!" and extending a delicate hand to each, indicating that, for the brief journey, they should take seats facing her.

"It shall be just we three," the countess pronounced and, as if on command, the carriage moved forward.

The day remained dreary and almost cool, though not uncomfortably so; rain nevertheless threatened, the air seeming sweet, redolent with the complex, ageless moisture of the Black Forest. The events of the morning were all to be indoors, so the weather was of no serious concern.

The coach proceeded at a quick pace for several miles down an obviously just-smoothed road and, as it reached the Rhine, slowed to permit the remainder of O'Leary's troopers to fall behind and then clattered across the arch of a relatively narrow, high wooden bridge onto the Île aux Épis, a nondescript wooded islet, reported to be ofttimes soggy but on this day at least dry, said to be located precisely half in the kingdom of the Bourbons and half in the domains of the Hapsburgs. Almost immediately, the coach drew up before an obviously just constructed structure, built to resemble a miniature chateau or perhaps a castle of sorts, located on the island, they were told, so as its precise centre straddled the borders of the two realms.

"*Nous somme ici!*" Countess Trautmannsdorf forced herself to smilingly pronounce the obvious as the door was smartly opened and there appeared the faces of a magnificently uniformed Prince Starhemberg, his knee-length, bright red coat heavy with braid, his orders and decorations gleaming, a shining pair of epaulettes at his shoulders, as well as the far more simply, clerically attired Abbé Vermond, the only two of her retinue who would accompany the dauphine into France.

The events that followed were, for Eileen, a moving, emotionally wrenching and ultimately numbing series of steps that would dramatically culminate in an unanticipated rush of emotions.

The pall of sadness, the sense of loss under which she felt she had been all morning was at that moment drawn back slightly, albeit briefly, as, just prior to the formalities—when Prince Starhemberg would finally lead Marie Antoinette into the neutral salon for the actual *remise*—the dauphine now stood in front of her and curtseyed deeply. "My dearest, my only Lady Eileen," the girl began slowly in her soft, German-accented French, her lips quivering, "I must now bid you adieu . . . although as we French say, it should and therefore shall be more correctly expressed as *au revoir*. . . ." She took Eileen's hands in her own, both trembling, and, as Eileen instinctively bent her height forward, the dauphine kissed her, her soft lips lingering on both of Eileen's salty, tearstained cheeks. The young woman held Eileen's hand tightly as she then moved her lips to Eileen's left ear, "Remember, you will always be my mama. Always."

Feeling Antoinette trembling, Eileen did not straighten immediately. "I have loved you, my darling, from the day, the very moment I first saw you, as a wee *cailín*," she smiled weakly, "to this day . . . and I shall love you forever, *my daughter*. Each day I shall pray for you. I . . ." Her voice faded as both now nodded and, oblivious to all who watched and would remember, instinctively, most reluctantly released each other's hands, and Eileen stood. As the dauphine stepped back, Eileen said softly, just loudly enough for her to hear, *"Au revoir, ma petite archduchesse,"* as they both managed to smile weakly through their tears.

Though she would linger longer with some than others—and with Eileen longer than anyone—the dauphine bid an individual farewell to each of the Austrians present, Eileen's eyes following her as she did.

The intensity of her immediate loss again fell heavily on Eileen's broad shoulders as she watched the dauphine, attended now by the countess and only the highest-ranking nobles of the Austrian retinue, approach the French courtiers, as a separate quartet of French attendants came forward, bearing what appeared to be a full ensemble of splendid clothing.

As the two groups of courtiers circled the seemingly diminutive princess, Eileen yet again found herself able to see above a number of the others, watching in disbelief as the girl's magnificent robe, in which she had been dressed for less than three hours, was removed, along with her undergarments and hose, her slippers even, and was efficiently, immediately redressed in what Eileen correctly surmised were French-made garments and accessories, all of which were indeed breathtaking.

Whilst the dauphine stepped towards the imposing pair of still-closed double doors that led into the drawing room itself, Eileen and others of the Austrian contingent watched askance as several of the French ladies pounced on and scooped up the dauphine's Austrian clothing, obviously seizing them as souvenirs of the occasion. Shaking her head, the fingertips of the tall Irishwoman's right hand went to her mouth as a number of the Austrians nodded at her from across the room, feeling she was expressing their collective opinion of the appalling behaviour of the French.

Suddenly, the doors were dramatically flung open by a pair of doorkeepers in the livery of Louis XV. Craning her neck, Eileen could see a room larger and more elegantly appointed than the one in which she stood, a gleaming, outsized table set in the precise centre, the walls also partially draped in dark tapestries. She would later confide to Art, "I pray they were mindless random decorations and I was grateful that the dauphine's knowledge of mythology, at least non-Irish mythology, is virtually nil, as one I believe depicted Medea, in the acts for which she is perhaps best known!"

And, as suddenly as the doors had been opened—the dauphine having stepped, alone but for an obviously solicitous Prince Starhemberg at her side, into the drawing room, indeed beyond the table set at the room's precise midpoint, into France itself—they were closed, sharply, "needlessly firmly," Countess Trautmannsdorf would always recall . . . and she was gone. The doors separating France from Austria, now separated as well the archduchess of Austria from the dauphine of France, and what had in an instant become her past from what would be her future, the known and proverbial from the unknown, the uncertain.

Virtually as one, the Austrians stood still, a massive sense of anti-climax overtaking the elegantly dressed group of men and women. After a while, a number of individuals finally began to move about tentatively, to speak softly amongst themselves.

Countess Trautmannsdorf and Eileen appeared to be spontaneously seeking each other out, when one of the double doors was abruptly flung open wide, crashing into the wall behind it, apparently by a flush-faced Count Mercy-Argenteau, the Austrian ambassador to the court of Versailles. As always elegant—today in a black velvet suit, his hair carefully powdered and perfectly tied, white hose, gleaming, gold-buckled shoes—he stalked briskly back into the again-hushed room, muttering, not quietly, in German, as well as, as those who could hear him thought, perhaps also in French, words roughly equivalent to "damned dog, nasty, dirty, *filthy* little animal!" as, barely stopping, his piercing black eyes sharply, anxiously scanned the group of courtiers. He was visibly relieved as, unexpectedly, they locked easily on Eileen, towering over most of those gathered and, his right forefinger pointing directly at her, he followed it until he stood before her, raising his eyes slightly to meet her own. "*Vous êtes la Dame* Eileen, *oui?*" he inquired, his harsh tone no longer evident.

Lowering her eyes slightly, respectfully, Eileen nodded in the affirmative.

"You have cared for. . . ?" and he cocked his head towards the salon.

Eileen nodded again, this time whispering, "Yes, Your Grace, I have . . . for not quite nine years, sir."

Nodding, again muttering—though this time, as Eileen herself heard, bilingual variants of "Good, excellent!"—the ambassador took Eileen's elbow firmly with his delicate fingers, leading her thus as they walked slowly now, explaining in a staccato of thoughts the source of his upset, Eileen's head cocked down in his direction.

The door that had been flung was yet again opened, this time very slowly; on the other side, almost in the centre of the room, stood a teary dauphine, alone, her trim shoulders shaking beneath her magnificent French raiment; she turned wordlessly, though obviously comforted to see her beloved governess.

Eileen stepped away from her escort and was quickly at her side. "My darling," Eileen said softly, extending her hand, which Marie Antoinette grasped, taking her other one as well. "What is . . .?"

Clearly exasperated, the count interrupted, albeit in a subdued, even gentle tone. "My Lady Eileen, you will *please*, on my behalf"—nodding, he eyed Eileen warily—"please assure Madame la Dauphine that, that . . . her . . . animal . . ."

"*Mops!* His name is Mops!" the dauphine interjected sharply, her almost shrill voice trembling as she glared at Count Mercy, her fingers now tight on Eileen's hands.

"*Oui,* Mops . . . Madame la Dauphine's *dog,*" the man resumed, now with some apparent effort, succeeding in remaining calm, ". . . that, contrary to what we had originally been led to understand by the French, *Mops* will indeed await Madame la Dauphine upon her arrival at Versailles."

Purposefully narrowing her eyes as she looked at him, Eileen nodded quite archly to the diplomat and, leaning down to the dauphine, her lips inches from the now French royal's right ear, whispered, "Mops shall be at Versailles, awaiting you, *my darling daughter,* if I have to carry him there myself." She then moved her head away from the girl's, standing erect, both of them, to his seeming relief, then nodding affirmatively at Mercy-Argenteau.

Turning away from the diplomat, looking directly down at the dauphine, "Now . . . be about your business, girl," Eileen said in English, repeating, in a faux harsh tone, the Irish idiom she had frequently used with her no longer little archduchess.

Instantly remembering, immediately understanding, she nodded and smiled weakly, managing, also in English, a barely audible, "I shall, yes . . ." then adding a whispered, "*Merci.*"

Though she had stepped back, Eileen again leant forward, impulsively adding, "Remember, Cork is far closer to Versailles than is Vienna. . . . I know not when, but please be assured I *shall* journey to see you. . . ."

The dauphine smiled gratefully.

This time it was Eileen who, in violation of countless tenets of French protocol, she was certain, gently kissed the dauphine on both cheeks, nodded and reluctantly released her hands after curtseying deeply, profoundly. She then withdrew, walking slowly backwards.

Eileen did not notice that the Countess de Noailles, whom Marie Antoinette would shortly critically christen "Madame Etiquette," had audibly gasped at what she had done, though, scarlet-faced as she was, the older French noblewoman nevertheless had then nodded stiffly in reluctant approval at the tall woman's faultless curtsey, her flawless withdrawal and, she conceded, her *extraordinarily* regal bearing.

As Eileen re-entered the Austrian room, her gold robes reflecting the multitude of candles aflame in a room that had grown darker as, outside, intermittent raindrops had desultorily begun to fall, Countess Trautmannsdorf immediately opened her arms to her, a quizzical expression on her usually benign face.

"Mops!" Eileen said, smiling ruefully as she gratefully stepped into the older woman's embrace, "Mops, he is Austrian; they . . . the French . . . they seemingly did not wish to permit him to be taken to Versailles by Madame la Dauphine."

The older woman's hands went to her cheeks.

"Our ambassador is an excellent diplomat, I believe. He merely wished me to assure Madame La Dauphine that, contrary to what they had been informed by the French, the wee little fellow would be awaiting her arrival at Versailles. It seems she trusted neither the French nor poor Monsieur le Comte!"

"And you did so, you were able to convince her, *ja?*"

"I did so, *ja.*" Eileen laughed. "I believe it shall be my final act of service," she added, her eyes unexpectedly filling with tears as the countess embraced her again, this time wordlessly.

A powerful silence had once again descended upon the group, including, momentarily, Eileen—though, unlike the others, she almost immediately sensed a remarkable feeling of . . . the word *liberation* quickly came to her, as did an equally strong urge *to be about her own business now.*

As she was the only one of the elite group who would not be returning with them to Vienna, everyone being aware that she was almost immediately to depart for Ireland, Eileen slowly circled the room and, beginning with the countess, curtseyed or at least extended a hand to and exchanged brief words of farewell with each of her Austrian confreres, the sounds of resumed conversations amongst the courtiers humming in the background.

As she reached, indeed as she actually had just placed her fingers on the brass latch of the door leading to the outside, to the Austrian side of the island, a remarkably abrupt silence filled the room. Sensing all eyes were on her, Eileen spontaneously turned, taking several steps forward, her again-moist eyes gradually circling the small assemblage, and, dramatically, curtseyed once more, deeply and slowly to the group as a whole. As she rose, applause began that would echo after—walking backwards, thinking, *this for the very last time*—she had stepped through and closed the door, marking the end for her of what she would for the remainder of her life characterise as being a truly extraordinary experience.

Once outside in the gloomy, dank late morning, Eileen began striding—effortlessly, deliberately resuming her once-customary "Kerry girl's gait," one that few had seen during her years in Austria—her long legs carrying her towards the bridge to the mainland. Spontaneously, she laughingly called aloud, into the still, cool, wet air, "Captain Arthur O'Leary! . . . Master Conor O'Leary! . . . Lady Anna Pfeffer!" By then smiling, as she reached the arch of what she now decided was a rather rickety-looking affair, she gathered up her elegant skirts and hurried across the swirling waters of the Rhine in search of her family, the bridge creaking even at her delicately slippered footfalls.

Almost immediately upon completing her solitary re-crossing of the Rhine, Eileen was greeted by a surprised young carriage driver, whom she had startled as he curried one of the two silver-grey horses, nibbling at the abundant grasses even as they remained hitched to the conveyance. Laughingly regaining his composure, he advised her that the plan remained for a small number of coaches to recross the high wooden bridge she had just traversed and gather the Austrians for their journey back to the abbey at Schüttern, where they had all spent the previous night.

Even before she could speak, he gallantly announced, "I nevertheless, Lady Eileen, should be pleased, indeed proud, to convey you alone myself, right this moment," which he did, opening the door and assisting her into the carriage with a dramatically expressed aplomb.

Once at the abbey, the now-former governess was almost immediately reunited with her handsomely uniformed husband, who had, whilst she was at the formal *remise*, formally turned over command of the detachment of cavalry he had led from Vienna, which had been a significant part of the dauphine's military escort, to his lieutenant. In addition, not only had O'Leary located Anna with little Conor in tow, but he had succeeded in having Eileen's beloved Bull—he greeted his gold-clad mistress noisily, and with much mane tossing and tail flaring—and the sturdy, yet-to-be named mare General O'Connell had selected for Anna brought around, along with the combined baggage carrier/coach, also compliments of the general. The vehicle was fully loaded with their clothing and personal possessions for their journey to Ireland, ably manned by two young Austrian soldiers whose excitement at the prospect of crossing the rest of Europe was palpable.

A look of relief on her face as she saw Eileen alight from her carriage, Anna, suddenly feeling uncertain of her status but with a need to share her thoughts, interrupted the couple almost in a whisper. "Sir, Mistress . . . I fear you must be aware that I am as thrilled as the soldiers there, I myself may be a bit . . ." and the O'Learys jointly embraced the beautiful girl with the golden blond hair, whom Eileen would henceforth proudly introduce as her *dearest friend*.

O'Leary added, "Certainly you are, 'tis nothing wrong in feeling such . . . and, when you are fully comfortable in doing so, you may henceforth address me as Arthur and . . ."

Eileen interjected, as if on cue, ". . . since 'tis my name, I should think Eileen would be an appropriate form of address, *ja*, Anna?"

They had all laughed as, looking up at the adults, so too then did Conor O'Leary, though several days would pass before Anna would fully cease using "Captain," "sir," "Mistress" and "Lady Eileen."

Facing a journey of almost 300 miles to Paris alone, with yet another 120-odd miles more from Paris to the port of Le Havre in Normandy, from thence by sea and yet again land finally to West Cork, the travellers collectively agreed to commence their trip immediately.

As the days passed, they all proved to be sturdy travellers and good company to one another, with generally benign and cooperating weather continuing as they arrived on the outskirts of Paris some ten days after departing Strasbourg.

Anna continued her ongoing observations and had resumed making written notes of this, *My Incredible Journey,* as she had written on the first page of her notebook. She felt the Habsburgs' lands were friendlier, as well as more dramatically beautiful than what she was seeing of France, and that the people living under the Hapsburgs appeared far more content than the Bourbons' subjects. She continually made comments to the effect that *I am unable to fully grasp that I am indeed journeying to Ireland! It is to me as were I travelling to the moon!* She alternated between being fully secure and suddenly uncomfortable in her evolving relationship with the O'Learys: *Today I addressed the Captain as "Arthur" and my cheeks turned red!* she wrote in her journal. It seemed more natural for her to speak with Eileen as *Eileen,* though, she recorded, without thinking, she still nevertheless frequently reverted to *Mistress.*

As they had been on the road approximately the same time as the new dauphine of France, who would arrive at Compiegne on the fourteenth of May and Versailles the following day, they purposely avoided entering Paris and would, as they continued their journey, circle wide of Versailles en route to Normandy. By prearrangement, O'Leary dispatched one of the soldiers, along with a carefully drawn map, with a message for Eileen's younger brother, Daniel Charles, now a captain in the Royal Swedish Brigade of the armies of Louis XV, who joined them this cool evening for a surprisingly sumptuous meal prepared in the woods east of Paris.

"And what of Hugh, brother, what news have you of him?" Eileen breathlessly asked as soon as the young officer had seated himself on a log, having just accepted a proffered glass of fine German—Eileen laughed as she poured it, with a flourish—wine.

"Of our dearest youngest brother"—who in January had departed Vienna to enter Dillon's Regiment of the Irish Brigade of the French army—"you shall now know all that I do, dear sister, brother: I believe the boy is as cloistered as were he a Cistercian novice, as inaccessible as were his handsome Irish Brigade uniform the rough white wool of the Carthusians. In short, other than General Dillon advising me as recently as this week that the boy is 'well, and progressing nicely, displaying all indications of becoming an extraordinary young officer,' I know no more. I have neither seen nor heard directly from him since he arrived with General O'Connell in late January."

Eileen nodded, to a degree satisfied, though she could not refrain from one additional question, the substance of and the answer to which the young Irish officer was immediately aware, scarcely before she had begun her inquiry—"But what of their correspondence, brother . . . now that she is *here*? What is to be. . ?"—Daniel playfully interrupted his sister. "As he previously advised you and the others in Vienna, I am told were any written communication for Monsieur Cadet O'Connell to arrive at the military academy from Madame la Dauphine at Versailles, it shall be delivered to and responded to personally by General Theobold Dillon himself, who has indicated he will explain respectfully the realities of Hugh's lowly status and express deep gratitude for Her Royal Highness's interest . . . etcetera, etcetera, *etcetera*!"

Daniel then laughed heartily, as did the O'Learys.

It was only after Daniel had, availing himself of the extended light of a gentle moonlit spring evening, left to return to Paris and the O'Learys were bedded down under an ancient oak tree—Conor snuggling close to Eileen, O'Leary's back to her own, with Anna close by—that, once again displaying her ofttimes striking prescience—*Sometimes . . . I have a certain feeling about things, is all* —Eileen reflected, *Have we perhaps laughed too easily, too soon?* She was well aware that after Hugh had left for France the young friends had already begun exchanging correspondence; indeed, Antoinette had informed her beloved governess almost casually that she fully intended to "summon," she had announced grandly, the young cadet soon after she herself was settled at Versailles . . . *and I have no doubt that Her Royal Highness will prove to be fully true to her word,* Eileen thought. Gently rocking Conor, she also recalled how frequently supposedly ironclad military processes failed to work as they had been planned. Shaking her head, she sighed and shortly thereafter drifted into a dreamless sleep, the topic forgotten and never revisited.

The following morning, the little group would circle north of Paris and then proceed on a road that would not pass Versailles, all of which would result in perhaps an additional day in their reaching Le Havre. Once there, Captain O'Leary, in his distinctive and striking red-jacketed uniform, was easily able to commandeer assistance in locating their vessel, which the earnest young Frenchman respectfully referred to as "the Irish trading ship." This caused Eileen and O'Leary to laugh, Eileen indicating to a somewhat puzzled Anna that "explain this I shall, my darling, 'twill be the first of many things Irish—great and small—with which you shall become intimate."

Master Michael Brosnan, himself tall, spare, leathery and with flaming red hair, one of the most trusted of the O'Connells' long-time ship's masters, greeted Eileen warmly and was almost as effusive as she introduced her husband and Anna. He let out a whoop as he caught a racing Conor O'Leary, reminding Eileen that there were now ten Brosnan children, only one of whom, the youngest, was a son. "Waited long enough to come, he did," the mariner laughed as he was greeting and then directing the soldiers to his ship. "'Tisn't much older than your lad!"

The baggage carrier was quickly unloaded and the trunks and satchels speedily aboard the ship, the soldiers feeling themselves flattered as

Brosnan directed his own crew to the task, offering the Austrians—and his men, as they completed loading—beer, bread and cheese, as Anna instinctively hovered about the little group, deftly translating between English and German to the friendly amazement of the Irish sailors and the Austrian soldiers.

After bidding a warm farewell to the young Austrian soldiers, the O'Learys and Anna were away on the next tide. They sailed almost immediately into a squall that became another squall and then a series of increasingly heavy rainstorms, though surprisingly absent of strong winds and waves, the often-turbulent waters of the Channel instead being gently heaving heavy grey-green. Though Anna had never been at sea before, she experienced little discomfort and expressed no concerns. She walked the decks frequently, looking, just looking, at the waves and the water, inhaling its briny scent for the first time. Art and Conor were each in his own way primarily but quietly bored; they, too, walked on deck, though there was little to capture the interest of a not-quite-two-year-old, nor that of his father, who, truth be told, vastly preferred dry land to any body of water, no matter how benign. Bull, on the other hand, was noisily unhappy, and Eileen visited him several times a day.

Midmorning of the third day, after departing the French coast, they were all, each for his or her own reason, quite pleased when the spires of Cork appeared quite suddenly out of a thick, foggy rain, the wind blowing from the shore sweet with peat fires, wet earth and the countless aromas of the harbour itself. The rain continued as they disembarked, as it would whilst the little party and one of the O'Connells' regular haulers, wended their way across a quickly greening County Cork to Macroom and thence briefly beyond, to a warm, albeit wet, welcome in the persons of Squire O'Leary and Catherine, at Rathleigh House, Eileen advising her curious little boy, "'Tis home, we are, my darling. *Home!*"

Versailles—June 1770

One steamy Tuesday morning in mid-June, a young courier, magnificently attired in the singular tri-colour livery of Louis XV, arrived at the sprawling, imposing École Militaire, whose elegant, largely interconnected collection of baroque-style buildings were coming to dominate the Champs de Mars on the Rive Droite of the Seine. He bore a weighty, almost-square crème-coloured envelope, which, despite speaking in soft Provençal tones, he firmly indicated to the shocked sentries, he was to "only deliver this" —his immaculately white-gloved fingers gently waved the rigid envelope— "to a Monsieur Cadet O'Connell, he being attached to La Brigade Irlandaise . . . this on the command of Her Royal Highness, Madame la Dauphine *herself.*"

The pair of regular French army officers to whom the messenger had first been directed were initially stunned, instantaneously appalled that their just-arrived dauphine would for any reason be communicating with *a mere cadet! a commoner! and not even French! In the* Irish *Brigade, no less!* Uncertain as to how to properly address the situation—unaware of there being any protocol in place, including any standing order of General Dillon setting out the manner in which the receipt of such a communication was to be handled and by whom—the young captain immediately sent men scurrying in several directions, all in search of *"any* Irish officer."

Within a quarter-hour, Lieutenant Seamus O'Kelly, a diminutive, compact junior officer of Dillon's Regiment, who was seconded to the military academy as an instructor of tactics, struttingly emerged from one of the dramatically styled buildings. Conscious of appearing far younger than his just twenty-one years, O'Kelly compensated by affecting an almost laughably officious manner, on full display as he stentorianously ordered the courier to "hand over that message," extending his gloved left hand.

"Ah, Monsieur Lieutenant, *c'est impossible!*" the now wide-eyed Versailles messenger exclaimed, his tone elevated, his expression one of shocked incredulity, reemphasising the communication's origin, again identifying its sender, then theatrically pressing the envelope to his bosom. O'Kelly shook his head, muttered something in Irish and indicated the man should remain *ici*, he ordered gruffly, his own white gloved right hand gesturing to the gravel on which they stood.

The next quarter-hour witnessed the communication's intended recipient's arrival—sweaty and dusty from the drill field, flanked by O'Kelly and a clearly displeased Major Michael Ó Néill, an officer in Clare's regiment, who had been located whilst dining with a French colleague. None of the Irish officers had ever heard of any order of General Dillon, or anyone else, as to what they were to do in a circumstance such as this.

Wordlessly, Ó Néill firmly plucked the envelope from the shocked courier's still softly gloved fingers, eyed it and passed it to Hugh. "Open it, cadet," he ordered in an even voice, speaking English.

Hugh turned it over and immediately saw what he knew to be Marie Antoinette's cipher, a delicately intertwined *MA* pressed into a soft blue splodge of wax, the seal created by which he gently broke, both officers noting the flicker of a smile on his sweat-sheened face as he withdrew the folded piece of fine, heavy paper. Holding the envelope in his left hand, the brief, beautifully scrivened note in his right, Hugh's eyes quickly scanned the message, which he immediately tendered to Major Ó Néill:

La présence de M. Cadet Hugh O'Connell est exigée par Son Altesse Royale, la Dauphiné, au Château de Versailles le samedi, le 16 Juin 1770 à deux heures de l'après-midi.

A separate postscript in English—carefully, though less-elegantly written, and on a more common sheet of paper—clearly intended for the recipient's superiors, indicated that the young cadet would be informally *introduced*—as opposed to being formally presented—to His Majesty, Louis XV, both of their faces evidencing shock, that he would dine with Madame la Dauphine and Monsieur le Dauphin, which caused O'Kelly's mouth to drop open and Ó Néill's cheeks to flame, and would be free to return to the Champs de Mars at approximately eight, or possibly even later, that evening.

"Most irregular . . . indeed, highly irregular!" Ó Néill observed, though—clearly seeing no alternative—handing Hugh a short, sharp pencil, he reluctantly indicated for him to scribble his acceptance on the blank card being proffered at that moment directly to the young cadet by the courier. This having been accomplished—*Oui, avec grand plaiser*, Hugh had written, signing his name with a flourish—the senior officer waved the messenger off, the expression on the man's face one of relief as he turned his handsome mount away from the military academy.

Even as the hoofs of the courier's horse clattered across the courtyard, before they had even cleared the ornate entrance gate that passed through the breadth of a building on the east side of the massive quadrant the school occupied, Ó Néill's commanding voice exploded in the stiflingly still air.

"O'Connell, what in the bloody goddammed hell is the meaning of this? Whilst we are at this, *who* in the bloody goddammed hell *are* you, man?" Ó Néill demanded of a now obviously uncomfortable Hugh, who, as quickly as possible, breathlessly related in a very general way his association with the former archduchess and, more particularly and in greater detail, his sisters' roles at the Viennese court. Less ruffled than he had been, albeit clearly shocked by the revelations, Ó Néill shook his head in response and sighed deeply. "I had no idea that you . . . that they . . ." His words drifted as he abruptly turned away, O'Kelly at his heels, speaking to him in a most animated fashion.

Uncertain as to what to do next, Hugh looked again at the near-rigid, card-like piece of paper in his hand and smiled, otherwise remaining mutely at attention for what seemed to him to be a long time, until he was dismissed, a still-distracted Major Ó Néill finally calling back over his shoulder a sharply spoken, "*Rejéte,* O'Connell!" As he began to walk away, Hugh slipped the message back into the envelope, rubbing his thumb over the broken seal, and thence into the inside pocket of his blouse. Reporting to his drill master, Hugh yet again stood rigid in the baking sun, answering a stream of questions, the young corporal's expression one of disbelief as he listened.

Hugh spent an awkwardly uncertain several days, though by the time Saturday arrived, and especially as he was being assisted into a near-flawless new uniform by a gruff, though not unkind supply sergeant, his knee-high boots being at the same moment blacked and burnished to a gleam by a boy whom Hugh had never before seen, his confidence was returning, *'Tis just Antoine, is it not?* he told himself. *She said she'd send for me once she'd arrived here, did she not? And so she has. . . .* He smiled as he drew on a new pair of fine dress gloves and tucked the no-longer-crisp invitation into the right pocket of his waist-length heavy wool red cadet's coat. The return of his self-assurance notwithstanding, even as he was departing his quarters, he could not help but wonder, as he had a number of times during the preceding days, *Could it be that Abby and Eileen may be correct? That everything*—everything?—*will be different now that she is dauphine of France?* He straightened his posture and strode towards the stables; *but . . . perhaps they err, perhaps 'tis still just Antoine. Could this not be the case?*

Accompanied by a clearly unhappy—aghast at the contrast between his slightly worn raiment and scuffed boots and Hugh's crisp new uniform, his gleaming boots—openly sullen Lt. O'Kelly, Hugh made what he calculated to be the seven- or perhaps eight-mile trek from the Champs de Mars through the rolling, mid-summer verdant countryside of the Île-de-France to Versailles with little conversation, his repeated attempts to engage his superior being met with a stony expression, such that even the invariably effusive Hugh was ultimately silenced. Only once did O'Kelly say anything, when, lowering his voice, he advised Hugh that one of his French colleagues had "confided in me"—as were it not generally common knowledge—that frequently in the summertime the royal family was elsewhere than Versailles, "usually the palace at

Fontainebleau," he volunteered, adding that it was only as the dauphine was newly arrived that the customary seasonal excursion had not been made. He then lapsed again into his emotionless silence.

It was only as they turned right off the road in the direction of their destination, the magnificent palace itself now looming not at all far ahead, that Hugh seemingly could no longer restrain himself. "When last I was here, I could not have ever imagined . . ."

"*When last you were here!*" sputtered O'Kelly, pulling up his horse sharply, incredulous at the remark, as he had never been even this close to the splendour that others had told him was Versailles. "When were you . . . ?"

"Oh, yes, sir!" Hugh beamed, interrupting guilelessly now, as they walked their horses. "'Twas with my uncles; I believe you must know Captain Daniel Charles O'Connell, of the Royal Swedish Brigade here"— O'Kelly nodded reluctantly—"and, aye, my sister's husband, he is Major Denis O'Sullivan, of the Hungarian Hussars, of . . ."

". . . of the armies of Maria Theresa, yes, O'Connell." O'Kelly sighed. "I am quite familiar with the Hungarian Hussars," he groaned wearily again, such that Hugh judiciously decided against mentioning either General O'Connell or Captain Arthur O'Leary.

The pair drawing ever closer to their destination, their horses' hoofs clicking sharply on the precisely laid, evenly patterned paving stones, as they made their way through the Court of Honour towards the intricate, stunning obverse of the rambling chateau, its massive church looming to the right. They could see a number of men and women scurrying into the courtyard ahead, such that by the time the horsemen had passed through an open, quite high wrought-iron gate and drawn up their mounts where indicated, a surprisingly large group had gathered in apparent welcome.

With no further thought of O'Kelly, who, appearing fully overwhelmed, quite at a loss as to what he should do, simply remained in the saddle, Hugh dismounted effortlessly, his horse's reins being taken from him immediately by a groom. Any lingering doubts dispelled in the moment, his focus now on but one person, Hugh took several clipped steps and instantly dropped to his right knee, his eyes on the instep of his left boot.

He heard a hurriedly graceful shuffle of petite, low-heeled shoes on the paving stones. Suddenly, the hem of her magnificent medium-blue summertime-silk robe appearing, the dauphine of France stood barely a foot from him, her right forefinger gently lifting O'Connell's chin, such that his eyes briefly met hers, before he lowered his lips to delicately kiss the proffered back of her hand, the only sounds being what had become a steady breeze and random fluttering birds.

The obligatory kiss completed, both smiled, and, to the horror of the courtiers present, the dauphine—and then her guest—immediately dissolved in genuinely warm, effusive, then almost raucous laughter, even as Marie Antoinette took Hugh's hand and raised him so that—as he had during the months they had shared in Austria—he towered over her, her eyes beaming as she again looked up at her dear friend, taking his other hand in hers. They stood thus for long moments, both smiling dreamily, until Countess Noailles rather officiously stepped forward. Hugh cast an eye at the older, magnificently gowned woman and nodded, slowly and respectfully, his full attention nevertheless remaining on his friend. Her face flamed. *Does he not know to bow to* me? the woman, who was sarcastically referred to as Madame Etiquette by the dauphine, fumed silently, her mouth agape as the dauphine gestured to her that she should step away.

Whether Hugh did or not was seemingly of no matter, as the dauphine, still holding his right hand in her own, had already turned him towards the palace, the pair immediately beginning what appeared to be a seemingly effortless, quite effusive conversation.

As they walked, their eyes and attention directed primarily on each other, a gaggle of courtiers was spread out behind the pair, a tall, vividly blond young woman, to whom Hugh would later on be introduced as being the Princess de Lamballe, the dauphine's closest companion since her arrival at court, walked elegantly backwards, her palms raised, keeping the small throng away from the dauphine and her guest.

Slipping through an entryway on the south side of the massive bulk that was Versailles, they crossed through a large hall, almost immediately emerging again into the brilliant afternoon sunshine. Followed now only by the Princesse de Lamballe walking some steps behind them, the pair strolled west, Marie Antoinette gesturing Hugh to gaze upon the intricate South Parterre and, beyond it, the Orangerie. Approaching what she'd indicated to him was the west front of the chateau, Hugh suppressed a gasp as the magnificent panorama of the vast expanse between the palace itself, the Grand Canal and, from thence, on towards the structure he would learn was called the Trianon appeared before them. Standing between the two pools that constituted the starkly beautiful Water Parterre, patting his arm with her delicate hand, Antoinette indicated they were now looking down upon the Parterre and the Fountain of Latrona, sparkling in the brilliant sunshine, and towards the Royal Avenue. "I shall show you these, as well as the Fountain of Apollo," she announced.

As Hugh was beginning to ask a question, already having noticed a retinue around and behind it, they saw that a carriage was making its way in the direction of the chateau. *"C'est le Roi!"* the dauphine exclaimed breathlessly, spontaneously again taking her friend's hand and not letting go, as the king's party draw closer. Antoinette tugged Hugh and they hurried down the magnificent steps.

As the compact carriage, which Antoinette would later tell Hugh had transported him from the Trianon, a small but elegant villa beyond the Grand Canal, though still on the immense grounds of the palace, drew to a gentle halt, King Louis XV, even now referred to as being the "handsomest man in Europe"—still dark-haired and trim, his complexion ruddy, his smile bright and full-mouthed—alighted. Antoinette released Hugh's hand, excitedly calling, *"Grand-père! Mon cher Grand-père!"* even as she raced towards the now-beaming sovereign. Even before she actually reached him, the young girl was chattering on, effusively gesturing towards Hugh, who stood silently some distance back, in genuine awe.

As he listened, affectionately indicating with his upraised palms for her to slow down, the simply light blue-satin–suited sovereign nodded several times, laughing warmly as the dauphine finally halted for a breath. He then gently turned his granddaughter-in-law back towards Hugh, the king nodding again as at that moment she had informed him of Hugh's prior visit to the palace.

Watching the pair approach, Hugh also took silent note that an attractive—at least from his vantage point—young woman who had arrived with the king, and who had only exited the carriage after he and Marie Antoinette had begun to move towards him, was walking briskly away from the coach, casting her eyes back several times as she strode alone up a gentle slope looking, he sensed, directly at him.

When he would later in the afternoon nonchalantly inquire as to the woman's identity, he was surprised when Marie Antoinette grew immediately serious and replied, in a tone both harsh and dismissive—a tone with which Hugh was totally unfamiliar—"*She* is *called* Madame du Barry and *she* is a stupid, crude and ill-bred courtesan, a commoner of the basest kind, who has seemingly captured the king's attention. She is someone whom you will understand is *nothing* . . . she is *no one!*" she continued haughtily, flicking her dainty fingers in a dismissive, trivialising gesture. After a moment, Antoinette explained, as if Hugh had any doubt, that she had already developed a deep animus towards she who was frequently referred to at court a simply "the du Barry," refusing even to speak to her. "We shall say no more of this," the dauphine then told Hugh, who silently nodded his understanding.

As the king and Marie Antoinette now drew near, Hugh reflexively dropped to his right knee, yet again sighting his left instep. He did not move until he saw that the king was standing before him, a rich voice commanding, "You may now rise, Monsieur Cadet O'Connell." Which Hugh did, directing a quick glance at his friend, who, her arm in the king's, smiled softly at him.

"We are pleased to welcome you, I understand, *once again* to Versailles," the king said in a softer tone, "and we are most grateful that you have placed yourself in our service, in the service of France, monsieur. We regret our inability to visit with you and your uncles when first you came here."

Hugh nodded; opening his mouth, no words came; he found himself for the moment dumb, truly tongue-tied. *This is perhaps the first time ever . . . for an O'Connell!* he mused silently, sensing himself being drawn into the monarch's piercingly black eyes.

It was only as he began to respond to a series of gentle questions, posed in the sovereign's deep, almost baritone voice—where in Ireland was he from . . . how long had he been in Vienna . . . how was he finding his academic and tactical studies . . . and, yes, General O'Connell was indeed his uncle—that Hugh regained his voice and his usual composure. Antoinette smiled as she saw him begin to gesture with his hands—*as does Eileen!* she recalled fondly—and as she sensed his speech pattern growing less terse, his shoulders a wee bit less rigid, his stance slightly more relaxed. She smiled even more brilliantly as she watched the king become momentarily, she thought, *less royal,* the monarch appearing to be genuinely enjoying his exchange with the tall young Irishman.

The king finally looked at Antoinette, nodded and smiled, advising the young soldier that "we must reluctantly take our leave, but please, monsieur, please do enjoy your time here and please know that you are always welcome at Versailles—and that you must return frequently to us!" Hugh bobbed his head and smiled, murmuring a soft *"Merci, Majesté,"* as, relinquishing the king's, Antoine again took his arm. As she curtseyed, he bowed to the departing monarch, noticing that his stride was almost diffident as he ambled towards the palace.

When Louis XV shortly thereafter rejoined his mistress in her apartments, speaking even as he entered the sumptuous sitting room, he shook his head. "Madame la dauphine, she appears most taken with her *young friend from home.*" He sighed, inquiring, "You could see him?" Du Barry nodding in the affirmative, the king continued, "I must say the Irish boy, he is certainly more impressive than my grandson will ever be, no?"

Du Barry unhesitatingly again nodded affirmatively, appending a simple "Indeed."

Meanwhile, a near-giddy dauphine had taken Hugh's hand. "Let us now go to the Gardens! You must see the fountains!" she said gaily.

Even as she was tugging at his hand, beginning to lead him away from the broad expanse of steps in the direction of the Versailles Gardens – and, in her mind, of *freedom* – the Princess de Lamballe stepped quietly to Marie Antoinette's side. Nodding almost imperceptively in apology to Hugh, she gently took her mistress's hand, creating several steps of separation between the dauphine and her guest, at which point she placed her arm at the dauphine's waist, thus turning both of their backs to the young cadet.

Leaning closely to her, speaking in a barely-audible voice, she began almost tenderly, "Madame, my dearest friend . . . I fear, indeed I most genuinely regret that I must remind you again of that subject about which we have spoken already several times today . . . ." Before Lamballe had even completed her thought, the dauphine's eyes were brimming, as she nodded stiffly, finally managing a soft, "*Oui.*"

Despite her gentle expression, the princess's voice, whilst remaining barely above a whisper, became assuredly definite, quite firm. "You must remember that you are now the dauphine of France, most assuredly now mere years away from becoming queen of France . . . and that you are wed! *Wed*, yes? You have left your family, your life, your possessions even, save for little Mops, behind . . . you have relinquished, willingly or not, everything—and *everyone*—which, and *who*, was once a part of your life. *Everyone*, Madame, *everyone!* And despite even who you are, not to mention the position to which you shall ascend, you can never, you shall never—*never*—regain anything—or *anyone*—from that life."

Though her eyes were by then dry, Marie Antoinette quiveringly nodded ever so slightly, even as her companion lightly kissed her hand and stepped, wordlessly, away.

Taking a deep breath, the dauphine finally turned and took several steps towards Hugh, who could not help but notice the flush on her flawless complexion.

They stood in awkward silence for a very long moment.

Finally, without intending to do so, Antoinette, after taking a deep breath, spoke *rather brusquely*, Hugh thought, "*Now* . . . you will know that all of this," she spread her arms broadly, "it was created by a gentleman, a masterful gardener named André Le Nôtre," she began. Even as she did so, anticipating Hugh's question, she realised she was uncertain when, so she smiled sweetly at her friend, ". . . many years ago."

Aided perhaps by what appeared to Hugh to be a genuinely-sheepish smile, some degree of balance slowly returned as they began to wander about the magnificence of greenery and fountains, the likes of which Hugh had never seen.

As a result, they spent the afternoon—at least to some extent—as they had spent many during what Antoinette had earlier referred to several times as "our magic months last year," walking, stopping, occasionally sitting on a stone bench or even perched on the edge of one of the fountains.

At one point, when Hugh impulsively took her hand, Antoinette appeared pained as she immediately, gently shook her head, quickly releasing it from her own; later, when Hugh turned and saw her dreamily gazing up into his eyes, he quickly averted them. Their moments of discomfit aside—they finally resumed talking, almost constantly, seemingly again effortlessly about anything—or almost anything that came into their minds—save that there was no mention by either of the other being *my dear, my very dear friend*. Confronted with reality, each appeared to the other to have seemingly concluded that the time for that had now passed.

In one of several lighter moments, Hugh nevertheless noted his friend's French had improved, that she seemed more certain, less hesitant and, as a result, their conversation flowed more smoothly. "Though I do miss the wee occasional Italian that you used to slip into our talks," he teased—to which the dauphine could only playfully punch his arm and laugh, "Oh, you—Hugh!" and giggle again—as she had so often done in Vienna.

It was only when the Princess de Lamballe quietly approached to gently remind the dauphine that the plan was to introduce Hugh to the dauphin upon her husband's return from his near-daily hunt, at which point they would all dine together, that the young friends realised their time together was ending.

The dauphine took this moment to formally introduce the princess and Hugh, Lamballe curtseying, Hugh bowing, both elegantly. Marie Antoinette would later recall that neither had taken his or her eyes off the other as they did so.

Indeed, even as the three of them stood chatting briefly, to his surprise—and to the dauphine's wide-eyed shock—the princess, quite nonchalantly and wholly atypical of her always very proper mien, not to mention her prudish reputation, continued to hold Hugh's larger, rough right hand between her palms—until, with a gentle, almost playful pat of her right hand and a lingeringly warm smile for Hugh, she quietly excused herself, at which point they once again exchanged a curtsey and a bow. This would be followed by a backward glance, clearly directed at Hugh, as she walked away. As to all of this, Hugh said nothing, though he noticed that the dauphine, who remained momentarily silent as well, had smiled wistfully—or was it sadly?

As they began their return to the chateau, walking at their own pace and again alone, Antoinette began, almost tentatively, "My husband, the dauphin, he hunts almost every day, from early morn until the evening. As the princess said, he is now returning, in order for me to be able to introduce you; he often stays out much later." Hugh sensed a sigh in her voice, his mind whirring, *Is she happy? Does she like this boy—this boy who would be the king of France? Dare I ask . . . ?*

"The dauphin is to join us in my apartments, to where our dinner shall be brought," she announced in a playful, grandiloquent tone, "I hope you will like him," she added, not at all playfully. She then explained that they customarily dined later, frequently much later in the evening, but that she had succeeded in changing the time for this evening's meal so as to permit him to join them.

As Antoinette escorted Hugh into her magnificent suite, she was clearly surprised to see that her husband had already arrived. Still in his hunting clothes, slouched in a high-backed chair, he was leafing through a book as the couple entered, Hugh immediately dropping to his right knee.

Seemingly taken aback by the tall young Irishman's gesture, setting the book down on the carpet, an annoyed Louis Auguste rose heavily, awkwardly, mumbling something that sounded to Hugh like the French equivalent of "Oh, get up, man!" which he immediately did, following which Antoinette smilingly introduced them informally. The dauphin offered him what Hugh felt was a surprisingly weak, listless handshake.

Eying each other critically, the two young men contrasted markedly:

Trim and handsome, Hugh was as resplendent as he could be in the cadet's version of the striking uniform of Dillon's Regiment of the Irish Brigade of France—the red coat brilliant, the subtle yellow and white facings elegant, only a delicate coating of gravel dust on his gleaming boots detracted from an otherwise flawless appearance. Standing not quite six feet and three inches, his thick, dirty-blond hair was tied in a tight queue, even the bow remained horizontally level. His posture reminded the dauphine of Eileen's: tall, elegant—*perfect*, she mused.

Though Louis was almost as tall as Hugh, one would not easily have seen it, as his posture was poor; he slouched, which only served to emphasis his portliness. His rough hunting clothes were dirty and mud-spattered, as were his boots. His hair was as dishevelled as his clothing.

To Hugh's surprise, the future king of France reeked of sweat and dirt, of blood—and perhaps even of scat.

Quickly, looking at Antoinette, he could see she was disappointed in, more likely even embarrassed by, her husband's appearance. Hugh felt genuinely sorry for her, to the extent that if he could have done so, he would have at that moment forgone dinner and simply returned to Paris.

She stepped, then leaned slightly towards the dauphin. Her voice soft, hushed, "My dear, would you perhaps care to bathe—or at least have a quick wash—and then change . . . before we dine?" the young woman hopefully inquired of her husband, who waved his right hand dismissively.

"I should like to dine *now*," he said brusquely. "I have had a very long day." He sighed deeply as he looked expectantly in the direction of his wife's small dining room. Antoinette gestured subtly to the staff and within moments the trio was seated at an elegant though not large rectangular table, Hugh flanked by the presumptive king and queen in what were apparently their customary seats at either end. As Louis had led the way into dinner, Hugh could not help but note his round-shouldered, shuffling walk.

It was only when Hugh inquired, "Did you enjoy a good day in the field, Highness?" that the heavy silence in the room was broken. Louis yawned and again waved his hand dismissively, sighing. "Actually, it was most unsatisfactory today: too hot the huntsmen said, though I felt they could have prepared better. . . . " his eyes appearing cloudy, Hugh thought, as he continued, "Though I did take one boar, a small, nasty one—butchered and hung awhile; we shall dine on it during the coming weeks," he advised his wife, who smiled weakly. Remembering Antoine's refined, almost dainty tastes in food in Vienna, Hugh immediately felt—correctly, he was quite certain—that the meat of a small, nasty boar was surely less than appealing to her.

Once the simple soup—almost a broth, favoured considerably more by the dauphine than by her husband—was served, spoons gently clinked and they began to dine. After a few moments, setting his spoon down hard, noisily, Louis squinted again at Hugh, leaning towards him. "So, you are Irish, yet you come here from Vienna, my wife tells me."

Hugh nodded and began to speak, though before he could, Louis— still peering, perhaps even more pointedly than before, again leaning towards him—observed rather than asked, "Why would you not remain in Austria, indeed why not simply stay in Ireland?"

Sensing in Hugh's slight hesitation perhaps a reluctance to immediately respond to the pointed inquiry, Antoinette attempted to begin an explanation. Even as she did, her husband was gesturing to the first footman: "Fish or fowl, preferably meat—I *must* have something of substance to eat!" his voice rumbled. Halting in midsentence, the dauphine averted her eyes, focusing on her empty soup bowl, as, with a gentle clatter of china and cutlery the soup service was cleared and the next course, consisting of a variety of shellfish, was served.

Perhaps he is simply hungry; hunger can surely make one ill-tempered, Hugh reflected, determining not to try to speak further to him until his host had an opportunity to eat. Hugh focused on that the food would be excellent, the wines perhaps surpassing any he had enjoyed in Vienna, quietly exchanging words with his hostess instead.

He smiled broadly as freshly baked croissants were offered, as well as that a quite ample silver basket, lined with linen and filled with the breads, was set before the dauphine. Their first croissants quickly consumed, Hugh smilingly accepted a second—as he would several others—from his hostess, recalling how she'd introduced him to the croissant in Vienna, saying it was amongst her "very, very favourite breads!" As they spoke, he also recalled hearing that the breads had first been made by bakers in Vienna in the 1680s, marking the defeat of the Turks who had besieged the city at that time, their unique crescent shape, a symbol of Islam, the feature of the invaders' flag. He nodded and smiled his approval as Antoinette advised that they were being referred to at court as *viennoiseries,* "Viennese breads." Louis remained impassive as to the conversation, though he ate a number of croissants.

Cutlery clattered gently—or, in the case of the dauphin, rather loudly—as several subsequent courses of relatively simply prepared roasted meats, poultry and fish were served, accompanied by a variety of steamed vegetables. The dauphine limited herself to the roasted chicken and several small slices of roast pork, drinking no wine but rather sipping lemonade.

As the meal continued, Hugh was finally able to quietly and simply explain his presence in France—relying primarily on that his older brother was already in the service of Louis XV and of the O'Connells' close commercial ties to the kingdom. The dauphin appearing satisfied, Hugh then attempted several times to further engage a once-again sullen Louis, the Frenchman's responses seeming near-surly, snappish and primarily consisting of *oui* or *non* expressed in a gruff, almost guttural tone. Once, when Hugh's eyes fell on Antoinette, he saw her cheeks flaming, and he felt she was about to cry. He impulsively began to reach for her hand, catching himself only at the last moment.

Antoinette completing her meal first, and then Hugh, who, in addition to the chicken, sampled roast beef, prepared rare, and a filet of a freshwater fish he could not identify, both having seemingly having eaten their fill, were finished well in advance of the rotund young man, whose appetite seemed *near-insatiable*, Hugh thought. He tried to avoid appearing as pained as he felt when he gazed at Antoine. *He devours food like a rough countryman, one who does not eat regularly.* As he continued to eat, Louis appeared to take little if any note that his wife and guest had finished and were quietly chatting, Antoinette having switched to her favoured water, one brought from Ville d'Avray, known for its purity, whilst Hugh drank several glasses of wine, as Louis finished his dinner.

At long last, pastries and coffee were served. Hugh found the array of what Antoinette referred to as *des pâtisseries* to be nothing short of magnificent, as they were presented on four suitably splendid three-foot-high, multitiered silver cake stands. Included amongst the striking offerings were Louis XI's favourite marzipan turnovers, as well as a variety of *choux á la crème*. It was the profiteroles that were displayed most conspicuously: The small round choux pastry buns, bursting with a variety of sweet crème fillings, were heavily glazed, most with chocolate, but others with vanilla or coffee-based icing, such that they all gleamed in the soft candlelight.

Antoinette indicated she would take a dainty bowl of chocolate rissole and a single one of Louis IX's turnovers whilst, to her smiling delight, Hugh allowed himself a broad selection from the splendid assortment, as well as two offerings of lime crème brulée.

As the young friends savoured their selections, sipping their coffee, Louis piled two plates high with pastries, chomping on several more even as he served himself, licking his fingers, appearing to Hugh to be trying to consume as many of the delicacies as possible in the shortest possible time. Embarrassed for the red-faced young man, Hugh finally—albeit reluctantly, for Antoine's sake—concluded to himself that Louis was oafishly gauche, very much to the point of being rude, at best socially inept and even then sadly tongue-tied and obviously uncomfortable, thinking, *future king or not, he is a dolt.* He contrasted his host to his grandfather, Louis XV, whom Hugh had found to be charming, personable and pleasant. *But not this sad fellow—in no way is he any of these!*

At his wife's gentle insistence, Louis, with obvious reluctance, at long last indicated he had completed his dessert. In response to the dauphine's near-urgent gesture, a trio of young footmen immediately moved to clear the table. Deeming the meal thus over, the dauphin rose, as, according to court protocol, so too did his wife. Hugh immediately stood as well.

Louis led his wife and guest into the dauphine's sitting room. As they halted, turning to each other in a semicircle the three began to speak at once, the single genuinely humorous event of the evening, permitting them to share a very brief collective laugh. Their stilted conversation was little more than momentary as, the apartments' doors having been silently opened for her, the Princesse de Lamballe now appeared in the entryway, her soft blue eyes immediately fixing on Hugh. He noted she had changed into an elegant, deep royal blue satin robe with a striking train so long that much of it remained in the corridor, as she did not enter the room.

Even as Hugh was still speaking, completing his expression of thanks to the couple, with a curtly mumbled "Good evening, sir," Louis turned abruptly, lumbering wordlessly past the princess, whom he did not acknowledge by word or simple gesture, leaving his wife and her friend to take a hasty, uncomfortably awkward leave of each other.

Hugh would long recall Marie Antoinette's genuinely pained expression as, hastening to join her husband, she turned her flushed face towards him. Nor would he ever forget his sense of the moment—perhaps more correctly, of the day itself, as he wrote in a brief note to Abigail the following day that, *it was what one feels whilst reluctantly watching the curtain being drawn on what had been a delightful play—or the same, upon completing, slowly, reluctantly closing a wonderful book.* It was only later that he would wonder if Antoinette had perhaps looked back again, realising that if indeed she had, she would have seen the princess, having immediately, elegantly taken his arm, leading him away—in the opposite direction.

As they strolled slowly through the now-surprisingly quiet—perhaps, due to the silence and, more so, the absence of the customary throngs, even more magnificent palace—Hugh walked at the pace the princess set, she clearly being in no hurry.

Her elegant train *wisping* over the marble flooring as well as the thick carpets, she now held his right arm firmly, with her free hand occasionally pointing out an objet d'art, in a number of instances effortlessly identifying the subject of a painting or sculpture. After she'd gestured to a portrait of Catherine de' Medici, advising in some significant historical detail as she did so, that Catherine had been queen of France as the wife of Henri II, the princess halted and grew momentarily silent, a playful, pixie-like expression creeping over her already radiant face, her eyes twinkling as she looked at Hugh.

Taking several steps more, the pair halted again, this time at the top of a dramatic staircase. To Hugh's surprise, the princess began speaking in softly, uniquely accented English—as to whether it was flavoured with

French or Italian, he could only fleetingly wonder—as she inquired, "So, my dear Master O'Connell, I trust you have enjoyed your day with the dauphine . . . and that you found your dinner to be a pleasant one." She smiled brightly, then dazzlingly, as Hugh diplomatically indicated that he had had a very pleasant time, expressing his thanks to her for her part in making it a "most memorable day."

As they slowly descended the steps, she continued softly, "I have grown so fond of your dear friend, the dauphine; she is such a wonderful young woman, so very kind to me." Pausing, Lamballe then advised Hugh, "So much of her life since arriving from Vienna has changed, sir. Her days are so full, she has virtually no time for friends," she added. Pausing again for a moment perhaps halfway down the staircase, she then, not at all subtly, indicated that, despite her high position in service to Marie Antoinette, she herself enjoyed a considerably less restricted life, even being permitted to travel occasionally into Paris, "which Her Royal Highness is not permitted to do, she and her husband having yet to make the required formal entry into the city," she said softly, her eyes lowered, as they descended the final steps in silence.

Clearing the last step, she effortlessly resumed in French, "So, you see, monsieur," "should you like, I may perhaps pay you a visit . . . at your school?" she said mischievously—almost coquettishly. "Would you enjoy that?" Hugh thought she was teasing until he felt her grasp on his arm become firmer, as she inquired, once again unsubtly, *"Ce serait agréable, non?"*

Hugh smiled broadly, returning to French as well. "That would be *most* pleasant, *yes!"* he assured her with a gentle nod and a dazzling smile of his own.

As they slowly approached the entryway where a weary-looking— and, as Hugh would discover soon enough, openly surly—Lt. O'Kelly awaited him, the princess assured Hugh that she would indeed make arrangements with his superiors for a visit, *"à trés bientôt,"* then laughingly—but quite seriously—promising him a large basket of baked delicacies, "As I believe the cadets' mess at the Irish Brigade, even that of the Dillons' proud regiment, it does not serve croissants, monsieur . . . much less profiteroles!" Hugh laughed aloud in confirmation of her surmise, as they stepped closer to the fully opened door, the fingers of a white-gloved servant's hand resting on the gleaming wood.

Even as Hugh began to step outside, where a groom awaited, prepared to immediately hand him his horse's reins, the striking young woman gently caused him to turn instead and face her, her golden-blond hair softly reflecting the flickering candlelight of the small vestibule, the flames dancing delicately in her eyes; raising them slightly, so she gazed into his, then kissing each cheek, she smiled, saying softly, *"Jusque-là, mon ami."*

Ignoring O'Kelly, Hugh bowed gently, nodding. *"Jusqu'à-là, en effet, madame. Merci!"*

Finally mounted, Hugh smiled at the princess once again, her eyes fixed warmly on him as she gazed upward at him; it was only after that did he, for the first time, see the seething, teeth-gritting fury on O'Kelly's face. Wordlessly, he turned his horse away from Versailles. He did not at all have a pleasant ride back to Paris.

Though he had been able to write and have delivered a very brief expression of thanks to Marie Antoinette, and—despite that, in responses to letters from Abigail and Eileen, he had also written brief notes to both of his sisters in the interim—Hugh's next substantial letter to Eileen, who remained his closest regular correspondent, was actually written quite a number of weeks later:

École Militaire, Paris
20 September 1770

My dearest Sister—

It is with sincere regret and deepest apologies that I acknowledge my recent resounding failure as a correspondent! The days, weeks and—dare I say?—months have sped by at an almost alarming speed, at least for one as young as I! As to your own days, etc., perhaps—filled as they are with spouse and child, the demands of a home and estate yet again—especially given the vast years which separate us!—I should think you are far more accustomed to this speedy passage of time than am I! I trust you and Arthur and Conor are all well. I think of you all often and fondly.

My schooling goes well, both the academic and military courses, though the latter are clearly given precedence over the former. This notwithstanding, you will be pleased to hear that I arrived at École Militaire quite well-prepared. I am advanced in my Latin— Greek is not taught—well beyond any of my fellows. I find—and my instructors confirm the fact—that my command of French exceeds any of my French brothers' of English. The Jesuit fathers similarly prepared me well in mathematics, though I do not aspire to military engineering as the numbers involved and their use seem beyond me. I am of course advanced in English drama and literature and doing well in those arts in French, though I have not as yet found any Frenchman who could replace Master Shakespeare! I am progressing, albeit slowly, in my studies of French history, of politics and society as well as of the military. I do thank you for permitting me to borrow the books you and the Abbé Vermond used whilst schooling the dauphine in some of these topics—at least I knew the names of some of the people and events.

Please tell my brother Arthur that I am well-practised in field drill as we march daily, most days in the morning, others morning and afternoon! My equestrian skills are, I am told, amongst the finest here, as is my shooting ability. I am learning swordplay— with the sabre, rapier and broadsword, even being taught specifically the use of the two-handed claymore, as used by the doomed Highlanders at Culloden—its hilt appears as a basket. The grim nature and purpose of the art and training notwithstanding, I find it quite enjoyable, and, dare I say, at times actually fun! I have told the heart-stopping tale of Denis O'Sullivan's wounding more than once, and the instructors say he must be an extraordinary horseman, an unsurpassed swordsman. I told them he is both, which made me feel most proud!

Also, if you would please tell Arthur that I am come to find the study of tactics quite fascinating—fondly recalling our beloved General, the Count—these titles are no longer humorous, are they? As when Mama would refer to them in jest?—as we sat on the floor with his wee soldiers, explaining to me the significant differences between those employed in foot as opposed to horse. That seems so very long ago!

I also quite enjoy the study of French military history, which is often taught as tactics. We recently spent several days immersed in what they refer to here as the Battle of Fontenoy-en-Puisaye—and you must know how proud I was as the instructor, after speaking at some length of the significant contributions of the Irish Brigade, indeed of my own Dillon's Regiment! to what he referred to as being a "decisive French victory"— even to costing Col. Jas. Dillon his life—singled me out, saying, "On this history . . . you may stand tall, Monsieur Cadet O'Connell, be proud of your regiment, indeed of your warrior race, sir!"

You will know that, barring some academic or other disaster I am told I am to complete my course of studies in May of 1772 and shall at that time be commissioned a sub-lieutenant.

I see the current Col.—also I believe possessed of the rank of a general officer beyond the regiment—Dillon but rarely, and have had no contact with him; his grandson, Arthur, whom I believe is perhaps four or five years older than I, is a junior officer serving these last four years or so as an instructor. He is a fine gentleman and a good teacher. You may be interested to know that he is already wed and spends most evenings at his home on what I am told is the very elegant rue de Bac, which is on the far side of the Seine. He and his wife are cousins and have a wee baby girl, not yet one-year-old. Mme Dillon's uncle is Archbishop Dillon of Narbonne—so well-established here in France are the Dillons! Perhaps brother Daniel and I shall see to it that the O'Connells are eventually similarly situate, though I know of no men of our even extended family who might aspire to holy orders!

I am certain you anxiously await news of your wee little archduchess. True to her promise and intention, the dauphine did indeed summon my good self to Versailles, this in June. I shall leave it to your imagination as to how this invitation was received by those in charge here when it was delivered by a liveried messenger from the palace!

Accompanied by a junior officer, I rode to Versailles on 17 June, a beautiful and warm day, and was greeted by the dauphine of France in the presence of numerous courtiers,

Versailles is, as you have heard, truly magnificent. We walked in the beautiful gardens, and there seem to be more splendid fountains in those gardens as there are in all of Vienna. Schönbrunn, whilst I shall always consider it beautiful, magnificent in its own way, is less opulent when compared to Versailles. I would find both the Hofburg and Schönbrunn as being more comfortable places in which to dwell, they seem more like a home than does Versailles. Etiquette or protocol, whatever term one would use, it is far stricter there, and I sense far more burdensome than similar types of rules under the empress. Yet, incredibly, 'tis frequently thronged with people—there is a stand at the gate where a man—virtually any man!—may hire a sword and, thus outfitted, be then admitted to wander freely throughout much of the chateau. Could you imagine this at Schönbrunn?

I met the king! albeit briefly. We spoke for several minutes, he was most kind to me and he shook my hand. He is, as is said of him, handsome; he has dark hair, very black eyes and a deep voice. Antoine appears to adore him, and he her.

After she showed me all the gardens and fountains, we went to Antoine's apartments in the palace and were greeted—I am not certain if that is the correct word!—by her doltish husband, the dauphin. It is only that I know that this letter will reach you via the Irish Brigade that I will say he is a rather odd fellow for a future king! He is brusque and seems awkward. I believe he has difficulties with his eyes, his vision as he squints a great deal. He hunts daily—for pure sport only, as I should think the palace is amply provisioned—and indeed came to dinner directly from the hunting grounds, his clothing and his person looking—and smelling—much like you and your clothing on the days you worked with the horses at Derrynane!

His conversational skills are horribly lacking and Mama would not tolerate his manners at table. He has an enormous appetite and Antoine and I had to wait whilst he finished devouring his many desserts.

I thoroughly enjoyed my time with Antoine and well that I did, as I have not seen her again, nor have I heard from her.

As you—and Abigail—told me they would be, things are indeed very, very different now that Antoine is dauphine of France. I have learnt that her life here is

far less her own than it was whilst she was a mere *archduchess of Austria &*
Lorraine. Her time is very circumscribed; they process to daily Mass; a number of
meals are even taken in public! She has little privacy, they appear to dress her up and
parade her about like a wee dolly. I did not, I felt I could not, ask of her if she is
happy, but I fear she may not be.

I do know she has come to Paris, this on the occasion earlier this month of what I
am told was a "masked ball"—which, to one such as I!—ignorant of such
entertainments—sounds rather peculiar, like some version of blind man's buff being
played to music? But, no, it is an actual ball, during which the participants dance en
masquerade. It still strikes me as being odd!

All in all, I have no regret that we were "very dear friends" in Austria and I
shall always have great fondness for her, but she is, as yet again you said she would be,
after all, now "Madame la Dauphine," who will someday become queen of France—
and no longer simply my dear friend Antoine.

Hugh paused, rereading, then thinking about what he had written.
Once again dipping, the quill he continued:

As you sometimes mention in your letters when you have done so, I have just now
sat for a few moments—not writing but rather, as you say, "reflecting":

Having done so, I believe I shall now tell you of a new friend whose acquaintance
I have made and, though on an extremely limited and restricted basis, whose company
I have now five times since June enjoyed. I must in truth say that she is well above my
good self in standing here, albeit not a queen will she ever become!

Her name is longer than that of any person I have ever met! You will know that
she is Marie Thérèse Louise de Savoie-Carignan, the Princesse de Lamballe! She was
born in Turin in 1749, so she is six years older than I. And, despite her youth, she is
a widow, having been wed but briefly to a prince who died.

I came to make her acquaintance as she has been and remains the dauphine's
closest companion since her arrival at court. I was first introduced to the princess the
day I went to Versailles and it was she who thereafter several times conveyed brief
written greetings to me on behalf of the dauphine. I have since come to believe,
however, that she was merely being kind in doing so and was never actually writing at
the behest of the dauphine.

During these months, those letters, written ostensibly on behalf of the dauphine, ceased entirely, whilst those of her own have grown quite frequent and more familiar. We share an enjoyment of books and reading and horses. She is quite tall, though not as tall as you, dearest Sister—is any woman?—and has golden hair, very like Anna's. (How is Anna? I hope she is well and likes Ireland. Please say hello from me to her.) And blue eyes; she has very blue eyes. And she speaks excellent English! So, we converse and correspond in both French and English, though she is helping me to improve my spoken French considerably.

She has visited me here five times now, most recently just last Sunday—thus being the individual whose "company I have now (that many) times since June enjoyed," as I wrote above. Each time she has brought hampers of pastries and croissants and food, all of which is most assuredly not the customary fare in our cadets' mess. Her visits, especially her "deliveries," have caused much of a stir at school, but—as she says—she is, after all, a princess . . . though the officers appear more curious than pleased when she comes. I hope she will continue to come here. I am, as you are surely able to conclude, quite taken with la Princesse!

On this highly positive note, I shall close—With great love and deepest affection always, from your devoted brother—

Before finally signing his full name with a flourish, Hugh reread his lengthy letter several times, smiling just barely as he came upon mention of the striking Savoyard, closing his eyes as he each time permitted his words *quite tall* and *blue eyes* to conjure a mind's eye image of the luminously blond, truly beautiful, he thought, Marie Thérèse Louise de Savoie-Carignan.

Rathleigh House, near Macroom, County Cork, Ireland—Autumn 1770

Following what had now become her customary brisk morning ride with Bull, Eileen was striding from the stables. Gazing towards the gleaming white-washed façade of Rathleigh House, she could only smile as through the already partially open front doorway burst little Conor O'Leary, Anna in pursuit. The nimble young blonde quickly captured him in full flight, laughingly gathering him in her arms, his little legs still pumping.

Hastening her stride, Eileen came upon them and feigned disappointment when her squirming son refused, as he frequently did of late, to "come to Mama."

Anna made a playfully dismissive motion with her free hand as she lowered Conor to the ground, "Ah, it is to the stables that we are bound, *Mistress*," she smiled at the title she no longer used, "Grandpapa told him one of the sheepdogs has had puppies."

As Eileen turned as if to join them in search of the puppies, her friend gestured again, this time back into the house. "Some kind soul has brought the mail from Macroom. It is on the dining table and I believe that you will want to read especially one letter—from your other little boy, Hugh!" Anna laughed.

Finishing tugging off her gloves, Eileen quickly entered the house and immediately went to the lower end of the large, gleaming dining table upon which was indeed piled a mound of newspapers, current from Cork, reasonably so from Dublin, but weeks-old from London, circulars and perhaps two dozen pieces of correspondence. Anna having set the one with Hugh's distinctive looping handwriting upright against the pile, Eileen immediately plucked it up, and, even before she sat, ripped it open, breaking its plain wax seal, failing to notice a piece of which had fallen on the carpet until she heard it being crunched by the heel of her boot.

Quickly gathering up the few pieces of hard wax, she sat and leaned back in what was Arthur's customary seat at table, withdrawing the several thick, rough pieces of paper, her dark blue eyes moving deliberately over her youngest brother's idiosyncratic script, nodding as she absorbed the news on the first page, on the top of the second.

It was only as she continued to read the second page, to the top of the third, that her eyes grew wide, as she purposely increased her reading speed—then stopped reading abruptly.

Laughing audibly, Eileen then spoke—quite loudly, actually—into the quiet late morning. "Bloody hell! She did it, *she actually did it!* She bloody well succeeded in getting her bloody little friend to bloody Versailles . . . practically before she was *bloody well unpacked!*"

She then stood, gripping the pages, speaking—still, she believed, to only herself, though unbeknownst to her, the girls in the kitchen pantry continued to listen and giggle—in a faux stentorian tone and manner as she grandly proclaimed, "*There are in place unalterable, irreversible and final orders of General Dillon! Should any man or men fail to follow them to the letter, their miserable lives shall be immediately forfeit, as they shall be hanged, drawn, quartered, beheaded and dismembered, the worthless remains of their mortal bodies then to be scattered to the ends of the realm, indeed to the ends of the very earth itself!*"—affectionately mimicking her brother, Daniel, who had solemnly advised them before they had departed France that, whilst he remained at the military academy, Hugh was and would continue to be as cloistered as a monk, General Theobold Dillon himself having seen to it that any communication from Versailles to Hugh would instead be brought directly to the general.

"Hah!" Eileen laughed aloud as she wandered outside, attempting to locate her husband, reading the rest of the letter as she walked. "*Hah!*"

Following her instincts, Eileen came upon Arthur—as he had joined Anna and his son at the cosy, hay-pillowed corner of the stables where Millie, a gentle border collie, as much a family pet as she was a valued working dog, had chosen to deliver her litter of six now furiously nursing puppies, towards whom Eileen leaned, and momentarily gazed, and smiled.

Upright again, she gently waved the pages of the letter at both adults; being careful not to startle the new mother and wee little babies, in a low voice Eileen playfully inquired, "Whom do you believe writes us"—she tapped the letter with her right forefinger—"of his summertime visit to *Versailles* with the *dauphine of France*, in the process meeting *the bloody king of France himself*, of strolling the gardens and the palace and there dining with the future king and queen of France, and . . . " She finally convulsed in laughter as O'Leary plucked the pages out of her hand, Anna shaking her head in mirthful amazement, her mouth agape.

Momentarily leaving an awestruck Conor to watch over Millie and her pups, the adults stepped just outside the stable door, into the bright sunshine.

"But what of the standing orders of General Dillon?" the pert young Austrian, only half-seriously, asked the couple, Eileen shaking her head again responding, "'Tis not the first time military orders have gone awry . . . is it, my darling?" she inquired of her still-reading husband, then good-naturedly repeatedly punching his shoulder, each time playfully demanding of him, "*Is* it?" Shaking his head, the young cavalry officer could only add, ". . . nor the last, I fear," and the three adults then laughed as one.

It was late that evening, well after dinner, the Squire, Anna and Conor all abed, the small household staff as well and the house silent, save for its own occasional creaks and murmurs that Arthur and Eileen swirled and sipped brandy in striking, Irish cut-crystal snifters whilst seated before a low fire in the small family parlour.

"Ah, Richard Hennessy, he distils a fine brandy, does he not, my darling love?" Eileen said to her husband after she'd enjoyed what was perhaps her third sip of the warming liqueur, which the one-time Irish Brigade officer had begun producing near Cognac in 1765, only just in the last year or so offering it for sale and consumption.

"He does indeed! 'Tis well for him and good for us that he departed the service of Louis XV to pursue what is obviously his true calling," O'Leary smiled, pleased that as soon as the initial charred oaken casks in which the dark, rich liquid had aged for almost three years had first been tapped and the brandy bottled for shipment, the O'Connells' vessels had begun returning to Ireland with cases of Hennessy's fine liqueurs. They were especially pleased now that, beginning with their own springtime journey from Le Havre, a pair of cases such as those they had themselves then carried to Cork would henceforth be regularly destined for Rathleigh's cellars.

By this late hour the couple had reread and were completing their discussion of Hugh's letter, agreeing that the reality of the young people's unalterably changed circumstances must have been a sad realisation for both Hugh and Marie Antoinette, though Eileen mused that "the lad's heart, 'tis clearly not at all broken by this." As to the topic of the apparently-beautiful princess, Art had, amongst a number of other things, opined, "I should think a young woman such as she will turn her attentions to someone whose immediate prospects are beyond being commissioned a sub-lieutenant in a foreign brigade of the armies of Louis XV."

As they shared a laugh, Eileen appended a soft, "One would certainly think so, my darling." Though even as she spoke, in her customary prescience her undeclared thought was . . . *though of this we cannot be at all certain. Indeed, I have some sense that we shall be hearing much more of this young woman.*

They then grew quiet, gazing together but separately into the gentle, low flames.

Eventually affectionately looking over at his wife, Eileen's expressive face appearing to him to indicate that she was at the moment faraway, O'Leary gently inquired, "So, my love, the lad—he writes of palaces and princesses, of masked balls and elegant dining in a setting perhaps even more magnificent than our Hofburg or Schönbrunn, aye? Could it be, my darling, that you might be missing such things?"

Eileen shook her head, dismissing whatever vision she'd been seeing in the flames and, turning, smiled warmly at him. Rising, taking a step, she immediately perched herself on her husband's lap, his left arm embracing her waist as, her right arm stretched across his shoulder, she rested her head against his, permitting them to once again silently gaze together into the fire. Eileen could feel Art's heart beating, they breathed almost in unison.

Finally, her husky voice gentle, she responded, "No, my dearest love, I do not miss any of it—not at all, as wonderful it was in Vienna, as lovely—indeed as magnificent!—as Versailles sounds. *This*"—as with a delicate sweep of her left arm she embraced all that was Rathleigh—"this estate, this farm is our palace, really ours—by the grace and favour of no one other than your dear father alone and thus 'tis truly our home.

"Never was I for even one moment at any Austrian palace happier nor more at peace than I am at this very moment."

O'Leary hugged her tightly. "Aye, indeed . . . nor I."

Eileen added turf and wood to the fire, whilst her husband refilled their sparkling glasses with Hennessy's subtly sensual elixir. They talked and dreamt long into the night of the life that lay ahead of them—in this, what they together firmly believed was and would remain their gentle, green part of the world.

An Deireadh

NOTES AS TO SOURCES

As was *Beyond Derrynane,* so too, is *Two Journeys Home* a work of fiction, and, once again, it has been the tantalisingly few facts that are actually known of Eileen's and the other O'Connells' lives that have provided the basic threads around which the tale itself is woven, into which strategic additions of numerous fictional and historical personalities and events have, I hope, seamlessly intertwined.

I have been a serious student of selected (including especially the Eighteenth Century) periods of the history of Ireland for most of my life; one significant aspect of this has been a continuing scholarly as well as personal interest in my extended family, many distant, and long-ago members of which, especially the characters of whom I write, I have "known" intimately since childhood. Some of the tales which I grew up hearing, and later reading about, have been the genesis for parts of both *Derrynane* and *Two Journeys Home.*

This notwithstanding, neither book could have been written absent a near-lifetime of reading and studying the works of a number of extraordinary historians and other authors, to all of whom – living and dead – an immeasurable debt is owed, especially to those noted below.

Though most of these works are cited in this same section of *Beyond Derrynane;* given my continued reliance on virtually all of them, in one way or another, in the writing of *Two Journeys Home,* at the risk of appearing repetitive, I feel it is only right to, once again, acknowledge the books and their authors.

In addition to family materials, old notes and the like, my formal research has included standard works such as the still-brilliant *Course of Irish History,* by T.W. Moody and F.X. Martin; *Contested Island (Ireland 1460-1630)* by S.J. Connolly and *Gaelic Ireland (1250 – 1650: Land,*

Lordship & Settlement), edited by Patrick J. Duffy, David Edwards and Elizabeth Fitzpatrick.

Raymond Gillespie's *Seventeenth Century Ireland* as well as Ian McBride's *Eighteenth Century Ireland*, both volumes in the Gill New History of Ireland series, and Patrick Moran's *The Catholics of Ireland under the Penal Laws of the Eighteenth Century* proved invaluable in permitting me to immerse myself in the period and, hopefully, to write, at least to some degree, as the seanachie told tales of ancient Ireland – as had the events unfolded only recently, rather than centuries before.

Daniel Corkery's *Hidden Ireland*; volume one of Mrs. Morgan John O'Connell's classic work, *The Last Colonel of the Irish Brigade, Count O'Connell and Old Irish Life at Home and abroad, 1745-1833*, Richard Hayward's *In the Kingdom of Kerry*, Malachi McCormick's detailed, indeed poetic notes to his extraordinary translation of *A Lament for Art O'Leary* (his Stone Street Press's hand-made book being a work of art in itself); Patrick M. Geoghan's two-volume biography of Daniel O'Connell, *The Rise of Daniel O'Connell, 1775-1829* and *The Life and Death of Daniel O'Connell, 1830-1846*; Sean O'Faolain's classic *King of the Beggars: The Life of Daniel O'Connell* and *Daniel O'Connell's Childhood* by Brian Igoe, which appears on *The Irish Story* website, have all played the same role for me concerning the O'Connells, the O'Sullivans, Derrynane and County Kerry.

These works have been augmented by John Crowley and John Sheehan's breath-taking *The Iveragh Peninsula: A Cultural Atlas of the Ring of Kerry* and *Derrynane House National Historical Park: A Guide to the Country Home of Daniel O'Connell* by Jim Larner (vice Alain Craig's prior version)

Jim Ryan's *Carrauntoohil & MacGillicuddy's Reeks: A Walking Guide to Ireland's Highest Mountains* was priceless in enabling, amongst a number of other things, my being able to trace Eileen's fictitious trek to Ballyhar in *Derrynane* as well as to write of the entire region with a greater degree of certainty.

Priceless background for the lives and careers of the Irish officers who appear in the book was provided by John Cornelius O'Callaghan's massive classic, *History of the Irish Brigades in the Service of France* which, in part, provided the actual genesis for the *Derrynane Saga* – as well as by Stephen McGarry's *Irish Brigades Abroad, From the Wild Geese to the Napoleonic Wars*, George B. Clark's *Irish Soldiers in Europe 17ᵗʰ-19ᵗʰ Century*, and the *Wild Geese – The Irish Brigades in the Service of France and Spain*, written by Mary McLaughlin and beautifully illustrated by Chris Warner.

In connection with the Vienna period, and in anticipation of the events unfolding and the characters (especially Marie Thérèse Louise de Savoie-Carignan, the Princesse de Lamballe) being introduced in Paris and at Versailles, I have continued to rely on *Maria Theresa: Biography of a Monarch* by Elfriede Iby, along with the extraordinary biographies of Marie Antoinette by Evelyne Lever (*Marie Antoinette: The Last Queen of France*) and Antonia Fraser (*Marie Antoinette: The Journey*), as well as Munro Price's *The Road from Versailles;* Carolly Erickson's *To the Scaffold*, Caroline Morehead's *Dancing to the Precipice: The Life of Lucie De La Tour Du Pin* (the daughter of General Arthur Dillon – who deserves an insightful biography of his own) and *Marie Thérèse, Child of Terror The Fate of Marie Antoinette's Daughter,* by Susan Nagel.

Though Daniel Charles and Hugh O'Connell's separate periods of study and training there pre-date Napoleon's by some fifteen to twenty years, early chapters of the extraordinary biographical work, *Napoleon Bonaparte* by Alan Schom, provided valuable insights into the history of and the academic and military training provided by École Militaire to cadets in the Eighteenth Century.

Robert K. Massey's *Catherine the Great: Portrait of a Woman* suggested Major von Klaus's mission to St. Petersburg, well as providing the various rationales for the Emperor dispatching him thus.

Internet-available essays by Brian McGinn ("St. Patrick's Day in Vienna, 1766") and by the unidentified blogger who maintains the fascinating blog site *The Blue Blot: notes, finds and fragments of research* ("The Ball of the Wild Geese – St. Patrick's Day 1766 in Habsburg Austria") were invaluable in providing otherwise unavailable detail for the referenced event.

I have collected and consulted copious numbers of booklets and smaller books, as well as notes made, at numerous locations in Ireland, France and Austria. The experience of wandering over the years from the sanctuary that Derrynane remains, in many ways little changed from the Eighteenth Century (many thanks yet again to OPW for their on-going efforts to preserve and enhance the area), as well as through the streets of Paris and Vienna, of Dublin and the countryside beyond these cities has proven invaluable. I must say once again that few experiences were as a fascinating as an afternoon "stables tour" at the Spanish Riding School in Vienna, its impact rendered even more permanent and vivid by the extraordinary book, *450 Years of the Spanish Riding School*, written by René Van Baken and Arnim Basche, published on the occasion of this milestone in this wholly-unique institution's colourful history.

ABOUT THE AUTHOR

KEVIN O'CONNELL IS A NATIVE of New York City, descended from a young officer of what had – from 1690 to 1792 – been the Irish Brigade of the French army, believed to have arrived in French Canada sometime following the execution of Queen Marie Antoinette in October, 1793. At least one grandson subsequently returned to Ireland; Mr. O'Connell's own grandparents arrived in New York in the early Twentieth Century. He holds both Irish and American citizenship.

Given this heritage, he has been a serious student of Eighteenth Century Irish and European history for virtually all his life; one significant aspect of this has been a continuing scholarly as well as personal interest in the extended O'Connell family.

As a result, in 2014, Mr. O'Connell began writing a series of historical fiction novels, now known as the *Derrynane Saga*. His first book, *Beyond Derrynane: A Novel of Eighteenth Century Europe,* was published by The Gortcullinane Press in July 2016, is in global circulation and has received a range of positive critical reviews, in the United States, the UK and in Europe.

The books, of which *Two Journeys Home* is the second of four projected volumes, trace the largely-fictional lives of several of the O'Connell family of Derrynane in County Kerry, Ireland in the mid-to-late eighteenth century, focusing on that of the Gaelic poet, Eileen O'Connell.

The *Saga* has been described as being "a sweeping, multi-layered story, populated by an array of colorfully-complex characters, whose lives and stories play out in a series of striking settings. Set against the drama of Europe in the early stages of significant change, the book dramatizes the roles – which have never before been treated in fiction – played by a small number of expatriate Irish of the fallen 'Gaelic Aristocracy' at the courts of Catholic Europe."

An alumnus of Don Bosco Preparatory School, he is a graduate of Providence College and Georgetown University Law Centre.

For much of his forty-plus year long legal career, Mr. O'Connell has practiced international business transactional law, primarily involving direct-investment matters, throughout Asia, Europe and the Middle East

O'Connell is married, has five children and ten grandchildren. He resides with his wife, Laurette, and their golden retriever, Katie, near Annapolis, Maryland, USA.

www.ingramcontent.com/pod-product-compliance
Lightning Source LLC
Chambersburg PA
CBHW031937130726
47905CB00008BA/2441